To Captain Jeff♡ W9-CCQ-461,
   It was a pleasure flying
with you. Really appreciate
you picking up my story +
giving it a read. Hope you
enjoy it!

City of
Destiny

A novel
by Brian T. O'Neill

BOOK PUBLISHERS NETWORK
Changing the World One Book at a Time

Book Publishers Network
P.O. Box 2256
Bothell • WA • 98041
Ph • 425-483-3040
www.bookpublishersnetwork.com

City of Destiny is literary fiction, as are all the characters within it.

10 9 8 7 6 5 4 3 2 1
Printed in the United States of America

LCCN 2017960631
ISBN   978-1-945271-87-8

Editor: Julie Scandora
Cover designer: Laura Zugzda
Layout: Scott Book and Melissa Vail Coffman

*To my colleagues in blue who lost their lives in service
to the community—gone but not forgotten.*

Tacoma was incorporated in 1884 and became known as the "City of Destiny" when it was designated as the terminus of the Northern Pacific Railroad.
– City of Tacoma website

PROLOGUE

Bare floor. Drab walls. A distant moan and rattle of metal. Smell of antiseptic overlying a pungent human stench. A labyrinth of hallways spread out ahead, and I took a narrow one that ended at a large metal door, which I opened with difficulty and not a little pain.

Yells turned to whispers as I emerged into a neon-lit lobby. I shuffled forward, boots scuffing the polished concrete, ignoring the group of uniformed cops openly staring at me. This was why I had taken the back entrance through the holding cells.

Fuck 'em, Cassidy. I gritted my teeth and limped away, repeating that little mantra until the muted conversations faded. A dark staircase led down to an area I had rarely visited. A puddle of light from an office ahead spilled into the corridor and illuminated an office window in which I caught my reflection.

Stringy brown hair wet with sweat, whiskered cheeks, and a hollow look in those grey eyes that made everything come rushing back at once. I turned away, rubbed my wet palms on my dirty jeans and cinched up my Kevlar vest. All in all, I've probably looked better.

"Don't tell that asshole anything, Cassidy!" a voice yelled down the staircase.

I turned around but couldn't identify the speaker. *Screw it,* I thought. *Let's get this over with.*

This area was reserved for administrative offices and thus was quiet in the early morning hour. I turned back towards the open doorway, and despite the temperature controls throughout the police headquarters building, a shiver of cold rose up my spine. It must have been the air conditioner. Or else the sign on the door.

Internal Investigations
Interview Room 2
Abandon All Hope Ye Who Enter Here

Okay, I made up that last part. But I'm guessing more than one poor cop had made the descent to this place with his balls shriveling. Or ovaries, for that matter.

I lifted a finger to scratch a nervous tic and recoiled from the sharp pain. Gently, I probed my left bicep, which turned out to be a sticky red mess.

Perfect. Fucking *perfect*.

Well, I thought, *if I looked like hell and felt like hell, I might as well visit the place, see what all the fuss is about.*

A cool breeze caressed my face as I stepped across the threshold. Apparently, hell had air conditioning. Either that or I had stumbled into the modern-day version of Dante's inferno, where it got colder and colder all the way to the bottom. And Mom said I'd wasted my college years on an English lit degree.

I stretched to my nearly six-foot height and forced a stiff leg in motion. *Abandon all hope? We'll see,* I thought as I entered what turned out to be a small room completely free of brimstone that smelled instead like new carpet and just a hint of . . . what was that? I sniffed again. Perfume?

A rectangular table in the center of the room took all of two strides to reach. Another blast of cold air from a ceiling vent made the hair on the back of my neck stand at attention. More images of Dante's enemies, buried up to their necks in ice, sprang into my head as I contemplated the man seated at the table, hands folded neatly and scowling at his watch.

The captain in charge of internal investigations, Charlie Doloviski, was a short, stocky guy with a florid complexion that gave the false impression of excitement. That was rarely the case with him, which was one of the reasons he had risen through the ranks. Charlie sat ramrod straight, lifting his chin to study me as if I were a particularly interesting microbe, though the look on his normally neutral face was that of an annoyed priest waiting to hear a particularly sordid confession.

Suffice to say I know that look.

Charlie wore an old tweed sports coat with shiny elbows, a crisp white shirt, and a bright-blue tie with what I assumed was a brand-new coffee stain, given the half-empty cup in his left hand. Finally, he afforded me a slight nod, causing wisps of thinning hair to rise and sway gently over his predominant forehead.

I'd known Charlie for years and knew this was all just an act, one he probably practiced in front of a mirror to transform his lovable but stodgy personality into the all-knowing prick one would expect to run internal affairs. Moreover, not only was Charlie a decent guy, he was, or at least had been, an able cop. It wasn't his fault he'd been given the role of hatchet man. Nobody wanted this shit job, so if he wanted to play the stereotype, so be it.

"Captain," I said by way of introduction.

"Detective Cassidy," Doloviski said, nodding again. He removed the dumb-ass glasses. "You're early. Good." He opened his mouth to say more and then closed it. For a moment, he seemed confused, as if he'd already lost his train of thought. Probably he realized this was not the time for one of his canned speeches reserved for the typical shenanigans—affairs and domestic abuse, excessive force, or alcoholism—that unraveled all the way and wound up on his desk. Nope, nothing like that, so I waited patiently for him to figure out his opening line. "Pardon me, Detective Cassidy," he said instead. "We have a guest sitting in on your interview this morning. This is Anna Best, a partner with the law firm retained by the police guild. Per policy, she'll be representing you today."

Exhaustion had made me miss the source of the perfume emerging from the corner of the room. A hand extended. Anna Best was tall, striking even. Her unlined brown skin made it difficult to gauge her age but was probably right around mine at forty. Unlike me, she was well-dressed in an emerald-green blouse and fitted tan slacks that accentuated her trim physique. But it was her wide, expressive eyes that caught my attention, focused on me as if I were the only person in the room, the world even. She blinked once, as if snapping a mental picture to be downloaded later, and took my hand in a firm grip.

"Sergeant Cassidy, pleasure to meet you." Her voice was husky and confident.

"It's Detective Cassidy, ma'am. Please call me Michael."

Best paused to process this new information, one eyebrow raised in Doloviski's direction. "I apologize. Looks like my notes are incorrect. And call me Anna," she added for my benefit.

"Shall we get started?" Doloviski said. The captain's tone was light but forced. At Best's urging, he fumbled with a napkin to clean the new stain on his tie.

"Jesus, Chuckie, can you let my client collect his thoughts for two seconds?" Best said.

I stared at them both in turn.

"Chuckie?" I blurted.

Doloviski, poor guy, actually blushed. "A *long* time ago the counselor and I were patrol partners," he explained with a nod in her direction.

Anna Best snorted. "Okay, *Captain*," she said, enunciating his rank in a way I would have found both shocking and humorous in other circumstances, "your email this morning was cryptic, to say the least. You ready to tell me what the fuck is going on?"

The captain looked as if he'd just sucked a lemon dry. "I wanted to brief you sooner, Anna, but your firm said you were on vacation and couldn't be disturbed."

"That's why they call it a vacation," she explained drily. "Now how about some background, so that I can properly represent my client?"

Doloviski shook his head slowly. "Sorry, but there is an issue of time involved here, and it's too long a story. You'll pick up the thread as we move forward."

Best shot him a look that would have boiled a potato. "That's hardly routine for an internal investigation—".

"This is anything but routine, Counselor," the captain interrupted, his voice hoarse. "You're going to have to trust me." Doloviski's expression was defiant.

Best took his measure and nodded, deciding not to press the issue for the moment.

After a moment of silence, my chin began to drop onto my chest. What could I say? It'd been a long day in a string of long, shitty days.

"Let's understand each other, Chuckie," Best said in a low tone that roused me by its severity. "I represent the police guild, which means I'm here to protect the rights of any cop who winds up in your crosshairs. You know it, I know it. So don't play me."

The captain tapped a pen on the table as he searched for the correct words. "Understood. Today is different. In fact, the chief didn't think your presence today was necessary. I suggested you were someone who could be trusted to act with discretion on a sensitive issue. I was right about that, wasn't I?"

"Guess we'll see, won't we?" she answered curtly.

"You're bleeding again," Doloviski said.

A moment passed before I realized he was talking to me. "Suture popped open," I said, my thoughts spiraling back to what felt like forever but had only been a few nights.

"What was that, Detective?" Doloviski's voice broke into my thoughts.

"What?" I answered. "Sorry. Thinking out loud."

They both stared at me.

"I'm okay," I added.

The captain shrugged. Then he reached into a coat pocket, retrieved a slender silver tape recorder, and rested it on the table. All attention immediately reverted to it.

"All right, if we're ready to begin," Doloviski said, "I've prepared a list of questions—"

"Captain," Best interrupted. She raised two fingers. "A couple of issues. First, it would appear my client is not physically ready for this interview." She glanced my way for confirmation.

I shrugged. "I'm okay." Even I didn't buy that, but it didn't matter at this point.

"Second," Best continued after giving me a skeptical look, "I shouldn't have to remind you that, according to the Garrity ruling, a police officer is guaranteed certain rights during questioning."

"Correct, Counselor. I was operating under the idea that this was not a jeopardy situation for Detective Cassidy, but I'm more than willing to address your concern."

Doloviski held the tape recorder to his mouth and pushed the record button. A light came on, bathing the bottom of his chin in pale green. "This is captain Charles Doloviski of the Tacoma Police Department. The date is May 19, the time 0626 hours. I am in interview room number two in the Office of Internal Investigations. Also present is Counselor Anna Best, an attorney representing the Tacoma Police Guild, and detective Michael Cassidy." He looked up at the corkboard ceiling. "The purpose of this interview is to hear the verbal account of Detective Cassidy with respect to case number 34322, an open homicide investigation."

Across the table, I sensed rather than observed Best's reaction. Nor did I blame her. Even when you're expecting to hear it, the word "homicide" lands hard on the ear.

Doloviski chose to ignore us. "For the record, the department is mandating the statements of detective Michael Cassidy in the following interview. His statements will not be held against him in any subsequent criminal proceedings. Ms. Best," he said, turning the recorder to face her, "do you consent to this interview being recorded?"

"Despite not knowing the details of this interview, I agree to it being recorded."

Doloviski nodded. "Detective Cassidy, do you also agree to this recording?"

"Yes." *What choice did I really have?*

"Very well, all parties agree to being recorded." Doloviski nodded again, satisfied, then set the recorder down and reached for a yellow legal pad. "I've prepared a series of questions to—"

Click.

Doloviski's hand froze, his pen hovering in mid-air. Slowly, he tilted his head toward the recorder, which I now grasped in a choke hold. "Explain," Doloviski said, failing to disguise his annoyance.

I took a deep breath. "Look, I know what you're going to ask me. I know the blanks you need to fill in. Simple answers to simple questions, a chronology of events, pin maps," I said, my voice rising in anger, despite my best efforts, "a list of people, all framed in their simplest fucking terms."

It was quiet in the room. I sucked in a few deep breaths. They leaned in, willing me forward.

"I'm worried that when I've finished answering those questions, you'll just slap it together in a way that only confirms the conclusion you've already reached. And you know what I'm afraid of?" I said, locking eyes with the captain. "That you won't understand a single fucking thing that happened." Hot tears leaked down my face as I leaned back, mad at myself for losing control. "You need context, Captain," I continued, "which means you need to hear the whole story. And I need to tell it. The question is are you ready to listen?"

Doloviski looked down at his notepad and checked his watch. Then he set the tip of his pen on the upper left margin of the yellow legal pad and nodded curtly.

"Okay," I said in a calmer voice, "then listen up because there's no way in hell I'm telling this twice."

I set the recorder back on the table and pushed the button. The green light blinked on.

PART I

It is not in the stars to hold our destiny
but in ourselves.
– William Shakespeare

CHAPTER 1

A PARKING LOT
MARCH 15 (TWO MONTHS EARLIER)
2230 HOURS

I hate stakeouts. Forget that Hollywood bullshit. The reality is that most undercover operations are case studies in boredom. Not to mention nagging bladders, the salty tang of other people's sweat, and the increasingly bad attitudes of hyperactive cops confined to a small space. Sure, I wasn't a detective anymore, which meant I didn't have to sit through this shit. But now that I had sergeant's chevrons, I had to do the responsible thing. Which tonight, unfortunately, meant sitting in a cramped, stuffy space with little to do for hours on end.

Though I had to admit that this time the ride was better. A lot better, in fact. The narcotics van seemingly had it all—state-of-the-art tech equipment, computer and surveillance consoles for two detectives, plus plush leather seats, a great sound system, and most importantly, a small fridge fully stocked with drinks and snacks. It lacked a toilet, of course, which was why I'd held onto the plastic water bottle. I was just pondering how much the taxpayers, or more likely drug dealers, had paid for the rig when the shooting started.

My head swiveled towards the sound. While I'd been daydreaming, or in this case, night-dreaming, a green Honda coupe had appeared on the corner across Pacific Avenue. The dark Hispanic features of our informant were clearly visible now that his hood had fallen to his shoulders as he stumbled backwards, his arms flailing.

Pop. Pop.

More shots. Unlike some I'd folks I'd seen when the shit hit the fan, our informant didn't let the gunman get a bead on him. He beat feet without waiting for an invite.

The detective behind me threw down her headphones, cursing as she shoved her hands over her ears. The boom mic must have amplified the gunshots. *Ouch.*

In the driver's seat next to me, the operational commander leaned his six-foot-six and 250-pound frame over me to get a better view. He was so close I could have counted the hairs on his chin, if he'd had any. As usual, Nate Orlando was as well-groomed and turned out in his tactical gear as a bride in her wedding dress. Not that I would have made that comparison when the guy could bench press most of the weights in the gym and shoot out a gnat's eye from two hundred yards. But I had pointed out Nate's curious attention to hygiene and fashion before, and it said a lot about our years of friendship that he hadn't pounded me into a gooey Irish pulp.

A set of binos appeared in his hands. He scanned the street, and I could almost hear his gears clicking. I tried to put some thought into my next move as well. As the district patrol sergeant, maybe I should start thinking about what the fuck to do.

With a snarl, Nate started the van, shoved it into drive, and buried the gas. I was thrown back into my seat as the van's tires sizzled on the parking lot asphalt. So I reset my game plan and buckled up. And held on.

The van surged forward with a surprising amount of power and plowed headlong through the manicured bushes. I doubted the bank manager would allow us to use the parking lot again, not the way the branches went flying past. We hit the sidewalk with the tires still spinning, launched off the curb. and hit the street with an impact that jarred my teeth.

I turned back towards the corner. The shooting had stopped. The informant was now running madly, hoodie flapping and arms flailing as he turned down the alley. Strangely, the green Honda, our target for the night's operation, hadn't moved an inch. An image of a carload of dopers laughing their asses off made my fists clench.

Nate yanked the van around in a tight turn. A bump and more cursing told me the detective in the back had hit the floor.

Shoulda' buckled up, I thought.

"Shots fired! Shots fired!" a voice broke through on the radio. "Target vehicle has fired on CI!"

No shit. There were things I should be doing, but those would have to wait until the damn van stopped. I took another look out the window as Nate prepared to crank the wheel around and pull in behind the Honda.

"Stop!" I yelled as a blinding flash of red and blue strobes atop a white Ford Explorer cut across our path. The expression of intensity on Officer Francine Echevaria's face made me smile, despite everything.

"'Bout time," Nate rumbled, spinning the wheel. He punched the gas again, spinning us rapidly through 180 degrees before tapping the brakes to stop the rotation. The van came to a halt near Echie's rear bumper. I let out a breath, mouthing a quick prayer.

The Honda still hadn't moved. *Weird.*

I shot out of the passenger door, my Glock .40 already in my hand. Nate slid forward carrying a compact H&K assault rifle that looked like a toy in his big mitts.

Echie's rig was thirty feet behind the Honda. She stood inside the well of her driver's door, a pistol in one hand, the PA mic in the other. "Driver, show me your hands now!" Echie said.

First one, then another thin brown hand slid out the Honda's left window.

"CI is back with me," a calm voice purred into my earpiece. It was the informant's handler, Detective Rafael Inigo. "He reports only one occupant in the vehicle."

I sidled up next to the patrol car's passenger door and rested my shooting hand on the rim. The adrenalin pounding through my body made the irradiated sights wobble ever so slightly. The radio volume competed with inbound sirens, while several sets of headlights backlit us—a classic fuckup, which I'd deal with later. Car doors slammed, followed by the sound of stomping feet belonging, I assumed, to Nate's detectives who had been on a loose perimeter.

All right, I thought. *We've got this shit figured out.*

Of course, it never turns out that way. For now it was Echie's show. I glanced in her direction as she brushed a few strands of long dark hair off her cheek, her face in profile lit up in flashes of light.

Focus, dude.

"Driver," she said, her voice deep and tinny over the PA, "reach out and open your door from the outside! Keep your hands where I can see them!"

More feet hit the pavement behind us. Uniformed cops, some of them mine, now moved up and took positions next to the plainclothes guys. Movement ahead caught my attention. The driver's hand reached for the door handle.

"I want more marked units standing by," Nate whispered into his collar mic. "No crossfire positions. If he bolts, no more than two in the chase. Everyone else prepare for containment."

There were several radio clicks to acknowledge this. As if the bad guy heard it as well, his hands disappeared back inside the car. The Honda's front tires spun, an angry buzz like an entire hornet's nest, as the rubber fought for traction. The car's hood floated back and forth until the rubber finally gripped the wet asphalt. The car shot forward, passenger door slamming shut, and the Honda roared away.

"Fuck!" Echie yelled. She threw her mic aside, holstered her gun, and jumped into the car. The door was ripped away beneath my arms a second later, and I staggered back. So much for tagging along.

More cops rushed forward, blissfully unaware that the main attraction had already decamped. Nate pushed through them, yelling directions, looking left and right for a car to take. In all, the bad guy had timed his departure pretty well.

Almost as an afterthought, I holstered my gun and jogged after Nate. Several sets of eyes followed my progress. It's hard to run and look dignified, but I did my best. Besides, Nate was my ride.

Since no one else had updated our situation, I keyed the little mic attached to the front zipper of my jumpsuit. "Suspect vehicle, a green Honda two-door, has fled southbound on Pac Ave," I said.

Echie's patrol car was over a block away, racing to catch up to the Honda. I surveyed the scene. Patrol officers were racing in both directions, some just arriving, some heading out to join the chase. Nate's more experienced detectives, whose undercover cars were not allowed in high speed chases, were settling in for some ass scratching and storytelling. It was your typical fucked-up mess.

"Detectives, hold the scene!" I yelled into the din. "Patrol officers, I want you in your cars setting up containment. Now!"

As the mob quickly reverted to a police department, an unmarked, black Ford sedan screeched to a stop not two feet away. The passenger door popped open.

"Get in," Nate grunted from behind the wheel. "You're on radio and lights."

I sat down without a word. Buckling up, I threw the switches for the siren and strobes, wondering where Nate had grabbed the unmarked Crown Vic. Somewhere, I assumed, another patrol sergeant was wondering why his car had suddenly vanished.

The big sedan slowly picked up speed. A block later, the tail lights from Echie's Explorer stopped shrinking. Nate kept steady on the accelerator, and we began to close.

"This is 4-Sam-3 in pursuit," I spoke into the car radio. "Take all other radio traffic to a different frequency. I'll be calling the chase."

The radio went abruptly silent. I continued, "We're southbound in the 6700 block of Pacific Avenue, second in line behind 4-Henry-2. The suspect vehicle is an old model Honda, possibly a Prelude. Our speed is," I glanced over at the dashboard, "approximately ninety-five miles per hour. The street conditions are wet, no pedestrians or other vehicles in view. I need the on-duty canine officer to fall in behind us. No other vehicles are authorized to pursue at this time."

I paused before inquiring, "We got aviation tonight?"

"Negative," the dispatcher replied.

Figures, I thought. We blew through an intersection. A white blur on the right told me the canine cop had joined us.

"K9-45 is in the chase," a bored sounding voice confirmed.

Not yet, you're not, I thought as the headlights popped into view behind us on the four-lane road and then quickly dwindled. We were right on Echie's tail, the Honda ahead running without lights, the wet road lending the sensation of gliding atop a wide black river.

I flipped open the dash-mounted laptop and scrolled through until I found the screen I wanted. On it, the patrol cars formed a loose half circle behind us. Well ahead, arrayed in a line along the city boundary, county deputies and state troopers, represented by other icons, were taking position.

"We have him penned in, sure as shit," I said, thinking out loud.

Nate grunted in response. I updated our status along with some possible locations for spike strips. After that, we'd revisit the whole felony-stop scenario. I was about to slap myself on the back when everything went to hell.

The first indication was the headlights from an oncoming car. Next, red brake lights flared on the Honda's rear, forcing Echie to stomp the brakes. Instead of following suit, Nate took his foot off the gas and steered a little to the right.

I keyed the mic. "We've got unknown traffic approaching, northbound on Pac Ave."

"Know what?" Nate said, breaking his silence. "This guy's got a plan."

The driver of the oncoming car, a minivan, became visible as we closed the distance—a woman's eyes, impossibly wide behind thick glasses, her mouth in a perfect O. The van's hood nosedived as she hit the brakes. The Honda spun sharply left, directly across the van's path just as the van's brakes locked up. The screech of the minivan's tires joined the Honda's in a chorus as the smaller car made such an abrupt U-turn that I nearly expected it to roll.

I stopped breathing, waiting for an impact. It didn't happen.

"Watch it!" I yelled, as Echie's car swerved sideways, directly into our path.

As usual, Nate had anticipated the sequence of events. With a single, savage yank on the wheel, he steered clear to the left, straightened out, and then stood on the brakes. Inside the minivan, not ten feet in front of us, a white-haired Asian woman stared at us in shock.

I had forgotten about the canine car, which now flew well past on our right, anti-lock brakes spasming. Nate didn't hesitate. He floored the gas, cranked the wheel, and spun us through a tight 180 degrees, even as the green Honda began pulling away in the direction from which we'd so recently come.

Echie's Ford Explorer was stopped next to the curb, smoke billowing out of the engine. The canine handler's SUV had blasted through a short wooden fence into a vacant lot. I shook my head, my emotions roiling between anger and relief. It was sheer luck no one had been killed.

As we closed the gap again, the Honda made a quick right turn onto a side street.

"Eastbound on 94th Street now," I said, hearing the shrill tone in my voice. "Christ, let's get this fucker."

"Leave God out of this," Nate said. "He's mine." He threw the car into the turn, taking it wide, and got back on the gas at the apex. The rutted road flowed beneath us. I jabbered into the radio again. Nate seemed to be waiting for something as he maintained our distance behind the Honda, which was veering back and forth on the narrow, poorly lit street.

Aside from all the poor life choices the Honda driver had made leading up to this point, he had actually done quite well behind the wheel this evening. But that streak ended when he took an abrupt right turn and made his first and last mistake.

The little car sailed wide into the opposite lane. Nate had held the Ford on the centerline, so he was able to take quick advantage. Braking in a straight line, he jabbed the wheel to the right and let the car drift inside the Honda's turning radius. Bumpers touched. With another subtle application of acceleration, Nate tapped the Honda's bumper again, finding just the right spot.

I dropped the mic and grabbed the dash with both hands. Nate punched the accelerator and cranked the wheel hard left this time, directly into the Honda. The green car filled the windshield for a brief second as we completed the pursuit intervention technique. The full weight of the Honda spun around the front of the Ford, which had become an over-large fulcrum, until the smaller car was flung off to the side like a piece of trash. *Physics rules.*

Acrid smoke obscured my vision, and the scent of burning rubber filled my nose.

The Honda rolled backwards, its transmission fried. Nate goosed the throttle and pulled in behind, effectively blocking it. The driver's door popped open just then, but Nate gunned the engine and smacked the Honda's rear. The door on the little green car slammed shut, the noise accompanied by a loud yelp from inside.

"Let's go!" Nate grunted, grabbing his miniature rifle and jumping out.

We ran in tandem up either side of the smoking vehicle. I stumbled once in the darkness, caught myself.

"Police. Show me those hands, my friend," Nate said on the other side of the car. His voice was calm but thick with menace.

The door on my side was closed and heavily tinted. Expecting it to be locked, I gave a savage yank, and it flew open. Playing my flashlight inside, I saw a small lump in the front seat, the driver, curled up in the fetal position, hands cupping his groin. A metallic object, gun-shaped, was inches away from his hands. Nate's beam crossed mine, reminding me that my area of responsibility was the back seat. He'd been a SWAT operator for enough years, so I let him deal with it.

I pointed my light towards the back seat. A chrome revolver floated out of the darkness.

Adrenalin flooded my system. I was immediately hyperaware of the barrel, which seemed to expand until it was all I could see. The moment stretched—if someone had told me later it had been hours, I would have shrugged and agreed. In my magnified vision I saw, or at least imagined I could see, the rifling grooves spiraling through the barrel itself all the way to the bottom where, and I swear this to be true, these ended at the smooth, rounded tip of a bullet.

And just like that, I was back in real time.

Gears in my head shifted. Muscles sizzled in anticipation. Though the moment had caught me awkwardly learning forward, every cell in my body screamed, "Move!" In response, I tilted my head back, raising my arms as if I were a gymnast doing a back flip. Flexing my muscles in a synchronicity so perfect the euphoria it produced nearly eclipsed my terror, I leaped backwards as if I'd shot out of a cannon, every thought aside from the motion itself blotted out.

Soaring through the air on a cushion of crackling energy, I heard the gun roar a single time. I registered pain just before the ground rushed up to meet me.

Lights out.

Chapter 2

"That," I said to my small audience, "was the beginning."

Anna Best's fingers poised above her laptop. She appraised me, and I knew what she saw. A client who wanted to talk; a client who was only going to make her job harder.

But there was still more to tell. A lot more.

"Are you all right, Michael?" she asked, her eyes softening.

I nodded.

"Is that how you injured your arm?" she asked.

I laughed, surprising both of us. "Yes," I said. "And no."

Best waited for more, but I didn't answer.

Doloviski tapped his pen impatiently on the yellow legal pad. "Do you need a break, Detective?" he asked.

"No, I'll be okay," I said. "Where was I?" Before anyone could answer, I held up a finger. "That's right. On the—

✴ ✴ ✴

Side of the Road
March 15
2245 Hours

A light rain fell. I tried to lift my head up, but an ice chipper sliced into my temples. Or not. Either way, my head hurt. I laid my head back down, and the stabbing pain became a lighter hammering behind my eyeballs. I slid an eye open. Rain coated my face, and I reached up to wipe it. Another bad move. A searing sensation tore through my left bicep. I closed my eyes and contemplated the falling rain.

Oh, and where was I, exactly?

A moment passed. Everything returned in a rush—the drug deal, the pursuit, the collision, Nate and I running up to the car—

Oh shit, I thought, panic squeezing my chest. *I've been shot.*

With quivering fingers, I explored my left arm. Sticky, wet, painful. Not in that order. My mind wandered, and I might have lost consciousness again. Then I became aware of a familiar voice, flat and filled with rage.

Nate's voice.

I rolled to the side and saw it happen. Nate's leonine figure stood above the Honda, impossibly large. His face was contorted, nostrils flared, lips pulled back in a savage grin that exposed gleaming white teeth against his dark skin. His eyes were black voids. Nate's whole being was a promise of imminent violence. It was the most terrifying thing I'd ever seen, more so because this was the same man whose compassion had propped me up in my worst days.

He spoke more sharp words, none of which I understood. Then Nate's little rifle coughed three times, so fast it was almost simultaneous. A second passed. Three more coughs. Then silence.

I had propped myself up on my right elbow but now rolled back to the dirt and gravel, spanking my head against a rock.

"Nate," I yelled, fighting to stay conscious as tunnel vision closed in. My voice was barely audible. I took a deep breath and yelled his name again.

There was no response.

Get up! Get off your ass! Struggling against the pain, I tried to roll over.

"Michael! For the love of God, stay down!"

"Nate?" I croaked in relief. "Nate! Are you hurt? What's going on? I heard shots! Are you okay?" This little speech made me light-headed, and I flopped back down. Double *ouch*.

"It's all right, my brother, it's all right. Two bad guys down," Nate said, noiselessly appearing next to me. "And I got help on the way. Where you hit?" he asked, his fingers gingerly examining my chest.

"Left arm," I gasped, too relieved to care about the pain until he stuck a finger in the wrong spot. I groaned. "Yeah, there. You found it."

After several seconds Nate said, "There's some blood but not too much. Looks like you just lost a little meat."

"I can spare it," I said, wincing.

"Little guy like you? Need every ounce you've got," Nate said, the hint of a smile in his voice. "Thank God, you're okay."

"Amen to that," I said, meaning it.

Nate got to work, unzipping the detachable sleeve on my jumpsuit. His knife made a *swick* sound as the blade swung out.

"Uh, what's the plan here?" I asked in case he was adding trauma surgery to his resume.

He ignored me, slicing the blade into the remains of my sleeve, cleanly severing the sergeant's chevrons I'd worked so hard to earn. His eyes, now quiet and full of concern, scanned my arm. "Yup, flesh wound," he pronounced.

I had been holding my breath. I exhaled, laughing.

Nate lifted a concerned eyebrow. "You losing it?"

"Hell no, brother," I said, laughing and wincing at the same time. "You remember when we snuck into that second-run movie theater back in high school?"

Nate let out a short, throaty laugh. "*Monty Python and the Holy Grail*. How could I forget? You made me see it three times," he said, pulling out a large gauze pad from the first aid kit, which had magically appeared in his lap.

The memory made me smile. "And the knight, the one who got cut into tiny pieces but wouldn't stop fighting because it was only—"

"A flesh wound, yeah, I get it." This time his smile was fleeting. "Can't say the same about those two in the car."

"Damn," I muttered. Somehow, I'd forgotten about the ones who had caused all this mess. Guilt, that familiar friend, nudged into my head and took a seat in the back row.

"We need to get this scene contained," Nate said, looking around. "Where is everybody?"

Damn good question. Sirens had been circling in the distance for the last minute or so. Had I updated our location? The question nagged at my brain, and I lifted my head. Then promptly passed out again.

Flashing lights. Sirens. Skidding tires. Running feet that reverberated in the ground beneath my head. Slowly, I roused enough to see that the blue crew had arrived. After making sure my initial shock was wearing off, Nate quickly took charge. He pointed in ten directions at once, sending cops scurrying. I watched a few guys from the SWAT team sneak up to the Honda and take a peek, the beam from their assault rifles like a monochromatic laser show. Seconds later, they backed away. Their body language told me that whatever they'd seen required no further action.

I contemplated life and death as a smoky mist rose over the Honda. "Giveth and taketh" and a hundred other epithets from a sketchy career as a Roman Catholic sprang into my head. But the only conclusion I came had no biblical reference.

Totally fucking surreal.

More cops arrived, most patrol officers in uniform and a few plainclothes detectives, one in a flannel shirt that looked suspiciously like pajamas. Crime scene techs, also looking as if they'd just rolled out of bed, bustled around stringing tape, snapping pictures, and breaking out boxes of equipment.

The shock and adrenalin were definitely fading. Unfortunately, that meant that numb body parts were waking up.

A few minutes later, Nate crouched down beside me. "The fire department was staging, and somebody forgot to call them in," he said. "Sorry you're still on the ground."

"No problem," I said. "I figure the longer I sit out here, the less paperwork I have to do."

He chuckled. In a low voice he said, "That was a close call, brother."

"Tell me about it, Nate."

He shook his head. "You don't understand. I saw the guy in the back seat with the gun. Saw you right through the car doors. And then," Nate's voice rose in pitch, "and then, you just . . . flew."

"Flew? Really?" I grunted, trying not to sound as nervous as this observation made me.

"I'm telling you, the gun hadn't fired, not yet. But there you were, launching yourself like a superhero! Couldn't believe my eyes," he said, his eyes wide in wonder.

My own observations, which not only included my little flight but Nate Orlando's brief role as the bullet-spraying Angel of Death, would have to wait. It would all requite some mental sorting.

We were quiet for a time. Nate couldn't let the topic go. He patted my uninjured arm. "Looks like the good Lord has some plans for you after all, Sergeant."

"Think so?" I asked.

"Damn, Michael, how long we known each other? You can barely clear the ground on a jump. You're so bad I used to think there was something wrong with your legs."

"It's a gift," I said, stifling a laugh against the pain it caused.

He chuckled. "You were in the grace of God, Michael. Do not kid yourself."

"Can I get an amen?" I responded, smiling.

"Amen."

I gripped his hand. It was cool and smooth. "I owe you my life, Nate. Again."

"You'd do the same, brother," Nate answered, the topic closed.

He stood up, nodded, and walked towards a gathering of detectives rubbing sleep out of their eyes. The Honda was lit up beneath high-powered lamps behind them. *Homicide,* I thought darkly. *Here to pick up the pieces.*

Another unmarked Ford turned onto the street, racing quickly up to the intersection and sliding to a stop. The door burst open, and a short, darkly handsome Hispanic man in a fitted grey suit emerged. He walked briskly, tie flapping, gleaming black dress shoes slapping the wet pavement. He nonchalantly ducked under the yellow tape, ignoring the cop trying to hand him a check-in clipboard. Rafael Inigo, gang expert extraordinaire, had arrived.

"Doesn't look too bad, Miguel," he said, leaning down and checking out my arm. "Long as you don't jerk off with your left hand."

"Ambidextrous."

Inigo laughed hard. With a wink, he was gone, heading towards the Honda and whatever was left inside. He stuck his head inside for less than a minute. Nate approached him as he backed away, and they walked over close enough for me to eavesdrop.

"They look familiar?" Nate asked, nodding towards the Honda.

"They're all tatted up with Sureno shit, Lieutenant. Don't recognize them right now, what with all the fucking holes, but they are definitely bangers. Shouldn't take me long to figure out who they are, which set they belong to."

Nate nodded once. Inigo returned to the Honda, and I forced myself to look more closely. The interior was dark and, from my position, a solid thirty feet away. Yet here I was.

Holy shit, had I jumped that far?

My eye caught something beneath the lip of the car door. When I recognized it, all thought of my improbable escape fled. Shivers racked my body.

It was a hand, limp and brown.

"You all right?" Nate asked, noiselessly appearing at my side.

"Getting cold, Nate," I lied. "Some asshole sliced up my brand new jumpsuit."

"Attitude like that, you won't be gettin' a new one."

The moment passed in silence. My tremors lessened. On a whim, I decided to cut myself a break. Sure, I'd survived, but it hadn't been skill, daring, or anything remotely noble. Hadn't my dad always said, *It's better to be lucky than good*? That made me feel better, at least a bit.

Over the next several minutes, I was treated by medics who rolled me onto a backboard and unceremoniously slid a needle into my arm. I recognized the soothing flow of morphine almost immediately, a sensation that made me feel infinitely better and emotionally conflicted, natural reactions for a recovering alcoholic like me.

Cops were milling around in a crowd of blue talking in excited, low voices, all gesturing towards three white-clad techs from the medical examiner's office. They were struggling with one of the corpses, stiffened with rigor into a ninety-degree angle. It wouldn't fit into the van until, with a practiced motion, they applied pressure on both ends and straightened the body with a grisly tearing sound that elicited wicked laughter from many of the cops watching the morbid scene.

I turned away, breathed in a lungful of cool, moist air. The stars swam above me, their slow gyrations across the cosmos a timely reminder of the inevitable fate of all us mortals.

That I was still alive gave me some small pleasure at that moment. At least until a familiar nagging question insinuated itself into my thoughts.

Do you deserve to live?

Yeah, I silently answered. *Hope so.*

CHAPTER 3

SIDE OF THE ROAD
MARCH 15
2258 HOURS

The medics had wandered away to argue about which hospital to take me—*The one that's warm and dry, fellas*—when two shapes approached, backlit by the fluorescent lights.

"Hey, boss," said the larger shape. "How you feeling?"

"Hey, James!" I clasped the thick hand of my senior shift officer, James Kapalu, trying not to wince as the squat Hawaiian squeezed my fingers in a vice.

Francine Echevaria's pretty face materialized out of the shadows next to him. Echie's raven hair was done up in a bun, wisps framing her olive skin like a masterpiece. My cheeks caught fire as she bent over me.

Instead of speaking, she simply studied me. Before she could read the message in my fully engulfed face, I turned my attention back to the thick-set Hawaiian.

"I'm all right. You?" I said, only then realizing that no one had asked how I was.

Kapalu laughed as if I were the funniest guy in the room.

I turned back to Echie, whose radiant smile caused my blood pressure to rise at an alarming rate.

"Lieutenant says you've got a through-and-through," Echie said softly. "How do you feel, really?"

"I'm okay," I repeated. "Thanks. What happened to that minivan back there?"

"The old lady?" Kapalu answered. "I gave her a ride home. She's real nice. She wanted to feed me. Can you believe it? Broke my heart to say no."

"You turned down free food just to do your job? Wow, this night is full of surprises," I said.

"Glad you're okay, Sarge," Kapalu said, smiling wide. "Think I'll head over and relieve the rookie handling the crime scene. Bound to have media out here soon enough."

"Sounds like a good idea," I said.

Kapalu gave me a wink before heading back into the noise and light. What was all the fucking winking about?

Echie just stood there, her proximity slowly draining my last few operational brain cells. My mouth was dry, my head woozy. *It's the drugs*, I thought, not even certain if the fluid dripping into my arm had any pain meds. I opened my mouth to say something I would have instantly regretted, but fortunately, Echie stepped back. The moment, if it had been a moment, had passed.

"Thanks for stopping by," I said.

A soft grin parted her lips, lit up her eyes. It looked as if she had just learned a secret. She waved, turned, and walked away. I followed her, appreciating the sway of her hips. She glanced back and caught me staring. With a mischievous smile, she disappeared into the blue crowd. I lay back on the stretcher and let the light rain cool me down.

Footsteps approached yet again. *Jesus*, I thought. *Is it office hours here?* A thick pair of hands grasped the side of my stretcher. They belonged to a man in his early fifties with a mane of silver hair. With his glittering eyes and smoothly shaved jaw line, dark wool coat adorned with a cluster of golden stars on the shoulder, he could have been a Hollywood star playing the role of police chief instead of the real thing.

"Evening, Chief," I said.

Randall Garcia shot me a look equal parts concern and pissed off. "Goddamn, Sergeant," he spat out, his neck muscles flexing as if he wanted to lift me off the gurney. "You gave us quite a scare."

"Could've been much worse, sir. Lieutenant Orlando saved my ass."

"Let's save the details for the investigation, Michael. Let's just count our blessings and leave it there."

He motioned over one of his administrative flunkies. "Please tell the goddam firemen to get my sergeant to the hospital now. As in right now."

Said flunky, a support staff sergeant, dutifully turned around and ran towards the ambulance.

"Thanks, Chief. I'll be okay," I said, surprised that I actually meant it now.

"Yes. Yes, you will," Garcia said, gripping my hand. "I'll see you soon."

Garcia turned and stamped over to the crime scene, intercepting Nate with a tap on the elbow. Nate lowered his head to the chief, listening intently, and then the two men fiercely hugged.

After a brief conversation, Nate unslung the rifle he'd so recently used and handed it over to Garcia who, in turn, passed it onto the newly arrived internal investigations commander, Captain Charlie Doloviski. It went into a large black canvas bag already marked for evidence.

I let my head sag back onto the gurney. Two medics finally came by and loaded me up into their rig. Ten minutes later, we drove into the cave-like bay at Tacoma General Hospital. I was rolled through the automatic doors with a whoosh of compressed air. We bypassed the waiting room where the cries of a young child, an old man's rattling cough, and guttural muttering in an indecipherable language slowly faded.

Minutes later, a nurse checked my vitals from the solitude of a private room in the ER. Her questions were interrupted by excited voices in the hallway. My eyelids dropped. Then closed.

The barrel of a gun followed me into sleep.

CHAPTER 4

INTERNAL INVESTIGATIONS INTERVIEW ROOM
MAY 19
0954 HOURS

Click. The green light on the tape recorder faded again.

I stared at it for a moment, suddenly lost. A cool, brown hand patted mine. I breathed deeply and leaned back in my chair.

"We need a minute, Captain," Best said.

Captain Doloviski checked his watch and nodded. "I need a cup of coffee. Anyone else?"

"Not if it's still that same old crap," Best answered.

A smile flitted across Doloviski's face. He stood up, checked his phone, and left the room.

"You looked like you needed a break," she said.

That was an understatement. I scratched the stubble on my face. "Look, Anna, I suppose there're a few things you need to know about me, things I don't feel like rehashing in front of the captain."

"All right," she answered. "Tell me as much as you can, but make it quick."

"It was about fifteen years ago," I began. "Probably right after you left, I'm guessing?"

She confirmed this with a nod.

I continued, "I was working swing shift in the Hilltop. You remember how crazy it was back then—crack and drive-bys—and you'd be too wired to sleep. My crew would meet up at the Spar in Old Town to decompress.

"I had just buried my parents," I said, remembering it as clearly as if it had happened yesterday. "Car crash. One minute they're alive, the next they're dead. It was my mom's fault. The old Irish curse," I mimed taking a swig. "She was behind the wheel when the car went airborne into the sound."

Thankfully, Best did not interrupt.

I pressed on, forcing myself through the telling. "The point is that I'm the son of an alcoholic, I know the signs. I should've seen where a few beers with my buddies could lead. Anyway, I was heading down that road. But then I met Therese. She was a server at the Spar," I said, standing and limping around the small room. Just the thought of her did this to me every time without fail. "She was from Montreal, pretty and lively and with a French accent, you know?"

Best nodded, the hint of a smile playing at the corners of her mouth.

"It took me a month to get up the courage to ask her out, and then it was like I'd stepped into a tornado. She was so full of life, passion. We spent all our time together—it felt like there was no one else in the world, only us. It was only two months before I proposed, but in that short period I lived a lifetime."

The memories threatened to overwhelm me. *Just finish it.*

"It took us both a year to discover the secret each other was hiding. Mine was liquor. Hers was depression. By then we were married. But we kept going, me spending time on that same stool at the Spar, her in the bathroom with her pills. When one of us checked out, the other was usually there to help. Until it got worse."

I took a deep breath. "One night, I was hitting my second shot of JD when Nate showed up. I thought he was there to give me one of his lectures, which had only made me feel guiltier and drink more. But no, he was there because I'd put him down as my emergency notification."

Best broke her silence with a single word. "How?"

"Pills," I answered, relieved to finally get there. "It was quick."

I rubbed my tired, moist eyes with the back of my hand. "I tried to follow her down, but liquor was slower. Got pretty close to the end of the line."

"What changed?" she asked.

I paused to consider the question. "I decided I wanted to live, I guess."

"Tough decision, under the circumstances," she said.

"I didn't make it alone," I responded. "Nate was there."

Chapter 5

As a rule, cops usually don't enjoy a lengthy retirement. By the time they put in their paperwork, the combination of shift work, a crappy diet, stress, any number of addictions and God knows what else has already snuffed out that happily ever after. Anna knew that. My own issues—anxiety and alcohol for starters—were as cliché as cops and donuts. Which I love, by the way.

Before she could respond, Doloviski reappeared in the doorway, sipping from a "World's Best Dad" coffee mug. There was a new stain on his shirt. He managed a tired smile as he pulled out the little tape recorder and sat back down.

"Ready to get back at it, Detective?" the captain asked perfunctorily.

Before Best could answer for me, I nodded briskly.

"Good," Doloviski said. He picked up the recorder and pushed the button. The green light flared.

$$\star \; \star \; \star$$

It was a wet slog up the steep viaduct to McKinley Hill. The tires on my cruiser lost traction more than once on the slick roads. A week after the shooting it felt good to be back at work. My arm was sore but healing quickly.

Leaving the arterial for a side street, I passed a phalanx of double-parked patrol cars and pulled over. A tap on the computer screen brought up the details of the call.

2335: (SUIWP) HM, 40s, RP neighbor re: possible shots fired upstairs; unk cause; possible (G)eorge

2337: 4H2 ONSCN

2339: 4H2 Req MED

2341: 4U1, 4U3 ONSCN

2345: TFD ONSCN

2348: 4U1 req SGT

Translation—sometime before midnight, anonymous caller, gunshot, possible suicide, paramedics on scene, Hispanic victim with possible gang ties. Summation—same old shit.

I tapped the arrival button, and my call sign, 4S3, appeared in green. I did a quick pat down of the dozen or so pockets in my jumpsuit, all filled. After five years in the detective division, it was hard to remember all the crap patrol officers had to keep handy. I grabbed my old, dented flashlight out of the charger and hopped out into the rain.

The dark, two-story apartment building was built hotel style, with walkways surrounding an inner courtyard. The wooden sign on the second story identified it as the Villa Fortuna Apartments. *What a shithole.*

I stepped beneath a crumbling archway and into the courtyard, navigated a cracked cement path strewn with fast food wrappers and dog shit. Yet in the midst of it all was evidence of normality—toys, a well-tended flower pot, a rocking chair.

A team of firefighters and paramedics trudged past, and I hailed the leader still scratching notes on a metal clipboard.

"How's the patient, Stan?"

Stan the paramedic rubbed his eyes and yawned. "Hey, Cassidy. Medical examiner is en route. We're just packing up."

"What was the TOD?" I asked, glancing down at the form.

"Time of death was," the paramedic paused, squinting at the page, "2345."

"Whoa," I said, checking my watch. "You were here, what, two minutes before you called it? You guys got a roast in the oven or what?"

"No," he answered, too tired to joust. "It took me two seconds to call it and two minutes to go back out to my rig and find a fucking pen that worked."

"Oh," I said. "Like that, huh?"

Stan gave a distracted nod. I patted him on the back and continued through the courtyard, stepping over a discarded microwave on my way to the corner apartment.

Francine Echevaria stood just outside, her heart-shaped face scrunched in concentration as she listened to a short woman wearing a tortured spandex pants and a T-shirt with a hand giving the bird.

"It was a fucking boom!" the woman yelled in a pack-a-day rasp. "It was so fucking loud I thought I was going to fucking die! I was like, what the fuck, you know?"

Echie looked up from her writing, saw me, and discreetly rolled her eyes.

"Did you see or hear anyone else before or after this noise?" Echie asked.

The woman took a deep breath and opened her mouth to speak.

But Echie interrupted. "And could you, again, please keep your voice down? There still may be people trying to sleep."

"Are you fucking kidding me?" the woman shouted back. "There's no fucking way anybody could have slept through this . . . I mean, I was like 'What the fuck was that?' and my kids were awake and screaming like they were gettin' fuckin' murdered! I mean what the—"

"Fuck. Yes, ma'am," Echie answered, still jotting notes.

I stifled my laughter. This obnoxious woman would, more than likely, be the only person willing to make a statement. The East Side was a tough area, not so much a melting pot as a chunky stew. There was not what you might call a mingling of cultures. People tended to stick with their own. Most of the residents were from either Eastern Europe, Southeast Asia, or Mexico, all living in an assortment of government tract duplexes, compact houses, and run-down apartment buildings like this piece of shit. This is where Echie had been raised. That fact had earned her a measure of respect from the community, as well as the department. And me as well.

I bent forward and whispered, "Where's James?"

"I think he's still inside with the . . . remains," she answered with a tilt of her head.

I nodded my thanks, stepped around them, and entered the apartment. My nostrils were instantly assaulted by a familiar stench. I backed out and took a couple of deep breaths before plunging back inside.

The apartment was small. The kitchen was an accumulation of seventies' cabinetry, a cracked Formica countertop, and a scorched hotplate on top of a stovetop. Stacks of dirty dishes filled every available flat surface, including the small kitchen table. But the trash that was strewn on the floor somehow stopped short of the living room carpet as if by an unseen wind.

A flat screen television hung on the living room wall, and a glass coffee table held remnants of a party—empty beer cans, a bowl of chips, assorted remotes, and a bong made from bluish-green glass. Directly before me stood a brown couch covered with bright colored pillows and a throw blanket in the colors of the Mexican flag. Most of the latter was stained a deep red. The coppery scent of blood and exposed flesh wafted up from it.

Beneath the blanket was a young man's mangled corpse.

My fingers reflexively traced a sign of the cross—forehead, chest, shoulder, shoulder—as I studied the dead man. His head was tilted back, but not so much that I couldn't notice how his skull was split in two down the centerline of his face. A thin, bloody mustache now dangled on either side of the cleaved space.

The corpse was centered on the couch, feet on the floor and dressed in a white wife-beater tank top, long denim shorts, and white Nike sneakers with royal-blue laces that all but screamed his loyalties.

A Sureno.

Gang member or not, the poor guy had met an early and bloody death.

CHAPTER 6

As you might guess, a bullet fired up into the chin is a fairly classic method of self-destruction, especially for men. The entry wound is typically small but very bloody, while the exit wound is a large crater on the top of the skull with attendant gore and surprisingly little blood. There is also massive discoloration and facial distention from the pressure of the round's passage, which sometimes pops out an eyeball or two. Yeah, it's not pretty.

But here was a new twist. Or should I say, a new angle. Instead of straight up and into the brain, the round's vector was tilted forward, cleaving the face symmetrically. The result looked more as if he'd been struck face-first with an ax, save for the telltale entry wound at the throat.

There was also the gun in his lap, or at least what looked like the end of a blued barrel poking out from beneath the blanket.

I considered what I was looking at, how it might have happened. Using my right index finger as a trigger, I rotated my wrist beneath the corpse's chin, simulating what could have been the dead man's grip. It was awkward, but not impossible. Maybe he'd been drunk or stoned. Maybe he'd had second thoughts, and the gun had gone off accidentally, or . . .

Another option suggested itself. I set it aside for the moment.

Turning my attention back to the entry wound, I observed a large flap of skin below the dead man's chin. I lifted it to the light with a pen. It was imprinted with a dark residue in the rough shape of a circle. Beneath that, on the frayed and blood-soaked edges of the flesh, were rough tattoos.

XIII

TTL

OSO

I stood back. There were more tattoos, all on his arms and hands—the smiling and crying masks known as the drama clowns, the phrase *La Vida Loca*, three dots in the web of his hand. All popular with Surenos. I made a mental note to discuss the tats with Rafael Inigo.

A hand touched my shoulder, and I nearly jumped out of my skin. "Jesus, James! Don't do that!"

"Medical examiner will be here in a few," Kapalu said, ignoring my outburst.

"What's your take?" I asked.

He seemed confused by the question.

"I know this looks pretty straightforward," I added, "but maybe it's not. Did you notice this?"

I pointed out the entry and exit wounds with my flashlight. I twisted my hand around, again mimicking a gun.

"You're not liking his grip?" Kapalu surmised.

"No, I'm not liking his grip," I said.

He shrugged. "Check this out," he said.

Using his long wooden baton to raise the bloody blanket, he uncovered the weapon, which turned out to be quite familiar.

I turned at the sound of footsteps. Echie entered the room briskly, her mouth open to speak. Instead, she shut it and stared at the object on the couch.

"Remington 870," I said.

The shotgun was well-known to police officers across the country, many of whom still carried it on duty. It had been years since Tacoma had switched over to rifles, but I still recalled how sore my shoulder had been after a day of firing it at the range.

"Yup," Kapalu replied. "With a modification."

He was referring to the Remington's barrel, which had been roughly hacked, shortening it by nearly a foot. A small, jagged piece of metal jutted out at the end.

"Sawed off. Federal crime," I said.

"Yup," Kapalu repeated.

Loud footsteps announced the arrival of yet another cop, a tall, handsome man, darker than Echie, with silver tints in his gleaming black hair. He wore an immaculate blue wool uniform and gleaming leather belt as if it were a royal robe. He took one step in the door and stared down his patrician nose at the corpse.

I ignored him for the moment. "What's your take?" I said again to Kapalu.

"That it's probably a suicide," Kapalu said. Then he shrugged, adding, "Unless it's not."

"What . . . the . . . fuck?" said the tall man, obviously angry at being ignored.

"Hey, Lieutenant," I responded neutrally.

The shift commander, Lieutenant Joe Barrajas, glared at each of us in turn, favoring Echie with a wink, and then stalked towards the couch as if he were about to chew out the dead man for sitting down on the job. "So what you're telling me," the lieutenant said caustically, "is that you think there's a shooter involved because, and correct me if I'm wrong, there's no way the dead guy flinched and blew half his face off along with a chunk of his tiny brain?"

To his credit, he'd picked up on the unusual wounds more quickly than I had. Didn't make me any happier about his presence, though. Having the shift commander at your scene usually meant you'd screwed up.

"Now, I'm not a homicide detective or anything," Barrajas continued in a conversational tone, "but I'd still like to know how this situation could be anything other than the colossally fucked-up suicide it appears to be."

That would be my cue. I took a deep breath and then launched into an explanation of the final option. He was silent as I trained my flashlight on the shotgun. With one finger held above the sawed-off edge, I pointed out the little curlicue of metal poking out. Next, I lifted the flap of skin off the corpse's throat, making a mental note to throw away the filthy pen, and exposed the detail I had noticed minutes before: a ring of black residue with a curlicue burn mark that was a solid match for the hacked end of the barrel.

Barrajas studied the ragged piece of skin for more than a minute in complete silence, examining it from several angles. "It looks," he said in a resigned voice, "like the trigger was backwards."

"You see it too," I said.

"The residue on that small section of skin shows us the exact position of the gun barrel when it was fired, thanks to the shitty job somebody did cutting the barrel."

"Which means . . . ," Kapalu said.

"It means that if this guy committed suicide, then he turned the gun backwards, tilted his wrist back, and pulled the trigger," Barrajas interjected, holding his own hand in what looked like a very uncomfortable position.

Kapalu whistled.

"Shit," Barrajas said in a disgusted tone.

I wisely chose silence. My boss scratched his big nose. Then he scowled. Again.

"Okay, here's the plan. You," he said, pointing a long finger at me, "need to get a crime scene tech out here ASAP. Then get on the horn to whatever dumb ass is on call over at major investigations and fill them in. If you want any help out here for your crew, then *you're* gonna have to convince the on-call that there's a problem with this scene. Got that?"

"I got it," I replied.

Barrajas glared at the corpse. "Chances are the hose jockeys stomped on every piece of evidence, but let's play it by the book. If major crimes doesn't buy into this shit, then it won't be on our heads. We clear?"

Everyone nodded. I issued a few orders, mostly unnecessary given Echie and Kapalu's experience, and they hurried out to their cars to grab equipment.

Which left just my lieutenant and me. The dead guy was better company. I was thinking of a reason to leave, but Barrajas held out his open palm.

"Look, Cassidy," he growled, "I didn't come here to babysit you."

"Good to know."

Given that he had just effectively washed his hands of responsibility of the matter, à la Pontius Pilate, I wasn't in the mood for an ass chewing as well. But I bit my tongue, proving that I can show discretion on occasion.

"I need to talk to you about a private matter," he continued, "and I think you know what it's about. Get hold of me later when your ass is squared away." With that, the lieutenant looked around a last time and headed for the door. Then he stopped mid-stride, spun slowly, and raised his head. I followed his gaze up to the ceiling where a rough hole about six inches had been blown out. Dangling from it was a chunk of blackened hamburger meat. "What . . . the . . . fuck?" Barrajas said again.

"I think we've located the tongue," I answered.

Barrajas glared at me as if I were making a joke at his expense. He stomped out the door, and suddenly I could breathe again. I turned to the rotting corpse and whispered, "That went well, don't you think?"

My brain churned through the thousand details that would now require my attention. Yet the shiver that rolled up my spine had nothing to do with cold blowing through the open door or the macabre scene before me. It was Barrajas's last comment.

But one thing at a time.

✶ ✶ ✶

The homicide sergeant was extremely unhappy at the wake-up call and tried his best to cut me off. In the end, he agreed to a solitary detective, bad news for me given how busy the shift had become and how much responsibility that dumped on my crew. Barrajas could easily have overridden this and ordered a full crew of detectives, but I knew better than to ask. He was covering his ass, of course. The powers-that-be would not look favorably on unnecessary overtime expenses, which would reflect on performance reports and promotional opportunities. Hindsight was the rule of the day.

There was an upside—that *one* detective would be Rafael Inigo, energetic and sharp, with an encyclopedic knowledge of gangs and worth a handful of slouches.

The medical examiner's office was equally helpful. *Sorry, still processing.* Kapalu was the only pleasant voice on the phone, though he made it clear he was too busy collecting evidence to chat.

I dialed the next number from memory.

"Barrajas," said a sleepy feminine voice.

It was no coincidence that Joe Barrajas, my caustic boss, had authorized a crime scene tech; his daughter, Desiree, was the first name on the call-out list. Fortunately, Des was my friend, as sweet as her father was rude, as forgiving as he was vengeful. Besides good looks, they seemed to possess few traits in common. And Desiree's look was the type you'd be most likely to spot on a Victoria's Secret catalogue. Not that I've ever looked.

"Hey, Des, I'm really sorry to wake you up."

"Michael? Is that you?" a silky voice spoke into my ear.

"Yeah."

"That's all right. What's up?"

"I've got a suicide with some red flags. I'm not getting much help from detectives, and I could really use your help. If you're up for it." I glanced at my watch for the first time in a while. "Shit, it's two in the morning. Sorry."

Her yawn sounded like the purr of a cat. "Of course I'll come. Let me get dressed and check in with dispatch. I'll get the info and see you out there in a bit."

"Thanks, Des. Really appreciate it."

Before she answered, I heard a single, loud snore.

"That was Nate saying hi," she said, the smile evident in her voice.

"Lucky guy," I said.

I sat there contemplating the phone for a while after hanging up. Instead of worrying about my crime scene, I was recalling my upcoming meeting with my boss, aka Joe Barrajas, aka Desiree's dad, aka I'm in deep shit.

Had their secret leaked? If so, the timing sucked. I stood and paced my small office.

Desiree and Nate had gotten married—eloped would be the appropriate word. Which meant that her dad, especially, did not know. Joe's temper was legendary, but it was never as hot as when a cop's eyes lingered too long on his daughter. Since Desiree attracted that type of attention like sugar attracts ants, it had made for many interesting moments within our dysfunctional little PD.

But Desiree was my friend, had been for years. Nate was no more or less than the best friend I'd ever had in this life. By comparison, my duty to Joe Barrajas was a professional obligation. Which had its limits.

I left my cramped office and headed for the main patrol area. Echie ambushed me before I could leave. Her eyes were red with fatigue, her calm demeanor evaporated.

"I'm sick and tired of babysitting that loud, obnoxious bitch!" she hissed through clenched teeth.

"I know, Echie, it's a shit detail," I answered truthfully. "Did she give you anything good?"

The tight lines around her eyes eased, and she dug out her notebook. "She heard some noises outside," she said, flipping through pages, "someone walking, maybe a soft knock on a neighbor's door. She was watching Jerry Springer, huge surprise. TV schedule has that coming on at 2230 hours."

"Gunshot was reported sometime during the next sixty minutes, right?" I said, thinking.

"Yes," Echie said.

"Good job," I said, meaning it. "Get one of the rookies to babysit her, and you can start typing it up."

"Sounds good," she said with the beginning of a smile.

Before I said something foolish, I headed for the exit. At the double doors leading to the parking lot, I recalled Joe Barrajas's request. I forced my unwilling feet to turn around, quite sure I was about to insert myself into an ugly family feud. But if I ignored Lieutenant Joe Barrajas, there would be worse consequences.

The station lobby was a vast space, lit at this hour by blue incandescent lamps, which gave it the nickname of Blue Palace. I trudged up the atrium staircase in the eerie quiet like a prisoner heading for the gallows. A solitary light burned in the lieutenant's third floor office, and loud voices boomed from it.

Per usual, Joe was having a loud conversation with the FOX News broadcaster, though his contributions were mostly "hell yeah!" or "fuck that!" When a commercial came on, I knocked.

Barrajas flung it open. "Come in, Sergeant."

I took the proffered seat. Barrajas took his time sitting down, shuffling through papers and looking uncomfortable. This was not leading up to the ass chewing I'd envisioned. Joe's rivalry with Nate, a one-sided affair in my opinion, was well-known and likely stemmed from the clock that was ticking until Chief Garcia's retirement. Maybe there was more to it. Race? Jealousy? Who could say. But as Nate's friend and Joe's subordinate, I was occupying a slippery piece of real estate.

"What's on your mind, LT?" I asked eventually.

He turned as if surprised I was still there. His dark eyes narrowed. "You're what, first generation?"

His voice was so low, the question so unexpected that it took me a moment to process. *What the hell?* "Um," I stammered. "Yeah, I am. Why do you ask?"

"Here's the thing you need to understand, Sergeant. Whether your parents are from Dublin or Beverly Hills really doesn't matter in this country. You know what does matter?"

I shook my head.

"Skin color. Simple as that. My family has been in this country for six generations, you know that? Fought in every war since the Spanish-American, worked hard, and got ahead. Like that means a damn thing!" he said, his voice hissing with sudden anger. He turned to me. "I was the only Mexican kid around whose parents didn't work in the fields. My father was an attorney, but the white kids lumped me in with the illegals and the berry pickers, called me beaner, or worse, ignored me. When I got older, my Hispanic friends joined gangs, sold drugs, went to jail. I've been a cop for thirty years now, raised a daughter, buried my wife, been a part of the community. Last week a guy at my country club thought I was the lawnmower!" Barrajas' eyes were wild, staring around the room as if trying to find the source of his anger. "Fuck them," he added, shaking his fists at the dark television. Joe walked to the window and stared out into the dark atrium. His chin fell. "The point, Sergeant, is that I can't escape the problems of my heritage. I must do as I see fit based on my place in this community, no matter what others think."

I was stumped. How could any of this possibly relate to me? Still, I didn't ask the question, knowing the answers would come soon enough. Barrajas didn't disappoint.

"My daughter," he said simply. "I want to know."

"What do you want to know, Joe?" If he was going to ask, I wanted him to say the words.

He cocked his head as if I'd just insulted him. "This isn't a cultural diversity lecture. This is me telling you there are things a father must do to protect his child from the world. I know what is in men's minds, what depths they will sink to gain what they want. And that is why I ask you again to tell me," he said, his voice now soft and almost pleading, "to tell me what has happened with my daughter."

"You haven't talked to her," I said, stating the obvious.

He shrugged off the question.

My eyes swept the bookcase behind him. It was stuffed with letters of appreciation, awards for service, commendations for valor, and certificates for training—the expected accumulation of thirty years in police work. But tucked in nearly every available crevice were photos, all of them featuring Desiree in various stages of growth—a child in her father's arms, college graduate in cap and gown next to her beaming dad, her first day on the job at TPD.

"All right," I decided abruptly. "I'll tell you."

CHAPTER 7

Desiree was a willowy teenager, gawky and demure when I first saw her. I was a rookie, unsure of my career choice, unsure of my skills, and generally unsure about everything, except that sergeant Joe Barrajas scared the shit out of me. Desiree trailed into the briefing room in the old station, her second home after her mother's passing. I didn't know that the veteran cops surrounding me had become her adopted family, but that was probably why they kept a close eye on me, especially when Desiree sat down next to me with a sly smile. She was usually around the station for the next few years.

Then Desiree finally headed off to college, a girl still growing into her looks, but she came back as a fully realized woman. Mature, intelligent, and with an off-kilter sense of humor that I found hilarious. But to say she had blossomed would be to sell it short—thick, lustrous hair no longer tied up in a ponytail, exquisite brown eyes, an hourglass shape that accentuated—dammit, you get the idea. Desiree was a throwback to the pin-up girls of yesteryear, a true beauty. Guys circled her like buzzards. Which of course brought Joe Barrajas to the boiling point on any given day.

Over the next few years, Desiree and I formed an easy-going friendship, mostly based on the fact that I never hit on her. Not that I didn't think about it, but I was either too shy, too married, or too immersed in my own issues. Or maybe I didn't feel like getting rejected.

Take your pick. What I learned as her friend was that Desiree was surprisingly lonely. She would hang out at the library or in bookstores, eat alone at home or with her dad. Her mom's death hovered between them like a storm cloud they both chose to ignore. It must have been tough for her, but beneath all that smooth skin and languid curves, Desiree was plenty tough and smart as hell. She told me that college had been as much escape from her cloying father as an opportunity to join the wider world. It was there that she found herself. She excelled in academics, made the dean's list, and finally found people who appreciated her for something other than a body, a face. With that accomplished, she decided to end her self-imposed exile.

The biggest surprise was her decision to seek a job at the police department, her childhood haven. Regardless, Desiree became a highly trained technician in the new Crime Scene Unit and started making a name for herself. Her homecoming was cause for joy. It all felt preordained.

But there were still issues. Her father picked up his possessiveness where he'd set it aside. Heads got knocked and feelings were hurt. Desiree took her private life off the grid. Outside of work, she became a ghost.

These were details Joe already knew. If he didn't, then he wouldn't believe me anyway. Since I was angry with him for using rank to force the story out of me, I didn't sugarcoat the details. With a mental apology to my friends—who knew this moment would come—I moved on to the brief love affair between Desiree Barrajas and Nate Orlando.

✶ ✶ ✶

A few months ago, I was sitting in a comfy leather chair in Nate's spartan office. His unit, Special Investigations, or SIU, was a neat little operation headquartered in a downtown high rise. He had access to a vast amount of seized assets, including a private garage filled with luxury cars all taken in drug raids and reserved solely for his detectives.

Nate and I had a long-standing appointment for coffee most days, and conversational topics varied—sports, religion, politics, whatever—as long as it didn't relate to the job. It gave me a chance to stay in the loop with him, while it gave him an opportunity to vent without it affecting his career. Not that Nate made any apology for his ambitions. Punching through glass ceilings was, for him, a blood sport.

His office door was always open, which is why Desiree was able to pop in and say a quick hello. That day I caught her scent, a whiff of cut flowers, a second before I heard her voice. Hers was surprisingly deep and infused with a quality I can only describe as feminine energy.

"Top secret discussion?" she asked.

I swiveled around. "Can't confirm or deny. How you doin', Des?"

"Can't complain. Morning, Lieutenant," she said, her eyes flashing as she nodded at Nate.

There was no response. I turned around. Nate's face was caught between expressions. I picked out surprise and wonder easily enough, but I did have trouble identifying the source of his twitching lip. It turned out to be nerves. My buddy, the former SWAT commander, whose reputation for being tough and fearless had plenty of examples, was nervous. Around a woman.

Holy shit.

In the awkward silence, Desiree's face communicated a subtle question in my direction. I just shrugged.

Nate finally regained his self-control, and the moment passed. He coughed and stood up. With extreme courtesy, he pulled out a chair for her.

I held my breath. As a rule, Desiree did not respond well to gallantry. I suspect she viewed it as a player's ruse. To my surprise, she just blushed sweetly and sat down.

"We were just talking about baseball," Nate said, his smooth lie shocking me yet again. "Michael here was trying to explain how to hit a curve ball, but I pointed out that since he has never in his life actually accomplished such a feat perhaps he should rely on the good opinion of others."

It was a lame attempt at humor, though not far from the truth in my case. Still, Desiree surprised me by laughing. Nate responded with a smile and a sly wink for her, but he was so unaccustomed to using said winking muscles that it took half his face to make it work. Being a trained observer, I decided something was going on.

In the past, when Nate was attracted to a woman, he just went right after her. No sly maneuvers, no word games. It probably helped that women would line up to talk to him. As a wingman, I was a bench warmer at best.

So, yeah, Nate's flirting was a rare thing. I could only wonder what other miracles the day might hold. Fortunately, Desiree didn't seem to notice the amazement plastered on my face. She had eyes only for Nate.

"So he says to the mayor, 'Well, I didn't vote for you,'" Desiree said in a fair impression of her father. "And the mayor tells him that his signature is on his paycheck. 'Fine,' my dad says, 'then just throw another goddam signature on this speeding ticket so I can get back to work.'"

That was my cue to head back to work, so I excused myself. Neither of them noticed when I left the office.

Had it been anyone else, I would have said the guy was smitten. But this was a different. Nate had never, and I mean never, pursued a workplace relationship because he considered it unprofessional. And in his mind, unprofessional behavior was blasphemy.

Under intense questioning the following day, Nate admitted he was smitten. For the first time I considered the possibility that my friend, a man whom I loved like a brother, might actually have found a woman who could distract him from his single-minded pursuit of greatness.

It still took some time for him to work up the nerve to call her. Their first date came the following weekend, and I was the only one who knew.

A month later, they were inseparable, and it was apparent my two friends were falling deeply, passionately in love.

Not that there weren't bumps in the road. A few weeks along, we were sitting in a Starbucks in my neighborhood when Nate confided his biggest worry—the department's policy against fraternization. Nate had not only written it but had also held a few cops accountable when their shit hit the fan.

"Hard to argue with my own writing," he growled at no one in particular.

"The irony is thick," I admitted.

"And what happens when Joe finds out, huh? For whatever reason, her father doesn't like me. He'd be thrilled to see me disciplined."

"So?"

"So?" he said, irked at my casual response. "I can take his distaste, his hatred even. Been doing that long enough, God knows, but what about Desiree?"

"What about her?" I asked.

He paused, looked out the window. "Feel like I'm coming between her and her father."

"Maybe," I agreed. "Seems like her decision, though."

Nate lowered his head to consider the point. "Still—"

"It's simple, Nate. Do you care for her?"

He looked up, confused.

"I repeat, do you like Desiree?"

At the mention of her name, his eyes lit up. "She's a jewel, Michael. She's beautiful, of course, but if you knew the depths of her intellect, her dry sense of humor, the—"

"I get it, Nate," I said, holding "I get it. Desiree is smart and gorgeous. I know that." I laughed, which seemed to piss him off more. "Look, bro," I said, lifting a palm, "everyone's in love with Desiree, and if you don't realize that, then you're deluded. But for some crazy reason she's chosen you."

Nate's expression softened.

I reached out and grabbed one of his beefy arms. "At least for the moment," I reminded him, "you're not her boss. You're not technically violating policy. You have the right to a life, assuming you want one. You do want a life, don't you?"

A smile slowly lit up his face. His teeth flashed, and he grasped my hand in a bone-crunching squeeze. He bowed his head, and I did likewise. Like the two kids we had been, sitting at his dinner table, we each whispered a silent prayer.

Mine was for luck. They both deserved a little of that.

After that, there was no stopping them. Despite the secrecy, or perhaps because of it, Nate and Desiree's romance burned hot and bright in the wet weeks that followed. They spent most of their time up north in Seattle where they dined by candlelight in Capitol Hill cafés, sipped wine in Queen Anne bistros, and, in eclectic Belltown nightclubs, danced into the early morning.

Nate and I had more or less adopted the life of stuffy academics, our private lives filled with working out, a few hobbies, and conversation. Not what some would call social lives, but our day job generated all the social activity we needed. Without his and Desiree's company, the hours passed slowly for me.

One evening I swung by his old house in the Hilltop. His mother, Rochelle, still lived there, and she was the sweetest, gentlest, and yet strongest person I'd ever met. The neighborhood had been gang central during Nate's childhood, though it had improved in the last few years. Rochelle had raised him alone, helping her only child find his way through the crucible of inner-city life with single-minded tenacity. Even after Nate had moved out, urging her to come along, she had remained, unwilling to abandon the friends she had made over half a life.

Seeing the old place reminded me of us as kids. Nate and I had been unlikely friends. He was a tall, gangly black kid, mature beyond his years with a major chip on his fatherless shoulders. I was a naïve slice of white bread with Irish Catholicism stamped into my DNA. Yet when Rochelle opened her door one day, the two of us were standing on the porch talking about baseball as if we'd known each other forever. She accepted our friendship with easy grace then, and she had remained an unwavering presence in my life ever since. I had spent most of my adolescence in their snug little home, an ironic haven for a white kid in a city too often divided along racial lines.

When Therese died, I had cried a thousand tears on Desiree's shoulder. When my parents had died, she had long since become my second mother.

I knocked gently on Rochelle's faded yellow door. It opened slowly, letting the familiar scent of cinnamon waft out. Despite her son's size, Rochelle was petite, a southern lady with genteel manners that did not go in for excessive displays of emotion. When she lifted her cheek for a customary kiss, I wrapped her in a bear hug and didn't let go.

"You're gonna break my back one of these days, Michael," she pouted until I released her. She made a big fuss of smoothing her printed dress, but I could tell she was pleased.

"Naw, you're too tough," I answered, handing her a bag of coffee beans.

Her smooth *cafè-au-lait* skin practically glowed when she lifted the bag to her face and took a deep breath. "French roast?"

I chuckled. "One day you're gonna ask that, and I'm gonna say no."

"And on that day I'll show you the door," she answered, her caramel-colored eyes twinkling.

Rochelle waved me to a chair, gathering her kinky grey hair into a ponytail as she moved deftly around the small kitchen. The beans rattled into the grinder, followed by the *burr burr* sound I found so soothing.

She handed me a mug of her usual espresso-thick coffee. We toasted.

"I was thinking," I said after the first sip.

"Always a good practice, I'm told."

"Well, I was thinking about this secret, Nate and Desiree, you know . . ."

Rochelle eyeballed me over her coffee, a look I'd seen Nate employ to great effect.

"Wait, wait!" I said, waving my palms in surrender. "Before you kill me, let me finish."

She held up a hand. "Now, Michael, don't you go jinxing those two. I have high hopes for Nathaniel, and a good woman is just what he needs. That boy's been alone for too long."

"You're right about that," I said, smiling. "What's the longest girlfriend he's had? A week? Two?"

She shook her head in mock disapproval and took another swig.

"It's just that I've never seen him put his career aspirations on the back burner for very long," I said. "I'm worried he's going to sabotage whatever he's got going with Desiree. You know how he is."

Rochelle set her mug down and squeezed my hand. "Of course I do, Michael. I know how he was, is, and could be." She stood up, sidled to the oven, and pulled the door open. The smell of sugary cinnamon made my mouth water. She slowly frosted the newly baked rolls, returning a few minutes later with a dinner plate overflowing with a warm, gooey proof of God's existence.

We lowered our heads in unison for a silent prayer. Then we dug in, greedily worshipping the blessed saints of cinnamon, sugar, and coffee.

I wolfed mine down, but Rochelle still set her fork down first, dabbing her mouth daintily with a flower napkin. "Michael," she continued as if we had not paused to devour a few thousand calories, "we all have our demons. Your poor sweet momma passed some onto you, am I right? Mine was a man, a handsome devil who gave me nothin' in this life but the son he never knew. Here's what we can't forget—sooner or later, life takes away most of the things we love."

In her soft words, I saw Therese alive, her beautiful fragility so near that I had but to close my eyes to touch her. Yet that wasn't the point. Rochelle had already guided me down this road once, and I had finally realized that my time with Therese had been a gift. A bitterly short gift of time, yes, but sweet.

Having known me so long, Rochelle read my changing expressions.

"You see my point," she said, dabbing her eyes now with the napkin. "Our demons will weigh us down, let us drown in our own tears if we let 'em. That's why we've got to learn to balance our gifts against our losses. Rochelle leaned back in her chair. "I pray for you every day, Michael. And I pray for my son as well. I pray that he and his pretty little gal can find some joy."

Her smile was radiant. I squeezed her hand.

"You and I just need to keep him on track," she added.

"You know you can count on me," I said. "It's just that, well, you know how the rumor mill works at the station. Desiree and her secrets, Nate and his reputation. It has me worried."

She shook her head. "It may surprise you, but I know a thing or two about reputations and secrets myself. When Nate's father wandered off all those years ago, don't you think people talked? Sure, they did. They were just as hateful and cruel as they could be, and the only ones they hurt were me and my little boy. Well, tell you what, he packed that burden around on his own shoulders like Atlas carried the world! He kept his mouth shut, kept his promises, and he never broke." Rochelle's face was flushed with pride, grew melancholy a moment later. "The day we quit fighting for the life we want is the day we don't deserve it."

I considered her words as I finished my coffee.

✶ ✶ ✶

The next evening I met up with Nate and Desiree at a waterfront restaurant in downtown Seattle. They were already seated at the table, sipping wine, their heads nearly touching as they spoke in low tones. I held back, unwilling to spoil the moment. Desiree finally spotted me standing by the door and waved me over. I hadn't seen either of them for a week, and we exchanged hugs before sitting down. It took us almost an hour of catching up before we looked at the menu. The meal was typical northwest fusion—Asian salads, a few spicy tapas, and smoked salmon. Sipping my customary lemonade, I stared at my empty plate in satisfaction.

"When you joined us," Nate said, "Des and I were talking about our childhoods. Turns out we have a lot more in common than I thought. We were both an only child raised by a single parent, both the first in our family to go to college."

"Know what your mom would say to that?" I asked with a wry grin.

"You looking for a medal?" we both answered at the same time. Desiree's laugh was clear and full of warmth.

"I can't wait to get to know your mom better," she said.

"And I can't wait to make your father understand how important you are to me," Nate responded.

A chill fell on the table. Fortunately, dessert arrived. I devoured the moistest piece of chocolate cake ever made. We argued over the bill until Nate challenged me to an arm wrestling match. I agreed, cheated as always, and paid the bill. The late evening foot traffic at Pike Place Market was still lively, even after its iconic booths had closed up for the day.

All too soon I felt like the dreaded third wheel and begged off.

"You're on graveyard, Michael," Desiree said, reaching for my hand. "How can you possibly be tired? Why don't you come dancing with us?"

"Are you kidding?" I answered. "I've seen you two move. Compared to that, I look like I'm having a seizure."

"He *is* a hopeless honky," Nate said, shaking his head.

"Racist," I said.

Nate gave me a big, uncharacteristic hug, a sure sign of his good mood. Desiree gave me a kiss redolent of jasmine and unresolved emotions.

I climbed the steep hill and looked back. They were sitting side-by-side on a park bench overlooking Elliott Bay. Nate got down on a knee—no small gesture for a man who prized his Brooks Brothers suits over most people—his face suffused with such joy it was evident from a block away. Desiree held his face in her hands, kissed his scalp. Nate buried his head in her lap, hugging her as if she were drowning.

I turned aside, overwhelmed.

On the way home, I punched in Rochelle's number.

"Know what I think?" I said without preamble.

"I'm sure you're gonna tell me, honey," she answered.

"I think he's gonna marry that girl."

There was silence on the other end. When Rochelle Orlando spoke, her voice held every bit of hope, worry, and joy that existed in the world.

"Praise God."

Nate made it official a few days later. We met on Sixth Avenue, a bustling street of restaurants, nightclubs, and shops far enough from the police station to ensure privacy. He entered the coffee shop dressed for success as always in a knee length camel hair coat over a white shirt, powder-blue tie, and black slacks. His large feet were wrapped in custom-fitted Italian leather shoes that probably cost more than my paycheck. The soles tapped softly on the tile floor as he approached my table, his face crackling with energy. He lifted the cup I had waiting for him and held it out.

"We toasting something?" I asked, amused.

"Yes, my brother," Nate said formally. "Desiree and I are engaged."

Despite my prediction, I was shocked. The man I'd known for years, a workaholic, a devoted cop, a man whose name was synonymous with "potential" had pledged his life to a woman? It was unthinkable. Then again, it wasn't just any woman, was it?

So I gazed up at this new man, this too-large dude with a smile so big it was about to tear the skin around his mouth. The truth finally set in as we touched coffee cups, and it was as if I'd absorbed the future through the gesture. My head filled with snapshots of a large, excited crowd, the exchange of vows, a new home, the sound of laughter and shouting, messy rooms, dirty diapers, kids' toys, 401(k)s, and, above all, Nate's wide-eyed look of surprise as he realized the full extent of the compromise he'd made. Then it morphed into the profound look of contentment that was now plastered all over his face.

We must have made quite the scene, two grown men hugging and dancing around the coffee shop. I didn't give a shit.

"Desiree's as excited as I am, believe it or not," Nate said after we sat down.

"Of course she is, bro," I said. "She's marrying you for your money."

His grin rekindled, and then it faded. "There's just one problem."

"Joe," I said.

"Yeah. She's convinced her father will sabotage this somehow. It's become a fixation for her."

"What does she want to do?"

"She wants to elope." Nate's shoulders slumped.

"Ouch," I said.

"No shit," he agreed. That rare curse was a fair indication of his feelings on the matter. He shook his head. "I can't say I get it," he continued. "I mean, I know we've had our professional differences over the years. I know I don't match his image of a son-in-law, but—"

"You're black," I said softly.

And there it was. The great divider, the killer of dreams, the wall that separated humans and would forever push them to view the world through a colored lens. Race.

We were both quiet for a moment.

"Nate," I said finally," you know how Joe is. Do you honestly believe he'll suddenly be okay with you as a son-in-law, a man outside his culture, a rival, someone he obviously doesn't even like?"

It was a bitter truth, of course. But Nate had handled this and worse his entire life. We might as well tackle it now and be done with it.

"I know that," Nate answered. "I'm being too optimistic, that's all. My happiness is, well, it's altering my perspective." He sat up straight. "As far as I'm concerned, Joe Barrajas is welcome to come to our wedding. But I will let Desiree decide the matter." A smile fluttered around his mouth. "She's already made most of the plans, anyway. Is that how it is with all women?"

I needed only a second to think about that. I shrugged. "If you wanna know about women, you're asking someone of the wrong gender."

"S'pose I am," he answered, his smile returning in full. "So anyway, she wants to get married in Vegas, hang out for a few days. After that, she'll figure out the best way to tell Joe."

"And you're gonna roll with that?"

It was Nate's turn to shrug. "Desiree gave me a choice—marry her in Vegas or not at all. I chose the lesser of two evils."

"If marrying a beautiful woman in a sunny vacation destination is your idea of evil, then you and I are due for another discussion on ethics."

"Which brings me to a related topic," he said with a glint in his eye. "I'm looking for a best man. You interested?"

I was thrown back twenty-five years in a moment. It had been raining softly the day Nate and I met, had rained through much of the ensuing years as we made our way forward, clearing the hurdles of manhood always together, one helping the other. He had been my best man. Now I would be his.

My heart pounded in my chest. I grasped the front of my shirt, unconsciously feeling the shape of the crucifix dangling from a silver chain while across the table Nate held its twin in his own hands. The crosses had been a gift from my mother, a devout Catholic who had finally overcome her own prejudices and accepted Nate into our home. We bowed our heads, mouthed the short prayer we'd learned decades ago in the cloistered halls of our Jesuit high school.

I put my chain away and appraised him. "How much does the job pay?"

Nate rolled his eyes, laughing.

"Just one condition, though," I added. "I'm not wearing one of those tuxes with all the bright colors. My fashion consultant says they make me look washed out."

"Brother, it ain't the tux."

Chapter 8

Barrajas listened quietly throughout my story. Which isn't to say he was pleased. In fact, each time I mentioned him in the context of the story, his anger filled the office. It felt as if I were standing too close to a flame. What this might mean for my immediate future I didn't know. Didn't care, really. He'd asked for it, hadn't he?

By the time I finished, he seemed to have collected himself. "I don't judge people based on race," he said, trying hard not to sound like he was pouting. "I don't care what color you are—marrying outside your culture just fucks everything up."

I didn't bother pointing out the implied racism in the remark; he wasn't listening anymore. What was also evident was that he didn't for a second believe his daughter had conspired to keep her relationship, not to mention her marriage, a secret from him. He was quiet, studying me. I waited him out.

"Something you need to know," he eventually said.

I nodded, quite sure that I didn't want to know whatever it was. After the bombshell I'd just dropped, it couldn't be good news.

"You remember when you were promoted? When the chief used the rule of three to pick you over Rafael Inigo?"

"I am well aware of that, Lieutenant. Why would you bring that up?" I asked, holding my anger in check.

"For what it's worth, you earned an enemy that day," he said with a neutral expression.

"All right, I'll keep that in mind," I answered.

I stood up. The lieutenant had already turned his attention to the TV, so I left without another word. I didn't stop until I was next to my car in the parking lot. My head spun, thoughts of Nate and Desire and their no-longer secret marriage, foremost in my mind. They would need to know right away. I gnashed my teeth with frustration, wishing she had been the one to spill the beans.

Well, the fucking beans were spilled now.

Then I recalled Barrajas's cryptic warning. Was he really just trying to one-up me, trying to put a little fear in my day by passing on a rumor about Inigo who, by the way, was at this moment on his way to help me deal with a tricky crime scene?

My cell phone chirped. Glad for the distraction, I checked the number. It was unfamiliar. "Cassidy, here."

"Hey, *el jefe*, it's Rafael."

Speak the devil's name and he shall appear.

I blamed Joe Barrajas for that thought. In fact, just hearing Raf's voice brought a smile to my face. Inigo had that effect on most people. He was a crafty guy, sure, but he was also witty and charming with that shit-eating grin that somehow made people like him. Also, he had investigative skills that were in high demand as well as a network of contacts—prostitutes, druggies, gang-bangers, and if you believed the rumors, worse—that made him all but indispensable. It was said he had eyes and ears everywhere, informants he had groomed, plucked off the streets or bailed out of jail. Inigo kept himself to himself, as my mother used to say, an enigma. But he was a good guy to have on your side when things went south.

"Morning, Raf. Didn't recognize your number."

"My personal cell, hombre. Forgot my work phone. It's probably sitting on my pillow, right where my head should be."

"Yeah, sorry—"

"Naw, it's all right. I'm already here at the Villa Fortuna, which, by the way, is a totally fucked-up name. *Mira*, Miguel! You shoulda told me about the dude's tongue! It hit the floor while I was standing there! I practically shit the bed."

I chuckled. "A little serendipity."

"Huh?" he said, yawning.

"A happy accident, that's all. Look, I know it's gonna be a busy night, but I appreciate the help. I'm heading up there now."

"Good." Inigo was quiet for a moment before continuing, "I got an idea how this went down, and I want you to hear it from *la boca del caballo*."

"My Spanish is rusty, but I think that means 'the horse's ass.'"

"You gringos are so funny."

"I'll be there in ten," I said and hung up.

Ten minutes later, I was back at the depressing little apartment building on top of the hill. It was quiet as a church without all the emergency vehicles. Only Kapalu's car and an unmarked blue Chevy sedan, Inigo's car, were parked in the fire zone.

A glowing ember inside the courtyard turned out to be the tip of Inigo's cigarette. The orange glow made his lean, angular face look hawkish, as if he were a bird of prey waiting silently for its next meal to scurry past.

We shook hands. The acrid tobacco smoke made my nose twitch.

"It's better than the smell inside," Inigo said, holding it away.

"Maybe, but those cancer sticks will get you one day, Raf. Can't live forever."

"It's either this or one of my ex-wives, Miguel. Either way I go out coughing up blood, right?"

"That is some dark shit, man," I answered, stifling a laugh.

"So's that *mierda* inside, Sergeant."

The mention of my rank changed the tone. I became intently aware of the chevrons on my sleeves. Inigo had finished ahead of me on the promotional list, and this was the first time the subject had been broached, albeit indirectly. My stomach churned.

"Look, about your shooting?" Inigo said, probably wanting to change the subject as much as I did. "I know it went south on us, but my informant had been kicking ass up until then, you know?"

"Yeah, I heard. Look, Raf, your guy was probably just in over his head that night."

"Yeah. My little *cabron* 'bout shit his drawers when the deal got fucked-up," he said. "I still don't know why those dudes took a shot at him. Could be he was just bangin' the wrong chick," he said, pausing to flick some ashes. "Anyway, I just wanna let you know I chewed his ass for not seeing that *puta* in the backseat. No more fuckups."

"It's cool," I said. "Let's just forget about it."

Inigo took a deep drag on his cigarette and nodded.

"I wanna get your take on the dead guy inside."

He nodded again and flicked his cigarette to the ground. "The dead hombre's known as Oso Negro, an original gangster with the T-Town Lokotes," Inigo said, his diction improving as he spoke. "SIU did an op five years ago and took down most of their OG's, including Oso, whose real name is," he paused to check his notes, "Antonio Ramirez-Sanchez. They called him the black bear because he sold a lotta black tar. SIU didn't catch him holding, but the feds popped him for felon in possession of a firearm. He just got out."

"No shit?" I was impressed. This was already more information than I could have hoped.

"I already made some calls and learned a few things about Oso. He had a tough time in the joint because his application to join the Mexican Mafia was—how do you white people put it?—not looked upon favorably,'" Inigo said, adopting a nasal tone.

"So, Oso got rejected by the mafia," I repeated. The Mexican Mafia, aka La Eme, was notoriously bad dudes. "Any idea why?" I asked.

"La Eme doesn't share its personnel rules with me. But if I were guessing, I'd say someone inside didn't think he was up to the 'blood in, blood out' standard. Most of their operation is run out of prison cells, but they still push a lot of dope and guns up and down I-5. Only way you can do that is to make sure nobody has the *cojones* to fuck with your program. La Eme is a gangster special force, Miguel, the big dogs," he said with a shrug. "For some reason Oso couldn't hang."

I thought about this for a moment, but Inigo wasn't finished.

"Picture this," he said, with a dramatic flair of his hands. "Oso's all bummed out cuz he didn't make the cut. When he gets out of the pen, he hops a bus to his crib here on the East Side. More bad news. His woman doesn't pick him up, so he has to walk home from the bus station. Then his key doesn't fit, so he has to knock on his own fucking door, right? And guess who answers? Some young dude from another gang! Hell, he's done a nickel in federal lockup. Why should his ol' lady wait for him? So he has to get his probation officer's help to find this shitty little pad here. Even though it's right in the middle of his ol' stomping grounds, none of his homies come by. Course most of 'em are dead or locked up anyway."

I followed this narrative, uncertain how he had found out so much so quickly. Or how much of it was true.

"Sounds like you're making a case for suicide," I said.

"You tell me," he said. "Finally, Oso buys himself a sawed-off shotgun from a Sureno up in Auburn. Maybe he'll pull a robbery, make a name for himself again. Prison was better than this, he thinks. But then he remembers how he got rejected by the mafia, and he knows he can't go back. So what does he do?"

The silvery moonlight winked out as Inigo lit up another cigarette.

I shook my head in disbelief. "How the hell do you know all this?"

"I hear voices, mijo."

"*Credible* voices?"

"They're the voices of the damned. They give me bad info? My swift sword of justice gets crammed up their ass."

I stared at him. He must have seen the amazement on my face because his grin was devilish in the burning light of the cigarette.

"Bullshit was part of my army training," he said.

"You served in Iraq, right?"

"Just bein' all I could be," he said bitterly.

"How'd it go?"

"I survived."

I left that alone for the moment. It was difficult to digest it all, though it did offer a reasonable explanation for suicide. "What about the exit wound?" I asked.

Inigo shrugged. "It *is* physically possible to commit suicide by holding a sawed-off shotgun backwards under your chin. You put your thumb on the trigger and pull, right? Stupid, yeah, but it'll get the job done. And how much dope you think they'll find in Oso's carcass?"

"Not a little," I admitted.

"*Mira*," Inigo added. "Look, I've already examined the scene with Kapalu. There's nothing left to find. At best we could call this a 'suspicious circumstances' death. I don't like it because it'll stay an open case, and the press will crawl up our asses. You wanna know what I think we should do?"

I nodded.

He continued, "We title it a suicide, let Kapalu file it. That way everyone forgets about it but us. Did your witness give you anything good?"

I had almost forgotten the obnoxious woman who'd frustrated Echie. "Nothing definitive. Possibly someone knocking on the door about an hour before the call came in."

"Hmmm," he said.

Yeah, it wasn't much. I gestured for him to continue.

"Let's call it suicide. If the medical examiner or the voices of the damned come up with anything, I can open it up with a keystroke. All right?"

"Sounds good, Raf," I said, surprised at how relieved it made me. "Let's do it."

In fact, his recommendation took most of the weight off my shoulders. Also, his promise to keep an eye out for further links was more than most investigators would offer. It had been a fool's errand, I realized. But at least it meant the system was working, right?

"Cool," he said. "I'm gonna clean up, grab my things, and head to the office. Since I'm up, I might as well write the fucking report."

We both turned at the sound of a car approaching on the gravelly road. A small white BMW slid in behind my police car.

"That's Desiree," I said. "I asked her to come by and help with the evidence collection."

But Inigo was already heading back towards the apartment. "We're gonna wrap this shit up in the next couple of minutes, Sergeant," he said over his shoulder. "No further assistance needed." Nodding towards the new arrival, he added, "Let her have some OT for slipping out of the sheets and putting on her makeup. Daddy won't mind signing the check."

Inigo disappeared through the door, shutting it behind him. *What the hell was that about?*

The abrupt attitude change confused me only for a moment.

Bet you took a run at Desiree, didn't you Raf? And I'll bet she shot you down.

I shoved cold hands into my coat pocket and walked quickly out to the street. Desiree's car engine was still running, her driver's window rolled down. A faint scent of jasmine wafted out. I inhaled deeply, anxious to rid myself of the lingering smell of death that had seeped out the apartment door. "Morning, Des."

"Morning, Michael. You sounded pretty excited over the phone, so I came straight from, um, home."

A stunning face materialized in the dashboard glow. Despite the hour, Desiree's thick hair was brushed, her meager makeup flawless. She blinked long lashes, studying me intently. I lowered my head to the window and spoke in a low voice.

"How is the new home shaping up? I always wondered how Nate would react to another human occupying his space."

"It's wonderful," she answered with a sincerity that was shocking.

"That's great, Des," I said truthfully. "Look, there's been a change of plan. I just finished talking to the case detective, and the initial ruling is still suicide. He says there's no reason to do a full scene. It'll be closed in a few minutes."

"Was that Inigo I saw talking with you?"

"Yeah."

Desiree stared out her windshield.

"He told me it would be inactive," I added, trying to convince her for some reason. "But he's going to put it in his pocket until the forensics are analyzed."

"All right, Michael. Now that I'm up, what can I do to help?"

"To be honest, I called you because the major crimes sergeant was being stingy with resources, and my crew was stretched thin." I didn't mention that her father had expressly instructed me to do the call-out. "Inigo just rendered his verdict—no crime, no foul—so I don't think there's anything to do."

"I get the picture," she answered with a nod. "So, how are things with you?"

I opened my mouth to speak, but an image of Joe Barrajas shut it as forcefully as a clamp. Again, Desiree studied me as if she were reading the news on my face.

"Michael?"

"Sorry, Des," I began.

"He knows?" she said, reading me as usual.

I opened my mouth again but only managed a nod.

"So there it is," she whispered. She bit her lip, her eyes lost in thought.

"Why don't you head home, Des? You've got enough on your mind. I'll sign your OT slip and put it in your box."

Desiree looked down into her lap for a moment, nodded, and started her car. She looked back once and mouthed a thank you. Her car pulled onto the ragged street. I watched until its red tail lights disappeared.

I smacked my frozen hands together. The first light of the new day traced a line of azure along the eastern horizon, signaling the end of a long, fucked-up night. Unbidden, the cleaved face of the corpse popped into my head. Shuddering against the cold, or so I told myself, I forced my legs into motion and headed for my car.

Miles to go, etcetera, etcetera.

CHAPTER 9

A cell phone buzzed loudly.

The three of us reached simultaneously for our pockets. The captain lifted his out and studied it, his expression blank. He rubbed his bloodshot eyes.

"It's the chief," Doloviski said. "I need to run up to his office. Why don't we take a break? It is now, " he glanced down at his watch, "1037 hours, and we are pausing the interview."

Doloviski clicked the recorder, and the green light disappeared. With it, I felt my own energy fade.

"I want to remind you both," the captain said, stifling a yawn, "that we've got to get through this today. Regardless of your own intentions," he added, staring at me, "there is an ongoing investigation in need of background information. I want you to think hard about what you're telling me. Keep it simple, but don't hold back anything of importance."

Without waiting for an answer, Doloviski hustled out of the room. His abrupt departure left me out of sorts. It took a moment before I heard Anna's voice. "Huh?" I said.

"So articulate," she said, a trace of humor crinkling the skin around her eyes.

"An attorney with a sense of humor," I said, studying her for the first time. "Who knew?"

"Sorry," she said, her gaze softening. "I'm not really good at holding hands and kumbaya. You okay?"

"Not really," I said. I rubbed my cheeks. "But I'm holding it together."

"Well, you look like shit," she said, standing up. "Wanna grab some coffee?"

We walked the short block to a nearby coffee shop. As soon as I poked my head in the door, however, I was engulfed in a wave of blue. A dozen cops pressed in on me, peppering me with questions. Anna Best stood behind me, her arms crossed and her eyebrows knitted in disgust.

"Fuck this," I said, backing out. "Let's go."

She followed me to the parking lot, where we hopped in her car, a big black Mercedes sedan.

"Gee, I wonder why you left police work," I said, impressed.

"Money isn't everything," she answered.

"Says the person with the money."

We shared a laugh. She asked for a recommendation for coffee. Fortunately, I knew just the place.

We drove downtown in comfortable silence. She slid into a spot in front of the County-City Building, a nine-story box housing most of the local government offices. A horde of caffeine-seeking politicians, jurists, and sheriff's deputies were pouring out the entrance, so we hustled ahead and managed to grab an open table in the back of an airy coffee shop with an incredible view of the mountains to the east. The rain-scoured sky allowed a fantastic view of the Cascade foothills with the glacial peak of Mount Rainier jutting above like a colossus.

Anna drizzled a sugar substitute into her nonfat, decaf latte.

I shook my head in disapproval. "What's the point?" I said.

"About what?" Best responded.

I attempted a sardonic smile, pointing to her drink. "That's what the baristas call your drink. No fat, no caffeine, no sugar, i.e., what's the point?"

She smirked. "Look, I'm already wide awake, and unfortunately I have a metabolism that shuts down the moment it comes in contact with fat, sugar, or chocolate. Not necessarily in that order."

"Fair enough," I said, chuckling and wiping the foam off my lips with my injured arm. I groaned.

"Whoops," she said.

"Sometimes I forget. Price you pay for not dodging bullets."

"Ah, the Superman complex I've heard so much about," she said. "Look, I know you've been talking nonstop for hours, but I hope you'll indulge a couple more questions. I feel like I'm operating in the dark here."

I sat up straight. The caffeine was already on the job. "Okay, sure. You can ask me questions. But I want you to understand something first. I didn't walk into Doloviski's chamber of horrors to salvage my career. I did it for my friends."

"See," she responded, "that's what I need to know. I have no idea what's involved here, but it's obvious the stakes are pretty high."

I had no reply for that.

"All right." Anna set her coffee down and picked up her notepad. "Forgetting for a moment what you just said—"

"I won't lie, if that's the implication. Not to save anyone, including myself." I looked out the window. "Ask away."

She scrolled through her notes. "Just two items. First, let's talk about Lieutenant Orlando. I was around only a few years, so I barely knew him. I need more background, especially regarding your personal relationship. I'll save the second topic for later, all right?"

I took a sip of the cappuccino, holding its warmth on my tongue, and begain. "Nate and I were born at St. Joe's only a few weeks apart. We grew up less than two miles away from each other, but until we turned fourteen, it might as well have been opposite sides of the planet. My parents were immigrants who raised their kids in middle-class America where Mom made lunches and Dad worked long hours, but at least there's a light at the end of the tunnel because you're the right color. Nate's family had a few hundred years of American life minus the dream, and living in the Hilltop was the only place his mom could afford after his dad split. People expected me to finish school, maybe go to college, you know. Irish Catholic? Join the fire department or be a cop. But Nate, well, aside from his mom, nobody expected much."

I studied my new attorney for a reaction. "Look, this isn't white guilt. You wanted to know about our relationship. You know what the

Hilltop was like back then. So do I because I spent half the time at his place. I heard the shooting, the sirens, all of that. Nate and I knew what alleys to avoid, knew when the heavy-duty gang-bangers would be out. The place was fucking cursed, but it was his home.

"When I first met him, Nate was this man-child, a tall, lanky kid with empty eyes that had already seen too much. If you prodded him, he'd jolt to life like an exposed nerve.

"I remember noticing him that first day of high school. Hell, I think everyone noticed the big, angry-looking dude from the Hilltop. They called him the scholarship kid, sometimes worse. Pretty rotten treatment, especially for a Jesuit school.

"Took a while, but eventually he opened himself up to learning, to life. Then it was like he was a starving man who'd stumbled on an all-you-can-eat buffet. When baseball season started, Nate went from curiosity to superstar.

"He was a natural—85 mph fastball and as good a swing as any fifteen-year-old kid ever had. That's where we met. I was a second-string catcher, the kid who spends the season picking splinters out of his ass or warming up pitchers. Tossing the ball with Nate became my favorite part of practice, even though I'd have to soak my hand in ice every night. I thought I knew everything about baseball, but he could reel off the batting averages of every player on the Tacoma minor league team. I thought I was a reader—Twain, Hawthorne, Shakespeare were some of my favorites—but he'd read them plus Camus and Chekov. I mean, who the fuck reads Chekov? The answer is the same kind of person who goes from atheist to committed Catholic in a year. But that was just Nate bein' Nate."

"Is that how he sees himself? As a Catholic?"

I nodded. "Nate became fascinated by the founder of the Jesuit order, Saint Ignatius of Loyola, this macho Spanish soldier who led a doomed campaign against the French in the sixteenth century. He was badly injured in the fight, and during the long, boring months it took to heal, he read a book about the life of Jesus. By the time he could limp away, Ignatius was a man of God.

"What impressed Nate most was that Ignatius never did anything halfway. He gave everything away to charity, hit the road, and spent the rest of his life ministering to the poor and sick. It's a pretty inspirational story, but that doesn't completely explain why Nate became obsessed with Ignatius's story." I chuckled.

"What's funny?" she asked.

"That was about the time he decided to become a priest."

"Really? A priest?" Best asked, skeptical.

"Obviously, he didn't. Turns out poverty, chastity, and obedience were deal-breakers, but my point is that Nate's mindset hasn't changed."

I continued, "Okay, fast forward to college. While I was off at U-Dub courtesy of student loans, Nate went to Seattle University on a full-ride baseball scholarship. It took me a bit longer to graduate, and by the time I did, Nate had a master's degree."

"Quite the overachiever," she remarked.

"Ya think?" I said, smiling. "Most people thought he'd wind up playing major league ball. When he passed that up, I assumed he'd head to law school, but all along he'd been telling everyone he was gonna be a Tacoma cop. It's just that nobody believed he'd do it until he actually went out and did it."

"Why?" Anna said quietly. "Why be a cop? If he had all those other options, why'd he choose the job?"

Knowing her history, I didn't take offense. "I wish I had a better answer, but the only reason he ever gave me was the one that normally comes out of the mouths of naive rookies. You know, to fight injustice, to make the world a better place, yada, yada, yada. I thought Nate was wasting his talents, just like everyone else."

"Yet he did it anyway," she said.

"Yup."

"And yet here you are."

"Yet here I am," I answered.

"How'd that happen?"

I grimaced. "One day I woke up with an English degree, no job, and no rent money. Nate was in the academy making wages, and I was sleeping on his couch. How does the saying go? 'It seemed like a good idea at the time.'"

Best's throaty laugh filled the room. "I know the feeling. And now?"

"To be honest, there are days when this can be the best job in the world, you know? Days when you feel like you're making a difference in people's lives, that you really matter. And then there are *other* days."

"*Those* are the ones that pushed me out," Best responded. She considered me silently for a moment before sliding a thick manila folder out of her attaché case. "Now that you mention that, I have your personnel file here. Care to give me a quick synopsis?"

"That's easy," I answered, setting my coffee on the table. Adopting a monotone, I recited, "Officer Cassidy is a dependable member of the department. He shows up for work on time and accomplishes his assignments in an acceptable manner. With regard to Detective Cassidy, see previous."

She opened her mouth to speak, but I raised a hand. "The file on Sergeant Cassidy, well, that's another matter."

"Yes, your demotion. We'll get to that. Let me ask you this, do you consider yourself unremarkable?" Best asked, setting her pen down and leaning back in her chair.

"In the land of the alpha male, yeah, that's a fair assessment."

"Look, Michael," she said, "I'm not here to psychoanalyze. I've spent a lot of time around police officers, and in my opinion, there are plenty of alpha males, guys *and gals*, who are unable to look past the drugs and crime to see the poverty and despair driving the behavior." She leaned forward in her chair. "I loved being a cop. I cared about the welfare of the people I met on the job, and that didn't include just the victims. The thieves, the addicts, the losers, all the people who self-destructed, taking their families down in the process. Unlike your holy saint, there came a point when I couldn't face them anymore, couldn't handle the hopelessness. As much as anything else, I went to law school to escape all that."

"Some escape," I said, indicating our current location with a nod.

Best leaned back in her chair with a wry smile. She tapped her pen. "Okay, last question."

"Fire away."

She took a deep breath. "When I arrived here this morning, I had no reason to believe it was anything more than a routine interview. Clearly, it is not. Your commanders think you know something important about whatever the hell is going on. They're desperate for you to talk, and I have no idea why. And," she continued before I could answer, "we've just spent the morning talking about Lieutenant Orlando's career, as well as his romantic relationship with Desiree Barrajas, a crime scene tech." She squinted at me through her reading glasses as if the answers were written on my nose. "What I want to know is this. Why are we talking about them?"

"They didn't tell you?" I answered, barely able to speak with the sudden knot in my throat.

"You heard Doloviski brush me off. So now I'm asking you. What the hell happened?"

"I just assumed you knew this whole time," I said, turning away. "I thought you knew."

"Knew what?"

"Desiree," I answered, Best's face suddenly blurring behind my welling tears. "She was murdered. And they think Nate killed her."

CHAPTER 10

INTERNAL INVESTIGATIONS INTERVIEW ROOM
MAY 19
1108 HOURS

Anna Best's heels tapped an angry beat as she marched down the hallway. Turning into the small room, she observed with some satisfaction that the noise had produced the desired effect. The police captain was squirming in his seat as if he were an animal caught in a trap. She swept into the room, riding a wave of indignation.

"Doloviski, for Christ's sake, why didn't you tell me?"

He winced as if she had struck him, but that didn't deter her. She folded her arms across her chest and gave him her best "don't fuck with me" look.

"How much did he tell you?" the captain asked miserably.

"A helluva lot less than I need to know!"

He held out his palms. "Then it should be obvious we have an unprecedented situation on our hands. The homicide detectives are jumping up and down across the hall. Everyone wants more information, which they think they can get by taking a chunk out of my ass, and the chief is trying to keep a lid on the details before this whole place explodes!"

Sensing the sincerity of his misery, she relented. "Look, Chuckie, I get it. You're in a tough position. But Detective Cassidy is injured and despondent. My job is to protect him through this process, and to do that, I need to know exactly what the hell is going on. What's the point of having me here if you keep hiding the facts?"

His hands gripped the edges of the table, knuckles turning white. It was clear her old partner was on the verge of really losing it.

"Goddammit!" He seethed. "Do you think I like all this skulking around? All this senseless bureaucratic bullshit I have to orchestrate? Hell, no! It wasn't my decision to withhold information from you of all people. But I wasn't given a choice!"

She counted silently to herself, and when she hit five, his rage vanished as if it had never been there.

"I apologize, Anna," he said in a calm voice. "I'm guessing Cassidy told you about Desiree Barrajas's mur-," another pause as his voice broke, "her death, so you understand what this means to us. This is one of our own."

"Can you at least tell me how it happened?" she asked.

"I'm afraid I can't," he answered, managing to sound contrite. "The details are classified for the moment while major crimes follows through on some leads."

"Fair enough, then what about the distraught detective currently cooling his heels in the lobby? Why do you need to talk to him in the first place?"

Doloviski exhaled. "We don't believe he's involved in the homicide, but his knowledge of the underlying circumstances is crucial for constructing the background of this case. Major crimes is working on motive issues, and well, Cassidy has a depth of knowledge with all the players." He raised his hands in exasperation. "I'm under huge pressure to get Michael on the record with what he knows, and it needs to be done yesterday."

"All right," she responded calmly. "You need to talk to him, and I need assurance that his statements won't put him in jeopardy—"

"The Garrity warnings give him immunity here, Counselor. You know that as well as I do."

"Then what's with all the deception?" she asked, her voice rising again.

"I apologize, Anna," Doloviski repeated. He blew his nose loudly. "I- I'm having a hard time staying impartial. I've known her, Desiree, I mean, since she was a baby. Joe used to bring her to the station, and we'd take turns bouncing her on our knees. That adorable little girl had fifty uncles, especially after Joe's wife died. He fell off the grid, and we didn't get to see Desiree for years. When she came back here after college, well, it felt like we were whole again. And to lose her now, like this . . ." He broke off and looked back up at the ceiling. Tears cut horizontally across his ruddy cheeks. He wiped his face and blew his nose again.

Anna sat down across the table. After a moment, she reached out and clutched his hand. They sat quietly for a while.

"So, you'll interview Cassidy and then what?" she asked, breaking the silence.

"Pass any relevant information onto homicide," Doloviski finished, releasing her hand with a squeeze. "Standard procedure. I just want you to understand the chief's point of view. This is a murder investigation involving a victim from our department, and the only current suspect is not only our most decorated police commander but also the chief's most trusted adviser. Aside from that, the domestic violence aspects alone demand a high level of privacy."

"About that, I'll need to know *something* about the circumstances in order to advise my client—"

"Again, I can't give you specifics about the murder itself," Doloviski interrupted, "but I can give you this." He pulled out a stack of paper from his satchel and slid it her way. "I'm sorry, but it should make more sense when you've read it."

Best raised an inquisitive eyebrow, waiting for more.

"If it sounds like I'm being cryptic, so be it," he said, lifting his hands in mock surrender. "But Cassidy's right about one thing."

"What's that?"

"We don't even know what questions to ask," Doloviski answered, nodding towards the report in her hand.

He pulled out his Blackberry and started tapping. She picked up the typed sheets in front of her. Curious, she lifted the first page and began to read.

Sgt. M Cassidy #0149   27 Mar 0633 hrs
Vehicle #70A (in-car video captured)

TACOMA POLICE DEPARTMENT SUPPLEMENTAL REPORT

> On 26 Mar at 2323 hours I was at my desk at the 4
> Sector Substation when the emergency tones sounded
> over the radio. Dispatch advised of multiple gunshots
> reported in the area of 40th and E. McKinley Avenue,
> a location that falls within my area of responsibility. I
> immediately responded four bells . . . .

Best skipped over the details, picking up Cassidy's report further
along.

> The three wounded subjects were in the center of a
> parking lot at the SE corner of 40th and McKinley
> Avenue, the site of a closed gas station. Two of them
> (later identified as the victims, Vic/Hernandez-Ortega
> and Vic/Prieto) were lying on their sides in the fetal
> position, separated from each other by approximate-
> ly three feet (see attached sketch). Blood had pooled
> on the concrete beneath the men, both of whom ap-
> peared to have bullet wounds in the torso. They were
> motionless. Neither had a pulse.
>
> I moved to the third subject, also a Hispanic male,
> who was approximately twenty feet south of the oth-
> er two. This subject (later identified as the suspect,
> Sus/Escalante) lay on his side. I quickly approached
> to check for a pulse, noting a small amount of blood
> soaking Sus/Escalante's shirt beneath his left breast.
> His carotid pulse was faint. I rolled him onto his back,
> and a small, chrome handgun dropped from his right
> hand. I immediately began chest compressions, and as
> I did so, blood bubbled out of a large, bloody wound
> on his chest.
>
> I administered CPR for less than a minute until relieved
> by paramedics from TFD. I secured Sus/Escalante's

firearm (later placed into evidence). I next placed a call to the on-duty commander, Lieutenant J Barrajas. He initiated a call-out of the major crimes unit.

I then moved to a position beside a city utility box located on the street corner that afforded a more complete view of the scene. The relative positions of Vic/H-Ortega's and Vic/Prieto's bodies, along with their respective entry wounds, suggested that Vic/H-Ortega and Vic/Prieto had been struck by rounds coming from Sus/Escalante's approximate location.

TFD terminated CPR and contacted the Medical Examiner's Office. Examining Sus/Escalante's injuries, I noted a large hole in his left breast consistent with an exit wound from a large caliber firearm. I rolled him over and observed what appeared to be an entry wound under and behind his right armpit: the fatal round likely penetrated the body at approximately a 45-degree angle, entering from Sus/Escalante's lower back and exiting his left front breast. This trajectory, given the relative positions of the three deceased subjects, made it unlikely that either or both Vic/Hernandez-Ortega and Vic/Prieto had fired the rounds that struck Sus/Escalante.

I discussed this inconsistency with Det R Inigo, the first major crimes detective to arrive. He advised me that he would follow up on the details and remain with the bodies until relieved by a technician from the Medical Examiner's office.

I next . . . .

"So, the gist of this is what?" Anna Best said, looking up several minutes later.

Doloviski put down his Blackberry and thought about the question. "This was a major incident, Counselor, a triple homicide in a gang neighborhood. Reporters dug into the story and discovered there'd been several recent shootings in the area. Anyway, the story took on a life of its own, and the public outcry was huge."

"Can't say I blame them."

"Neither did the chief. As usual, everybody had his own ideas on how to fix it. The police guild wanted us to saturate the area with extra patrols, staffed with cops on overtime, of course. The city council wanted to hold community meetings. The command staff looked at all the options and decided it required immediate and decisive action."

"Which meant what?" Best asked, anticipating his response.

Doloviski shrugged. "You know the deal, Anna. There's no padding in our budget. We had to make do with what we had, so—"

"So you reshuffled," she said.

Doloviski frowned. "We reallocated resources, yes. We reactivated the gang unit, put a commander with plenty of experience and strong leadership skills in charge, and gave him a powerful mandate."

"What does that mean in English?" she asked.

"It means," he said, trying to control his frustration, "that we wanted him to be proactive, to make arrests, to put butts in jail."

Best smirked. "You wanted him to crack heads."

"If we're speaking metaphorically, then yes," he answered. "We trusted the commander's discretion."

"Okay, so there's a gang problem," she pressed, "I get that, Chuckie. I'm just having trouble putting all of it together—gang violence, the murder of a police employee, a secretive internal investigation." She lifted her hands up in frustration.

Doloviski gave a tired nod. "I understand, it's a—"

"A long story," a voice interrupted.

She turned around. Detective Cassidy stood in the doorway. His eyes were bloodshot, his cheeks red and feverish. He leaned against the doorframe as if he might fall.

"That's why I'm here." He sat down heavily, grunting as he did. He continued, "I want you both to understand something. I need answers more than anyone. And I can't find them alone."

CHAPTER 11

INTERNAL INVESTIGATIONS INTERVIEW ROOM
MAY 19
1117 HOURS

I read the expression on Best's face and concluded that they'd discussed Nate.

Best said, "I take it you don't believe your friend Orlando—"

"No," I interjected, trying to contain my temper.

"Ready to go back on the record?" Doloviski asked.

Holding my gaze, Best nodded. He tapped the machine, and the fucking green popped on.

"All right, Captain," Best said. "I assume the same legal protections regarding my client's testimony remain in place."

"Yes, of course. Let's move on," Doloviski said. He gave me an expectant look.

I took a deep breath and stared at the recorder, losing myself in its glow.

✱ ✱ ✱

PATROL BRIEFING ROOM
APRIL 9
0757 HOURS

"Well, if it isn't Sergeant Swiss Cheese."

I'd been trying to slip through the crowded briefing room unnoticed when the booming voice brought all attention my way. *Shit.* It was Gerry Montgomery, of course. The man was a first-class asshole whom I usually ignored. This time I tried to think up a snappy comeback, something that would shut his fat mouth and, more important, divert attention away from me. But my cranium was apparently filled with barbed wire and sawdust, so I bit my lip and found a seat.

"If he's Swiss cheese, what does that make you, Montgomery? A pot of fucking fondue?"

This surprising outburst was followed by a roar of laughter. I didn't know who'd backed me up, but Montgomery's reaction was priceless. His doughy head spun in circles looking for the anonymous jokester, his tiny mustache twitching as if he were a mouse sniffing out the aforementioned cheese. *Fuck him.*

In the three weeks since the shooting, I had finally begun to work through the typical anxieties. Insomnia had been the worst of it. Every night I would lie awake for hours, only to fall asleep and relive every bit of the nightmare right up until the muzzle of the gun appeared, pointed right between my eyes. Then I would find myself hovering above the yawning barrel for what felt like hours. Finally, I would spiral slowly down into and through it, tracing the rifling along the barrel's hollow interior. Then I'd wake up with a racing pulse and a dry, acidic taste in my mouth.

It was not fun.

That changed a week ago. I went out to the shooting range to requalify and ended up chatting with the range master, an old hand who'd survived more than his share of close calls. He pointed out the obvious.

"You just had tunnel vision, Cassidy. You saw the gun in the front seat, and your mind couldn't refocus. It happened to me, too. Once."

Left unsaid was that you usually don't get a second chance. This accurate assessment had been seconded by Nate, who was likewise no stranger to critical incidents. "It happens, Michael. Get over it."

Shake it off? Really, that's it?

It wasn't very touchy-feely, but the message did allow me some perspective. In the end, I simply decided that life was lived in the forward direction. Whether I could shake it off remained to be seen, but I was doing okay.

And I had no intention of making that same mistake again.

The loud conversations in the briefing room suddenly ceased when Chief Garcia strode up the aisle. His hair was coiffed into a white helmet, his barrel chest thrust out like a prizefighter, but he was loose enough to pat a few shoulders and made some casual remarks on his way to the podium.

"Good morning," Chief Garcia said, swiveling his head around the room. "Since this is bedtime for some of you, I'll make my announcements brief. Would one of you be kind enough to wake up Sleeping Beauty?"

Nervous laughter rippled as a sergeant in the front row, a thin Asian guy who worked graveyard shift in the North End, was roused with a sharp elbow. He raised his blurry eyes, glanced around the room, and in an unperturbed voice said, "Please continue, Chief."

Hearty laughter followed.

"Thank you, Sergeant. As I said, I'll keep this brief."

The white screen behind and to his left lit up. A bright blue PowerPoint slide appeared: "Tacoma Police Department: Gang-Related Crime Statistics."

"As most of you are already aware, we're dealing with a new round of gang violence. The Four Sector alone has had several shootings in just the past few weeks involving rival Sureno sets. Make no mistake, this is a turf war, pure and simple. But this one is particularly brutal and thus far very bloody."

Chief Garcia clicked through several more slides filled with data, most of which I'd collected myself from East Side crime stats.

"As you all know," Garcia said after cycling through the last graph, "gang members came very close to claiming the life of one of our own recently. We're all glad to have Sergeant Cassidy back at work."

Murmurs of approval buzzed around the room. Hands slapped me on the back. I swallowed, embarrassed at being the center of attention. Yet for all that, the moment hung, suspended by a goodwill that caught me by surprise. The experience left me briefly light-headed. I blinked. The chief was still smiling, so I gave him a thumbs up.

He looked around the room again. "I know many of you possess a much broader knowledge of street gangs than I do, but it's imperative that we all be on the same page. I've asked Detective Inigo to give us a brief synopsis of the current gang situation. Detective?"

Inigo materialized next to him wearing his customary grin. He was freshly shaved, hair gelled, and wearing a tailored blue suit atop a crisp white shirt and light blue tie.

"Thanks, Chief," Inigo began, looking for the world like a motivational speaker. "All right then, ladies and gents, let's get right to it. Sureno, Spanish for 'southerner,' was the name given to the country's largest gang by their creator, the Mexican Mafia. The mafia, aka La Eme, or the Black Hand, was formed in the California penal system decades ago. This crew only recruited the worst—the bad-asses, the killers. Not much has changed since then."

Inigo's voice took on the clipped, professional cadence of a seasoned lecturer. "Since La Eme mostly existed in prisons, they wisely decided to create an external presence. Decades ago, they gave their blessing to a few Hispanic street sets from LA and incorporated them. These became the Surenos, a reference to the Southern California turf they claim. There's an estimated 150,000 Surenos, though the actual number is anyone's guess. The reason there's so much fighting between sets is that their traditional rivals, the Nortenos, have only a fraction of the membership. So yeah, it's Sureno versus Sureno.

"In the last few years La Eme, through the Surenos, has forged ties with Mexican drug cartels and built a large West Coast drug distribution network. That includes our area, which has the benefit of deep-water ports and an interstate. What it lacks, however—gang injunctions—makes it prime real estate for any gang member in hot water down in LA."

Inigo paused on a slide displaying a smirking Hispanic youth dressed in royal blue, brandishing a gun and flashing gang signs.

Detective Inigo continued, "The Surenos represent themselves on the street with the color blue and the number 13, a reference to the thirteenth letter of the alphabet, *M* for mafia."

He advanced to another slide. "Most of the tagging is done by the new recruits, the kids with something to prove. It's nothing more than advertising, but it also implies that we don't own the streets; they do. Here in Tacoma, we've got a couple of very active Sureno sets—Brown Pride Killas, aka the BPKs, and a few old-school TTLs, the T-Town Lokotes."

A last slide depicted a skinny Hispanic youth surrounded by several larger gang members whose fists were clenched as they advanced on the smaller boy. "This little *pendejo*," Inigo swore, "is getting jumped into the Surenos. His ass whooping will last thirteen seconds," he said, adding with a smile, "more or less."

Inigo turned off the projector and stepped back as Chief Garcia moved forward.

"That's about it," the chief said. "Any questions?"

Not a single hand went up.

"Okay, ladies and gents," Garcia said, "now that we know what we're up against, here's what we're going to do about it." He held a sheet of paper up before the silent group. "The command staff has designated a new gang unit. It will be composed of two squads, one uniform and one plainclothes. If you are interested in putting butts in jail and getting rid of this plague on our city, then please submit a memo to its new commander, Lieutenant Orlando."

I spun around. Nate was leaning against the back wall, his face damn near inscrutable. I was surprised he hadn't confided in me, but my disappointment was lost in the surge of pride I felt. This was a high-profile assignment. Moreover, it spelled out the chief's thoughts on whom he believed would be his replacement in the next year or two after he pulled the pin on his career.

"I said I would keep it short," the chief continued, "but I will leave you with this. Regardless of what the gang members believe, these streets are our streets, not theirs. We paid for them in blood and sweat. The gang bangers need to get the message."

Murmurs of agreement followed the chief as he stepped away from the podium. The assembled cops, mostly sergeants and lieutenants, stood and headed for the door. I stood stiffly, stifling another yawn. Just then a matronly African-American woman with white hair leaned in and spoke softly in my ear.

"Michael, Chief Garcia would like a word."

"Sure thing, Cathy," I said automatically.

After delivering the message, Cathy Bowerman, the chief's secretary, walked briskly up the aisle. She pulled up next to Gerry Montgomery, who was in a heated discussion with Inigo. She ignored Montgomery's glare, spoke her few words, and walked away.

Suddenly anxious, Montgomery heaved himself to his feet and scurried after her like an overgrown rat following the cheese. Have I mentioned I don't like the guy?

I trailed a few steps behind, curiosity the only thing propping my eyes open. Nate and the chief were talking in hushed tones as we marched up.

"Gentlemen," the chief said, "I wanted to continue the day's topic in private."

We both nodded as if we had a choice in the matter.

"Sergeant Cassidy," Garcia said, looking my way, "I've spent the last few days discussing the best candidate for the new unit's plain-clothes supervisor."

"Yes . . . sir," I answered, completely confused by this trajectory.

"You have a strong reputation in investigations, and you've done solid work in patrol these last few months. Most important, you're familiar with many of the players on the East Side, which is obviously where most of the problems are originating. Based on that, we'd like to offer you this assignment."

My mouth opened, but nothing came out, which was fortunate because my brain kept repeating *Holy shit!* It was an assignment most sergeants would kill to have, and I tried to summon up something to prove that the chief wasn't offering it to a moron. When brain finally came out of vapor lock, I managed to sputter, "Thank you, Chief. I guess I'm your man."

"Excellent, Sergeant. And congratulations. I think you'll find the job a challenging one. It certainly won't be dull."

We shook on it, the chief squeezing my hand in his manicured vice.

I risked a sidelong glance at Nate, but his eyes looked past me. They were suddenly wary.

I turned around, and my smile faded. *Joe.*

My soon-to-be former boss, Lieutenant Joe Barrajas, stalked towards us, hands clenched in fists and eyes on fire. He finally seemed to notice that he had become the center of attention, so he pulled up and wiped the scowl off his face. He crossed his arms, highlighting the swath of golden stripes—one for every three years of service—running up his shirtsleeve from wrist to elbow.

Garcia looked at him expectantly.

Barrajas cleared his throat.

"Seems to me that the gang problem is as much about race as it is about crime," Joe said, enunciating each word as if it had been rehearsed. "You and I both know that, Randall. You can't jump into this kind of mess without knowing the community."

"You feel you're better qualified for Lieutenant Orlando's job, I take it," the chief said. Garcia's tone was neutral, as if he were a physician talking to a mental patient. Or maybe that was a cheap shot on my part. Whatever.

"Of course," Barrajas continued, emphatic. "For Christ's sake, shouldn't the unit at least have a commander who can speak Spanish?"

"Lieutenant Orlando, would you care to respond to that?" Garcia replied without turning his head.

Nate lifted his chin, his arms stiff at attention. "Lieutenant Barrajas, I'm African-American, obviously. My mother's people are from Alabama, been there for generations. But my father was Cuban, and I embrace my Latin heritage. I intend to use it to build stronger relationships within the Hispanic community, the same community where I hope to raise my own children. But first and foremost, I am a police officer. Like you."

I was impressed at the speech, more so because it was delivered entirely in fluent Spanish. Nate was poised and confident, while Joe, on the other hand, seemed to wilt a little bit with each new word. It was clear he hadn't known about Nate's Spanish skills, which had been cultivated in college, rather than picked up from his long-gone deadbeat dad. Joe was defeated, and his body language admitted as much. But it was all too pathetic for me to enjoy.

The chief broke the awkward silence by stepping forward and squeezing his old comrade by the shoulders. "Joe, I understand the depth of your feelings on this matter. I also gave some thought to the discussion you and I had yesterday."

The discussion was quickly bypassing the "too much info" barrier and moving into an awkward level. I was reminded of the cloying and distasteful sensation I'd had when my parents started their drunken foreplay on the couch while I was on the chair next to them munching on Cheetos.

Nate, whose attention was fixated on his new father-in-law, obviously felt differently. He and Desiree both had a lot to lose if Joe were to remain an enemy.

Garcia stepped in close to speak to Barrajas. The silver-maned chief looked short and stocky next to the Barrajas, whose jet-black hair was so thick with oily gel it was a damn good thing he didn't smoke.

"Joe," the chief said, "we all love Desiree, but she's an adult with the right to choose her own partner. I told you yesterday, and I'll tell again; I believe she made the right choice. Nate's a good cop, a good leader. More importantly, he's a good man. I hope you'll see that in time."

Barrajas' eyes burned. "You talk about my daughter to me? A daughter I cared for alone after her mother died? A daughter who married without my knowledge? And you want me to be happy? I—" His mouth slammed shut on the remainder, and he spun on his heels and walked with slow dignity down the aisle and out the door.

We all watched him leave in silence.

The chief looked around at the group. "Detective Inigo, did you have something to add as well?"

We all turned towards the back wall where Rafael was slouching, arms crossed and wearing a rare sheepish expression.

"My apologies, Chief," Inigo said. He grinned, displaying his brilliant white teeth. "Just checking my messages."

Garcia raised a suspicious eyebrow, but Inigo's infectious smile made him shake his head in mock exasperation. "All right, come on over, Rafael. I believe Lieutenant Orlando has some news for you as well."

I was the only one to catch the flash of despair in Nate's eyes as he pulled them away from the doorway. Truth be told, it rattled me to see him so deeply affected. But when he turned to address Inigo, any trace of concern had vanished.

"Detective Inigo, it seems we have a need for someone with a particular skill set, someone who knows Hispanic gangs, the players, the rules. Sound like anyone you know?"

"Intel work suits me fine, Lieutenant," Inigo said, feigning surprise.

"You anticipated the job well, Detective," Garcia noted, chuckling. "Which brings us finally to you, Gerry. Since we disbanded your pro-active squad to form the gang unit, you need a new assignment."

Montgomery leaped to attention, his back rigid.

"Hopefully, you have no objections to becoming the gang unit's new uniformed supervisor," the chief said.

"That would be fine, sir," Montgomery answered in a high voice.

That was the signal for a round of handshakes. I managed a brief, uncomfortable grip with Montgomery. Inigo stepped up next.

"Working together, huh, mijo?"

"Looks like it, Raf. You'll keep me out of trouble, won't you?"

"Ah, no. I don't think so," he replied, winking.

"How's *your* Spanish?" Garcia asked, shaking his hand and leaning in to speak quietly.

"Passable, sir," I lied.

"We'll see," Garcia said. He leaned in and spoke directly into my ear. "Stay on top of your game, Michael."

In other words, *Stay off the booze.*

"I will, sir. I promise," I replied as butterflies fluttered in my stomach.

Inigo and Montgomery followed the chief out, leaving Nate and me alone in the darkened room.

"You could have warned me," I said quietly.

"Yes, I could have," he said, his face doing that sphinx impression. Which I hate. "But I didn't. Why is that, you think?"

"You know how much I love riddles," I said, scratching an ear in frustration. "Well, if I had to guess, I'd say you wanted me to look genuinely surprised."

"Why would I do that?" he asked, all innocent.

"So that the chief, Raf, and Montgomery wouldn't think you and I discussed it beforehand."

He nodded. "Which is one of the reasons I picked Montgomery. To balance that out."

"Why *did* you pick me? Just because we're friends?"

Nate gave me a disgusted look. "Don't be dense, Michael. Of course that's why."

I had no response to that surprising admission.

He shook his head. "Do you know how many guys would kill for the job you just got? The last thing I need is some ambitious hotshot looking to make a name for himself at the expense of the mission. Yes, you are my *friend*, the best and most loyal friend I ever had, could ever have, in fact. You are also a very competent cop who doesn't seem to appreciate his own talents. I need someone who can think on his feet and is loyal to me and the mission. That's you."

I have never been good at accepting praise. I could joke that I don't get many opportunities, but the truth is I'm more responsive to criticism. Don't know why.

"You with me on this?" Nate asked.

"Yeah . . . yeah, I am. And thanks."

He clapped my shoulder.

"Sorry it didn't turn out better with Joe," I said.

"Me too. Maybe one day he'll consider his daughter's happiness before his pride."

"Really? You think Joe will ever accept you into the family?"

For a second, Nate's eyes betrayed the depth of his disappointment. "No," he grunted. "Never."

CHAPTER 12

Stakeouts. Hate 'em. Or have I said that already?

I stretched my legs out on the passenger seat of the unmarked Jeep Cherokee and wiped away the moisture from my fogged-up windows. But there was little to see in the East Side neighborhood, which had become a ghost town in the last hour. Our buyer was two hours late. Right on "doper" time.

"Target sighted," a voice whispered in my earpiece.

"Finally," I said aloud for the sake of my back seat passenger. I turned around and gave the shadowy form a thumbs up.

Like a spider unfurling itself from its web, Matt Hagstrom stretched his gangly legs and breathed a sigh of relief.

"Hey," I said, "you didn't have to accept the invite."

His response was a harrumph.

I smiled as I plucked a pair of binoculars out of the charred remains of barbecued ribs and glanced back to make sure Hagstrom was staying out of sight.

The whip-lean and lanky gang prosecutor was roughly my age with bristly blond hair, thin, stylish glasses, and cheeks so freshly shaved he looked as if puberty were still on the horizon. But Matt was one of the good guys, even if he was as serious as a mortician and possessed a courteous formality that I imagined could get old. Yet Matt was passionate about his work. It had taken zero arm-twisting to get him to tag along.

I adjusted the lens on the binos, and our informant came into focus. He was Mexican, a rare middle-aged drug dealer with a shaved head and wispy goatee like a rat's tail. Despite having little English, he had what we needed most—Sureno ties. I didn't trust him, of course, but I trusted Rafael to keep him in check.

The informant was leaning against a fence next to a shuttered storefront wearing Sureno gear—bright blue soccer jersey and a bandana around his bald cranium. That didn't automatically make him one of the gang. In this neighborhood, blue was always a good first choice. And second, third, and fourth.

"What happens next?" Hagstrom said, squinting.

I didn't answer right away. Our target for the night had just materialized, amorphous until he stepped into a beam of light from a nearby porch.

"Looks like Loony to me," Inigo said softly over the radio. "*Más tarde.*"

"Better late than never," another detective whispered.

"The skinny kid is the target, I assume," Hagstrom said in his deep, clipped tone. He didn't have one of the expensive earpieces, so he relied on me to keep him in the loop.

I nodded, putting a finger to my lips. We were plenty far away, but I wanted Hagstrom to be aware of his surroundings. If it was Loony, he was a short, wiry kid in his mid-teens with a royal blue baseball hat clamped over his head. It was snug enough that it pushed his ears out, making him look more Bugs Bunny than badass. The thick gold chain rattling around his neck and the over-the-top swagger only made him look more ridiculous, like a too-tall kid who just got his training wheels off. When he stopped in front of our informant, exposing high cheekbones and a sturdy Mayan nose, I recognized him from pictures handed out during the briefing.

"Yeah," I whispered, "that's him."

Our informant ignored Loony's arrogant demeanor, reaching into a jacket pocket and nonchalantly withdrawing a wad of cash. He held it forward, just out of reach.

"Jesus, don't toy with him!" I hissed. Kid or not, Loony was on our radar for his propensity to shoot people who pissed him off.

Fortunately, Loony did not seem put off at having to reach for the money, thus ensuring a good photo op for the surveillance tech. With the binos dialed in, it was easy to spot the plastic baggie that emerged from Loony's pocket and from there into our informant's larger hands. Business concluded, Loony and informant passed each other as they sauntered away in opposite directions, though I couldn't help but notice that Loony had dropped his swagger in exchange for speed.

"And now," I said, once the two were out of sight, "to answer your earlier question, my crew will follow the dealer home, get his vehicle information and address, and write up the report."

"Voice and video?" he asked.

"Yeah. It'll be the standard package, and you'll have it on your desk by tomorrow morning."

"Outstanding," he said, nodding his head.

"Yup, that's why we get paid the big bucks."

Despite the breezy confidence of this statement, I was still acclimating to the new job. Fortunately, I had a great crew of detectives—Type As, all of them, each with more dope experience than I had—not to mention a healthy budget and a broad objective. And we were off to a good start: seven ops, twenty kilos of coke, twelve pounds of BC marijuana, and so much heroin that we had needed more storage lockers. Moreover, we grabbed everything we could from the dealers, including four cars, a condo, and a cool Cobalt twin-screw cruiser its crew used for smuggling black tar heroin. On top of that, cash seizures were around a hundred thousand dollars, give or take.

And all I—we—had to do in return was get the Surenos to stop the damn shooting.

To be fair, much of the credit belonged to our intel specialist and informant wrangler, Detective Rafael Inigo.

Hagstrom spoke in my ear.

"What was that?" I asked.

"I said do you mind if I ask a personal question, Sergeant?"

I gave the tall prosecutor a curious look. "Sure, but in that case you better call me Michael."

He didn't smile. "Don't take this the wrong way, Michael, but how long has it been?"

I flinched at the question. "Uh, I'm not sure how to respond to that. Are we talking about sex?"

He shook his head once but said no more. There was a curious mixture of weariness and melancholy in his blue eyes, along with a trait I had noticed in the line of his jaw, the motion of his hands. Though we had spoken only a handful of times, I concluded that Matt Hagstrom was what cops privately referred to as "a determined motherfucker."

And just like that, I realized what he was really asking.

"Nearly ten years," I answered.

Hagstrom deliberately ran a hand through his thick bush of hair, eyes locked on mine. I waited in silence. "There is a vibe someone like us gives off, you know?" he said.

I nodded, though I didn't necessarily agree. I'd been sober so long I no longer thought in terms of "us and them." Either way, if he were suggesting we shared an addiction, then I certainly hadn't picked up on his vibe. "You?" I asked.

"Been on the wagon almost fifteen. Again," he said, holding up a palm, "I don't mean to get too personal, but when's the last time you attended a meeting?"

"AA?"

"That or any of the other groups of which someone in our situation might avail himself. I ask because this unit is a big deal downtown, at least at the moment, and if you don't mind me saying, stressful situations like this can be a trigger for . . . well, you know."

It had been some time since anyone had spoken to me in such a straightforward manner. *Could he be right?* I wondered. *Was I getting cocky in my sobriety?*

Hagstrom seemed to sense my train of thought. "I just want to make sure you're aware so you can be on guard. Nothing more."

"Yeah," I answered, exhaling. "Thanks."

"And this conversation is just between you and me." He leaned back in his seat, his eyes hidden.

A moment passed as I digested the information. The silence was not awkward.

"Think your guys are ready for a warrant roundup?" Hagstrom said.

It took me a moment to process the change in topic. My unit had been conducting operations like this one almost every night for two weeks, none of which had ended in an arrest. It was frustrating but purposeful. Too many gang-related dealers getting popped would arouse the suspicion of an already paranoid population. Thus, keeping a low profile meant holding off on the arrests until each transaction had been vetted by the prosecutor's office and signed off by a judge.

Matt's question implied that all our work had, thus far, met the expectations of the criminal justice system.

"Yeah," I said, shock turning to excitement. "Oh, hell yeah, we're ready!"

GANG UNIT OFFICE
APRIL 21
1405 HOURS

The next day's perpetual drizzle tapered off as I arrived at the office. The gang unit occupied the second floor of a modern building downtown, a space normally reserved for law offices, stock brokerages, and other members of the business elite. I felt out of my league, but that didn't stop me from appreciating the lush carpet and fine wood furnishings, not to mention the high-speed web access.

I could get used to this.

Walking into the cubicle area, I immediately sensed that the cat was out of the bag. The place was packed. Montgomery's crew, mostly young officers dressed in their crisp, new black camos, milled among the detectives' desks trying and failing to show how calm they were. Somebody had spilled the beans, obviously. I didn't really care as long as the bad guys didn't know the day's agenda.

It was roundup time.

Gerry Montgomery stood in a far corner, hands in his pockets, looking as if he had just swallowed something nasty. I ignored his pouty face, even though it resembled a constipated puffer fish.

Nate gave me a nod from the back of the room and walked towards the podium. All eyes followed his progress expectantly, and he did not disappoint. Nate launched into his briefing with all the emotion and rhetoric of a preacher, the throng of cops his willing converts. Why not? We all believed that what we were doing was that incontrovertible, unassailable right thing to do.

The operation itself, he told his hushed crowd, would be straight-forward. Track down the dozen or so gang-bangers who had sold us dope. Arrest them. Take them to jail. The End.

It was a no-brainier operation, involving everyone's favorite work pastime—putting bad guys in jail. Copies of the warrants, complete with pictures, were passed out, and everyone was perusing them when Echie stood up.

"None of the guys on this list belong to East Side Criminales," she said. "Why isn't the biggest and most active Sureno set in the city even on the list?"

It was an insightful question and one that I had asked myself only a few days prior. Instead of answering, Nate motioned towards Rafael Inigo sitting at his desk in the back.

He shrugged. "These aren't Boy Scouts, Officer Echevaria," he said in the patient voice of a wise elder lecturing a young upstart. "Every name on that list is a banger and a felon, and the last thing on their mind is gettin' jammed up with us. Which is why," he said, using his most infectious smile, "we have to be very careful with our informants. As you pointed out, ESCs are the big dogs at the moment. That's why none of my little *perros* wanted to get jammed up with them." He shrugged again, adding, "I can make 'em do only so much."

It was the same explanation he'd given me. Not only did it make sense; it also jibed with everything I'd seen thus far. Still, the East Side Criminales were a growing enterprise feared by more than a few of their rivals. *One thing at a time. They'll get their turn.*

I watched Echie absorb the answer, her eyebrows knitted in concentration, her mouth curled in obvious dissatisfaction. She sat down, though not without raising one of those manicured eyebrows in my direction. The blush that lit up my face felt like a third-degree burn.

Nate wrapped up the briefing and roared, "Go get 'em!"

A chorus of whoops arose, only fading as the squads split up and filed out to the garage. I trailed along behind to make sure everyone got in his assigned vans. Montgomery climbed into the front passenger seat of Echie's van, and I decided I disliked him just a little bit more.

Nate was the last out the door. Surprisingly, he clasped my hand and gave me a brief one-armed hug before jogging to the last van and sliding his thick frame behind the wheel. The wide passenger door was still closing when he shot forward and out the exit.

Ten minutes later, I was behind the wheel of my vehicle, squinting against the first ray of sun slicing through the overcast. The arrest warrants were fanned out on the passenger seat, each one bearing a color photo of a young man, each of them similar enough that they could have been related. All were Hispanic kids in their teens or early twenties, though some had shaved heads, others wispy mustaches. A few bore pale scars on their light-brown faces, several boasted tattoos, including one whose bruise-colored tattoo of a snake curling up and around his scrawny neck made me wonder what in the hell he'd thought when he first checked himself in the mirror. What made them all so similar, however, besides their youth and ethnicity, was the cold contempt etched into their features. They were kids, sure, but each one still led his own violent crew.

I eased back into my seat for the short drive onto Sureno turf. A wide, four-lane arterial near the train depot was populated by street people, most of them shuffling back and forth in search of their next fix. One caught my attention, a skinny ghost of a woman perched on a street corner with the pocked flesh and hollowed-out cheeks of a meth addict. Her gaze lingered on me as I drove slowly past. She pursed her lips in distaste, her message silent but obvious. *Move along, cop.*

I gave her a friendly wave.

At the base of McKinley Hill, I turned and drove south past the Tacoma Dome on my left, while on the right the long, sinuous car museum looked like a giant space worm gorging on a steady line of humans.

At the top of the hill, a few modest houses gave way to apartments and the first of the East Side's many projects. Despite the ubiquitous gang tagging, many of the residents had spruced up their homes, hanging flowers or cultivating gardens in the tiny spaces provided. It was a reminder that there were plenty of decent people living here, folks who needed respite from the assholes who considered these homes a mere stage for their stupid, homicidal games.

Students began to fill the streets. I grabbed some coffee to re-set my head, standing in line behind workers holding empty lunch pails and speaking rapid Spanish. It was still early afternoon when I hopped back in the car. The radio started to squawk. It was Inigo calling in the first target. Soon after, he found another.

Per protocol, my plainclothes team stayed clear of the take-downs. Most of us, including me, however, couldn't resist spying on the action from a block or two away. I cruised slowly through an alley across from a boarded-up shop just a few seconds before Nate's black van skidded to a stop in the middle of the street. The wheels were still spinning when the side door flew open. Their target was just walking past the alley not twenty feet from my front bumper when he was suddenly engulfed in the black swarm, his whole body disappearing without a sound. As one, the group hustled back to the van, and the doors slammed shut as the van shot forward. Seconds later, the street was as quiet as if all that crazy shit had never happened.

The gang cops were clearly enjoying themselves. The radio banter was energetic, even chaotic. When one of the bangers made a break for it, his saggy britches couldn't handle the straining. Six or seven fit young cops dressed like ninjas chasing a waddling gangster would, no doubt, be the talk of the neighborhood for days to come. By midnight, we had all but one subject crossed off the list. It had been a good day for fishing, and Nate began winding the operation down.

I had not found a single target and was damn frustrated. I pulled up to an intersection with shuttered storefronts, my head on a swivel. Gang graffiti painted nearly every surface. A lone figure stepped out of the shadows beneath an awning dressed in dark clothing, his face and head covered with a hood.

The light turned green. No one was behind me. The man took another step in my direction, lifting his head to take my measure. He might as well have been holding a "Drug Store—Open for Business" sign. His head tilted down towards my window, but his face remained in shadow. Then something caught his attention to his right, and he turned, exposing his profile. He had a round face with dark skin, high cheekbones, a strong nose and big lips. There was a scar on his left cheek, which hooked below his left eye and slashed across his nose.

I hadn't noticed the scar the previous night. But I recognized the face.

The face disappeared, the figure melted back beneath the awning.

I picked up the remaining arrest warrant as I pulled away and studied Loony's photo. *Gotcha.* Silently, I thanked my new friend, Matt Hagstrom, for rushing the last report through the courts. I called it in. "George-60 has Pedro Ruiz-Munoz, aka Loony, on the southwest corner of McKinley and Fifty-Sixth Street."

Nate's deep voice broke in. "George-60, this is George-North. Both arrest teams are in the jail sally port. You need to call patrol."

"Copy, that. Switching frequencies. See you at the jail shortly."

I switched over to the busy patrol south channel and hastily asked for backup. Tense minutes passed. *Loony will still be there,* I thought. I hoped.

The waxing moon cast a silvery light on the street. From a vantage point a block away under a leafy tree overhanging the street, I spotted a patrol car make a quick turn and pull up a few yards short of the corner. James Kapalu hopped out. I itched to hit the gas and make the arrest with him but knew that would earn me a ration of shit for breaking protocol.

Loony was a stick figure, barely visible beneath the awning as James sauntered up. Alone.

I had assumed Kapalu was riding with a partner tonight. It wasn't like the experienced vet to jump without backup, but maybe nobody was available. *Fuck it,* I thought, putting the car in drive and creeping forward.

The next few seconds passed in slow motion. I was only a hundred feet from the corner when Kapalu stepped beneath the awning, his shadow merging with Loony's into an amorphous shape that instantly began to writhe and jerk. A second later, they spilled backwards into the light. Kapalu was locked onto the skinny kid from behind when the two hit the pavement hard.

I was only fifty feet away now, foot shoved on the gas, adrenalin spiking, eyes focused.

A flash of reflected light. A blade.

CHAPTER 13

I don't remember throwing the car in park before leaping out, but I do remember how those last twenty feet seemed more like a mile through shifting sand. James had a beefy arm wrapped around the kid's scrawny neck as the silvery shimmer of light slashed across James's forearm, tracing a thin line of moonlit blood as it passed.

I stepped up to the sidewalk as James's cry split the quiet. Ten feet to go, my right hand found and released my gun. The knife arced again, too soon.

A third shape materialized behind Kapalu, a long object held high. It came crashing down before Loony's blade struck, before my gunsights were centered. A sickening thud resounded, somehow drowning out Kapalu's yells, cutting off Loony's wheezing breaths, and stopping my heart in my chest.

The next sound was the tinkle of metal as the knife hit the ground. Loony's limp form followed it.

Then silence.

Kapalu and I stared at each other, incredulous.

"*Buenas noches.*" A Cheshire grin emerged from the shadow. Rafael Inigo held a black baseball in a two-fisted grip. He used the blunt end to nudge Loony, but the kid didn't move. To say I was shocked at Inigo's sudden appearance would be an understatement. I half expected him to put a boot on the kid's melon and ask me to take his picture.

"Rafael," Kapalu said in a weak voice. "Thanks, man." Then he slumped to the ground as well.

I caught James's head before it struck the cement. I eased him gently down, setting his knees up to keep shock at bay. He had a nasty gash on his right forearm that was rapidly leaking blood. He was still conscious. I found a small towel in my car and had him clamp down on the cut.

Inigo called for an ambulance while I checked on Loony. His pulse was faint but steady.

"Still breathing, eh?" Inigo said, frowning.

No one spoke for a moment.

"Jesus Christ," I said, finally.

"No shit," Inigo added, his smile ratcheting up again.

"Ow," Kapalu muttered.

✷ ✷ ✷

An hour later I was sitting next to James inside the ER.

"Déjà vu?" he said, lifting his head briefly from a magazine.

"Little," I admitted.

He nodded and returned to his reading.

The young resident sitting between us glanced up from his stitching, curious. When I didn't respond, he shrugged and went back to his sutures.

A harried looking nurse pushed aside the curtains and leaned over the resident's shoulder. She scrutinized the resident's work carefully, patting him on the head like an indulgent mother. Then she dropped a sheaf of papers on the table next to Kapalu. "He'll be good to go in a minute, Michael," she said. "Must be déjà vu for you, huh?"

"Seems that way, Jill," I responded.

The resident's curiosity was apparent as he looked at each of us in turn, but no one had the energy to explain.

Kapalu pulled a pen from the pocket of his blood-soaked uniform. He scratched his signature across several pages using his left hand and then handed it back to the nurse with a rare smile.

"Tough guy," she said, her eyes crinkling as she hurried out.

"I'll be out front, James," I said, standing up. "When you're done, come on outside. I'll take you back to the station."

Kapalu grunted, not bothering to look up from his *Sports Illustrated*.

I walked out past the nurses' station, waving at the familiar faces, and strode through the hallway. It reeked of antiseptic. *Why would anyone work here?* The waiting room door swung open to a different smell, that of sweating and anxious humans. I held my breath all the way to the exit where the doors whooshed open on a whisper of compressed air. I took a deep breath in the ambulance bay and contemplated life.

"Hey, sailor. Looking for a party?"

I spun around, startled, my hand automatically reaching for my gun.

Francine Echevaria sat behind the wheel of a black Ford Mustang, dash lights illuminating her mischievous grin. She held up her hands up. "Sorry to surprise you," she said, though she looked anything but sorry.

I laughed. It felt good. I tried it again.

Echie wrapped an arm around the passenger seat. Her hair, which she normally wore in braids, fell in dark cascades around her olive face. I caught a flash of deep-red lipstick.

"What're you up to?" I asked, trying not to sound like I was thirteen.

"Just left the station and currently heading to the Spar for a drink," she said, accentuating the last word with a curl of her mouth. "Raf said you'd be here and told me to swing by. Why don't you join us? The whole team will be there."

My response was immediate and unplanned. Panic. A rush of blood rose up to my face. I took an involuntary step back.

"Everybody's getting together . . . thought you'd want to come along," she added, her confusion and disappointment evident.

She didn't understand. *Dammit!* The fault was mine, of course. I had been sober for so long that my alcoholism had fallen off most people's radar. There had been plenty of new folks during that time who, like Echie, hadn't known that part of me. "Sorry, I'm just a little shaken," I said lamely, glancing back at the entrance to the emergency room.

Her hurt expression shifted to concern. "Oh, is it James? Is he okay? I thought it was minor."

"He bled a lot, but you know him. He'll be okay. It was just a rough night, that's all. Sorry, my mind was on other things," I said.

Maybe if I kept apologizing, this whole scene would rewind. But instead the door behind me hissed open, and Kapalu emerged. His skin was sallow, his eyes red, and he cradled his injured arm in a sling. Still, he beamed when he saw Echie.

"Hey, James, how you feeling?" Echie yelled.

"Never better," he responded.

Echie and I shared a laugh.

She pointed a finger at Kapalu. "You feeling good enough to have a drink before heading home?"

"That'll go down well with the drugs. Where we going?" he said, already walking towards her car.

"The Spar. Right now. I'm buying. Come on, I'll give you a ride," Echie said.

"That's nice of you," I said to her.

"With all that blood loss, he'll be a cheap drunk," she answered with an impish grin. "You joining us?"

As most experts will tell you, the male brain has an off switch located directly below the belt. That anecdotal fact is the only excuse I offer for the following response. "Sure. I'll see you there."

"All right then," Echie replied. She leaned back in her seat, satisfied.

Kapalu handed me his bloody uniform shirt and vest as he walked past. The rest of his gear, destined for the evidence locker, was already in my rig. He patted me on the back and slowly lowered himself into the passenger seat while groaning.

Way to milk it, James, I thought. Then Echie dropped the clutch, and they were gone. Which left me suddenly lightheaded. That's when I began to reconsider my rash decision. *What in God's name had I done?*

Alcoholics have triggers—watching football, smoking cigarettes, that type of thing. For me it was always hanging out in a bar with friends. This was a really, really bad idea. But it was also complicated, given that this was as much a work-related gathering as a social one. I was the sergeant, the boss, the leader of my little club of overachievers.

Celebrating our success as a team was not only accepted; it was expected. How could I say no?

Simple. N-O.

Self-deception has always made me nauseous. My slowly churning stomach reminded me of the wasted mornings, afternoons, nights, and days lost in a whiskey binge, each one beginning with the arrogant conviction that I could stop at one. Or two.

But the truth was, is, will always be this: there is not enough liquor in the world to quench my thirst.

So it would be a mistake to go.

Yet I was unable to stop myself. Why? What fucked-up rationale existed that could propel me towards a scenario that could cost me so much?

The answer was hard to admit, even to myself. I was lonely.

Pathetic, sure. But at least this was the truth. At the moment, when I most needed the willpower to say, "Thanks but no thanks," my inner strength had been sucked into the aching, hollow place inside me. I used to fill that hole with booze, especially on the nights when all I could think of was Therese, holding her cold hand in mine, her eyes staring at nothing, her chest unmoving as she lay splayed out on our bathroom floor. I shuddered, releasing the image. Still, the mere thought of my drafty house, of spending another night of solitude in my monkish life, was too much to bear. More than that, I convinced myself, who can say no to a pretty woman?

Still I wavered. I seriously considered calling Matt Hagstrom, even pulled out my phone. But I already knew what he'd say, so it stayed in my pocket. I stared out at the quiet street, my decision made. *Into the fucking breach.*

CHAPTER 14

THE SPAR TAVERN
APRIL 20
2322 HOURS

Old Town clings to a bluff overlooking Commencement Bay. Its rotting piers, rustic lampposts, and Victorian homes were all quaint reminders of its days as a bustling port of call. Where the wives of sea captains once paced back and forth on widow's walks or shopped at the fish market, there now existed a small but vibrant assortment of restaurants, shops, and offices, most boasting a stunning view of the Cascade Mountains rising above Puget Sound.

The night was too dark to see any of this, of course, but tonight I would have paid it little attention. Every fiber of my being was aware of the door ahead, the one that opened into the Spar Tavern. Despite the warm and welcoming glow emanating from the frosty windows, the squat brick building was the site of some of my worst moments. I was still contemplating my next move when the cab of my truck suddenly seemed to shrink. *Screw this. Let's go.*

My boots slapped the puddles forming in the fractured sidewalk. Before I could talk myself out of it, I pushed through the door and entered the Spar.

And back in time.

Whether it was the quality of the light on the old brick walls, the smell of greasy food and spilled beer, or the loud, slurred, but happy conversations, it felt . . . good.

The bar was crowded as usual. The few tables were occupied, as were the bar stools. A raucous group was clustered around a pool table. Even if I hadn't recognized every face, I could have picked them out as cops just by the way their elbows jutted out as if they still wore their gun belts, still spoke in voices used to commanding attention.

Smack!

I spun around, my butt stinging. Echie stood behind me, her eyes shining beneath a layer of black bangs, her cheeks flushed. She raised her hands again, laughing at my shocked expression.

"Glad you could make it, Michael," she added with a wink.

"Me too," I answered, smiling wide. And I meant it.

"There's our man!" said a loud voice behind me.

Rafael Inigo gave me another hard slap, this one on the back.

I made the round with handshakes and fist bumps. Holding court at the pool table was a tipsy Kapalu, whose story was undoubtedly improving with each telling. I scanned the room, eyes locking with Inigo. I nodded my thanks, and he bowed in dramatic fashion, still sporting that shit-eating grin.

Over his shoulder, I spotted Gerry Montgomery. The asshole was nursing a beer by himself at a booth, bushy eyebrows knitted together as if he were having a difficult bowel movement. Beneath his Seahawks jacket, his uniform shirt was visible. *Correction, lazy asshole.*

Inigo pulled me unsteadily through the crowd of twenty or more, amidst a cloud of whiskey breath, to the head of the pool table. Intuition and experience told me something bad was about to happen. Inigo whistled through his fingers. All heads in the bar turned towards him as he raised a full glass of whiskey.

"Ladies and gents, I'd like to propose a toast." He still had a grip on my hand, and I felt a second tickle of anxiety as everyone hoisted a drink.

"A toast to the newest and baddest unit in this here po-leese department!" Inigo yelled.

There was a chorus of hoots and clapping. He finally released my hand but only to shove a full glass of dark whiskey into it. With barely a pause, he added, "To the gang unit!"

As the cheers rose up around me, I stared down at the round surface of liquor. My stomach went through a spin cycle. My legs wobbled. Every glass went up and down, except mine.

But Inigo wasn't finished. "And to the guy who led the charge, our fearless leader, let's raise a glass to Sergeant Michael Cassidy!"

The clapping and shouting increased in volume. Rough hands slapped my back as the first rhythmic swell of "drink, drink, drink!" rolled through the bar. In a stupor, I gazed around at their young faces, men and women in a smorgasbord of color. These were my brethren. This wasn't about the booze; this was about camaraderie, about stepping up and being counted, about trusting people, having their back. Yeah, it all sounds like one big, fat cliché now.

In the moment, though? All I can say is it felt real.

I swirled the dark amber in my glass. Maybe piety wasn't for me, I thought. Maybe my future was in my hands right now.

"Fuck it," I said to no one. "Into the breach."

And I lifted my glass.

The whiskey went down as if it were water. The bar erupted in cheers. Beside me, I sensed Inigo's presence, his wide smile. An arm reached around my waist. Echie was there, her brown eyes bright and full of promise, her shape fitted into my own like a key in a lock.

The sensation of euphoria lingered for several seconds. Then my gut dropped as if I'd fallen off a cliff. I broke free of Echie and scurried for the bathroom.

I flung the door open, not caring who was inside. I slipped in a pool of urine, nearly falling on my ass. I found my balance against the door of a stall, rushed inside and dropped to my knees. Grasping the wet sides of the bowl, I buried my face as the first wave hit. My stomach spasmed again almost immediately. And again. My body screamed for it to stop, while my mind forced me onward. The bowl filled with the remains of dinner. I retched, finally empty, until I couldn't breathe. Then I gasped a lung full of foul air and laid my cheek against the rim.

This, I realized with absolute clarity, used to be my life. My wretched life.

Once my breathing slowed, I spat out the last drops of liquor, and my stomach seemed to settle a bit. I wiped my hands on my pants and tried to stand up. I got as far as one knee when the door behind me swung open.

"I knew it. Goddam alkies never change."

Gerry Montgomery's voice was like fingernails on a chalkboard. His presence was literally the worst thing I could have imagined at that moment. No doubt he'd been ecstatic when I'd swigged my drink, had probably pissed his pants with excitement when he saw me run for the restroom. I imagined this was the happiest moment in his entire fucked-up life.

Fuck that, Cassidy. You did this to yourself.

This thought was followed by a brief moment of self-loathing. Then I wiped away the vomit and leaned back. Montgomery was by the sink, feet apart and arms folded across his broad chest. He was the personification of gloating. Worse, the contempt in his eyes made me feel lower still, as if he were the master viewing his chattel.

The bastard had me this time. Obviously, he thought so too because he pointed a thick finger in my direction. "I tried to tell them what you were," he spat, "that you couldn't handle the simplest goddam task when you were a patrolman, that you didn't deserve a promotion. Ass kisser like you, what should I expect? Then they give you the choicest assignment in the department, and here's what happens."

He leaned forward, all smugness. "I'm not the least bit surprised."

I had to admit he had a point. But since I was kneeling in a piss-stained bathroom stall with strings of vomit clinging to my shirt after torching years of sobriety, I was in no mood for his bullshit. What did he know of my life, anyway?

Alcoholism is my curse, a miserable hand dealt from the bottom of the deck. It had broken me, spilled every part of my being onto a thousand filthy floors. Hadn't I paid enough for my sins?

No, I told myself. *You're a fucking mess.*

"This is it for you, Cassidy," Montgomery pressed on. "I know about your deal with the chief, how you weren't supposed to take another drink if you wanted to keep those stripes. Well, you can't bullshit your way out of this one. You're fini—"

I tuned him out. The lingering effects of the minimal alcohol, which had escaped the purging, had finished cycling through my system. My head abruptly cleared. Blood rushed into my limbs. I stood, resolved at last.

Montgomery's mouth snapped shut, and he faced me like a predator, eyes narrowed to slits, unsure if his prey were as helpless as he'd expected. I took his measure, risking that even a moron like Montgomery wasn't stupid enough to carry a gun into a bar. That would get him fired, jailed even. If he were, so be it.

"I don't appreciate the speech, Montgomery," I said, my voice raw but steady. "You're going to apologize. Now."

"Apologize?" Montgomery replied in a mocking tone. "Just who the fuck do you think you are, you dru—"

I took a single step and lashed out. My right fist landed solidly, snapping his thick head sideways and very nearly breaking my knuckles.

Sure, I could have walked out, but that wouldn't have changed anything. I knew Montgomery would follow through on his words, as well as I knew the truth of them. Arrogant Neanderthals like him placed far too much value in their own authority, using their badge— or in Montgomery's case his sergeant's stripes as well as his size, his strength, whatever—to bully their way through life. I'd taken crap from guys like him for years.

No more. Plus, I'd be lying if I said I hadn't daydreamed of the image of Montgomery's long, thin strands of hair flying out and away from his head as it rocked sideways, my fist following through cleanly. I kept my head in the game, instantly sensing the opportunity for a follow-up to the stomach.

Instead, my fist unclenched, and I waited. His recovery was very quick.

"You fucking loser!" Montgomery sputtered, rubbing his chin and staring at me as if I were some strange new species. Contempt became shock until rage swept over his florid face.

I chose my words carefully. "For the record, I truly don't give a shit what you think of me." This is how you bait a bear, right? Oh well, in for a penny and all that. "If you think you're man enough to make your point, then this alcoholic is ready to go," I concluded.

That did it. He surged forward, his meaty hands clenched into fists. I'd expected the charge. Without thinking, I slipped into training mode, sidestepping him in the close quarters. His bullish charge propelled him past me, and I used this momentum to advantage. Grabbing a shirtsleeve, I pulled it across my body like a ripcord. He spun, unbalanced, landing unceremoniously at the base of the toilet. My defensive tactics instructor would have been super proud.

Unfortunately, Montgomery had caught himself before he got doused in vomit water. With one hand on the slick floor and another on the toilet paper holder, he propped himself up.

I backed away from the stall. "We can stop this little dance right now, Gerry. Whaddaya say?"

Montgomery's only response was a howl. He heaved himself to his feet, but this time he was much quicker. And this time he caught me.

His shoulder took me right in the chest, tossing me backwards like a bowling pin. A split second later, my head exploded in sharp pain when I hit the restroom door. I stumbled backwards, vision darkening. A large blur appeared. Montgomery bowled me over with a savage tackle to the chest.

We landed in a heap on the floor, his massive weight suspended over my chest. My head sang with pain. Pinpricks of light danced across my vision. He rolled off me, and I caught a breath.

Relief was short. The first in a rain of blows landed on my tortured stomach. I grunted in pain. My gorge rose up yet again.

Disembodied shouts drifted through my pain and nausea. I floated, barely aware until my fingers scratched against dirt. My left arm was alive with pain. I opened my eyes to an image of a gun barrel, the muzzle wide enough to step through.

A blow caught me on the chin. My head snapped back. The fog of confusion vanished, and I became aware of my surroundings. Panic and a welcome shot of adrenalin caused me to lash out with my fists. I made contact with lumpy flesh and bone—a cheek?—and followed through.

The flurry of blows to my gut halted immediately. I opened my eyes. Faces hovered above me. Voices spoke simultaneously. I blinked, wondering why James Kapalu was staring at me, his wide oval face hovering inches above.

"Take it easy, Sarge. Just take it easy."

Good advice. Resting my head on the hardwood floor, I took stock. There was a lump on the back of my head, but it wasn't bleeding. My right fist was swollen and raw, my stomach sore.

Stupid, stupid, stupid.

Echie's concerned voice interrupted my assessment. "Christ, Michael, are you okay?"

"I'll live," I replied, rolling over onto an elbow.

A crowd huddled around me, their excited voices like shattering glass. My attempt to piece together events was interrupted by a siren. For the first time in my adult life, the noise scared me.

Oh God, what have I done?

CHAPTER 15

Click.

Anna Best held up the small recorder, the light now red.

"It's two o'clock, Captain. May I suggest we take a break before finishing up this interview?" she said.

Doloviski glanced at his watch with a surprised look and jumped to his feet. "All right, let's take a break and meet again at . . . 1500 hours?" Without waiting for a response, he added, "I'd like to finish up at the courthouse downtown, if that's all right with the two of you. I need to be available for the chief and the prosecutor the rest of the day."

I gave him a wary look.

He didn't flinch. "Regardless of what you and I might believe happened," Doloviski said, "we're both looking for the truth. No matter what that might be. That is what we're both after, correct?"

I just shrugged.

Best looked back and forth between us. "All right, Chuckie, downtown at 1500 hours." She stood up, muttering, "Although why you can't just say three o'clock is beyond me."

I limped after Best to the parking lot where we climbed into her Mercedes. The bucket seats were like a feather bed after sitting in a hard chair half the day.

"I know a good place," I said.

"What?" she asked, confused.

"I know a good place," I repeated, "for lunch."

"All right."

I eased back into the plush leather, adding, "Hope you like Mexican."

We drove for several minutes, finally turning onto the main arterial that bisected the East Side. The street was lined with small storefronts, half of them empty, and a few tired old homes. I pointed ahead to our destination, a cream-colored food truck parked at a corner lot. The bright reader board had pictures of food, making my mouth water. I considered when I'd last eaten but couldn't recall.

Best pulled into the lot, her eyes widening as she stared ahead at the boarded-up gas station behind the food truck. I followed her gaze to the criss-crossing street signs at the corner.

"Is this . . ." she began in a hoarse voice.

"Yeah."

She nodded and said no more. I was surprised, given that I'd brought her to the scene of the triple homicide she'd so recently studied. Was she imagining the details—the taut nerves of a few dozen gang-bangers, rapid gunfire, followed by the soft thud of bodies hitting the ground. It was happening to me even as I sat there. Best rubbed both hands along her pant legs, the only tension I'd seen from her all day.

The food truck was backed into a corner, a handful of people queued up beneath its faded awning. I stared at the weed-choked concrete, my hand on the door latch.

"Makes it more real, doesn't it?" I asked.

She didn't answer right away. I could tell she was more than a little pissed off with me, but her professionalism appeared to be winning out.

"I don't much like surprises, Detective."

I nodded.

"But I suppose you're right," she added.

Despite everything, I chuckled. "I'll admit murder isn't great for the appetite. Sorry for the shock."

She raised an eyebrow. "I'll add it to my bill." After a pause, she continued, "But I'd appreciate it if you'd order for me, all the same."

"Done," I answered.

She reached for her purse, but I hopped out and greeted the two young Latinas behind the counter. Both had family and friends who wore Sureno blue, but like so many good kids in the neighborhood, these young women were too busy to screw around with that bullshit.

A few minutes later, I returned with two steaming burritos wrapped in aluminum foil, infusing the car with scents of barbecued steak, onions, and mole sauce. My attorney's dark eyes lit up.

"All right," she said without preamble. "Where to?"

"I know a quiet place to eat," I answered. "And don't worry; nobody died there. At least no one I know."

I guided her back downtown. We found a space in the shadow of the County-City Building and walked up to the main entrance. I badged the security guy while Best waited in line at the metal detector.

We passed through a wide hallway of polished gray marble before halting before a tall and ornate wooden doorway stained a dark mahogany. I produced a key that looked as if it had been cut during the Eisenhower administration. Best read the aged bronze sign on the wall, "Superior Court Chamber 3."

I jiggled the key in the lock, pulled the door open.

She peered inside anxiously. "Are we going to get into trouble here?" she asked.

"Nope," I said. "The judge is on vacation. I'm friends with his clerk. It'll be cool. Better than sitting in a stuffy break room."

The courtroom was lined with more huge slabs of the same swirling gray and black marble while the benches, desks, and chairs were a dark cherry wood. It was, in all honesty, a grand room.

Best spun around slowly, taking it all in. "I haven't been in this courtroom in years."

"But you *are* an attorney, right?"

She gave me a frosty look. Then she sat down at the desk reserved for the county prosecutor and rubbed a hand across the varnished surface. "I used to dream about sitting at this desk," she whispered.

"Why didn't you?" I asked. "Prior law enforcement? They would've hired you in a heartbeat."

"Usual reason," she said, sitting up straight and setting her attaché case on the table. "A bigger paycheck."

"Ah, the dreaded lure of disposable income," I affirmed. "That's why I got into law enforcement."

We both laughed, our voices echoing. Then I handed her a burrito, and we ate in silence.

A couple of minutes later I was done. I burped. It echoed loudly off the bare walls. "'Scuze me," I said, wiping my mouth.

Anna Best burped loudly in reply. "Highest form of compliment." She patted her belly in satisfaction. "Thanks."

"Sure."

"I took that class," she said a moment later.

"Huh?"

"The defensive tactics class. I remembered that when you were talking about fighting Montgomery."

"Yeah? That was a long time ago. All I remember now is that skinny old instructor always repeating the same thing, over and over."

"Training mode," she said, obviously remembering. She shook her head. "You're right about one thing, though. Montgomery was always an asshole."

"Got that right." I leaned forward and sat up straight. "Back to business?"

"Yes," she answered, checking her notes. "I want to go over the bar fight in a little more detail. Especially what happened after. I want to make sure the department doesn't revisit the incident with future discipline. You were punished, I assume?"

I winced. "You could say that. But I thought the Garrity ruling protected my statements."

She continued to take notes. "If I never trust administrations to follow their own policies, then I'll never be surprised when they don't."

"Amen," I answered.

"Okay, let's talk about that night. Lieutenant Orlando was your immediate supervisor. What did he do?"

It took me a moment to put those unpleasant details together. "First, patrol arrived. They knew it was a cluster fuck right away, so they called the sector sergeant. She listened for two seconds before calling Nate in. He already knew about it and was on his way."

"Who told him?"

"I'll let you figure that one out. As for what Nate did when he got there, well . . ." I paused to consider how to respond. "If you don't know him well, it's hard to sense when he's angry. He has amazing self-control, and he can mask his anger really well when he needs to. But I've known him since we were kids. I can read the tea leaves, and when it spells troubl,e I usually back the hell up."

"And was he really pissed off that night?"

I nodded.

"Why do you think he was so angry?"

"Simple," I answered. "Anything that happens within his chain of command is a reflection on him. Honor above all else. You know the drill."

"Sounds like a lot of cops I know," Best affirmed.

"Yeah, but with him it's an obsession." I leaned back. "Jesuit high schools are a breeding ground for idealists and intellectuals, both of which describe Nate. He thinks of himself as a soldier on a holy mission."

She nodded, unimpressed.

For some reason that irked me. I continued, "That night outside the bar, Nate said I'd disgraced the unit, the department, myself. All true."

"And then he suspended you?"

I nodded.

"And Montgomery?" Best asked.

I couldn't prevent a fleeting smile. "Nate chewed his ass good. Gerry looked like he wanted to dig a hole and climb in."

"Wish I could've seen that," she said. "What happened to him?"

"He put in his paperwork the next day."

"He retired?" she said, sounding surprised.

"Yup. Seems he could dish it out but couldn't take it. Anyway," I continued, "when everybody else was gone, Nate waved me over. I gave him my car keys, my badge, my gun. If he'd asked, I would've ripped my heart out and given it to him." I exhaled. "Sorry. That was as near the bottom as I've ever been."

Anna looked up from her notebook, her eyes thoughtful. "I can't shake the sensation that this was all a bit too personal. Is there something I'm missing?"

I shrugged. "Let me finish and judge for yourself. We jumped in his car. Instead of driving me home, he took us up into the Hilltop, back through his old neighborhood. It was his way of reminding me, or maybe both of us, where he came from." A touch of anger crept into my voice. "Like I hadn't already been right there with him for much of it."

I continued, "Then Nate drove us onto the interstate. We're coming up on the T-Dome when he pulls onto the shoulder and points toward the brush."

"What was there?" Best asked.

"At first all I noticed was a raggedy old blue tarp covering a bunch of trash. A homeless camp. I had no idea what he wanted from me, but I knew we were there for a reason. Then I spotted it. An old road sign, worn away and nearly on its side but still clinging to the dirt like a weed."

Anna Best's pen scratched across her paper.

I forced myself on. "The sign said, 'Welcome to Tacoma, The City of Destiny.' That's it. That's all. I looked at Nate, and he was calm. I realized he wasn't really mad at me, or at least not only at me.

"Then he told me about the first time he left Tacoma. He was eight years old when he and his mom rode the bus to Seattle. I can only imagine how different it must have looked—the Space Needle, the skyscrapers, the waterfront, Seattle Center. So many new things. On the bus ride home, he told his mom he'd move them both there someday. She surprised him by saying no.

"'You don't walk away from your problems,' is what she said. There were plenty of good places, good people in Tacoma, and if he up and left, well, he'd just be taking the easy way out. That wasn't the son she was raising. The man she wanted him to be would be strong enough to fix whatever he thought was wrong, and that included his hometown. So he took another look out the window and saw that same view he was showing me: the downtown factory buildings huddled up against a mud-colored waterway, the smokestacks along the tide flats coughing up gray clouds, and his tough little neighborhood perched on top of the hill surrounded by a moat of freeway. He and his mom passed that sign at that moment. For him it was a premonition."

Best had put her pen down to listen.

"Nate doesn't do things halfway. He devoured school, religion, sports, but those are just the framework of his ambitions. If there were a picture inside that frame, it would be that sign, that prophecy that pushed him to achieve." I shook my head. "He could have had anything he set his mind to. A shot at the majors. A free ride to law school. You name it. Instead, he put everything he had into fighting the one thing that haunted his childhood. Crime." I sputtered to a stop, a bit self-conscious. "Sounds pretty crazy, I guess."

"No, not crazy. It's a very admirable goal," Best answered. "But also egotistical."

"I disagree."

She raised an eyebrow. "How so?"

"Does keeping a pledge made at the age of eight make one egotistical?"

She digested this. "You obviously hold your friend in high regard, Michael. What's clear to me is that you do so to your detriment. Everything is about *his* vision, *his* achievements. What does that make you? His loyal henchman?"

"If you recall," I answered, defensive, "Nate saved my life. Not once but twice. I owe him everything."

Her eyes probed mine. "And how would that change if you found out he actually did kill his wife?"

I was suddenly blinded by a white-hot rage. Looking away, I began counting up to ten. I hit twenty before calming down enough to speak. "My answer is this. I'll never believe it." I shook my head, getting up and heading for the door. "There's still more you don't know. By the time this is finished, you'll understand."

"Michael," she whispered, her voice perfectly audible in the marbled room, "I'm your attorney, and what you tell me is privileged. I'd like a straight answer. Do you know who killed Desiree Barrajas?"

I turned back.

"*That* is a good question."

CHAPTER 16

Seated in a small interview room on another floor, Captain Charles Doloviski checked his watch again. He forced himself to relax. Lunch sat like a lead weight in his stomach. Excessive caffeine and the pressures of the investigation were contributing to a now-raging case of acid reflux. As tired as he was, sleep was a luxury he could ill afford. Even when he had the opportunity to catch a wink, his imagination would immediately produce an image of Desiree—as a baby, a gawky teen, a young woman, and finally, a corpse in a coffin—and all thought of sleep would vanish.

More than anything, he wanted to be done with this unspeakable task. Detective Cassidy's story hurt him in places he was trying to protect. The younger man's grief was difficult to witness, and he cursed Garcia for forcing him through this. Yet he had always been a loyal cop, one who knew his duty. Like it or not, this was his job.

And it sucks, he thought bitterly. *Maybe it's time to retire.*

For now, the important thing was to keep his hands on the wheel, make sure everything went smoothly. The chief's friendship with Lieutenant Orlando was a liability, one more reason to stay the course. He rubbed his bleary eyes and considered grabbing more coffee, but his gut still felt as if it were being shredded by a cheese grater.

He sighed and checked his watch again. Where the hell are they?

His notes were spread out in front of him, including the totality of Detective Cassidy's tenuous career. In truth, Michael Cassidy had been a solid, often exemplary cop and a promising sergeant right up until that ruinous night at the Spar Tavern. He recalled the chief's disappointment the next day, knew how much stock he had placed in the younger man. Cassidy had been stoic throughout the brief internal investigation, though it was clear to everyone that his heart was broken. Doloviski had to remind himself that the disgrace had come from Cassidy's failure to abstain from liquor, a promise he'd made to the chief.

Yes, it was a shame how it had all turned out. He looked down at the file on the desk in front of him, each page intimately familiar. He looked up when the *snit-snit* of high heels on carpet announced his old partner's arrival.

Anna Best breezed into the room, took it in at a glance. Her nose wrinkled in distaste.

"I know, I know," Doloviski said defensively. "This room is mostly for public defenders and their clients. It gets cleaned with disinfectant once a week."

"It's overdue," Best answered, sitting down across from him.

Doloviski shrugged and flipped open his notepad. Cassidy trailed in, settling himself slowly into a folding metal chair. The sling was gone, though he still cradled his injured arm.

When the two were seated, Doloviski removed the digital recorder from his pocket and set it on the desk. For several seconds, all three of them stared at the toxic little box. He pushed the button, and a sickly green bathed the tabletop.

"All prior conditions still apply," Doloviski said in a monotone. Let's get started. Detective Cassidy, would you be willing to answer questions—"

"Sorry, Captain. If you want to hear my side, you'll need to bear with me," Cassidy interjected in a muted voice.

Doloviski let out a quiet sigh of resignation. He nodded, added a verbal "all right" for the recorder, and leaned back in his chair to hear what he hoped would be the end of the story.

CHAPTER 17

If you've never had the pleasure of attending alcohol rehab, here's what it looks like: drab paint on bare walls, plastic chairs from the decade before you were born, little posters with inspirational sayings that would make the average person want to stick his head in a noose. Institutional fun at its finest.

There's a lot to bitch about, but I was also painfully aware of why I was here two weeks after my suspension.

We were in group, a kumbaya circle in my opinion, listening to a woman with a hornet's nest of hair and a wheedling voice that made me want to slit my wrists. With my teeth. Group sessions were all like this—a repetitive litany of self-hate. The great paradox of addicts is that the abuse we heap on our bodies and spirits is matched only by our narcissism. It's as if we're all a bunch of divas, each of us demanding a spotlight only to bitch about how fat we look.

Which is why I usually speak very little in group. If I wanted someone to hear my venting, Matt Hagstrom had already offered and accepted. I had become deeply appreciative of his support, his ability to listen without judgment.

"I'm tellin' you, Matt, this is driving me crazy," I'd told him the night before. "I feel like I washed up on the island of misfit people. None of them seems capable of handling the slightest stress in their lives without leaping off the wagon."

"I hear you, Michael." His voice was soothing to my jangled nerves. "They're trying to piece themselves back together, just like you."

"I know, I know."

"You know what I'm going to say next, don't you?"

"Be patient," I whispered back.

I heard my name and glanced up.

"I said is there something you'd like to add, Michael?"

My group leader was a fussy man with a frizzy gray Afro à la *Welcome Back Kotter* and the hefty WASPish name of Edwin Burbridge. His ghostly pale face and wispy pseudo-beard, which didn't quite hide his lack of a chin, were forgotten when he turned his attention your way. He had a set of deep-brown eyes, magnified by thick reading glasses, that seemed to be looking past the you sitting there to the person you were trying to hide. The first time Edwin skewered me with that look, I had come away haunted by an image of myself. The alcoholic. I had resolved to exorcise that image of myself.

Despite his appearance, Edwin was a kind man. And he had caught me out this time. Before I had time to think, he had locked his brown orbs on me. Words started spewing forth from my mouth, and I was unable to stop. Soon the tumbling words became coherent sentences, which eventually formed a fractured story. It was as if a pressure valve had sprung in my head. After that, I let it all out, from my mother's alcoholism to my wife's death, from my struggles to eventual sobriety, and finally, to the awful night that had led me to their circle.

I finally emptied out and settled back into my chair, immediately self-conscious. Everyone in the circle, a dozen or so hard-core alcoholics and Edwin, was leaning forward, intent. I searched their faces but saw no contempt, no judgment there. Only sympathy.

A young but grizzled war veteran with a prosthetic leg saluted me. A heavily tattooed woman in her twenties smiled through her tears, her pierced lips quivering. A trucker with a leather vest and thick belly dabbed his eyes. One by one, I acknowledged their concern with as much grace as I could muster.

After the meeting, Burbridge motioned me to his office. I followed him, still in a mild state of shock. He sat down and picked up a form from his desk, pulled a pen out of the pocket of his billowy Hawaiian shirt, and signed the form with a flourish. Without another word, he handed it over.

I read it in disbelief. I was done.

Minutes later, I was on the street, the paper clutched in my hand as if someone might take it. Jogging to my truck, my feet hovering inches above the sidewalk, I kept clutching the form to satisfy myself it was still there. I hopped in and tossed the wrinkled sheet into my glove box.

I was going back to work. *Hell yeah!*

And just like that, I took the big step back into my old life. My lawn needed mowing, the dishes were piled up in the sink, and there were a million messages on my phone. Adding items to my to-do list was the ultimate buzzkill. *Hell yeah.*

✶ ✶ ✶

The Road King leaned deep into the sweeping curve. The rumbling of the big V-twin shook my spine as I steered the Harley onto the off-ramp, slid my hand off the gas, and coasted up to the intersection. The light turned green at the perfect moment. I goosed the throttle, throwing my weight smoothly into the corner. The bike gained speed down the slight grade. Another green light beckoned me. I took it as a good omen and twisted the throttle again.

It had been just a few short hours since I'd signed out of rehab. After grinding through mundane tasks, the rarity of a sunny spring day and the Harley tucked into my garage made me set the to-do list aside. Fresh start was written all over the road.

The wind found a gap in my lips, filling my cheeks with air. A spontaneous grin caught me by surprise. Well, if the god of green lights was shining his or her beacon down upon me, who was I to argue?

I pulled into the station at a more reasonable speed—it didn't seem wise to provoke the gods of police work so soon—and turned off the engine, coasting into a spot.

I entered the station a little less jaunty, the familiar sights and smells immediately putting me in a different frame of mind. After all I'd been through, however, I couldn't help wonder if I still belonged here.

Two patrol officers were talking in loud, animated voices outside a holding cell. Inside was a scrawny guy wearing mangled jeans held up with rope, frothing at the mouth as he took drunken swings at invisible demons. Another few steps took me past a small huddle of detectives dressed in suits and holding court next to an ancient coffee maker. Nobody paid the least bit of attention to me as I strode by.

What had I expected? A lynch mob? A ticker-tape parade?

I began to relax.

The elevator stopped at the top floor. The administrative offices were at the end of the hall, a stroll that took approximately five years. My thick leather coat was suddenly warm. Then hot. Ten seconds later, I had the new world record for flop sweat.

The real estate up here was pungent with authority, reserved for those with years of experience and a strong stomach for politics. Yet few cops understood who the real movers and shakers were, the operators behind the scenes who held the reins of power. One of those quiet leaders sat behind the desk in front of me.

Cathy Nguyen, the chief's secretary, looked up from her computer. Her hair was yanked back in a severe ponytail, her dark eyes magnified behind bifocals. She wore an expression of mild distaste, as if she were about to swallow something sour. When her eyes focused, however, she smiled. And it was as if the sun came out from behind a cloud. "Michael!" she said, her joy reverberating in my bones.

Cathy was a fixture in the department, having served a progression of chiefs dating back well before my time. She knew, as they say, where the bodies were buried. She was also good people.

I smiled back. Then I laid a folded envelope on her desk.

She glanced down, noting the sender, but did not reach for it. "Michael, it's so good to see you!" she said, removing her glasses and looking me up and down. "You've lost weight. Have you been eating?"

"Been working out some. Had a lot of time on my hands. You look lovely today."

"None of your Irish-ness, please," she said, waving the comment aside. "What brings you in on this fine morning?"

"Just turning in my release form. My counselor says I'm lazy, and I need to get back to work."

She nodded her agreement. Then, with the authority granted to her by herself, she sliced open the envelope and scanned my form. Five seconds later, it landed atop a stack of similar forms on her desk.

"I'm way ahead of you, Michael," she said, reaching into a drawer. "I knew it wouldn't be long." Cathy pulled out a single sheet of paper. "First the bad news."

I took the proffered page. Skipping the boilerplate, I found the words that summed up my fate.

> It is the decision of this disciplinary board that Sergeant Michael Cassidy's actions on the night in question were grossly negligent and a clear violation of policy. Therefore, following his medically authorized return to work, he will be demoted to his previous civil service rank of police detective and reassigned to graveyard shift as the on-call investigator.

Nguyen studied me for a reaction. While it would have been prudent to keep my thoughts to myself, this was not unexpected news. In fact, I had already decided to accept the outcome, no matter how dire. Despite Cathy's warning, the news could have been worse.

"I'm fine with it," I said, exhaling. "I'm grateful I still have a job."

"That's a healthy attitude," she replied sagely. She reached out and squeezed my hand. "Now read the bottom."

I scrolled down to the last sentence above the chief's bold signature.

> Per the negotiated union contract, the name of the demoted employee, Michael Cassidy, will be placed at the top of the sergeant's list for future consideration by the Chief of Police.

I grunted. "I suppose this is meant to be a carrot?" With a shake of my head, I lowered the paper. "Think I'll just focus on being a detective. I'm a bit rusty." The words had come out of their own accord, but it felt like the truth. The tension that had built up began to drain.

"Good for you," Nguyen said. She reached into another drawer and withdrew a badge.

"Recognize this?" she asked, extending it to me.

It was my old detective badge. Or at least it had been mine not that long ago, before my promotion. I took it, rubbing the metal for luck.

"Welcome back, Detective."

"Thanks, Cathy," I replied, blinking my eyes against the sudden dust storm that had caused them to leak. I fastened the badge onto a leather holder and clipped it to my belt. Was there anything else in this world that could give a man—or woman—such a sense of pride?

Not hardly.

A tickle on the back of my neck made me turn around.

The police station was a newer building, with an open lobby that ascended all the way to the skylights atop the fourth floor. Around the rectangular atrium wound a series of walkways connecting the various hallways, offices, and meeting rooms. At that moment, it seemed as if every occupant of the building was standing on those walkways staring. At me.

The scores of eyes made me feel as if I were naked. My pulse kicked up a notch.

Recalling the swell of pride that had been there only seconds before, I dug deep in search of, I don't know, an inner strength. That seemed cliché, so in the end I simply surrendered to the collective scrutiny. With my arms at my sides and head held high, I awaited their judgment.

Come, stare at me, my fellow cops, my brethren, you judgmental motherfuckers! Take your best shot!

I stood there until the ticklish sensation passed. The normal murmuring and footsteps resumed. Everyone seemed content to go about his or her business, like blue-suited ants in a glass jar. Whatever the fuck that was, it was over.

I backed up, lightheaded.

"Looks like everybody's moved on," Nguyen said softly, her eyes bright behind her glasses. "How 'bout you?"

I nodded, sure of myself. With a wave, I headed for the elevator. The words of a long-ago training officer echoed in my head.

Pick your broken ass off the ground and get back to work.

Not exactly Shakespeare but close enough.

The elevator doors opened at the lobby. It was hours before my new shift started. Normally, I would have sought Nate's counsel, but he and I weren't on good terms. At least not yet. I was confident we could rebuild our trust over time, so I set it aside for the moment.

Then I remembered that the sun was still shining and my bike was outside. I had a sudden craving for the rumble of the Harley, a quiet country road, a stunning vista of the mountains, and a juicy burger at a roadside diner. My steps quickened as I headed for the exit.

When I reached the narrow hallway leading outside, my feet turned instead into a dark alcove. On a small sign next to a plain door, the words "Crime Scene Unit" were etched boldly in silver letters.

I knocked softly.

A woman's voice breathed, "Enter."

The forensics office was a windowless suite of rooms that served as laboratory and high-tech computer center for the department's crime scene technicians. At the moment, there was only a single occupant. She was seated at a cubicle beneath a poster of the rock band Kiss in their trademark makeup, long black hair, pimped-out spandex, and platform shoes.

My visit was well-timed. The woman was engrossed in the dual computer screens where a set of latent prints was displayed. With each tap of the mouse, her head bobbed up and down, nearly in tempo with heavy metal music blasting out of two tiny speakers on the desk, her singing woefully off-key.

I'd learned two things early on in my friendship with Desiree Barrajas. The first was that the aforementioned music—punk, thrash, eighties heavy metal in that order—was her greatest passion. Second was her obsession with her job. When Des was working a case, she lost all track of time and place.

This was no exception. She seemed to have forgotten that someone had just entered the lab. Not wanting to interrupt, I stood back and peered over her shoulder. She was comparing a couple of finger-print samples, one bearing a stamp from the jail and the other partial prints from at most three fingers. The cursor hovered over the tiny details of the latter as she searched through the unique patterns of loops and whorls to find similarities. She stopped to type notes after each click of the mouse, reminding me of how painstaking and detail-oriented her work was. Fortunately, Desiree was the best we had.

When she finished tapping, she slowly turned away from the screen. In profile, her high cheekbones and unblemished olive skin were striking, and she clutched a pencil in her full lips that never needed lipstick. Desiree wiped a single hair from her face, exposing long fingernails painted a dark red. Finally, she noticed me, and her quick expression of shock gave way to a beautiful smile. Her languid chestnut eyes expressed both surprise and welcome. "Michael, it's so good to see you!" she cried, wrapping me in a bear hug.

"You look great!" I said, and she did. She often showed up to work in clothes better suited to a construction zone, but that had changed when she had started dating Nate. He was a clothes horse, always on the lookout for the latest Italian dress shoes, new shirts from Brooks Brothers, a Rolex to add to his collection. Sure, he looked good in all that expensive shit, but Desiree looked better. Today she wore an austere cashmere sweater of silvery blue and a long black pencil skirt above supple, black equestrian boots. The outfit flattered an already voluptuous figure. I tried my best not to stare. Oh well.

She looked me up and down in turn. "You've lost some weight."

"Stress diet," I said, shrugging. Her eyebrows knitted in concern.

"Yeah, I haven't been eating much," I admitted. "But I'm working on that. How are you?"

Sensing my eagerness to change the subject, she turned and pointed at the prints. "Some latents from that triple homicide. You were on that one, weren't you?"

"Unfortunately, yes," I answered.

"I just came across them in another file," she said with a shake of her head. "They were misfiled and never processed. I swear, too much falls through the cracks around this place." Her eyes softened. "We've missed you."

"We?" I asked quietly.

"Yes, *we*, Cassidy!" she replied with heat, "What did you think? That your best friend would just forget about you? Christ, are all Irish that dense?"

"Racist," I said, grinning.

She gave me an exasperated look.

I wagged a finger. "There's an old Irish saying—"

"Shocking."

I ignored that. "Never get a Latina fired up," I said in a decent impression of my dad's brogue.

"That's not much of an old saying," she said, rolling her eyes.

"I'll admit it's not one of our best."

"Anyway," she said with a bold flourish of her arm, "we're a passionate people."

I held up my hands in mock surrender. She sat down on the edge of her desk and gestured for me to sit. I took her chair and spun in a slow circle.

"So when do you get cleared to come back to work?" she asked.

"Now. Tonight, actually."

"Really? That's fantastic news!" she said, beaming.

"Thanks, I think so too—"

"I sense a 'but' there."

"Pervert," I said, still spinning.

She rolled her eyes again.

"But," I said in a more serious tone, "I'm back to being a detective."

"Yeah, I already knew that."

"What?" I said angrily. "Is there a public forum for announcing administrative secrets?"

"I think I need to bring you up to speed," she answered, pushing up the sleeves of her sweater and crossing her arms.

"Please do."

As she spoke, her confident tone reminded me of the first time we'd met. She had wandered into the briefing room one day while I was working swing shift. She was on break from college, but judging by the ease with which she fit into the camaraderie and banter, you would have thought she was a twenty-year vet. It took several minutes of staring and whispered questions to find out that the gorgeous visitor was my boss's daughter.

Since I was one of the few newbies already married, I steered clear of the train wreck that occurred five minutes after she left the building. That locomotion was supplied by every single cop—and more than a few married ones—while the immovable barrier was my shift sergeant, Joe Barrajas.

After several nights, I finally introduced myself. Her breezy confidence vanished, and she regarded me with suspicious eyes and an icy tone. I could tell that in her eyes, I was either a buzzing nuisance or a predator. Either way, my attention was unwelcome. For the first time I realized that living inside a face like that might actually be isolating.

It took a year or two before she really considered me as something other than one more hound dog barking at the door. By the time she hired on as a crime scene tech, we were already friends. It was only months later that my wife died, and I found myself leaning on her friendship. Desiree had a quirky sense of humor and could ruin a joke by laughing all the way through the telling. She once surprised me with tickets to my first ever Kiss concert, and despite singing loudly in that surprisingly horrible voice of hers, she was invited backstage. I was totally up for it, but she politely demurred. In reality, I wasn't part of the invite.

So, yes, Desiree was enticing and beautiful, and for many years she was available. Why didn't I take another step?

Because we were friends.

I tuned in again when I realized she was no longer speaking. "Huh?"

"No problem, Cassidy, I'll just repeat everything I just said," she replied in a perfect imitation of an annoyed teenager.

"Sorry. Faded out for a minute there," I said.

She smirked and then sang the chorus of a truly awful death metal song. I plugged my ears until she switched off the music.

"Here's the deal, Michael," she began.

The fallout of my suspension had started the next morning. The chief's first move had been promoting Rafael Inigo into my former job, a decision that neither surprised nor bothered me.

"The chief had no choice," she continued. "There's too much at stake. On top of the violence, there's the media, the city council, and the neighborhood groups all demanding action, all second-guessing every move Garcia makes. Whether you or I agree with it, putting someone with Rafael's knowledge and skills has a certain logic to it."

"I get it. It's not a problem," I said, unable to summon any amount of outrage. "Maybe he should've had the job in the first place."

"Michael, you're sweet, but you can be so dense," she said, softening the comment with a wry smile. "Don't you see? You were the perfect fit! You knew the East Side, the community leaders there trusted you, and the rank and file respect you. Inigo may be popular, but everyone knows he's always running some scheme. He lacks leadership traits, which is why he was passed over in the first place. He was at best a second choice."

She gauged my reaction, but for me it was all moot. Desiree continued, "His sergeant's slot is temporary, but if he keeps the rank for six months, well—"

"Then it becomes permanent. Yeah, I know."

"Doesn't sound like you care that much," she said.

"I've used up all my rage on the mirror, Des. I can't fault Raf for taking advantage of my mistakes. And I'd look pretty lame complaining about *his* promotion when the reverse could have been said about me six months ago."

"I understand. It's just that, well," Desiree said, looking away. "Nate and Inigo are getting pretty tight. He's got a lot of influence over Nate at the moment—"

"Look," I interrupted gently, "I'm not jealous of the guy. Nate's my best friend, but that doesn't mean I'm the only one he should listen to. Hell, he never took any of my advice anyway."

Desiree gave me a hard look. "Everyone sings Nate's praises to the heavens, but that doesn't mean he's perfect." She paused as if to consider her words. "You, more than anyone else, keep him grounded. If it weren't for your friendship all those years growing up, I don't know where he'd be right now."

I rubbed my chin. "Pitching in the majors? Fortune 500 CEO? Ruler of a small kingdom?"

"Staging a coup against the government?" she added, chuckling.

"All right. Not that I necessarily agree, but I see your point. So . . ."

"So," she paused, uncharacteristically chewing on a manicured fingernail, "my point is that I'm not sure that Inigo is good for Nate."

I could read Desiree fairly well, and I sensed she was concealing something. And then I remembered Inigo's reaction to Desiree's arrival the night of the gangster's suicide. I was probably right in assuming Rafael had made a move on her, which she would have summarily shot down for a number of reasons. If true, I doubted that she would have confided this to Nate. The collateral damage would have been substantial, and God knows she put up with enough of that from her dad. Further, knowing Desiree, if she wanted to talk about it, she would broach the subject herself. But she just sat there waiting for me to work it out in my head.

"Okay," I said, setting that aside, "I don't know what I can do to help Nate. If you haven't noticed, he doesn't want to be seen with me in public."

"Yes, yes, his career, of course," she responded in an exasperated tone.

"As much as he's done for me, I don't begrudge him that."

"Fine, but I'm going to discuss all this with him. Nate wants, he *needs* to know how you're doing."

"Thanks, Des," I said, meaning it. "Meanwhile, at the Batcave—"

"Yeah, I heard you were assigned to graveyard. How wonderful," she said, smirking. "Sleeping by day and haunting the dark streets of the city by night."

"All that and a paycheck," I said, standing up to leave.

"Welcome back, Michael," she said, giving me another hug. "And happy Cinco de Mayo."

"*Gracias, señora,*" I answered. "I forgot."

As I turned for the door, she cranked her stereo again. "Detroit Rock City" followed me out the door.

The sun was still shining when I walked out of the station. My black Road King beckoned with images of a mountain and blue sky, the wind in my face as I chewed up the pine-scented miles. Barely breaking stride, I slid a leg over the saddle and grabbed my helmet off the handle bar.

The tall form of the graveyard commander strode towards me, his stride stiff and his expression dark. He halted in front of my bike, blocking me. His face was pale, his eyes bloodshot, but his tailored lavender dress shirt and pressed khaki pants were immaculate.

"Hey, LT," I said.

"*Detective*, I need a word," Barrajas said.

I couldn't help notice the stress he'd placed on my rank. Never a good sign.

He continued, "It's come to my attention . . . not that I normally pay attention to rumors—" He stopped abruptly, face contorting in disgust. "Fuck it," he continued quietly, his eyes narrowing. "I can't do politically correct, so let's you and me talk, man to man."

What fresh hell was this? I nodded.

"Since your suspension, I've been hearing rumors . . . rumors about my daughter and that fu—" Barrajas paused again, "About Lieutenant Orlando."

He paused again, evidently expecting me to wade in. When I remained silent, he frowned.

He lowered his voice to a whisper. "They say your friend married my daughter just to spite me, that he doesn't love her, that—"

"Wait—"

"I know, I know." Barrajas waved my objection aside. "I'm not an idiot, Cassidy. I know my daughter. Desiree is beautiful, intelligent, and kind—even an asshole like your friend can appreciate that. It's obviously bullshit. But there are rumors she's spending her evenings with someone else."

I'd heard enough. I stood up as straight as I could over the bike seat. I was good and angry now and decided it was my turn to vent.

"Desiree is my friend, Lieutenant! Her integrity is beyond question," I said, my rage building. "Why the hell do you need to hear this from me? This is *your* daughter! How can you believe such shit?"

Barrajas motioned for me to keep my voice down.

Instead, I folded my arms and said no more.

He studied me as if he were trying to read my mind.

Let him, I thought. *Maybe he'll see what I'd like to do to him right now.*

"You're telling me the two of you are *just* friends?" He gasped out the last words, his fists clenching and unclenching.

"What the fuck?" I stuttered.

It didn't take long to connect the dots. I'd been off the radar for weeks, Nate and I weren't talking, and rumors were obviously swirling.

Plus, it was suddenly obvious that Joe must have followed me out after I left Desiree's office. By the time the gears in my brain quit grinding, I had been mute for several seconds.

In that time, Joe mistook my silence for guilt. He took a single hostile step forward. Our noses were inches apart.

I lowered my arms to my sides. Defenseless, I summoned up every ounce of conviction I possessed. Enunciating each word, I said loudly, "I would never do that."

The lieutenant's eyes disappeared beneath his thick brows. His scrutiny felt like a strip search, and a particularly vindictive one at that. I did my best not to sweat, knowing weakness would only convince him of my guilt.

"Never?" he spat out.

"No," I responded immediately. "Never."

"I would like your word on that," Barrajas said.

I stood at rigid attention. "You have my word as a man, Joe. I've never touched your daughter."

Barrajas took a step back. Just like that, the moment was over.

"This is coming from Inigo, you understand," Barrajas croaked. "He's the source."

"How do you know?"

"Because, I didn't just fall off a fucking fruit truck, Cassidy," he snarled. "It's all whispers, but it's coming from Inigo's people, including that useless pile of shit, Montgomery." Barrajas raised a critical eyebrow, adding, "That asshole would still be pissing blood if I'd hit him."

"Well, then I'm sorry I didn't hit him harder," I answered acidly.

"Never mind that," he said with a wave. "These aren't just department rumors. People in my community, people who know Inigo, came to me with this shit," he said, biting off each word. "You understand why I had to talk to you. This is a fucking disgrace!"

I considered that. "Okay, what was Desiree's reaction?"

He looked away. "We haven't spoken."

"I see."

"Look, Cassidy. I don't dislike you." Barrajas said, looking out at the parked cars. "I thought you had the potential to be a decent sergeant someday. I'm sorry for your problems, but they're *your* problems. My daughter is my life, and now she's been taken from me by a man I do not respect, and her reputation is being trashed by a sick little fucker who isn't good enough to polish her boots."

Barrajas swung around abruptly and took a long step towards the station. His shoulders were slumped with the weight of his worries. I actually felt sorry for the guy.

He turned back. "I'll tell you one more thing."

"Yeah?" I said, certain I didn't want to know.

"Rafael Inigo ain't your friend."

After his little tantrum, I decided to ignore Joe's advice. His judgment was suspect at best. He walked off in a huff, and I sagged into the saddle. So much for my good mood.

Time passed as I considered a question I thought I'd already answered, one that now seemed to contain far more weight.

Where the hell am I going?

CHAPTER 18

TACOMA POLICE HEADQUARTERS
MAY 8
2054 HOURS

Unlike most people, I don't mind the station at night. It's often quiet enough that I can get a lot of work done. And when I start to get restless, the place will suddenly explode—drunks and druggies mouthing off, busy cops racing in and out, and the occasional federal task force rolling through on some secret squirrel mission. Everything happens quickly, and it makes for a lot of excitement. My first training officer, a crusty old graveyard cop with an unnatural love of the BeeGees, used to sing "It's the night fev-uh, night fev-uh" so loud he'd drown out the siren.

This, my first night back, was no exception. After the bizarre ass chewing from Joe Barrajas, I'd taken a cheerless ride home and fidgeted around the house until it was time to head back to the station. I returned early with plenty of time to decide that my new office in the investigations area was too far removed. I needed to be closer to the beating heart of the station. Night or day, that meant patrol.

So I claimed a desk in the corner of the patrol area's cubicle farm. It offered a view of everyone coming and going. More important, it made *me* visible to *them*. Being a team player went a long way with cops, especially the younger ones stuck on graveyard.

I was scrolling through the few hundred emails I'd missed during my banishment when loud voices interrupted. I checked my watch. Shift change. Patrol officers poured out of the locker rooms, their voices mingling with the familiar squeaks of worn leather and the sizzling electrical discharge from Tasers being tested. Radios clicked on, announcing their battery charge with a staticky chirp. This was home, the noises as welcome as the crackle of firewood in a hearth. I lapped it up for another moment before turning my attention back to the screen.

A shadow crossed my vision.

"Whaddaya know, Cassidy?" This from a thickset man in a rumpled jumpsuit with a short brush of white hair. He looked quizzically down at me, his eyebrows arching almost to a right angle.

"Yeah, what's going on? Looks like you're moving in," added a thin, immaculate Asian woman behind him. She was a stark contrast to her large, red-faced partner, except for the perfectly matched grey crewcut.

"Hey guys," I responded. "Just mingling with the common folk."

"Sucks what happened, Michael," offered crewcut one.

"Montgomery's an asshole. You shoulda kicked his ass," chimed in crewcut two.

"That seems to be the consensus. Sorry I couldn't oblige. Water under the bridge now."

The odd couple—who were not really a couple, given that both were happily married to women—did an about face and filed into the briefing along with a couple of dozen other officers. I trailed in last and took a seat in the back.

The duty sergeant, a trim, middle-aged, white woman with a stern expression, stepped briskly to the podium. The sergeant tapped her pencil several times, waiting for the room to settle with a withering glare. Then she began reading off a clipboard in a low monotone, regurgitating the day's activity in a manner repeated across thousands of police agencies across the country. She paused several times as a particular detail was targeted with jokes, rambling anecdotes, and the type of dark humor endemic to cops.

Thirty minutes later, I was antsy, like an altar boy at the end of a long church service. But when she mentioned more gang shootings and a new record for homicides, I paid close attention. The details were fuzzy, but the violence was familiar. Who had I been kidding? The violence would never stop. I'd been fighting a rising tide with a bucket, and all I'd accomplished was to slow down the inevitable. There may have been some sour grapes on my part, but like it or not, it was now somebody else's turn to take on the Surenos.

Or so I thought at the time.

As always, the last few minutes of the briefing devolved into a bullshit session. My mind drifted until I noticed the room had gone quiet. Everyone was staring at me.

I sighed.

"All right, *Detective*," the sergeant said, stressing my new rank. "Whaddaya know?"

"Not much," I answered. "Been too busy having a meltdown, or haven't you heard?"

Laughter accompanied this. "See," I continued, "it happened like this. Once upon a time—"

The laughter turned to groans.

"All right, all right," I said. "Two weeks ago, we were doing a warrant sweep on the East Side. It went pretty well. My unit met up at The Spar after work. I allowed myself to get talked into going. Someone put a drink in my hand. I tossed it back." I swiveled, taking in everyone's eyes. "That was a mistake. I'm an alcoholic. It was true then and it's true now."

A young cop at the front of the room opened his mouth and then shut it.

I nodded at him. "You want the rest?"

The room was silent.

"Well, there I was, face down in the toilet, puking my guts out in the men's room, or at least I think it was the men's room," I add to a few chuckles, "when Gerry Montgomery came in and found me in the aforementioned condition. He made some comments, which I didn't care for, and we had a few words. Then we knocked each other around for a bit." I stopped abruptly.

The room was quiet again.

I coughed once. "I won't bullshit you. It was humiliating. It was a personal and professional shit storm. And it cost me." I tapped my sleeve where my sergeant's chevrons had been.

Then I studied their faces, surprised to see the same expression of silent understanding that had been present following my meltdown in rehab. It was uplifting.

"I'm willing to take my lumps, though, even if it means working with the dregs of the police department. Or worse," I finished with a sorrowful shake of my head, "graveyard patrol."

Lifting her palm, the patrol sergeant silenced the yells and hoots. "Then you'll fit right in, Cassidy," she said.

On that note, most officers stood and filed out. I stuck around to chat with some of the newbies. Then I spotted Rafael Inigo standing in the doorway, hands folded across his chest and a look of amusement curling around his mouth. He waved me over.

I walked back to my desk. Inigo was already there, sitting in my chair with his feet up.

"Helluva speech, Miguel," Inigo said, with a slow clap. "Not what I would have said in your place, but not bad."

Despite both Barrajas's concerns, I felt a surprising sense of camaraderie with Inigo. Whether it was his decision to seek me out or his connection to my estranged best friend and my former unit, I didn't know. Inigo certainly had a polarizing effect on people. "I hope you never have to give that speech, Sergeant," I responded.

Inigo's grin dimmed slightly. He recovered quickly, though, his smile returning to max wattage. "Hey, you know how it is around here, mijo. One day you're up and the other guy's down," he said, holding one hand up over the other. He switched them. "The next day, who knows?"

"Ain't that the truth," I admitted, extending my hand. "So I guess congratulations are in order."

Inigo hesitated for only a second, not long enough to make it awkward. "*Gracias, Miguel,*" he answered. "And thanks for the stripes."

And just like that, we were both laughing. He offered me my chair back and grabbed another one for himself.

Inigo scanned the room. "Wow, I like what you've done with the place."

"I'm still waiting for the area rug, the armoire, the hunting trophies, a big wall clock—"

"Yeah, well you won't be in such a good fucking mood when you're still sitting at this desk a year from now," he said with a sour expression.

"What do you mean?" I asked, caught off guard.

"What do I *mean*?" Inigo asked, leaning forward. "You think I started out in major crimes? Shit, I got my dick's badge when your training officer was wiping your ass, hombre. Nobody shook my hand and welcomed me to the fucking club. No, it was more like, 'Hey, junior, we need an asshole for graveyard, and you're just the right size.' Six fucking years I spent in that seat." His lips pursed in distaste. "I knew I'd be doing the same shit for the rest of my career if I didn't figure something out. That's why I started working snitches. Think that helped? *Mira*, the other dicks just pumped me dry and sent me out for more."

A cloud crossed Inigo's face. "Finally, I say, 'Look, you wanna hear from my snitches? Then here's what you're gonna do for ol' Rafael." He leaned back. "That was the only reason I got off graves before I went bat-shit crazy and ate my gun."

I held my tongue, knowing this flash of temper would pass.

"All I'm sayin' is you need to learn what passes for currency around here," Inigo continued. "Some got their connections. Me, I got information. But you? You're in the shitter, Miguel. Bet no one's takin' your calls. What's that leave you with? Good manners? A sense of nobility? Take a look around and see where that gets you."

He spun slowly in his chair, shaking his head. "You took a goddam bullet for them, and they tossed you a shit sandwich. Mijo, how long you gonna eat it before it starts to taste bad?"

"That's one way of looking at it, Raf. I suppose we could debate my situation for a while, but unless I'm wrong, you're leading up to something."

His smile reappeared. "You may be naïve, but you ain't stupid. This fucking desk is a dead end."

That sounded like an opening of a negotiation, but I didn't bite. "As much as I appreciate the support, there's not much I can do about it."

"Ah," Inigo said, lowering his head as if he were praying. "All things are possible when the angels are on your side."

"What the hell are you talking about?" I said, laughing.

Inigo's expression flipped back to serious. His constantly shifting attitude was really throwing me off.

He responded, "There's a reason you're sitting here wiping patrol's ass at oh-dark-thirty instead of working major crimes on day shift."

"Yeah?"

"Believe it. When's the last time you talked to Orlando?"

"Not since my suspension," I said, masking my disappointment.

"That's what I thought," Inigo said with a sage nod. "He's distancing himself from you, hombre. If he'd given you the slightest bit of support, it would've been enough. You'd be on days working fraud, maybe even the Burglary-Robbery unit." He rolled his eyes. "So you got a fucking drinking problem. You think you're the only one? C'mon, there're no saints in this place." Then he clasped his hands in prayer again. "'Cept his holiness, of course."

Meaning Nate. In truth, I had already guessed what Inigo was confirming, but hearing it out loud still stung. Nate had always been my sounding board, a friend who knew me better than myself. And vice versa. For the first time in our decades-long friendship, I felt a twinge of resentment.

The room had grown quiet as the graveyard cops drifted out to the parking lot to start their shift.

"Let's jump ahead to the point, Raf. I'll go first." I leaned forward, hands clasped. "I like being a cop. I like being a detective. I don't mind being on graveyard shift. In other words, I'm good."

"Good?" Inigo answered softly, his face blank.

"Yeah, good. And to answer your next question, good is not great."

Inigo raised an eyebrow.

"Great," I continued, resigned, "was running a squad of overachievers, setting up complicated ops, making arrests that really mattered . . ." I paused, embarrassed at the surge of emotion in my voice.

"Yeah?" Inigo urged.

"Yeah," I answered, leaning back in my chair and nodding. "That was great."

Inigo's eyes were unreadable. He glanced around the now-empty room. "Okay, San Miguel," he said in a voice full of mischief, "there may be some things I can do to get you back on the path to righteousness. All is not lost." His eyelids were at half mast, his fingers steepled. "Here's the problem. The lieutenant is mostly upset because his reputation took a hit after your little misunderstanding in the bar."

He grimaced, as if he'd just swallowed something nasty. "*Dios mio*, you could steal the man's shoes off his feet, and he wouldn't give a shit. But say shit *about* him? Scorched earth, mijo. Scorched earth."

He shrugged. "I can do a couple things for you. First, the lieutenant and I will have a discussion in which I bring up your name. His holiness has a lotta pull around here, that is for goddam sure. There are other ears I can whisper into. Maybe I find the right one, and who knows?" he said, gesturing with outstretched arms at the dark room. "Maybe you give up this little slice of heaven for a vacancy in, say, major crimes."

"Your old spot in homicide," I whispered, utterly failing to hide a sudden surge of hope.

"Co-rrect. Still vacant."

It was a huge opportunity. There was no waiting list for the homicide slots. It was strictly invitation only, a mark of networking skills as much as investigative achievement. The detectives assigned to major crimes did the boiled-down form of police work that I loved. It was intense and gritty, the pace at times unrelenting and exhausting. But it represented the highest level of our profession. Raf studied me quietly as I considered the offer, his expression that of a cat eying a juicy mouse he's caught in a corner. Or maybe I was being paranoid.

"You know, I'm willing to do my time here," I answered finally, "but I'd be lying if I said your suggestion wasn't tempting. The question is—"

"You wanna know why?"

"Well, sure."

"Simple, Miguel. You can handle major crimes. You did right by me, and you deserve another shot."

"Thanks," I said, waiting for the other shoe to drop.

Inigo's smile grew. "You and I have something in common. We both know what it feels like to lose a promotion we think we've earned, and we both know what it feels like to be in charge of a squad of—what did you call them?—overachievers?" He laughed softly. "That's a bit fucking generous, but I'll give you this—it has its perks."

I acknowledged this with a nod of gratitude, adding coyly, "So, this is your way of ensuring I won't try to win back my stripes?"

The broad smile faded. His thin face took on a calculating look. "That's your choice, *hombre*. I can't stop you from doing a good job, now can I?" The hard expression eased. "But hey, maybe they realize they can't live without Sergeant Inigo, huh? And if you're lucky enough to make homicide," he said, tapping his index finger on my desk, "maybe you'll like it."

It was clear, studying his trademark smile, that Inigo had thought this through. He did a good job of hiding his true feelings behind that shit-eating grin. Then, as usual, he abruptly changed the subject. "And I hear a homicide job isn't the only thing you want, eh?"

"Oh yeah?" I answered, caught off guard.

"Detective Michael-Francis-Irish-Sister-Mary-Catholic-Mass-Cassidy," Inigo said, shaking his head. ""You want what every man wants. You want a woman."

I was already laughing before he finished.

"And I have a friend," Inigo said, putting his finger to the side of his nose, "you will like."

"Seriously, Raf? A setup?"

"No, *hombre*. You already know her. And judging by the hormones shooting back and forth the other night, you like her plenty."

He snorted at my obvious confusion. It took me a couple more seconds to make the obvious connection.

"You're talking about . . . Echie?" I stammered.

Inigo's lips parted, and his white teeth gleamed. "Ah, Miguel, you know it's like high school around here. Nobody has any secrets."

"That's . . . ," I began and then shut my mouth.

"Look, mijo, I ain't trying to get in your business, but I think you two have a shot. And altar boys like you need all the help you can get."

I didn't bother pointing out that I had, in fact, been an altar boy. He would have found that too amusing, but when Inigo handed over the scarf, I took it reflexively, still confused.

"I know the Latinas in this department, Miguel. Francine, she likes nice things, you know? Something you need to keep in mind if you wanna hang with her. Mira," he said, pointing at it, "I've seen her eye this scarf, so I picked it up for you a couple days ago. You give this to her, tell her it matches her eyes or some shit like that, and you, hombre, are in the fucking saddle."

Inigo's eyes danced as he spoke. As no other response suggested itself, I reached for my wallet.

Inigo waved it away. "Just give it to her, Miguel." He grabbed his bag and stood up. "In the meantime, I'll be talking to some people."

He strode out without another word.

I leaned back and exhaled. *What the fuck just happened?*

The answer was not pleasant to consider. By accepting his offer to help promote my career, I had become entangled in the sordid business of influence peddling. But who was I kidding? My relationship with Nate had never been anything but helpful to me, even if I hadn't asked for it. Nate had even told me as much when I'd been assigned to the gang unit.

Drawing on my extensive Catholic experience, I wadded up the growing ball of guilt and stuffed it into a crevice in my head. Sure, it would fester there, along with a hundred other guilty thoughts, but as I stroked the soft woolen scarf, I decided I didn't care.

For my first day back, it was certainly proving interesting.

Over the next few hours, I fought through a digital stack of paperwork. When I finally glanced at the clock, I realized it was almost midnight. Swing shift would be calling it quits shortly.

A door popped open down the long hallway to my left. Bored, I turned around.

It was Nate.

He was dressed in black fatigues. A phone was stuck to his ear. His head turned slowly in my direction. He saw me and froze. Seconds passed. I felt an upwelling of emotion. All thought of resentment and frustration vanished, and I was just about to get up when his expression went dark. His eyes narrowed, seeming to look past me.

I spun around, curious. There was no one else in the room. Yet when I turned back, I was shocked to see real rage on Nate's face. It was the first time in years that I'd seen his anger directed at me. I tensed, sensing real danger.

Without a word, he turned on his heel and walked away. In just a few long, purposeful strides, he went around the corner and out of sight.

I leaned back in my chair, my heart pounding as if I'd just run a race. It took several minutes before I calmed down enough to resume working.

Eventually, I settled into the task of writing a follow-up report for Matt Hagstrom. The prosecutor wanted more background on the triple homicide, which meant backtracking through my notes and rereading the entire case file. The details absorbed me, allowing me to forget Nate's strange reaction for the time being until loud voices broke my concentration.

Five black-clad gang unit officers walked past the cube farm on their way to the locker rooms, assault rifles slung over their shoulders. My heart skipped a beat when I saw Echie among them. She was partially hidden behind a cop with broad shoulders and a big chest. She laughed at something he said, and I wanted to kill him.

Whoa, fella.

We hadn't spoken since my suspension. I'd been too preoccupied, that is, too embarrassed, to call. She reached up and patted the man's beefy shoulder and then, *Oh God!* walked directly towards my desk. My panic was so adolescent I wouldn't have been surprised if I broke out in acne.

Echie moved with a brisk, self-assured step, arms swinging wide to clear all the crap sticking out of her gun belt like any cop. But further comparison to the rest of us knuckle-draggers was nullified by the subtle sway of her hips, an unconscious but extremely sexy aspect of her that I felt all the way down to my Y chromosome.

She caught me staring again, of course.

This time I didn't flinch, despite the frosty look I got for my trouble.

She halted a few feet away and rested her right hand on her firearm, her body language all cop. Her cool appraisal made me feel like warmed-over roadkill.

"How've you been, Michael?"

I noticed her use of my first name. *Is that good or bad?* We were now on equal footing, more or less, which didn't bother me in the slightest. In fact, it gave me a small thrill to hear my name fall from her lips.

"Not bad, Echie," I answered, trying not to sound as if I was going through puberty. "Just catching up. First day back."

"Yeah, heard you got released."

I wasn't sure how to respond to that, so I just nodded. "How about you? You don't seem your normal happy self."

"Went to a funeral today. Family."

"I-I'm really sorry to hear that," I stammered. I was definitely out of the loop. I knew little about Echie's large family, most of whom lived on the East Side. Hadn't there been mention of a shooting at the briefing? I bit my tongue before asking that stupid question. She seemed to read my thoughts. Slowly, her eyes lost their accusatory glare.

"Thanks," she answered, closing the subject. An awkward silence followed.

"Look, I hit a low point there for a while," I said, not liking the sound of that. "Shit, I was humiliated if you want the truth. That's why I didn't reach out to anyone, you included."

Her neutral expression didn't waver as I spoke.

I took a deep breath and pressed on. "I owed you more than just silence for the last two weeks. It was just foolish pride. For that I'm sorry."

She crossed her arms. I squirmed. The silent contest continued. This was worse than my recent battle of wills with Joe Barrajas.

"And well," I said, talking now just to fill the silence, "I guess I have a hard time talking about my problems because I figure nobody in her right mind would want to get involved with, with . . ."

"An alcoholic?" she answered, rescuing me.

"Yeah."

She let her arms fall to her sides. "You know, I liked having you as a sergeant. You weren't arrogant, and you weren't lazy. You knew your shit."

Praise was the last thing I'd expected to hear. I tried to think of a response and came up empty.

Echie took a step closer. "But more than anything, I think you actually care about people. Sometimes it's hard to hold onto that in this job, you know?"

I did know. More than once over the years, it felt as if my humanity were being stripped away by the ignorance and malice that immersed me on the streets. It was hard to hold onto faith in this line of work, but for some reason, I still thought people were worth the trouble. Coming from Echie, a tough cop, I took it as high praise. I was still forming a response when she bent her head low, her face inches from mine.

"You're a good man, Cassidy." Her lips curled up. "Sometimes."

The proximity was electric. For the first time I didn't turn away from her bold look, her pretty face framed by sculpted eyebrows over light-brown eyes that seemed to be laughing at a private joke, her light-brown skin with lips as . . . as . . .

I was never a poet, but for the first time I understood what artists meant when they talked about their muse. I lacked the words to convey how Echie's presence made me feel at that moment. Yet I drank in her essence like cool water and willed my simple thoughts directly into her mind.

My God, you're beautiful.

We were so close now I could have reached out and pulled her into my lap. That scandalous thought made it all the more intense. Her eyes flicked towards something behind me, and the moment was over. She stood up.

"What's that?"

The severity of her tone jolted me. I spun around, suddenly anxious. The only thing on my desk that didn't belong, however, was the silk scarf Inigo had dropped there hours ago. I had totally forgotten about it. "This?" I said, unsure how to handle the situation. I tried an innocent grin. "Oh, nothing."

She stood back and folded her arms across her chest. Her train of thought was clearly chugging down the wrong track. Without thinking, I grabbed the scarf and suavely draped it across my forearm. *Just like Inigo*, I thought with a mental wince.

"It's just . . . it's something I thought you might like," I stammered. *Smooth, Cassidy. Real smooth.*

She gave me a second round of the crossed-arms-raised-eyebrow look. I tried not to squirm. The day was shaping up to be just one long Spanish Inquisition.

Finally, Echie smiled. Cliché or not, the sun came out.

"Why, Detective Cassidy, I had no idea you cared," Echie said in a passable southern accent. She took the scarf and held it up to the fluorescent light, her delight obvious as she stroked it. She mouthed a silent thank you.

It nearly distracted me from my objective. "You, uh, you free for lunch tomorrow?"

"Why, yes, I believe I am."

"Great," I responded.

I hadn't thought past this point, so another moment passed as I scrambled for words.

"We have an op that starts tomorrow at 1700," Echie said, jumping in to help. "You want to meet somewhere?"

"Yeah, uh, that's a good idea." *Me speak good.*

"How about that new Argentinean steakhouse on Sixth Ave? It should be warm enough to eat outside on the deck. Would be nice to get some sun," she suggested.

"Sounds good," I said, though at that point having lunch on the surface of the sun would have sounded fine. "Thirteen hundre—I mean, one o'clock?"

"Yes, Detective, thirteen hundred hours sounds fine." She gave my knee a gentle squeeze, but when she stood up, her smile had vanished.

"Just so you know, Michael, I've never dated a cop before."

I nodded.

"It's hard enough being a woman around here, you know. And my family, well," she continued in a somber voice, "let's just say it's not a good mix."

"I understand," I said, adding, "I think."

She laughed, her eyes dancing with mischief. "I'm just giving you a little heads up, Cassidy. That's all."

What could I do but smile? "Consider me fairly warned. But I'm curious why you're changing your own rules."

She understood my question immediately. "You're different," she said, tilting her head to study me. "You don't push that alpha male crap. You're honest."

Before I could respond, she circled the scarf around her black fatigue shirt, her dark eyes suddenly aflame. "And now that you're outside my command chain, you're fair game."

Then Echie did a slow pirouette and drifted towards the locker room. I watched her walk away, my mouth dry, my mind totally blown. How long had it been since I'd asked a woman out on a date? Had it always been this hard?

All in all, getting shot was less stressful.

CHAPTER 19

I rolled into bed around six that morning. Several sleepless hours later, I was still wide-awake. *Shouldn't you be sleeping?* the digital clock taunted.

I shoved the fucking thing off the nightstand.

It was Echie's fault, of course. Every time I closed my eyes, the darkness would become a canvas where her picture would appear—a cascade of dark hair, curving hips, pouting mouth. And other details best left to the imagination.

Finally, I threw back the covers and got out of bed. I padded into the living room and picked up my guitar. At first the nylon strings seemed foreign to my fingers, but soon enough I found myself strumming a flamenco tune, Echie's hands whipping around her face in my imagination. A discordant twang brought me back. I studied the broken string, wondering idly what she was doing right now.

Hell with this. Dressing quickly, I hopped into my truck. The mundane chore of driving actually helped, and by the time I got to the gym, I felt like myself again. Throwing around weights released the last of my nervous energy. With muscles aching pleasantly, I jumped on a stationary bike and rode until the sweat poured off. On the way home, I consulted with Bob Marley.

No Woman No Cry? Sorry, brother. Too late.

On the short drive to my little craftsman home in the Proctor District, I felt relaxed for the first time in a while. I passed beneath ancient oak trees standing watch, limbs bent in homage to the century-old Victorian mansions lining Old Town, their lawns strewn with a carpet of cherry blossoms.

After a quick shower, I agonized over my paltry wardrobe options, finally settling on the least worst choice of a maroon golf shirt, tan slacks and a pair of ankle-length black boots I wore riding my Harley. I tipped an imaginary hat to the stranger in the mirror and headed for the door.

I was five minutes early walking into the rustic, wood-wrapped restaurant. The smell of sizzling meat and spices made my stomach growl as I followed the hostess outside to a small square table facing the street. I sat down, slid on an old pair of Ray-Bans, and ordered a lemonade. The spring sun was warm on my skin. Through the tinted glasses, the bustling street was awash in gold.

Echie's arrival was preceded by an engine's snarl. Her black Mustang pulled up to a vacant spot directly in front of me, the top down and the Gipsy Kings spilling out of the speakers. She shut off the engine and brushed the raven strands of hair from her face. In no hurry, she tilted her mirror and pursed her lips, sliding the lipstick around in a sensual oval. Glancing around, I realized that several people were watching the performance, including a teenage busboy with a stack of plates in his arms who was staring at her as if she were the first woman he'd ever seen. I couldn't blame him a bit.

She got out of the car wearing the scarf. Wrapped around her neck, the blue-brown silk was a superb contrast to her sleeveless, cream-colored dress with a hemline that thankfully showed plenty of Echie's smooth, muscular thighs. I tried not to stare, especially at the way the little dress hugged curves normally hidden beneath a layer of Kevlar. Alas, I failed.

Last, Echie put on a pair of sunglasses. When her indigo-tinted gaze scanned the restaurant and picked me out, I felt as if I'd won the lottery. I gallantly raised my lemonade in salute.

Take that, every male on the planet.

She strolled to my table, and I stood to greet her. She gave me a lingering kiss on the cheek.

"You look . . .," I began, but my language skills decided to take the rest of the sentence off.

Echie's smiled in delight, clearly enjoying the effect she was having. "You clean up good, too," she said, but we both knew she was just being nice. "Maybe we should go shopping sometime."

"I'm shooting for most improved dresser," I said. "First step is setting the bar low."

She laughed along with me, and just like that, we were both relaxed. We made light conversation as we sipped drinks, Echie opting for a dry white wine. By the time the food arrived, she was talking animatedly about her interests—horses, tennis, and, oh my God, baseball!—and I was more than halfway in love. When it arrived, the food was superb. We shared tangy bites of *lomillo*, the signature hanger steak grilled to perfection, along with a plate of polenta and sautéed vegetables, as our knees touched under the table. The waiter congratulated me on my taste, though a sly wink let me know he wasn't referring to the food.

Finally sated, we pushed our plates away. The silence was easy and pleasant. I left a big tip for the clever and overly attentive waiter, and we walked outside. The air felt energized. When Echie reached out and grabbed my hand, I thought I would burst.

"Take a drive with me?" she said.

My answer was a smile that nearly split my stupid face in two. She grinned impishly and jumped in the driver's seat. I hopped in next to her. My body shuddered when the engine started, its deep throaty purr as erotic a noise as any car I'd ever heard as it leaped onto the road.

I snuck a furtive glance at Echie, her tan limbs moving athletically as she drove, and snapped a mental picture. I tilted my head back, lifted my eyes to the sun, and swore to remember this moment for the rest of my life.

She drove us down to the shoreline for a spectacular view of the bay, the Cascade Mountain range hovering above like a jagged wall. The snow-capped peak of Mount Rainier finally made its appearance as we neared downtown. Passing a line of theaters, antique shops, and eclectic restaurants, she parked in front of a new condo complex, where she turned towards me, her lips an open invitation. I accepted.

Taking my hand, she led me inside the building. We kissed again in the elevator, this time more passionately. We stumbled inside her condo, where I marveled for a nanosecond at the expansive view of the waterway and mountains.

Then our bodies came together. I touched her gently at first, enjoying her sighs and moans. It had been so long for me that my lust felt like a lead weight from chest to groin.

Without thought, my hands slid up her legs, hiking up her skirt. I softly caressed the skin I found, brushing across the slit of her panties and eliciting another deep-throated moan. I continued exploring, first outlining her hips with my fingers, then moving my hands up her dress to lightly rub the exquisite breasts hidden beneath. As my fingers ran over her nipples, she cried out and shoved me away. Roughly, she pulled the dress over her head and came at me.

Echie and I fell on the bed together. We kissed and stroked one another, our hands moving everywhere as if trying to capture the other's image through touch. I forced my eyes open, letting them drink in her caramel skin, full breasts with brownish-pink nipples, tiny triangular patch of hair pointing downward between flawless thighs.

She was breathtaking. I looked into her light-brown eyes, saw my reflection, and pulled her to me. She clutched my back as I slid into her, finding a moist warmth in her body that felt like coming home.

We spent ourselves in the coolness of her bed, our bodies undulating in the rays of sun streaming through her window like sails straining against a warm wind.

∗ ∗ ∗

I left her two hours later with a soft kiss. The two-mile walk back to my car gave me an opportunity to process the various emotions battling for attention. I was exhilarated. I was delirious. I was . . . out of words.

A few hours later, I was back downtown. I parked my new ride—a dark blue Chevy Impala preferred by police agencies and little old ladies—in the shadow of the jail. The building was separated into several pods, each one dropped into place as if a blind giant were playing with monochromatic Lego pieces.

Next door, the County-City Building was already spewing hordes of people out its front doors. Attorneys in expensive suits, police officers in a variety of uniforms, civilians wearing everything from pressed shirts and slacks to sweaty tank tops and tortured spandex all passed by in a wave of humanity watched only by a small contingent of hollow-eyed homeless jingling their cups.

Rather than let that view ruin my day, I turned west towards the sun, a red disk rapidly descending towards the horizon, its rays striking the emergency lights of police cars lined up symmetrically in the parking lot.

I didn't feel like myself. What I felt like in that moment was jumping up on top of those cars, walking back and forth along the twinkling line of lights and preaching a new gospel. *Hear, O sinners, the Word of Michael. Love one another! And I mean get busy, people! Forget about all the other shit that doesn't matter! Just have sex!*

When the moment passed and I remembered I wasn't the first guy on the planet to get laid, I determined this was all Echie's fault. Again. She was a virus that had invaded my mind, eating away at the rational part.

I only hoped there was enough brain matter left so I could do it all over again.

Then I remembered why I was at the courthouse. Matt Hagstrom had wanted to discuss my latest report on the triple homicide, which I thought was a waste of time. The official conclusion, that all involved parties were deceased, had been released. But Matt struck me as a detail-oriented guy, so I wasn't surprised he wanted to hash things out one more time.

A man in a dark coat and jeans stepped out of the single-level garage and sauntered towards me. Rafael Inigo wore an LA baseball cap and a smirk that struck me as the proverbial cat with the canary in its mouth.

Did he know something I didn't know? Did he know something about me he shouldn't know? *Oh shit, had he been watching me just now?* I thought, worried I might have actually started to dance while entertaining those bizarre thoughts.

"Hey, Ser-geant," I said, trying for a smirk of my own. But I couldn't pull it off.

"Hey, De-tec-tive, whaddaya know?"

"Not much, Raf."

"*Lo mismo.* Same here, Miguel. But why so early to work? Couldn't sleep?" Inigo said, his last question filled with innuendo.

"No. No, I'm sleeping just fine," I lied. So he did know something. Christ, this guy was worse than the NSA. I continued, "I'm meeting with the gang prosecutor about that East Side triple murder."

"Hell, that was a good night for us!" he said with obvious good humor. "You gotta love it when the bangers wrap up the case *and* thin their own herd. Who's the overachiever in the prosecutor's office?"

"Hagstrom. I think he wanted to talk about the shooting angles."

"Hagstrom, huh? Sharp dude, I hear." His expression went blank, as if he'd turned off a switch. "Hope he's smart enough not to fix something that ain't broke."

"Yeah, well, I don't mind coming in early for a meeting if it means getting off a little early. Hard to sleep through days like this."

In a soft, almost apologetic voice, Inigo said, "*Es verdad*, Miguel. Word is you might have other things to do in bed besides sleep, eh?"

"What the fuck are you talking about, Raf?" I asked, losing my fraying temper.

"Easy, mijo, easy," Inigo soothed. "You're not the only one whose personal life is a little more public these days, you know?"

I couldn't argue with that. Everyone in the department knew about Inigo's divorce, a nasty business. His soon-to-be ex-wife had lifted some fairly damning, not to mention pornographic, information from his phone and sent it out as a group email to the department. The identity of the women—three female cops and one cop's wife—was obvious. The fallout had included a locker room brawl, surprisingly between two female officers, three divorces, and a flurry of work for the Internal Investigations Unit. Somehow, Inigo himself had emerged relatively unscathed, a fact that only enhanced his reputation. I had no idea how he'd pulled that off.

Inigo continued, "I mean, these rumors come with the job, right? No shame in it for you, Miguel. It's good for a man to plow the field now and then." His voice dropped an octave. "Good for a woman too, you know."

I looked around for a hole to leap into.

"No kiss and tell, huh?" He shrugged. "I respect that, I really do. It's just that I watch you get out of the car, stare at the sky like Romeo, minus all the bullshit words, right? And I can't help think that there, by the grace of God, is a man who just got a piece."

It would seem I had been wrong about the source of his information. No one had followed us around. Inigo had simply dangled the bait, and I had risen to it like a largemouth bass.

"Sucks when everybody knows your business, eh, Miguel?" he said.

I nodded. "I'm not really comfortable talking about it, Raf. I'm new to the dating scene, and, well . . ."

"I feel you," he interjected. His teeth flashed white. "It's a pain in the ass but a sweet one, am I right?"

I laughed. "She is amazing, that's for sure. And hey, before I forget, I want to thank you again for the sca—"

"Not here, not here," he said, holding a finger to his lips. "Too many ears, *sabes*? I hear you, all right?" He slapped me on the shoulder and said in a stage whisper. "Just be nice to her."

"Can do." I was struck by a thought. "Hey, I thought the undercover unit was supposed to steer clear of the jail."

"Me? Get burned?" Inigo's dark eyes danced. "*Mira*, just about every piece of shit with a bandana in this town knows who I am."

"Yeah, okay. Whatcha got going then? Picking up the bad girls as they walk outta jail?"

"You wound me, Detective," Inigo replied in a nasal voice. "Naw, training class. Gotta show the youngsters how it's done, you know. They need ol' Rafael to teach 'em the tricks."

"Stop, please," I said, rolling my eyes.

Inigo chuckled but then dropped his smile. "Hey, man, I'm just gettin' in your business because you gotta stay ahead of the rumor mill. If you don't know who's saying what, then they're talkin'—"

"About you," I finished.

"Believe it."

"Where's everybody else?" I asked, meaning the rest of the unit. Mostly meaning Nate.

"Naw, they're all back at the shack, hatching schemes. I'm heading there now." Inigo turned to leave and then looked back over his shoulder. "Let me know how the meeting with Hagstrom plays out, all right?"

"Yeah, sure. And good luck with the new job."

"Good luck with the *chica*, Miguel." Inigo winked and walked away, the heels of his dark brown cowboy boots scraping the asphalt.

The lights of a gold Mercedes flashed as he stepped up and then hopped inside. I watched him pull away, amused and a little relieved. A black Escalade with opaque windows was parked behind Inigo's empty spot. I recognized it immediately.

Nate's car.

It was one thing for an undercover operative, even Inigo, to show up in the jail parking lot. It was quite another matter for Nate, the strictest commander in the department, to do the same. Setting the tone for everyone else was his leadership style. I looked up at the building towering ten stories above, wondering what was so important.

And while I'm asking questions, why did Inigo just lie to me?

A stray thought, unformed, slid through my mind. I tried to grasp it and examine the contents, but I was too damn tired to marshal my thoughts. It vanished along with my excitement.

I lifted my head towards the west, needing to feel the sun on my skin again. But a bank of newly formed clouds was busily swallowing the last of the evening light.

CHAPTER 20

I walked into Hagstrom's office still rattled.

As usual, Matt was behind his desk, head bent over the computer screen. The prosecutor was dressed immaculately in a charcoal three-piece suit, crisp white shirt, and tie a matching color to those ice-blue Scandinavian eyes of his. He peered over the top of his bifocals, his pupils appearing bigger still.

"Hey, Matt. What's shakin'?"

He tapped a few more keystrokes while I grabbed a chair. Though it was nearly quitting time, his face was scrubbed and clean-shaven, his short brown hair slicked back. I shook my head, thoroughly disgusted with the perfection that was my new friend.

"What's that look?" he asked, shoving his keyboard aside and turning his full attention on me.

I shrugged. "Just my darker side urging me to kill you for being so freakin' squared away."

"It is both blessing and curse," he admitted, managing to look both world-weary *and* hygienic.

That made me chuckle. Hagstrom took off his reading glasses and rubbed his eyes, leaning back in his chair so far I thought he was going to fall. "Thanks for coming in, Michael."

"Anytime. What's on your mind?"

"Your report was clear and concise," Hagstrom said, standing up and shutting the door to his office.

"Do I detect a note of surprise?"

Seated again, the prosecutor rolled his head to the side. "Don't be coy. We've both read a lot of police reports. There are no Shakespeares on the force."

"Something tells me you're sugar-coating that."

He nodded. "That way I don't have to refer to them as sloppy, rough, or fucking illiterate."

"Yeah, well they really missed out when they chose not to spend tens of thousands of dollars on an English degree." Out of curiosity I asked him, "You like prosecuting gang cases?"

Hagstrom paused before answering. "Two years in, I'm still getting used to it. Frustrating job. I have yet to find a single credible witness in any of my cases."

"Well, you know what they say. 'Snitches die in ditches.'"

Matt nodded. "Snitches are bitches."

"Snitches get stitches."

He held up a hand. "First, let's agree that the discussion we're about to have has nothing to do with our relationship outside of work. Let's set aside that entire topic, all right?"

"Fine with me," I said. "I'm talked out at the moment."

"Here's my problem," the prosecutor continued, "your last report clearly points out the discrepancy with regard to ballistics—"

"I'm no expert, Matt," I interrupted.

Hagstrom waved off my concern. "This isn't rocket science. It's the O.K. Corral. Three gangsters die in a shootout. This is an indisputable fact. If you were to testify, I would only ask you to take me through your observations of the victims and their wounds, maybe have you point at some crime scene photos, the usual shit. I could use a forensics expert for everything else."

I nodded. "Fair enough. So what more is there to talk about?"

Matt stood up and paced behind his desk. In the cramped space, he looked like a giraffe, his head bobbing up and down with each step. He probably wouldn't appreciate the comparison, so I kept it to myself.

"The point," he said, still pacing, "is not that you need to convince a jury that gang bangers wanted to kill each other. They'll accept that without you proving it. The problem I've got is that everyone thinks this case is resolved, when there are still red flags."

I was thankful when he finally stopped pacing and sat back down. It was making me edgy.

He added, "The only person I need to convince of that right now is sitting across from me."

I blinked. "Me? What are you trying to convince me of?"

He threw up his hands in frustration. "Dammit, Michael, you saw the bodies. You saw the angles." He clicked the mouse and began reading off the screen. "Entry wounds through the chest of the two deceased lying next to each other, Hernandez-Ortega and Prieto, are consistent with shots fired from directly ahead, which would make Escalante the likely assailant. Escalante's single wound was the result of a round which entered at an angle inconsistent with the relative position of either Hernandez-Ortega or Prieto."

Matt set his glasses on the desk. "I could read more, but why would I? You're the one who wrote it."

I held my tongue. He shook his head.

"Okay, let's review. Keep me honest," Hagstrom said, standing again. "Escalante is squared off against the other two, holding his burner like so." He held up his right arm, pointing the index finger as if it were a pistol. "He shoots at Hernandez-Ortega and Prieto. They're hit and fall to the ground. But let's say that one of them gets a shot off, okay?"

"All right," I said, willing to go along with him. My line of reasoning had been discarded in the face of major crimes' assertions to the contrary. The details of the report were my first impressions, which at the time I assumed would be examined and confirmed by investigators. That hadn't happened, but by then, it had become somebody else's case.

Obviously, Matt didn't share my blind faith. As he ranted, I couldn't help but think that, in his fervor, he sounded less like a prosecutor and more like a conspiracy theorist. Or maybe he was just that frustrated by the investigation. In truth, I was getting swept up in his theory—or was it my theory?—as he recited the details from my report.

Hagstrom faced me, his left foot forward in a proper shooting stance. When he pointed his right index finger at me, I struggled not to flinch.

"Since Jaime was right-handed," he said, "this is a likely position for him, wouldn't you agree?"

"Sure."

"All right, then here's the problem you saw that night," Hagstrom said. "If Hernandez-Ortega or Prieto had fired the shot, the medical examiner said Escalante would have to be in this position."

Maintaining the same shooting stance, Hagstrom pivoted 180 degrees to face the opposite direction. He looked over his shoulder at me.

"In your experience, Detective, have you ever seen a gang member, or anyone else other than a trick shooter in a circus, shoot in your relative direction from this position?"

I stared at his back, speechless. The office faded, replaced by darkness. In my mind's eye I saw the parking lot, the details barely visible in the dim lighting, the silence peppered with sirens. I could see Escalante's crumpled body looking so impossibly small it would have been easy to miss without the growing pool of wetness around him.

For the briefest of seconds as I'd stood over him, his life's blood draining out, I had wondered why the wound in Escalante's chest was so large. Now I knew that it hadn't been an entry wound after all. The bullet had fragmented and blown a cavity out of his sternum on its way out, shredding his heart and spewing arterial blood everywhere.

And I knew then that the prosecutor was right; the gunfire that had ended the life of that young man had not come from his two dead rivals. It had come from somewhere else. Someone else.

Matt waited patiently as I worked through it. He loosened his tie and continued, "There's one more thing. According to the medical examiner, the entry wound was under Jaime Escalante's right armpit and was consistent with a standard 9mm round. Whatever the caliber, the bullet or bullets passed through his body. They were never recovered. Detectives found a .32 and a 9mm pistol on Hernandez-Ortega and Prieto, respectively. If we can't find the rounds that killed Escalante, if we can't prove that Prieto didn't fire those rounds, then there is little more I can do."

So, what are you going *to do?* I wondered. We were getting to the point of the meeting.

"Normally I would send a follow-up request to the lead investigator."

"And?"

"And I did that two weeks ago. The response was . . .," Hagstrom paused, rubbing his gleaming chin. "Well, it wasn't helpful."

"I see," I said, getting angry.

"Do you, Michael?" he said, catching me out. "I have a *closed* homicide investigation because the case detective says all the shooters have been identified. But I have a medical examiner's report and your supplemental that fails to line up with those results. And on top of that," he said, his voice betraying his frustration, "I have a boss who's already suggested I'm wasting taxpayers' money on this."

I held up a conciliatory hand. "I read you, Matt. For what it's worth, you've convinced me there's more to this. But I'm not a homicide detective. Why bring this to me?"

"Because the lead detective and the investigations commander are cock-blocking me," he said, running a hand through his gelled hair. "What I need is assistance outside the normal chain, someone with investigative skills and inside knowledge about the crime itself."

I stared at him, mute.

Hagstrom pressed on, "I need to definitively determine whether Jaime Escalante was killed by his dead rivals or," he added, softly tapping an index finger on the wall, "someone else."

He gave me a sharp look. "I need answers, *Detective*."

I considered what he was asking. My anxiety cranked up. "Matt, you know I've been demoted," I sputtered, "I'm on shaky ground here. For God's sake, they've got me processing booking reports on graveyard shift! You want me to cherry-pick an investigation already closed out by major crimes? Do you know how big a policy violation that would be?"

"Matter of fact, I do," Hagstrom answered simply. "A rather large one."

I laughed at his audacity. "One question."

"Shoot."

I wrinkled my nose, wondering if the pun were intended. "Who was the case detective?"

"Detective Rafael Inigo."

Despite everything, the answer still shocked me. Homicide investigations were doled out on a rotational basis to the fifteen or so major crimes detectives, which meant the odds of Inigo being assigned this particular case were low. The stray thought that had escaped me earlier fluttered past, still out of reach.

"Fuck it," I said, nodding at Hagstrom. "I'll look into it."

Instead of looking pleased, however, the prosecutor's expression was grim, his voice deadly serious.

"Watch your back."

CHAPTER 21

The steep incline to the top of McKinley Hill was rain-slick. Behind me, the port's floodlights painted the road a dull orange, while the headlights of approaching cars made me squint. I felt the first throb of a headache.

Compared to the skull-splitting headaches of my drinking days, however, this one barely registered. A good day's sleep would fix it. In the meantime, I swirled the bittersweet dregs of a cappuccino around my mouth as I thought again about my meeting with Hagstrom.

A part of me, the chickenshit part, wanted nothing to do with what could be a career-ending mistake. But I'd given him my word. *Why the hell had I done that?* I suppose that was a rhetorical question, given the contrasting details about shooting angles, missing rounds, and thus Inigo's questionable decision to close the case.

Which raised yet another question—why did Inigo always seem to pop up like a genie every time some banger fired a gun?

He's the gang intel guy, the left side of my brain argued. *Isn't that his job to know?*

Not a fan of coincidences, buddy, my right brain responded.

I sucked down the foam, hoping to drown out the little voices in my head. Even so, the number of Inigo's timely appearances were beginning to stretch credibility. I scratched my head, unwittingly wiping foam on my face.

I hate fucking riddles.

Which meant I could rely only on objectivity, logic, and evidence. In other words, good old-fashioned police work. First stop, the scene of the crime.

The location of the triple homicide was well-known and not just for superb street tacos. If I were to tap the location into my car's laptop, it would trigger a notice to dispatch that would be met with an immediate inquiry. I didn't want to answer those, thus I didn't want anyone knowing my location for the next hour.

Unless I were willing to lie through my teeth—which I was neither interested in doing nor certain I could pull off—it was better to stay off the grid with this. If I were found out, my recent run at infamy would only hasten a swift and sure exit from police work. I could probably keep Matt's name out of it, but my name, along with my career, would be mud.

It was a lot to think about, so I turned on the radio and let Bob's son Ziggy Marley change my mood. A few minutes later, I flicked off my headlights and steered the gutless sedan into the corner lot. I shut the engine off and listened.

The muted sounds of the neighborhood—the crackle of a high voltage wire, unintelligible voices from a nearby television, music heavy with trumpets and accordions, which I always thought of as Mexican polka, blaring out of a staticky radio—drifted in through my open window.

Stepping out into the rain-cooled night, I surveyed the familiar, blighted gas station. The business had been shuttered for months. Virtually all the glass windows had been shattered, the front doors ripped off their hinges, all replaced with particle board. The concrete parking lot itself looked as if a bomb had gone off about a foot beneath it.

I quickly picked out the spot I was looking for; the stains were still visible after more than a month. As I approached, the hair on my arms stood up. The narrow beam of my flashlight wasn't enough to keep a rising dread from creeping up my spine.

Afraid of the dark? asked a reasonable voice in my head. But the part of my brain that considered the possibility of ghosts and monsters flitting around in the pitch black a real possibility was too chickenshit to respond.

Despite that, I kept walking. A few more steps took me to the dark patch on the ground where Jaime Escalante's blood had spilled.

If I'd allowed myself to dwell on the spooky factor, I would've jumped back in my car and gotten the hell out of there. But one of the benefits of an active imagination is the ability to project oneself into a fictitious reality. With an exertion of will, I dredged up my memories of that night.

The sounds and images, the smells and other sensations that assaulted me when I originally rolled up on the shooting scene slowly materialized. Next, Escalante's ethereal body appeared, wrapped in the fetal position and hovering an inch or two above the dried bloodstains on the ground. I held the image in my mind and gave it more substance.

The other two kids, Hernandez-Ortega and Prieto, had died not ten yards away. I picked out two more dark spots, five feet from each other. It would have been a couple of simple shots for Escalante, even had he employed the typical gang method of "spray and pray." It would have been hard to miss from this distance, and by all accounts, he had not missed.

Recalling Hagstrom's posture, I took a position similar to Escalante's—left foot forward and right hand extended. In shooting circles, this is known as the isosceles stance, so named because of the triangle made by the feet and hands. Using my thumbs as makeshift gunsights, I aimed.

What sounded like footsteps made me freeze. I spun, simultaneously turning off my flashlight and yanking the real gun out of its shoulder holster. I slid quickly to one side, away from my last position. I scanned the darkness, my night vision blown. Adrenalin mixed unpleasantly with caffeine. I stifled a burp.

Nothing.

A minute passed. I continued scanning with eyes and ears. Apparently I'd been infected with a nasty case of the heebie-jeebies. Steadying my breathing, I shuffled back to the Escalante's stain, recalling the details from the ME report. The bullet fragment had struck

Escalante behind the right deltoid, lacerated the left lung and the aortic valve, and exited through his left pectoral muscle.

I closed my eyes, willing myself again into a relaxed state. I imagined the bullet as it was fired, rifling inside the barrel spinning it rapidly, holding it steady as it raced for Jaime Escalante's torso.

I could actually hear the round now. Its passage sounded like a miniature storm as it tore through the air. I felt a searing heat as it penetrated the spot where Escalante had stood, right where I was now standing. My heart thudded in my chest in sympathy, my lungs burned, my tongue tasted blood.

Somewhere on the edge of my consciousness, I sensed the yawning gun barrel from my nightmares. So close.

I forced my eyes open.

The night was still dark, the sky still wet. I shivered again, this time with my whole body. My hands were at my sides as I stumbled backwards on wobbly legs. My back struck a flat, upright object. The shock of impact cleared my head.

Slowly, I stood upright. The fuzziness crept from my vision. Thankfully, I was still alone. Turning around, I studied the object that had kept me from falling on my ass. It was a green metallic box, chest high, a city utility box. I remembered it vaguely from that night, recalled propping my feet up against something sturdy while performing CPR on Escalante. When the paramedics had shoved me aside, I'd backed up and bumped into it.

I gave it a pat of appreciation.

Once again, I surveyed the scene, imagining the three combatants in their relative positions. The light rain soaked through my thin jacket and jeans. *Shit.* It didn't require a rocket scientist, or a ballistics expert for that matter, to figure out that the shooting angles, entry wounds and the gang-bangers' locations could not be explained by the current conclusion.

Which meant . . . say it, Cassidy. *Damn. Someone else shot Jaime Escalante.*

Someone was getting away with murder, which totally pissed me off. I stared around the lot, inexplicably worried that the killer might still be here. With a shudder, I got back to the next burning question: where had the killing shot come from?

There were no grassy knolls hereabouts. Just apartment buildings too far away, except for a skilled shooter or a seriously lucky shot. Both were unlikely, so I concentrated on the only other option.

The boarded-up gas station was close and, most important, the storefront faced at an angle that juxtaposed with Escalante's fatal wound. I narrowed my eyes, trying to visualize Escalante alive and upright. A translucent mental construct of him appeared hovering over the bloodstains in a rigid shooting stance. Staring through the apparition, I sketched out the bullet's vector beginning at the exit wound and moving in a direct line to and through the entry point. When I realized I was staring directly at the boarded up window to the left of the station's front door, I squinted to get a better look. There were slits between the sheets of particle board, any of these wide enough for a rifle barrel to poke through.

Cover and concealment. The perfect spot.

My eyes glazed over. I summoned up the characters again, as if I were directing a movie. Two more pale, shimmering forms rose up, the avatars of Ortega-Hernandez and Prieto. Like Escalante, they were motionless until I willed everything into motion. There was a flurry of erratic movements. Escalante's ghost drew and fired several shots; his two victims slowly sank to the ground and evaporated.

Directly behind Escalante, a head bobbed up behind the station window, the features too fuzzy to identify. Like an eel protruding from a hole in the coral, a slim, elongated barrel slowly extended out of a gap in the wood pointed at Escalante. A wispy cloud was the only clue that it had been fired. Like everything else, the bullet moved in slow motion, traversing the short space and entering its target below the right armpit. Another followed, striking the same spot.

That was as much confirmation as I needed. But my imagination continued rolling film, and I watched in morbid fascination as the bullets tore through Escalante's ghostly flesh, slowing considerably. His body crumpled to the ground, but any horror I felt was eclipsed by the realization that the bullets' trajectory had altered and were coming straight at me.

The tips glowed a brilliant white.

A part of me knew this was bullshit, a figment of my imagination. But the same irrational voice in my head that had been speaking to me since I was a kid, whispering haunting thoughts in the dark, had taken over. My legs trembled, threatened to buckle. My fear was real, even if nothing else were.

Feeling both stupid and terrified, I hurled myself sideways, ignoring the *what the hell am I doing?* question, out of the path of the phantom rounds.

I hit the ground and rolled once, standing up neatly. Then I spun around, fear gone. There was a reason I had let this all play out. So far, my lost memories had done well filling in the missing details, and I wanted to see it finish.

The first bullet was beginning to fade when it struck the utility box. The second one hit an inch or two lower. Both vanished.

I shook my head, groggy, and took a couple of unsteady steps. This wasn't the first time I'd let my imagination run wild—call it self-hypnosis—but it had been the most consuming. I bent over the utility box, noting two distinct gouges in the dark green paint. A flash of gray metal beneath the chipped and slashed paint was already beginning to rust. Both bullet marks were a hand's width from the spot I'd imagined the rounds striking.

Here, at last, was the proof Hagstrom wanted.

I pulled a small digital camera out of my pocket and snapped a couple of pictures. I'd give Hagstrom a call in the morning. He could come out here and make the discovery himself. The only thing that bothered me still was that the rounds had not been found. Either the shooter had picked them up, a unlikely possibility given our quick response to the shooting, or someone else.

Who?

"Sup?"

I spun around, gun already out, heart blasting in my chest. My flashlight clicked on a split second later, illuminating a shaved head and a narrow brown face. A kid.

Reflexively, I barked, "Tacoma Police. Show me your hands!" I had one eye on him, another peering into the darkness behind him. If I'd had a third, I'd be checking my six. I cursed my lack of awareness.

The kid wore a thick down coat that hung nearly to his knees, with jean shorts extending a few inches below and shoes so white they seemed to glow. His eyes were lost in the shadow, but his jutted chin and casual slouch made me think *banger*. It was confirmed by the blue bandana dangling from his waist. He certainly didn't give a shit about the gun pointing at him.

Fortunately, the kid pulled his hands out of his pockets and held up empty palms. He crossed them over his chest and tilted his head as if to say, "Your move."

I lowered the gun but kept it in hand. The alarm bells were still going off in my head, so I reached for the mic on my vest to call for backup.

The young man spoke again. "You're Cassidy, right?"

My hand froze on the mic button. I took another, longer look at the slim face in front of me. He threw back the hood. Somehow it looked familiar.

"Do I know you?" I asked.

"No, you don't know me," he answered, lazily stringing the words together into, "nawyoudonome." Speaking more clearly, he added, "You know my aunt, Francine Echevaria."

Jesus Christ, you're kidding me.

"Lemme get this straight . . . Echie's your aunt?" I asked, incredulous.

"Yeah."

"What's your name?"

"Ernesto."

"Ernesto, okay." I said, looking over my shoulder again. "What can I do for you?"

"Naw, dawg, it ain't like that. See, you're the one in the shit. Not me."

"That right?"

"Yeah." The young man lifted his hand to cover his eyes. "Yo, turn off the light."

Since the kid's night vision would be ruined for a bit, I decided to be nice.

"All right, here's the shit," Ernesto continued in a whisper. "There's a fucking war going on right now, dawg, and you're in the middle."

"War? Between the Sureno sets, you mean."

"Yeah. There's some shit you need to know. Everyone's hard up for the East Side business, shootin' it up left and right. Some scary shit, ya know?"

"Yeah, it is," I responded. "But what does that have to do with me? I'm not even working gangs anymore."

"Don't know, but it don't matter. The OGs, they been talkin' 'bout you, sure as shit, dawg. Say that some top-shelf *ese* wants you gone."

My bowels flushed with ice water. "What kinda top shelf you mean?" I answered, trying to keep my voice from rising an octave.

"The fucking mafia. La Eme."

My brain snapped as if it were a rubber band that had stretched too far. *This can't be good.* Normally I adhere to the rule of "never let 'em see you sweat." We were past that point.

Ernesto correctly judged my silence as fear. With a nod, he stated the obvious, "Stone-cold killers, dawg."

"Okay," I answered with a nonchalance both of us knew was bullshit, "I get what you're saying. Any idea why?"

"I don' know," Ernesto replied. "You musta crossed somebody up."

Duh. "So why tell me?"

Ernesto squirmed, and for a second I could see the remnants of the boy hidden behind the gangster's mask. "My mom always says I need to watch out for *mi tia*, make sure none of the homies get on her, you know, her bein' a cop an' all. My mom says *mi tia*, my aunt, she likes you." Ernesto shrugged. "Something happens to you, it'll be bad for her."

"That's it?"

The boy nodded, slouching even further.

I holstered my pistol and extended my hand. "I know you're taking a big risk, Ernesto. I just wanna say thanks."

I gave the kid credit for shaking my hand, even if his grip was a wet noodle. Before he could disappear back into the darkness, I said, "Hold up. You help me, I help you." I took out a business card and handed it to him. "Call me if you ever get into trouble out here, all right? You don't have to hold onto the card, just keep the number handy."

"What kinda trouble?" he asked, wary.

"Depends on the kind of trouble you get into, doesn't it? If you get picked up by the police, I'll try to help you."

"For real?"

"Absolutely. And . . .," I paused, unsure of how to say the rest, "you can give me a call if things get, you know, sideways with you and your homies."

He stared at me, silent.

"It happens Ernesto, you and I both know that."

"Blood in, blood out, thas the way," he responded quietly.

I shrugged, unwilling to argue the point. He fiddled with the card for a moment before shoving it into a pocket but not before I caught a glimpse of ink in the webbing of his right hand. A gang tat, most likely. He took a single step back into the shadows, and before I blinked, he was gone. I let out the long breath I'd been holding for the last ten minutes. Christ, what a night.

On the way back to the station, my phone rang. I checked the number and smiled. "Hey, Echie."

"Hey back at ya, Cassidy. Whaddaya know?" Her voice was soft and teasing.

"Heard a thing or two," I answered. For some reason I decided against telling her about my mysterious conversation with her nephew, assuming he was telling the truth about that. "You?"

"Same old. Where you lurking tonight?"

"Nowhere in particular," I answered with a pang of guilt. "I'm a free-range cop."

Her laughter was light and silvery. We talked about nothing in particular for a few minutes, the sound of her voice effectively soothing my jangled nerves. But I kept checking my rearview mirror anyway.

"Hey, what are you doing tomorrow night?" I asked, trying to sound as if I could care less. As usual, it didn't fool her.

"Tomorrow is Saturday, right? Lemme see . . . think I have a date."

My heart lurched. I was silent for several seconds, struggling for a response. She probably assumed I was slipping into cardiac arrest, so she let me off the hook with a laugh.

"With you, Michael," she said in a voice that was both seductive and innocent at the same time. How do women do that?

"Oh, right," I answered.

"What did you have in mind?"

"You ever seen the Rainiers?"

"Hmmm, the beer or the mountain?"

"No—"

"I'm kidding! Yes, I've been to a Rainiers game. In my family, baseball was the only excuse for missing Sunday mass."

"Really?" I said. "My parish priest used to say that if baseball were a religion, nobody would miss church."

"All right, a Rainiers game sounds like fun."

"Great. I'll pick you up at five," I said, excited already. "You need a helmet?"

"A helmet? What for? Do I get to play?"

"No, but it's against the law to ride a motorcycle without one."

"Oh," she replied, the smile evident in her voice. "I don't have one of those. You got an extra?"

"I swore an oath to protect and serve, didn't I?"

"Of all the sexy things you could have said," she said, laughing again, "that wasn't one."

I hung up, grinning like an idiot. The world outside my windshield had turned into a dark gray soup. Rain sprinkled the windshield as I recounted our conversation. I decided to ask her about Ernesto tomorrow. *But only when the moment was right.*

I took a last, lingering look in the rearview mirror. The street was empty, the ambient light swallowed up in nothingness. Abruptly, I felt exposed. The laughter we'd shared just minutes ago was suddenly miles away.

CHAPTER 22

A MOUNTAIN ROAD
MAY 12
1840 HOURS

The throttle rolled smoothly, and the big V-twin let out a deep bass note that scattered birds from their perches and shook my seat pleasantly. The Harley took the turn greedily, and I leaned in. The road fell away before me, a steep downgrade that afforded a postcard view of Rainier, the mountain's bluish white shoulders crystal clear after a night of rain and a cloud hanging above the peak like a crown.

I squeezed the throttle again and raced downhill. It had the desired effect. Two arms encircled my waist, and I felt her warm shape meld with mine. Echie was, it seemed, enjoying herself.

We'd had another fantastic meal, this one at a downtown bistro, before taking this circuitous route to the baseball game. In actuality, we were less than a half hour east of town. We pulled into Cheney Stadium, a picturesque ball field situated in an urban hollow surrounded by green hills, as the garbled lyrics of the "Star-Spangled Banner" spilled out. I jumped off and held the bike steady while Echie dismounted, her cheeks flushed and her hair tousled in a way I found very sexy.

"You like it, huh?"

"I like," she answered, her eyes dancing and her voice animated. "I thought it would be just like driving, but the wind . . . I haven't felt that kind of rush since I was in a pursuit. Plus," she added in a sultry voice, "you're fun to squeeze."

"I'll add that to my resume," I replied, happier than I'd been in, well, a long time.

We walked into the stadium holding hands.

It was a tight game. The visiting Fresno team was the first to blink, blowing an easy infield defensive play. The error sparked the beginning of a long and explosive rally by a young, aggressive Rainier's bench. We got caught up in the fervor until the productive inning ended on a controversial call. Echie took loud exception with it, and when I made a half-hearted defense of the ump, she turned her ardor on me.

"The infield fly rule? You think that's what the infield fly rule is all about? Holy shit, Cassidy, have you ever played the game?"

When she realized I was teasing, she kicked me in the shin.

In the parking lot after the game, we stood next to my bike waiting for the parade of cars to end.

"So when we get to my sister's house," she warned, "they're gonna look you up and down like you're a piece of meat, all right? Don't be nervous, it's just a Mexican thing."

"'S all right," I said. "Irish bacon is top shelf."

Honestly, I was looking forward to hanging with her family. Outside of Nate's place, I hadn't been invited to a family gathering in years, let alone a tight-knit bilingual one. For the last week, I'd secretly practiced my Spanish with the young girls at the Mexican food truck, hoping to impress the Echevaria's family.

I had also discreetly found out that Echie indeed had a nephew named Ernesto. That topic was on the agenda for later.

Following Echie's directions, I turned off the arterial and rolled down a quiet lane parallel to Pacific Avenue. She pointed to a small, tidy one-story on the corner. An amber porch light cast a soft, cozy glow, beckoning me. I geared down, adding brakes and flicking my right turn signal.

I never saw the car that hit us.

My first indication was the tortured squeal of spinning tires and the frenzied growl of an engine at maximum output. It was right behind us. It had been waiting. For me.

Fear threatened to wrap my mind in an icy bubble. Instead, I projected my awareness out, using the scant seconds remaining to advantage. I rolled on the throttle, letting the Road King accelerate.

My intent was to minimize the closure rate, but if I could stay ahead of him . . .

The engine behind me sang a higher note, and I knew my minimal efforts wouldn't be enough.

Echie squeezed me hard right before the crash.

When it came, the impact tore her arms loose.

My teeth rattled as I was swatted off the bike by a giant hand, flying through air that seemed to crackle with energy. The pavement below slipped past below like a body of water seen from an airplane at high altitude. The milliseconds stretched out until my short flight was finally arrested by the unforgiving blacktop.

I landed awkwardly on my chest and catapulted back into the air like a skipping rock. Arms flailing, I gyrated helplessly a few inches above the pavement, landing this time on my side. I rolled. My helmet struck the ground, once, twice. My head clanged as if it were a nerve-coated bell.

Consciousness slid away. Drifting in a red haze, a bright light and a stabbing chest pain roused me. Pinpricks of light obscured my vision even as my head cleared. Ironically, these turned out to be real stars.

I caught movement in the corner of my eye and turned to look. Bad idea. Pain shot up my neck. My internal clock told me little time had passed since I'd passed out. My eyes opened to a man-shaped silhouette standing over me.

Male. Short. Medium build.

He cocked his head sideways, looking at me as if I were a stubborn weed. With a quick motion, he dropped to his knees. Rough hands reached inside my leather jacket and found the pistol I carried in a shoulder harness. He gave it a savage yank, nearly lifting my entire body off the ground. It remained firmly in place, however, thanks to the holster's built-in safeties.

He uttered an unintelligible curse in Spanish. I considered telling him to fuck off but lacked the energy. He reached in again, fingers deftly examining the holster. Seconds later the gun slid out. He lifted it to the light and examined the gun. My gun.

With his face exposed beneath the street lamp, I tried to piece his features together—sneering mouth, short, bristly black hair, high forehead, thick eyebrows, and a wide nose squashed onto his face like a small apple. As he stood up and stepped between my splayed legs, his identity clicked into place. Then he lifted his right arm and the cyclopean muzzle of my own gun stared down at me.

I turned away.

"Fucking *chota*," he said in a guttural voice.

The words barely registered. Far from giving up, I was trying desperately to tap into the adrenalin that was saturating every limb, every pore of my body. I bathed in it, my thoughts racing at hyperspeed, my muscles tensing. I readied myself.

Focus.

He was saying, "You shoulda—"

I lashed out with energy gathered deep in my core. My legs uncoiled, wrapping around my attacker's feet and pinning his knees together. With my butt acting as a fulcrum, I lifted my upper body off the ground and thrust my fists at him. My hands found the gun, clamped down, and shoved it aside.

A single squeeze on the trigger would mean my death. With Echie's name ringing in my head, I wedged my right thumb in the space between the trigger and the rear of the guard. An instant later, the bastard squeezed the trigger, catching my thumb in a metal pincer. The gun didn't fire.

But it hurt like hell.

Using my left hand, I grabbed the slide. If he were able to get a shot off and somehow miss, at least he couldn't chamber another round.

Fighting against the searing pain in my right thumb, I used both hands to push the gun muzzle up towards his face, intending to tear it from his grip. The exertion cost me, however. Pinpricks of light, not stars this time, danced across my vision. I gasped for breath. The gun thrashed wildly back and forth, neither of us gaining an edge. Slick blood, probably mine, oozed between my fingers.

I had to give the son of a bitch credit. He was strong.

Switching strategies, I heaved my body to the right. With his knees pinned, he rolled with me. Caught off guard again, he still held tight to the gun as he fell on his side. Locked together as we were, I felt the impact as well.

It knocked my thumb out of the trigger guard.

The gun fired.

We both froze.

I felt no pain. A second later, I heard the click of the firing pin on an empty chamber. He'd aimed this second shot at my head, but somehow I'd managed to hold onto the slide and keep the next round from clambering.

After I recovered from the shock, the explosive energy that had enveloped my body began to dissipate. The first tremors of exhaustion rippled through my muscles. When that happened, it would be all over, a thought that brought Echie's face into clear focus.

I yelled a profanity, my voice cracking. All those years of defensive tactics training, which I'd done begrudgingly, came back with shocking clarity. I released the bastard's legs and scuttled forward, my butt lifted off the ground. Spitting, flailing, and kicking like a madman, I did everything I could to loosen his grip on my gun. He fell for the ruse, focusing all his attention on that while I used the opportunity to settle my back on the ground.

I kicked forward. My toes brushed his ears as they passed, clamping down tightly on his neck with my knees. I squeezed with every ounce of desperation. Only when he realized his next breath wasn't coming did he begin to waver. His body twisted and writhed, his eyes shut and mouth gaping. Then a fist the size of a melon came hammering down into my groin.

I was ready for that. Even if that hadn't been part of training, keeping one hand free to protect my balls was instinctual. I blocked one strike after another, holding his neck in a pincer while his whole body jerked back and forth. Yet the frantic motions did have an effect—my left hand began to loosen on the Glock's slide, which was already slippery with blood. Though I was desperate to grab the gun with both hands, I knew that as soon as I did he would hammer my testicles into my throat. That would be the end of the fight.

Though my position was secure, it was less so with each passing second.

Doubling down on my position, I used every ounce of my rapidly diminishing strength to cut off his airway. His fist kept up a rapid fire into my crotch. The pinpricks of light—not stars this time—appeared again. It was now a competition to see who would black out first. If I lost, I'd be dead.

But what about Echie?

Thinking her name brought an image of her standing over me, scarf entwined around her neck, her dark brown eyes looking deep into me. She had seen something inside me, some quality that I had not yet identified. I suddenly found it in an explosion of energy. My heart rate increased, head cleared, and the soreness in my leg muscles vanished. I pressed harder, wanting to stop his breath, stop the blood from reaching his head, wanting his useless heart to stop beating. In that moment, I wanted more than anything to kill this man.

His punches began to lose their force. I kept up the pressure even as the blows subsided. After an interminable period, it stopped. His body went limp.

Still I didn't let up, worried that he was faking. I couldn't keep this up forever, couldn't start over if he gained consciousness. But over the next few seconds as he remained still, I began to realize what I was doing. I was killing him.

"Finish it."

I opened my eyes and looked up. One half of Rafael Inigo's lean face was visible, the other half lost in shadow.

"Finish it," he repeated.

I released my grip. My muscles spasmed painfully, still wrapped around the unconscious man's neck.

Inigo grunted. "Shit. Okay, I got this, hombre! Leggo!"

He roughly pulled my cramped legs apart and rolled me over. My head dropped to the pavement. My eyes were wet, my breath ragged. I took stock and decided that everything hurt.

I felt like shit. But I was alive.

Had I been in better shape, I might have been more than a little anxious about Inigo's sudden appearance. Eventually it occurred to me that I was not yet safe, so I tried to get up. My left arm collapsed under my weight, numb. I reached across and probed with my other hand and discovered the flesh beneath my left shoulder was wet and ragged. The truth brought out a single, hysterical cackle.

Damn. Shot again. In the same arm. You gotta be fucking kidding me.

And then I remembered something I never should have forgotten.

I screamed her name. "Echie!"

"Quiet, Miguel! Quiet!" Inigo hissed.

I ignored everything—the crash, the fight, his traitorous words—in my desperate need to know she was all right. No matter what happened, if she could just be okay, then I could accept everything else.

Suddenly, it was all too much. My pounding head became too heavy, and I collapsed on my side. As if in a dream, Inigo's slim silhouette waded out of the blur, standing above my attacker's motionless form. I was surprised to see that the man was awake, his face contorted in pain.

With the two of them together, I immediately recognized him. Inigo's informant. I'd last seen him running through an alley, chased off by the trigger-happy Sureno who would later put a bullet in me.

He was Inigo's informant, but was that their only relationship?

My body began to tingle, the numbness fading along with the initial shock. The first shard of serious pain announced its presence in my arm. My thoughts clarified.

El Feo, I recalled. *The ugly one. That's your street name.*

Nate had said Inigo kept this guy on a short leash, which did not bode well in this circumstance. Such a helpful guy, our Rafael. Always willing to share an informant or a favor.

Always first on the scene. Coincidence? *Bullshit.*

The final truth was anticlimactic. Perhaps my subconscious mind had already figured it out, had tried to warn me. At some level, I should have begun to suspect Inigo's motives at the time of that suspicious suicide. But I'd been too dense to connect the dots.

I thought again of the poor guy's face hanging in ruined pieces. Now it was plain that the only thing suspicious about that "suicide" was the identity of the killer who'd pulled the trigger. Had Inigo done it? More likely he'd had someone else do the dirty work. Maybe this poor bastard.

By the time those thoughts played out, Inigo had drawn his sidearm. El Feo stared up at the barrel, his ragged breathing loud in the sudden stillness.

"Fucked-up again, hombre," Inigo said without inflection. "*No mas.*"

The blast from Inigo's gun was preceded by an eruption of blue flame that disappeared in the darkness. El Feo's chest lifted imperceptibly. My ears rang from the blast.

Of all the night's horrors, this cold-blooded execution was the biggest shock of all. It was as if someone had suspended gravity for a moment and I were floating away. It wasn't that Inigo had taken another man's life but that he had done it with no more concern than if he were taking out the trash.

Inigo kicked El Feo's motionless body, nodding as if he had crossed something off his grocery list.

Then he turned and looked at me.

Inigo's face was no longer in shadow. The Cheshire grin was gone. His emotions were easy to read—a death threat written in capital letters. He looked as if he were swallowing something he didn't like, and he stalked towards me as if he couldn't wait to spit it out.

I turned away from the sight of Inigo's corruption. The rain-scoured night sky was clear, and for the first time in what seemed like forever, the stars above the city, my city, were twinkling. The stalwart North Star stared back down until it was blotted out by the muzzle of a gun.

I turned away.

A police siren warbled. Then another, this one closer. Porch lights flickered on. Hesitant voices from nearby homes drifted my way. Several seconds passed without me being shot.

I rolled onto my back. The throbbing in my left arm allowed me to focus on my situation.

Inigo had disappeared.

I set that not unimportant detail aside, turning instead to look back. My motorcycle was on its side next to the curb, one cracked headlight emitting a fractured beam. I followed the light across the street where, on the ground next to a parked car, lay a dark, motionless lump.

I blinked. A helmet materialized.

"Echie!"

My yell seemed to rebound off the houses. A moment later, footsteps pounded towards me. The wailing sirens doubled in volume as several patrol cars rounded the corner in tandem.

I kept yelling until my vision narrowed to a gray tunnel, though not before I watched a Mercedes sedan cross the street behind the oncoming police cars.

CHAPTER 23

I hate hospitals.

It's not that I don't appreciate the life-saving skills of the doctors and nurses or the high tech gizmos they use to cut out tumors, repair hearts, and enlarge penises. Maybe I sound unappreciative, but from my perspective, it's just hours of painful tedium amidst incessantly beeping machines, a line of people with long needles, food that tastes like plastic, and an antiseptic smell so pervasive it's still in my nose a week after check out.

Which is why, despite my eyes being shut, I knew exactly where I was. I opened my eyes—which seemed to take the better part of a day and felt like sandpaper rubbing across the inside of my lids—to blinding light. I blinked and an amorphous shape began to materialize.

I caught a hint of jasmine. "Des?" I said in a wrecked voice.

"I'm here, Michael."

Cool fingers lightly traced my brow, forehead, and scalp. It was blissful. My eyes eased shut. I drifted in and out, letting time carry me on a ponderous current. When I awoke, Desiree was still there staring quietly out the window.

"How?" I grunted.

"You're in rough shape, sweetie," Desiree answered softly, anticipating most of my questions. "A lot's happened, but you're going to be okay."

I twirled a finger. *Keep going.*

"You sure you're ready for everything? You look beat."

"Feeling better," I said, and I was.

"All right. Let's start with Echie," she said. "She was transported here, too—here is Tacoma General, by the way—with a mild concussion, bruised ribs, and a fractured wrist. They took her into surgery to repair the wrist, and now she's in recovery. I looked in on her, and she's sleeping. She's going to be fine."

When Desiree broke this welcome news, it was as if an over-inflated balloon of stress just popped inside my head. I was so relieved that for a moment I forgot to breathe. When I did, I exhaled loudly, blowing out the malignant tension that had taken root the moment I'd been knocked off my bike. My eyes blurred. *She was going to be all right.*

"What was that, Michael?"

I must have spoken aloud. "Can I see her?"

"Not for a while, I'm afraid," she answered, shaking her head. "You're on a morphine drip, in case you missed it. No broken bones but lots of bruising. Thank God, you were wearing a helmet. The IV can come out shortly. If you tolerate pain meds and food, you could be home tomorrow."

I looked down at my left arm. It was wrapped in gauze from shoulder to wrist and fastened tightly to my chest on a sling.

"Oh," she said. "I forgot about that."

"Know what?" I said. "Me too." *Seriously, how fucked-up are you if you forget being shot?*

The absurdity of it all made me laugh. Then I laughed some more. Fortunately, Desiree's sense of humor was as twisted as mine, and her braying laughter filled the room. My anxiety sloughed off, and I only stopped laughing when my head began to pound.

Drying her eyes, she continued, "So, about your arm. It looked pretty bad when I got to the ER. You bled a lot. The bullet took a chunk of flesh, and you'll be on antibiotics for a while. No permanent damage, though."

"Cut back on the weights; got it," I said. Already I was feeling stronger. "What else?"

"Well," she said, trying to gauge how much to tell me. "You do know Rafael shot and killed the man who attacked you, right?"

I bit back my reply. Despite all of my faith in her, confiding my suspicions—screw that, my certainty!—about Inigo's intentions could put her right in the middle of this ugliness. That was not something I was willing to do anymore.

"The scene is still being processed," she continued, though it was clear she knew I was holding back. "I spent a little time out there myself before coming to see you."

"I'm glad you did," I replied. "Thanks, really."

Her smile lit up the room. "Before she went into surgery, Echie told detectives that the suspect's car rammed you from behind. Everyone assumes he disarmed you after the crash and then shot you. Your Glock was the only firearm recovered."

"How much of this did you get from *him*?" I asked, unable to keep the anger out of my voice.

"Inigo? Minimal. He took off just as patrol was arriving, saying he was in pursuit of a second suspect."

"There was no one else," I said. "Let me guess. No one's heard from him since."

Her eyes narrowed, but I kept my mouth shut.

"You remember things differently?" she asked lightly.

"Maybe," I said.

She waited for more, but I was done talking about Inigo. That homicidal fucker had no reason to bother Desiree, and I wasn't going to provide him one. Besides, I had other problems. Contrary to what everyone believed at the moment, Inigo had gone off the grid. But he had used what little lead time he'd had by throwing up smoke screens to keep anyone from seeing what he'd really done. Which meant that anything I said at this point could be passed off as delusions resulting from my injuries.

You got a nasty bump on your head, Detective. You were confused, and it all happened so quickly. Here's a lollipop.

A man had been murdered. True, El Feo had been a bad dude who would have shot and killed me, but I didn't get in this business to enforce the law of the jungle. Inigo had to answer for what he'd done.

And if my assumptions were correct, killing his former informant would be just one of many crimes.

With a start, I realized that I'd been ignoring my visitor.

"Sorry, Des," I said. "Think I drifted for a minute. Must be the drugs."

She gave me a shrewd look that suggested she didn't believe a word. But instead of browbeating me, she held my hand for a bit longer. Her palm was warm, her smile tender, and I felt a welling of emotions for this wonderful woman who was my friend. Had I opened my mouth to express what I felt, I'm not sure what would have come out.

My God, how I wish I had.

She returned to the topic. "To wrap it up, the ME has the body, and the crime scene will wrap up in a couple of hours. There's not much more to tell." She frowned. "About your motorcycle . . ."

"Don't worry about it," I interrupted.

Priorities are a funny thing. I've heard that near-death experiences change people's perspective but always assumed I was too experienced to buy into that cliché. Hell, most police officers I know have danced on the edge a time or two, and none of them was in dire need of a group hug afterward. You visit the shrink, fire a few rounds at the range, and get right back in the saddle.

Only now that I'd nearly been killed again, my emotions were a little . . . buggy. The last thing I was worried about was my bike.

She nodded. "Okay. So, you know about Echie's condition. You know a little bit about the crime scene, or as much as I know—"

"Major crimes guys will probably drop by soon. I'll just pump them for info."

"I'm sure you're right. Oh, I almost forgot," she said, smiling. "For the time being, you've got your own little security detail."

When she saw my puzzled look, she turned towards the door.

"James?"

A brush of dark hair poked through the doorway. James Kapalu's lazy smile appeared. He tossed a quick salute and backed out again.

"Chief's orders. Probably understandable given the circumstances, don't you think?"

"Sure," I answered, though the thought that I might need a bodyguard did not make me feel any safer.

"All right. So, what else can I tell you?"

I hesitated and then asked, "Do we know who the bad guy is?"

"All I know is that he's been identified. He had some fake ID in his car, but a couple of detectives said they recognized him. That's all I've been told, and probably all I will be told. You know how it is."

I nodded. It must have been a shock for Nate and his unit when they learned that the guy that had ambushed us and tried to kill me was one of their own informants. I had an inkling that the water would only get muddier over time.

In all, I was grateful to have missed the last few hours, but it was time to get back in the game. I was wondering about my next move I when I noticed Desiree was preparing to leave.

"Des—wait. Have you seen my phone?"

"Oh, I almost forgot," she answered, reaching into her purse. "It was in your pocket when you got here."

She handed it over. "You got a bunch of texts while you were out, all from an unknown number. I looked at one or two. Hope you don't mind, but I just wanted to make sure you weren't missing anything important. You should take a look at them before the detectives get here. They'll probably want to confiscate it."

I scrolled through the missed calls and indeed there were several from a phone number I didn't recognize.

need to chek ur back tonight!!!

If the first one left me perplexed, the second one made my blood pressure spike.

M is on ya dawg!!!!!

It had to be Ernesto.

I quickly scanned the rest, remembering that I'd turned my phone off before Echie and I had left the baseball stadium.

Which meant that if I'd left it on and read the texts . . . Screw that. There was no point wasting time on what-ifs.

"Thanks for letting me know," I said, pointedly placing the phone on the bedside table with the screen facing down.

"Of course," she responded. "I'm just glad you're okay, Michael. And don't worry, Echie will be fine."

"Thanks for that, and thanks for being here. It means a lot to wake up and see a friendly face."

"You're getting a lot of practice at that, aren't you?" she answered with a wry smile. "Is there anything I can do before I head home?"

I had anticipated her offer. "I really need my laptop computer. It should be in my car, wherever they put it. If you have the time, I'd greatly appreciate it."

"I'll go right now."

She fished the keys out of my folded pants and then left with a breezy smile.

I rubbed my stubbly chin and considered my next move. Somehow, I'd made an enemy within the Mexican Mafia. How had I managed to do that?

If Inigo were part of this—a near certainty—then it had happened while I'd been in the gang unit. The only aspect that didn't jibe was that violent street gangs weren't known for their long-term grudges. They were young hotheads with short fuses, unlikely to wait even a few weeks to explode.

But, I admitted to myself, *La Eme was a different breed.*

A chirping noise from the now-empty bag of intravenous fluids next to my bed startled me. It was a déjà vu moment, a reminder of the last time I'd been here with my left arm wrapped in gauze and D5W dripping into my veins. There was a connection between those two incidents. El Feo, the dead informant, had been present at both. So had Rafael Inigo. But the frustrating part was that I had no clue what it all meant.

My thoughts revolved back to Echie. I imagined her lying weak and injured not far away. A rush of guilt, like a spring storm, struck me in the chest. It was immediately followed by a rage so powerful I was on the verge of passing out. The monitor next to the bed began flashing.

Deep breaths. *I don't have time for this,* I told myself. *Besides, the guy who did this is already dead.*

It was little comfort, knowing El Feo was merely a thug following orders.

Whose orders?

I suddenly wished that Nate, not Desiree, had been there when I'd woken up. His agile mind would have easily pieced together all the random details and leaped ahead to the conclusion.

I picked up my cell phone.

Yet I couldn't make the call. Despite all our years of friendship, he was still keeping his distance. Like it or not, I felt obliged to respect that. Besides, he would be far too busy with the shooting to talk about what was largely a personal issue.

There was still another reason I set the phone down. I was ashamed of all the times I'd had to lean on Nate over the years. Just once, I wanted to be able to handle a major crisis without asking him for help.

There was still plenty for me to think through anyway. Maybe I couldn't connect the disparate information into a coherent theory, at least not yet, but there were still plenty of questions that needed answers. And I knew where to look. All needed was my laptop computer.

Which made my current situation, hooked up to an IV with pain killers altering my already weak state that much more frustrating. I banged the bed frame.

"Hurry up, Desiree!"

✳ ✳ ✳

A phone buzzed. I opened my eyes. Despite everything, I'd dropped off to sleep. The phone was silent now, but this made me recall Ernesto's flurry of texts. He clearly knew more than I did, yet I had forgotten all about him. This day was as fucked-up as I apparently was.

While I grabbed for the phone, I pictured the kid, his hooded face all but invisible under the moonless, rainy night he'd taken me by surprise. That scene played out in my head, and along with it came that irritating sensation I'd missed something. I saw myself extending the business card to him at the end of our conversation, watched him reach for it and . . . there.

There, in the webbing between the thumb and forefingers. A tattoo.

My subconscious somehow filled in the fuzzy details, leaving a clear picture of three letters etched vertically alongside his thumb.

ESC

The implications of this cycled through my drug-addled brain state. Unless coincidences were reproducing at a mathematically impossible rate, then Ernesto's status as an East Side Criminales—the only Sureno set Inigo's informant couldn't penetrate—was what one might call a clue. I considered the possibilities, none of them pleasant.

First, Rafael was our point man for street gangs. For some reason his hand-picked informants were avoiding any transactions with the East Side Criminales, the city's largest and most violent Sureno set.

Second, our hard-working public servant appeared to want me dead. *Why?*

Three, a member of ESC said I was being targeted by his set, the only one that had gotten a free pass during our operations. It made little sense to me, but—point 3.5—it might to Ernesto.

I grabbed the phone and began reading his texts, which included the last, which undoubtedly had been the one to wake me up. Christ, the irony.

Why the fuck you not listen to me!!! That puta call me from jail yesterday sayin some dark shit!!!! Mi tia better be ok dawg!!!!

The kid's terror was like a punch to the gut. He'd tried his best to warn me, but I had been too busy screwing around. But this last reference to a phone call, and from the jail? What the hell did that have to do with this?

Before calling Ernesto, I needed more information. Phone calls and jail records were—

"Michael?"

"Hey, Des," I said. "Was just thinking."

"Sure," she said, laughing. "I could tell by the way you were scowling."

It was good to hear her laugh. She produced the laptop, and I thanked her profusely while greedily powering it up.

"I'm going to go update Nate," she said.

I nodded, barely hearing. Only later did I realize that she had expected something from me, a reaction of some kind. But I was already too engrossed in my computer to notice, never looked up as Desiree Barrajas walked out of my life.

And I'll never forgive myself.

CHAPTER 24

A couple of hours later, a nurse came in and took more blood, hung a new bag of juice, and checked my vitals. Convinced I was still alive, she whisked back out again. I had made a little progress in my research, and now it was time to get some help. I tapped out an email to Matt Hagstrom.

Among his many talents, the prosecutor had a vibrant network of law enforcement types—from mayors and police chiefs to civic-minded businesspeople and, more to my interest, a group of regional gang experts both in police agencies and in the prison system.

Since emails were discoverable, I kept my request circumspect. That finished I opened the police department's gang intel file, a searchable database filled with every report, photograph, and bulletin related to criminal street gangs. For a tense few seconds after entering my password, I wondered if my access had been terminated. Then I was in.

The screen lit up with a cartoonish image of a brick wall tagged with the names of the city's gangs. I clicked on SURENO, and a regular window popped up. It was an alphabetical list of the local sets, each one with a folder. I knew exactly what was in most of those because we had used those extensively during the gang sweep. Along with a brief on the gang's structure and geographical boundaries, the information contained an extensive history of predicate acts—crimes attributed to its members—and, most significant, a roster. This intel treasure trove was mostly Inigo's work; at least the son of a bitch had been thorough.

I perused each one until finally clicking on the icon for the East Side Criminales. What I found, or rather, what I didn't find, confirmed my suspicions. The file itself was bare—no history, no leadership, no known members, not even a rough estimate of its numbers. It was almost as if the East Side Criminales didn't exist.

There was only a single document in the file. It contained two pictures taken and uploaded by a patrol officer; both were views of the same wooden fence with gang tagging running horizontally across. The first one read:

After days and weeks studying similar tagging, tattoos, and all the other pseudo-cultural bullshit relevant to the gang lifestyle, the translation was actually simple:

It was the ubiquitous claim for turf, in this case the East Side Criminales. But what caught my attention, of course, was *Dawg*. Ernesto's repetition of the term, not to mention his gang tats, were a fairly good indication that he was the artist.

The second picture was obviously taken at a later date. *ESC* and *Dawg* had been crossed out, an overt threat, replaced by *BPK* and *Loony*, respectively. It was no shock that the Brown Pride Killers bore some animosity towards Ernesto's set, but seeing Loony's moniker there made the whole world shrink just a bit. A memory of his broad Mayan face appeared, his face contorted just before Inigo dropped him with a baseball bat.

There was a twisted logic to it all, but only if I were to consider what should have been unthinkable—that Rafael Inigo, decorated detective and now police sergeant, was a shot-caller for the East Side Criminales. Twisted or not, at least it made sense.

Instead of adding Inigo's name to the empty ESC roster, I logged out. Then I flipped through Ernesto's texts before tapping out a short response.

Call me.

A minute passed, then two. The phone vibrated.

"Cassidy here."

"Yeah, dawg. This is foolish. I don' wanna talk to you."

"I know that. Just wondering if Loony ever came at you." I waited patiently, almost able to hear the gears grinding in his head.

"Think you know somethin', huh?" Ernesto finally answered, unable to mask his anxiety.

"Yeah. Not too many Surenos out there throwing up 'dawg' on fences. You know this Loony character?"

"He just some fool, ya know? Anotha' *puta* in anotha set. What do I give a shit? Heard you guys beat his ass anyway."

I abruptly changed the subject. "Look, I still want to help you, Ernesto."

"Don' need no help."

"Really? Seems to me you're in pretty deep. Your set is gettin' mixed up with some real bad players. What if your friends find out you talked to me? What if they think you're responsible for El Feo's death?"

"I got nuthin' to do with that!" Ernesto yelled. There was silence for several seconds. In a scared voice he added, "You gonna snitch me out?"

"Of course not," I said hurriedly. "I'm just saying that you're in over your head. You know La Eme is—"

"Don't even talk about them, dawg," he said in a haunted voice.

I reminded myself Ernesto was still in his early teens, still impressionable. A reckless gang-banger, maybe, but he was still a kid. "Look, Ernesto, I owe you. I think one of the reasons you approached me is that gang life is getting too hot," I said.

I let that sit for a moment. When he didn't respond, I prodded, "Am I right?"

He answered in the weary voice of someone years older, his voice ragged. "People be gettin' shot all over the place. I got friends who're dead, ya know? Now *mi tia's* hurt. I don' want this no more, thass all."

"I can get you out of there, set you up somewhere safe," I pressed. "But you gotta do the right thing. The smart thing."

"All right, all right," Ernesto replied. "If you can get me outta Tacoma, then I'm down."

"Good," I responded.

"But you want something from me first."

The kid had read me like a book. I made a mental note to watch what I said. I *would* do right by him.

"Yeah, I do," I said. "There're a few things that need to be put in place to make sure no one comes after you."

Fortunately, Ernesto had already made up his mind. Over the next few minutes, he opened up about the phone conversation that had prompted his panicked texting. The caller had been a man named Luiz, though it quickly became clear that this was also the name of the newly departed El Feo, whom Ernesto described as a hired gun, an enforcer who performed so-called wet work for a number of drug traffickers. Luiz had shown up in the area within the last few months, just before the East Side had exploded into violence. Though Ernesto, a low-ranking member of his set, probably didn't know the specifics about Luiz's role, he had nevertheless received a phone call. Luiz had been picked up for drunk driving and needed bail money. Ernesto had been terrified, especially when he'd had to tell the enforcer he didn't have the cash.

"And that's it?" I asked.

"Yeah," he said. "Naw, wait. He wanted me to look up a couple of dudes."

"Names?"

"Gettin' to that. He rattled off a couple so fast I didn't catch 'em. Didn't feel like tellin' him to back up, ya know?"

"Yeah," I answered, impatient.

"The only one I made out was Hoora."

"Hoora? What the hell is that?"

"Not what, who," Ernesto said, clearly frustrated.

Oh shit. "You mean Jura, like a Sureno's street name."

"Yeah, dawg."

There was a reason the hair on the back of my neck did a little Irish jig. That name meant something to me. "Did he say anything else?"

"Yeah," Ernesto replied. "He says, 'You tell those dudes that if they want me to handle their shit they better get me the fuck outta here.'"

"And did you get hold of this Jura?"

"No, that ain't how it works. I called somebody else and tol' 'em what was goin' on. I got a phone number, no idea whose, then I called Luiz back and gave it to him. That's when I started texting you."

"Why text me?" I knew the answer but still needed to hear it out loud.

"Shit, I gotta spell it out? Look, I tol' you already. This dude, Feo? He was here to take *you* out!"

I saw myself, prone on the street, injured, helpless. Above me stood the man hired to kill me. El Feo. Ugly Man. The phone in my hand blurred red as rage obscured my vision. Instead of throwing the fucking thing at the wall, however, I closed my eyes and breathed in. Then out. Then in. My anger drained slowly, but I swore that I would not let this pass.

"Enough, let's talk about you," I said. "The main thing is to get you out of your situation and into a safe place. I'm going to talk to a friend of mine who can help handle this sort of thing."

He grunted. *Close enough.*

"One more thing, Ernesto. I'm really sorry your aunt got hurt. I did my best to protect her. I want you to know that."

Ernesto surprised me by chuckling. "I know, dawg. They already talking 'bout what you did to that fool. Look, I gotta go."

The screen on my phone went dark.

Outside, the rain whipped the windows as I considered all the possible translations for *Jura*. The accepted one was an oath, but it could also have a few other meanings. None of those mattered because on the street *Jura* meant only one thing.

A cop. Inigo.

The only item of this that bothered me was the obvious nature of the moniker. Seriously, they just call him the cop? Was Inigo so confident he could pull all this shit under our noses that he practically telegraphed his involvement?

Hell, yes. And up to this point, his arrogance had been justified.

My fists clenched and unclenched. My arm throbbed. I accepted the pain, thinking about Sergeant Rafael Inigo, aka Jura, and how it might feel to squeeze his neck in my hands.

Oblivious to my anger, the rain continued to fall.

✶ ✶ ✶

Matt Hagstrom's email responses popped up a few minutes later. The first confirmed that one Luis Gutierrez, whose moniker was indeed El Feo, had been a guest at the county lockup hours before eating a dirt sandwich.

Hagstrom had delved even deeper, locating several of Gutierrez's outgoing phone calls and downloading each one onto a digital file. My pulse raced as I clicked on the first one.

The sound of heavy breathing was interrupted by a ringing line. A click announced the disconnect. The next file was the same, as was the next. Gutierrez apparently used up his whole Rolodex trying to find bail money. Drug enforcers aren't the most popular guys on the block.

There were only three voice files left when Ernesto finally answered. Luis Gutierrez spoke. It was that same harsh voice of the man who'd tried to kill Echie and me. It was all I could do not to throw my laptop across the room. I started the recording over and paid attention this time.

The conversation progressed exactly as Ernesto had described it. I couldn't imagine talking to a demon like this guy, especially at his age. The kid had probably pissed himself afterward.

The next file started with what I assumed was a jailer yelling for Gutierrez. When he came on the line, Ernesto hurriedly recited a phone number, which I quickly copied. It was oddly familiar.

I clicked on the last file and found what I wanted.

Voice 1: "Who's this?"

Voice 2: "Feo."

Voice 1: "You fucking *puta*. Why you calling me on this line? *Dónde estás?*"

Voice 2: "*Estoy en el carcel.*"

Voice 1: "Jail? You're in fucking jail?!"

There was a torrent of cursing in Spanish, and the line went silent for several seconds.

Voice 1: "I don't think you have any information that the department wants, sir. Do not call again."

Click.

Despite all the logical conclusions that had helped me construct a plausible theory for recent events, it was still a shock to hear Inigo's voice on the recording. Though he hadn't confirmed the nickname, Jura, the likelihood created a physical sensation that spiked my blood pressure. An alarm bell attached to one of the drip lines stuck in my arm began to ring.

I lay back in bed and tried to relax. Hagstrom would tell me I needed to do yoga. My nerves told me I needed a drink. My head informed me that neither would be happening.

So Rafael, or should I call you Jura, how long have you been playing both sides? When did you decide that the ESC, La Eme, and a contract killer nicknamed Mr. Ugly were more worthy of your loyalty than your fellow cops?

And why did you kill your man? Just tying up loose ends?

I glanced down at my notes for answers but the only item that caught my attention was the phone number. I grabbed my phone and punched it in. A name came up.

Well hey, Raf. Should've guessed it was your number.

Inigo had told me this was his personal phone number on that night he'd come out to help with the suspicious suicide. That was obviously one more homicide to add to his running tally.

I hated to admit it, but Inigo had been superbly convincing. He had true charisma, enough that he could convince people to ignore reason or talk them into doing things they wouldn't otherwise do. For example, ignoring forensic evidence of a murder.

That was all me.

I'll admit I'd been overwhelmed with the responsibility of handling a potential homicide. Inigo had sensed my lack of confidence in my opinion and had done nothing more than nudge me towards the easy choice. He gave me plenty of reasons to shut down the suspicious suicide, though none of these was sufficient. Taking a conservative approach would have required a lot more painstaking work with plenty of stress for a rookie sergeant. But it would have been the right thing to do. I just hadn't done it.

There was more blame, too. Blind to his duplicity, we had also seriously underestimated his ambitions.

I took satisfaction in only one aspect of this mess—the tremor in Inigo's voice when he realized that Gutierrez had called his personal phone from a recorded line at the jail. How I wish I could've seen his face. That would have been worth something.

The question before me now was, what would Inigo—a narcissistic manipulator—have done after that phone call?

Simple. He would have sent a proxy to bail out Gutierrez, someone whose identity and face could not be directly linked back to him. That sounded right, but how would I find out whom Inigo had sent?

The answer was in Hagstrom's next email. It contained a single attachment, a video titled, "Release Area Video Feed."

Matt and I were clearly on the same wavelength. The video began buffering, and then the screen went dark. A moment later, a grainy black-and-white feed from inside the release room showed a single corrections officer at a counter. Numbers on the bottom of the screen ticked off the time.

The digital reincarnation of Luis Gutierrez walked into view from the left, his wide sneer in profile, his stocky, hulking body relaxed. The jailer set a bag on the counter and unceremoniously dumped out the contents. After a quick inventory, he pushed the pile towards Gutierrez.

Then someone else walked into view from the opposite side. Average height and weight for a man, face and clothes lost in the dim light. Whoever it was, this man was not Rafael Inigo. That had been too much to hope for.

The newcomer must have spotted the camera because his head was down and turned aside. The video immediately switched to a new camera angle, and the unknown man's features came into stark relief. I hit pause and studied him intently. No matter how hard I looked, though, it was clear that I had no idea who this was.

He was an intimidating figure, nevertheless, dressed in a dark stocking cap and tight-fitting clothing over the lean, muscular frame of a boxer. Bushy brows hooded eyes that constantly flitted back and forth, scanning for threats. One hand reached up and stroked a scraggly black goatee, the only unique feature in an otherwise unremarkable Hispanic face. But here comes the melodramatic part. This guy just exuded malice.

Fortunately for all of us, true sociopaths—the kind who'd stick a knife in you without a second's hesitation as long as they knew they could get away with it—are rare. I had sensed this same violent, hungry expression only once, years ago when I'd been assigned to the sexual assault unit. It was the least popular job in investigations, a proving ground for new detectives since we were the ones who had to listen to the gut-wrenching tales of women and children who'd been molested or raped by some severely twisted humans. One predator in particular, a serial rapist with a penchant for adolescent boys, had looked at me with the same dead eyes that were now in the middle of my laptop screen.

I pushed the play button again. The man produced a thick wad of cash and handed it to the jailer. He counted it, nodded, and pushed a buzzer. Luis Gutierrez, who should have waited for his trial, followed the other man out the door.

How was this man connected to Inigo? What role did he play? And who the hell was he?

A last email from Hagstrom had arrived while I'd been watching the video.

Hey Michael,

I heard you were injured. Again. What is it with you? You must be feeling well enough, since you're email-ing me in the middle of the night, but please fill me in when you get a chance.

Switching back to the theme of your emails, I discov-ered a few interesting items concerning that scary fellow who posted bail for Luiz Gutierrez. I ran a cropped photo from the video through the jail's facial recognition software and came up empty, so I sent the photo off to a contact at DOC, a guy with a photo-graphic memory that is borderline creepy. Seriously, he remembers every gang-banger locked up in the state pen in the last twenty years. Suffice to say, he rec-ognized your guy.

I'm going to give you a name and no more: Juan Rodriguez. If you want more, you'll need to call me.

MH

That was ominous, especially for a button-down guy like Hagstrom. Since he was up anyway, I decided to give him a call.

"I hear you're doing an encore impression of Swiss cheese," Matt said, who sounded as if he was wide awake.

"Morning sunshine," I said. "It's only a flesh wound."

"Spare me your Monty Python references, please. It's way too early, and your accent is an abomination. What's the situation with

Luis Gutierrez?" He said the name slowly as if he were reading it. "I hope he had nothing to do with you being shot because I argued against his bail amount."

"As a matter of fact, he *is* the guy who shot me—"

"Dammit! I'll—"

"Look, Matt, there's no need to go head-hunting. He's dead," I said, not wanting to elaborate. "What I need is more info on this Juan Rodriguez character."

"All right," he said, obviously dissatisfied. "But you are wading in over your head on this one."

"I figured that much," I noted wryly.

"Juan Rodriguez, aka 'El Moto'—"

"No shit, El Moto? The Machine?" I asked. "What's that supposed to mean?"

"I assume it's a reference to his particular skill set, which is probably the reason he is on Homeland Security's watch list," he continued, "which I learned when my phone rang and some federal automaton with zero sense of humor asked me why the fuck I was inquiring about so-and-so when I clearly lacked clearance to mop a federal floor."

That was intriguing. I'd heard from other law enforcement types who'd received similar calls after conducting a routine check. Most of the individuals they were researching had been flagged on the "No Fly List." A few were probably potential terrorists.

And then there was this guy, the Machine.

"Sorry I dragged you into this, Matt," I said, meaning it.

"Uh-huh," Hagstrom said. "In any case, I didn't send you everything because if I'd put it in an email, the NSA would have been crawling up my tight little sphincter as we speak."

When I failed to reply, he chuckled darkly. "Now you see what I mean," he said.

"Is there anything you *can* tell me about this El Moto guy?"

"Sure," Matt said. I heard papers rustle. "Locked up in the federal pen twice, once for interstate drug distribution and another time for manslaughter. Hit our state radar as a felon in possession of a firearm a few years ago, but he's been off the grid since."

"Doesn't sound any worse than plenty of guys here in town," I said. "Any guess why he'd be on the feds' watch list?"

"They don't share that type of information with a county laborer such as myself. Everything I just gave you came from my contact at state corrections."

"Got any more?"

"Apparently Rodriguez is a legit member of the Mexican Mafia," he said.

Which only proved my theory that there were no coincidences.

"You there, Michael?"

"Huh? Oh, yeah."

"Well, my contact said that Homeland Security sometimes tags people with a suspected connection to international organized crime," he added, his voice heavy with insinuation.

"You're talking about the cartels," I responded.

There was a pause. "This does not bear further discussion over the phone."

"I agree. Hey, thanks for getting on this so quickly. You have no idea how much it helps. When I get out of here, I'm gonna buy you a bucket of coffee. No, I'm gonna buy lunch."

"I doubt that," Hagstrom responded, laughing. "You can't afford my tastes, Detective. How's your head after all that's happened?"

"I know what you're asking, and the answer is I'm fine. Really."

"That's good to hear. You have enough on your plate as it is. These are some bad players you're messing with. Best be careful."

I hung up, even more disturbed. What Matt told me fit all too well. The DEA had long suspected the cartels were working with La Eme, using the latter's distribution system to smuggle narcotics up and down the West Coast. Nate's former narcotics unit had frequently worked with the feds, especially when the dealers were involved higher up the food chain. It stood to reason that any change in the status quo—California's gang injunctions and the increasing violence over its drug turf came to mind—could force the network to shift its business. Such a transition would, at least in the beginning, create a violent ripple effect throughout the affected area.

God help me, but that sounds familiar.

Loud footsteps in the hallway broke my concentration. I heard Kapalu's subdued voice, then the curtains around my bed were rudely shoved aside, and Joe Barrajas appeared. His eyes were red and moist, his normally light-brown skin a grayish pale. He truly looked like shit.

"Cassidy. You awake?"

"Am now," I said, unwilling to fake pleasure at his sudden appearance.

He nodded, either failing to hear or ignoring my tone. He scanned the room, though the vacant look on his face told me he saw nothing.

After nearly a minute of this strange behavior, I decided to break the silence. "How's graveyard shift?"

His head spun as if I'd startled him. Again, he didn't respond. Finally, as if he had made a difficult decision, he sat down. "What is it with you and hospitals?" he asked, ignoring my question.

"Free food? Who can pass this up?" I answered, annoyed. "What's happening out there right now?"

Barrajas's eyes shone with a hint of his normal fire. "After that cage fight of yours? It was pretty fucked-up for a while, but once Strand and his boys showed up, things got squared away in a hurry."

I grunted. I knew that Barrajas and Jack Strand, the major crimes commander, were close friends, so I wisely chose to keep my opinion of the officious prick's helpfulness to myself.

Barrajas took a seat at the foot of the bed. For a second, I considered kicking him off, but again I deferred. In his current state, he probably would have ignored me anyway.

"The bad guy's worm food. Inigo's doing, I hear. Wonder what the real story is there." He cocked an eyebrow, but I refused to take the bait. He shrugged. "The media is stalking you, Detective. They're lined up at the nurse's station right now. I don't have to tell you that you're not authorized to talk to them."

"You're right, Lieutenant, you don't need to tell me that." A guy can take only so much crap.

"I just don't wanna see a photo of you on the front page."

At that moment, I couldn't have cared less if they posted a picture of me, or my pale ass, on the front page. I shrugged, which turned out to be a rude reminder that the pain pills weren't keeping up.

Barrajas didn't seem to notice my discomfort, but his red-rimmed eyes finally locked onto my bandaged arm. "Holy fuck, Cassidy! Did you get shot in the same arm?"

I stifled the "duh" forming on my lips, opting for a dramatic roll of the eyes.

"That explains it," Barrajas said.

"Explains what?"

"Some of the rookies were taking donations to buy you a shirt with a bull's-eye on the sleeve."

I didn't respond because I didn't give a shit. Gallows humor came with the job.

"Is there any word on Echie?" I asked, changing the subject.

This only riled him up again. "Those fucking motorcycles are death machines, Cassidy. Don't you know that?"

"I seem to recall you were a motorcycle cop once upon a time, Lieutenant," I answered coldly.

Barrajas leaned away as if I'd smacked him. For a moment, I actually wondered if he was going to cry. "I'm sorry, I'm sorry," was his only reply.

This was a noteworthy moment in Joe Barrajas's testosterone-fueled life, at least in the years I'd known and worked for him. But I was too shell-shocked and exhausted to give it much consideration.

He recovered quickly and pulled out a large book from beneath his coat. "I have something I want you to take a look at," he said.

He set a large, leather-bound book in my lap with the words "LINCOLN HIGH SCHOOL" printed on the cover.

"Are we taking a stroll down memory lane, Lieutenant?"

"You'll see," he said grimly. He flicked through several pages, only then noticing the computer in my lap. It was paused with Rodriguez's face on the screen.

"What the fuck?" Barrajas whispered as if he'd seen a ghost.

Oh shit. How would I explain what I was doing without lying to his face? His reaction continued to play out on his face—those bushy brows forming a triangle over his bloodshot eyes, his teeth slowly grinding back and forth. "What the hell is it, Joe?"

"It's him," Barrajas whispered darkly.

"Him? Who?"

"That's the fucker from La Eme," he hissed, rudely shoving the screen towards me.

The temperature in the room seemed to drop. The wind-lashed rain struck loudly against the windows. Barrajas's hand trembled as it hovered inches above his holstered gun.

"Who is he to you?" he asked.

"I'm just figuring that out now, but—"

"Tell me!" Barrajas demanded.

I took a deep breath. "As far as I know, he's a violent felon, Mexican Mafia like you said. I've just learned all this, so I really haven't confirmed—"

Barrajas considered this with a dazed expression. Without asking, he shoved the wheeled nightstand away and set the old year-book next to me on the bed. He flipped through it until he found a dog-eared, well-worn page. It was Desiree's senior picture, her expression doe-eyed and innocent, her beauty not yet fully formed. Barrajas turned the pages angrily this time, hammering an index finger atop the photo of a Hispanic boy with an expression of barely controlled anger.

Juan Rodriguez. *El Moto.*

Barrajas spoke through gritted teeth. "You know something I don't. I want to know. Now."

I nodded wearily. But before I could begin, Barrajas put a finger to his lips.

"We need privacy," he said, parting the curtain and moving to shut the door. Before it clicked shut, a blue-sleeved arm adorned with four bands of gold blocked it. Slowly, the door opened, and Chief Randall Garcia stepped into the room.

Barrajas stepped back from the door with the look of a kid caught cheating on a test. I sat up in bed, absurdly self-conscious of my greasy hair and whiskers. Then I happened to notice the chief's appearance.

Garcia was a mess. His uniform coat was soaking wet, as were his jeans and black running shoes. Poking out beneath his jacket was a plaid shirt I realized were pajamas. His hair, normally combed and blown to shiny-white perfection, lay in tangled wet clumps, while every line in his forehead and cheeks stood out in stark relief. The chief's eyes were filled with plump tears that spilled down his cheeks and cascaded over his lips, and that same fear I'd felt as a child when my father had broken down at my grandmother's deathbed returned in full.

Stepping inside, the chief seemed to fill the entire room with his grief. I tried to steel myself, but Garcia turned instead towards Joe and placed his large hands on the taller man's shoulders. The two men, who had known each other for decades, were silent for an agonizing handful of seconds.

"Joe," Garcia said, breaking the silence. "Joe."

Barrajas was mute, his body rigid. He was a cornered animal with a feral expression, and he instinctively tried to pull away. Garcia just gripped him more tightly.

"It's Desiree, Joe."

Barrajas remained motionless, staring at the ceiling as the chief brought him in for an embrace.

The air was close, the room suddenly too small. It was all too surreal. Maybe the drugs were just fucking with my head. My throbbing shoulder cut that hope to shreds. There was no escape from the tragedy that was playing out.

Then Garcia unleashed the words that would resound in my head for the remainder of my pitiful life.

"She's dead, Joe. Desiree is dead."

PART II

The world breaks everyone, and afterward, some
are strong at the broken places. But those that
will not break it kills.
– Ernest Hemingway

CHAPTER 25

Desiree Barrajas's world was darkness.

Her eyes roved near and far. The absence of light made it impossible to judge distance, but floating in the inky void somehow alleviated the panic, the strangulating pain. She began to lose the tenuous connection to her body, and though the sensation was strange, it was not unpleasant. She glided forward, the motion effortless.

A flood of images—creations of her imagination—appeared against the backdrop of nothingness. Green pavement and sunshine. A tennis court. She recalled now the lithe sensation of movement as she rushed the net, kissing the ball with a dizzying spin, and afterward a grunt of paternal approval. Then the light touch of rain on her skin, the smell of salt water, and a glimpse of sunlight breaking through the clouds. The quality of light in the morning seen through the spires of a cabled bridge. The delicate clink of wine glasses, the red liquid suffused by candlelight, her own reflection in her lover's dark eyes. A ring appearing in his hands . . .

The image wavered as if behind a flame, only to be replaced by a string of faces, each one appearing briefly as if in a slideshow, each accompanied by a textured layer of emotions. Apathy, love, fear, excitement.

The last face was that of a man, his hair the color of dark sand, his eyes a clear blue, his mouth crinkled in a sad smile that filled her with an unexpected tenderness.

Then he, too, faded. She was no longer floating but racing forward, though direction seemed unimportant in the abyss that spread out before her. Her anxiety all but gone, she allowed the motion to take her, and she imagined herself a powerful bird gliding under a moonless night sky.

All at once, the blackness was shredded with violent bursts of light and noise. With a rude shock, she was suddenly thrust back into her physical body.

Pain returned, at first as tiny pinpricks. It intensified quickly, becoming a searing heat. She let out a voiceless cry of terror that was instantly smothered.

A harsh glare. Pain. Shapes moving. Pain. Muffled sounds and lungs writhing. More pain. Desiree became aware of a coarse fabric covering her face. She was suffocating.

Her panic became a lit fuse. It detonated with a mute scream that ripped through her being without release. Her body convulsed, the need to breathe a primal force that only multiplied her agony.

With a last shred of conscious thought, she tried to will herself back out of her body. She began to recede.

The first subtle release of pressure yanked her back. A stream of miraculous air slid into her lungs, making her body flex as if she'd received an electric shock. Before she could fully inhale, the smothering pressure redoubled. Cut short, the pain clamped down tightly on her tortured lungs even as she savored her last, exquisite breath of air.

I'm dying, was Desiree's last conscious thought.

With that realization, she found it profoundly simple to loosen her mind from her body as if she were shedding a coat. Her thoughts and memories remained intact, but the corrupting fear and pain receded more quickly this time.

She was again floating in a calm black sea. With an exertion of will, she shot forward.

Faster and faster, her speed accelerated in synch with her desire. This new realm, she somehow understood, had no limits. She imagined wings, and they were there. She soared, still moving at unspeakable speed, along a ripple of warmth. She soaked in it and felt cleansed.

A slight tug from behind made her pause. Without turning, she sensed the wispy cord snaking back in the direction from which she had come. Turning away a final time, Desiree Barrajas flew on, barely noticing when the cord binding her spirit to the world severed.

CHAPTER 26

Now that I had finished talking, the sounds that penetrated the interview room's thin walls leaped out at me. The clink of ancient boilers, the scuff of passing feet, even the syncopated breathing of Doloviski and Best seemed too close. The claustrophobia vanished when I noticed the tears threatening to spill out of the captain's red eyes. Embarrassed, I turned away, my attention drawn to the tape recorder and its pale green light. It seemed to urge me on, but I was finally spent.

Doloviski blew his nose loudly. "Thank you, Detective Cassidy. With your permission," he added with a nod towards my attorney, "I have just a couple of questions."

Anna Best's quiet gaze lingered over me, making me aware of my appearance—scabs and bruises, ripped shirt and jeans, fresh blood from the damn sutures that had ruptured again. I felt like yesterday's roadkill, so no, I didn't want to answer a couple of questions. But the thought of my friends, Nate and Des, crushed my self-pity into pathetic dust. I wrapped my fragile spirit into a stoic shell and waved the captain forward. Anna's appraisal continued, and I could tell she saw through the façade. Not for the first time, I wondered how women like Rochelle, Echie, and Desiree always seemed to handle life's gut punches so much better than men.

"Detective," Doloviski began, "can you give me a brief account of your interaction with Lieutenant Barrajas after you were released from the hospital?"

"He came by to see me a couple of days after I got home from the hospital," I said. Then I considered the reason for his question and asked my own. "You haven't talked with him, have you?"

"No," he responded. "Lieutenant Barrajas has been on bereavement leave since his daughter's death, and he's not responding to us. Not that I blame him under the circumstances."

"So you need me to fill in the blanks. Again," I said.

Doloviski acquiesced with a sheepish expression that made me feel sorry for him. He was actually a decent man.

"Joe was a wreck when I first saw him," I said. "Hadn't eaten or slept since the news about Desiree's . . . since the news."

"What did he tell you?" Doloviski prompted.

"He said that Captain Strand's guys had arrested Nate, that Nate wasn't talking." I rubbed my cheeks to wake up. "I was out of the loop, still recovering, still dealing with the fact that she was gone. This was news to me. And the worst kind."

That had been a horrible day, even by the unending cycle of shitty days since. Talking about Nate's dilemma would only piss me off more.

I continued, "Anyway, you asked about Joe. He couldn't sit still. Kept talking about Nate, how he had known it would end this way for the two of them. What the hell could I say to that? There was no information from anyone, not from the cops who found her body, the detectives assigned the case, the prosecutor's office. I had no idea what happened to her. So I just let him vent."

The captain's face reddened, but he said nothing.

"I know, I know," I said, brushing it aside. "Protocol. You don't have to explain it. But not knowing has been really, really hard."

"I understand," he said. "What were your thoughts when you heard about her murder?"

I could tell that Best was about to interrupt me, so I plowed ahead before she could. "Nobody wanted to talk to Nate more than I did. I was still in the hospital during the autopsy, the funeral, and the burial. I had a thousand questions only Nate could answer, but thanks to Strand, Nate was in isolation. Suicide watch, for Christ's sake. But you already know that."

Doloviski opened his mouth to speak, closed it. The silence stretched. Finally, he murmured, "Please continue."

"After a couple of days, I told Joe what I thought," I said, leaning forward. "Nate had nothing to do with Desiree's murder. Blaming him was part of the plan—"

"What plan?" Doloviski snapped.

"The mafia," I said, impatient. "This is all about drugs, Captain. Her death is directly linked to the gang violence that started all of this shit."

Doloviski took this in without reaction. Then he asked in a flat voice, "Did Lieutenant Barrajas believe you?"

"Would you?" I answered. "No, Joe didn't believe me. But he did agree that there were things we could do. Since we were out of the loop, we could ask the questions that no one else was asking. Even if Joe and I weren't on the same page, we were still looking for the same thing."

Doloviski gave me a pessimistic look.

"The truth," I said, my voice firm. "So we started with the one person linked to the past and the present. Juan Rodriguez. El Moto."

I put my hands on the table, unclenching my fists. "I haven't heard his name mentioned once, even though he's a known gangster and a former classmate of Desiree's who just happened to bail Luiz Gutierrez out of jail a few hours before he tried to fucking kill me and Echie!" I stopped shouting and saw that my hands were clenched into fists again. Anna stood, but I waved her away. I had been dealing with this rage for what seemed like a lifetime. I set it aside again, knowing that eventually there would be a reckoning. "The point I'm trying to make is that there are no coincidences."

Doloviski quietly jotted notes.

"Don't you see?" I continued, pleading my case to Anna. "Rodriguez knew Desiree, probably had a thing for her. He comes back to town years later, and he's a big shot with La Eme. He finds out the cop in charge of shutting down Hispanic gangs is married to the prettiest girl from high school. BAM!" I yelled, startling the others, "she dies!" I rubbed eyes that felt like sandpaper. "How hard is it to connect the dots?"

Doloviski looked up from his notepad. "Does Lieutenant Barrajas believe that this Rodriguez character was responsible for his daughter's death?"

"We talked about it plenty. I won't say I convinced him, but he understood there were too many loose ends." This last was a jab at the murder investigation, which up until this point had been a colossal failure. In my opinion, sure.

Doloviski rolled his eyes. "I'm sure you can appreciate the sensitive nature of this investigation, even if you ignore the legal perils of a sideline inquiry. You'll know more in time, and maybe then you'll understand. For now, I just need you to fill in the blanks. Please continue."

"Fine, keep your secrets, Captain." *Deep breath, Cassidy.* "As I said, Joe and I made some phone calls, talked to a few people, and eventually put the puzzle together." Energized, I unfolded my arms and stood up. This was what I'd been waiting for all day.

"It starts with the Mexican Mafia. They've been running the Surenos for decades, but California's new gang injunctions shoved the Surenos off their turf. The feds have been picking off their high-ranking shot callers as well. The bottom line is they need another location on the West Coast for their narcotics distribution.

"So La Eme sends out its scouts," I continued, "guys like Juan Rodriguez, to find the best spot. He knows the area, wants to make a name for himself. Somehow, he hooks up with Rafael Inigo, the guy who knows all the gangster lowlife in town."

That detail finally captured Doloviski's attention.

I continued, "The two make some kind of pact. Rodriguez needs nothing less than complete control of the gang turf to keep the drugs rolling smoothly. That means only one gang set can be on top. Inigo can make that happen. For his own reasons, he chooses the East Side Criminales. Then he and Rodriguez start stirring up the hornet's nest.

"The renewed gang violence forces the department to tackle the problem. Predictably, we resurrect the gang unit. Rodriguez and Inigo anticipated this, knowing Rafael would be an obvious choice for a slot. This meant they'd have one of their own on the inside. That's right, Inigo is one of theirs, a gang-banger known as Jura, 'the Badge.' It was his job to make sure we never touched the ESC."

I had effectively captured Doloviski's interest, so I continued, "Sergeant Inigo brings in Luis 'El Feo' Gutierrez as his informant, a guy who also just happens to be the mafia's contract hit man. El Feo buys dope from every set but ESC. We make arrests and pat ourselves on the back. But all we're doing is helping the Mexican Mafia dismantle the competition because the East Side Criminales are their puppets.

"Let's look at numbers." I held up two fingers. "Those two Orlando shot in the car." Another finger went up. "The one Inigo knocked out with a baseball bat." I raised the last two on that hand and one on my injured side. "The three who died in the East Side gunfight. What did they all have in common? They were all ESC rivals, all shot-callers whose gangs stood in Inigo and Rodriguez's way. And you want one more? I'll bet when we reopen that suspicious suicide—you remember, the banger who blew his face in half?—I guarantee we will be able to add his name to that list."

I stretched my arms wide. "ESC is now the alpha dog on the East Side and the South End. Between them, Rodriguez and Inigo did this. They cleared a path for the mafia. I'd lay odds that the bloodbath on the East Side is about to dry up. Pretty soon, the politicians will declare victory, the neighborhood activists will be heaping praise on the department, and Sergeant Inigo will be in line for a commendation. Meanwhile, the Mexican Mafia will be running dope out of a new drug distribution center in their new place, a city with everything it needs—a busy seaport, a train and trucking hub, an interstate, and let's not forget, a minuscule federal presence and no gang injunctions."

Anna lightly tapped on her keyboard. Doloviski's pen scratched across his legal pad.

When they both looked up, I pressed ahead, "That's what Lieutenant Barrajas and I surmised. But there's more to it."

Doloviski sat up straight. He folded his hands in front of him and cocked his head expectantly.

"Why did someone try to kill me?" I asked. "Was it because the gang unit was such a pain in their ass? No way. Inigo's clever. He's got guys like Gutierrez and Rodriguez running around doing his dirty work. It's all under control. So why come after me?"

I continued, "Consider the first major Sureno shootout, the one with three fatalities. The forensics and firing lines didn't support the investigative conclusions, but the case was closed all the same. The gang prosecutor was dissatisfied and asked me to redo my report on the case. From there, the evidence of another shooter was easy to find because it had been there all along," I stressed. "But the discrepancies were never investigated by the assigned detective." I folded my arms across my chest, trying to keep the righteous indignation out of my voice. "I'll give you one guess who that was."

When no one rose to the bait, I rolled my eyes.

"Inigo, who else?"

Doloviski wrote for a bit longer and then waved me on.

I stared up at the ceiling. "The fact that I stuck my nose into that damn shooting investigation could explain why someone came at me. But I believe the real reason is intensely personal."

"You're saying that you were targeted as some sort of vendetta?" Doloviski asked, his skepticism obvious.

"I am. Are you forgetting whose name came before mine on the sergeant's list, Captain?"

Doloviski's eyes narrowed.

"Hear me out," I said. "First, Inigo knows I'm a recovering alcoholic, so why would he shove a drink in my hand at the precise moment it would be extremely awkward for me to say no? And yes," I added bitterly, "I failed that test all by myself. I accept that. But Inigo set me up, knowing full well I would be humiliated, demoted, and possibly suspended."

"Was there a second point?" Doloviski asked.

I hesitated before answering. "I saw his real face."

"What do you mean?"

"The night Gutierrez ambushed me," I replied, "Rafael somehow turned up. Just as he always has. How? Because, just like every other time, he knew it was going to happen." I put all the conviction I had into my voice. "I know I've said this before, and I know you may not believe me, but he assassinated Gutierrez. That shit-eating grin masks a cold-blooded son of a bitch who can execute a helpless comrade with no more thought than it takes to pull the trigger." My stomach roiled with acid. "And I'll tell you one more thing. If the residents hadn't called in that night, if patrol hadn't shown up so quickly, Inigo would have put a bullet in my brain."

"You believe that?" Doloviski asked soberly.

"I looked up and all I saw was the barrel of his gun," I answered, locking eyes with the captain. "Do you believe *me*?"

Doloviski cleared his throat. "You're aware that in Sergeant Inigo's report he claimed you were unconscious when he arrived, that he killed Gutierrez in self-defense before you woke up?"

"We've already been through that bullshit."

"If I'm not mistaken, Gutierrez wasn't a rival of the East Side Criminales," Doloviski said. "According to you, he was contracted by the mafia to handle problems for them. If Inigo was so closely allied with that gang, as you say, what possible reason would he have for killing Gutierrez in cold blood?"

"As I wrote in my report," I answered with forced patience, "Inigo was upset Echie had been hurt. I don't think he'd planned for her to get caught in the crossfire. Apparently, Gutierrez had already screwed up enough and had become a liability."

Doloviski's pen continued scratching on his pad.

"Joe Barrajas believed me," I said.

"And what did the two of you do?" Doloviski asked.

Now we were getting to it. "We went looking for Inigo."

"You did what?"

Startled, Anna Best chimed in a second later. "That's enough, Detective. Don't say anything else."

I shrugged. "It's a moot point."

"What do you mean by that?" Doloviski demanded.

"I mean," I continued before Best could interrupt, "that the man has gone underground. He's found a hole, jumped inside, and pulled it in over his head."

The captain's face was flushed. He was probably rethinking the immunity he'd offered me on tape. *Tough shit.*

"Inigo was our only link to Rodriguez, so we needed to find him first. We checked all over town. You'd be surprised how many people know Rafael. *All* kinds of people. Turns out he's a regular at every strip club and biker bar, even collects a little protection cash. The same goes for the prostitutes working by the Dome. Unless every one of them is lying, none of them have seen Sergeant Inigo in the last week."

Doloviski sighed in exasperation. "All right, fine. Our investigation has covered much the same ground. We didn't jump to the same conclusions, but when he failed to show up for his shooting review, we decided there were enough unanswered questions. I've had several detectives looking for him to no avail."

"One more reason to have me in the hot seat here, right? To see if I know where Inigo slithered off to."

Doloviski shrugged. "I won't deny that was a large part of it. I still have a job to do, Detective, and that includes preventing an illegal inquiry from interfering with the official one. You seem to be very adept at that."

Though his words were strong, the poor man just sounded tired.

But I was getting riled up. "If Strand's detective's had been looking in the right place, I would've stayed well out of it!"

The captain's body seemed to deflate, and he added more quietly, "You know that's not how it works, Michael."

"Look, Captain," I said, trying to get back on track, "I'm not here to complain about the bull's-eye painted on my back. I can deal with that. What I can't deal with is that the people I care about are getting hurt."

"How is Officer Echevaria?" Anna Best asked.

I let the captain respond.

"Francine was released from the hospital and is recovering at home. She'll need some physical therapy before returning to work."

Best nodded at the news. "Good for her."

"She's a tough lady, a good cop." Doloviski said, more to himself than to his old partner.

I had already heard this. Though it was good news, guilt still weighed down every thought of Echie.

Doloviski tapped his pen and then nodded as if he had made a decision. "This terminates the internal investigations interview with Detective Cassidy."

Doloviski pushed the power button on the recorder. The green light winked out for good.

"I'm going to share something with you," Doloviski said, extracting a thin manila folder from his briefcase. He set it on the table and removed several typed sheets of paper. "This is the written transcript from Officer Echevaria's interview. I'm going to let you read a portion of it, but," he said, staring at both of us in turn, "I would like to keep this just between us."

It was a surprising offer, since Charlie was as strict as they come. Beneath all the straight-laced bullshit, I sensed there was a compassionate man, one committed to doing an unpleasant job as best he could. I wondered if I could have done as well.

"Agreed, Chuckie," Best responded for both of us.

Frowning at her, Doloviski handed over the report and held his palms out in an invitation. I scooted my chair next to Anna's for a better view.

> Echevaria: Yes, my cousin, Bianca Sanchez visited me. We hadn't hung out together for a while, but she was tight with Desiree. This must have been right after the murder.
>
> Interviewer: Was there anything in your conversation with Bianca that might relate to this investigation?
>
> (Pause)
>
> Echevaria: Well, maybe.
>
> Interviewer: I know this may cross into personal issues, but at this point we can't rule out any line of questioning.
>
> Echevaria: I know, I know. Okay, so we started talking, and almost immediately she brings up the scarf.
>
> (Pause)
>
> Interviewer: What scarf?
>
> Echevaria: It was a scarf that Michael, I mean, Detective Cassidy gave me as a gift. She asks if she can see it, and when I pull it out of my jacket, she starts to cry. I know it's a crazy time, but what's so tragic about a fu—, sorry, a stupid scarf? She asks me where I got it, and I tell her. At first, she doesn't believe me, so I ask her why the hell—sorry—would I lie about

something like that? When she realizes I'm telling the truth, she freaks out.

Interviewer: What did she say?

Echevaria: She said it's Desiree's scarf.

(Pause)

Interviewer: Did she elaborate on that?

Echevaria: Yeah. Like I said, Bianca and Desiree spent a lot of time together, shopping at the mall, getting their nails done, all that girlfriend stuff. Desiree showed her my scarf a couple of months ago, said it was the first present she got from Lieutenant Orlando and that it was her favorite thing in the world.

Interviewer: So she wondered how you got it?

Echevaria: Sure, of course. I told her that Cassidy gave it to me before our first date. I said he must have picked it up at the same place Orlando did. You know that they're really good friends, or at least they were. Anyway, I told her it couldn't be the same one. I mean, why would Desiree give something like that to him?

(Pause)

Interviewer: What did she say to that?

Echevaria: She said that Desiree stopped wearing the scarf a couple of weeks ago, and when Bianca asked her about it, she said it was missing. Well, that makes me upset, of course.

(Pause)

Interviewer: I know this is difficult, but please go on.

Echevaria: All right. So Bianca tells me there's a rumor going around that Cassidy was having an affair with Desiree. I say bullshit to that. Bianca says she's just passing it along. Fine, I tell her, though now I'm pretty mad. She says she heard that Desiree and Nate supposedly weren't getting along. I knew Des and Michael were always confiding in each other. I mean, I knew they were friends, and I figured that's how rumors get started, you know? Bianca says she didn't believe any of that shit—sorry, stuff either, but she felt

I should know what was circulating. Especially with that story about the scarf.

Interviewer: And that was it?

Echevaria: Yes. No, wait. I asked her if she ever confronted Desiree about the rumor. She hadn't. That made me mad. I mean, when a good friend's name gets dragged through the mud and you don't even have the guts to let them know about it? And now it's too late. Desiree's dead. (Pause) She's dead. So what does any of it matter?

(Pause)

Interviewer: Do you need a minute?

Echevaria: No, sorry about that. This is just tough to talk about.

Interviewer: I understand.

Echevaria: Anyway, I wasn't angry with Bianca. I mean, what's the point? What's done is done. So I ask her where she heard the story, and she says she got it from her girlfriend Teresa.

Interviewer: And that's it?

Echevaria: Yes. Wait, no. There is one connection you might want to check out.

Interviewer: What's that?

Echevaria: Teresa? She's dating a cop.

Interviewer: Who?

Echevaria: Sergeant Rafael Inigo.

This only confirmed everything I knew. Despite that, reading Echie's words consumed me with grief. I had lost Desiree, had been strung along by Inigo. But Echie had been collateral damage, wounded physically and emotionally just because she'd made the mistake of hanging with me. Though scandalous rumors were commonplace at the PD, this bit of news made me furious. I wanted to punch the wall, but I already had enough aches and pains.

And now was not the time to lose it. "Thanks for sharing that, Captain."

Anna gave me a suspicious look, as if I were hiding something. *Only rage.* Doloviski stood and gathered his belongings.

"Counselor" he said formally, "I want to personally thank you for being here. I knew this was going to be a difficult day. For the record, the department is not seeking any discipline against Detective Cassidy, especially for his part in an unauthorized investigation," he said, looking down his nose in my direction.

He cleared his throat again and checked his watch. "If you have any questions, call my cell, Anna. Maybe we can grab some coffee when this is over. For now, I've gotta run."

Best looked startled by the abrupt conclusion. She found her voice quickly. "All right, Captain. Of course, it's not my business to intrude on a police investigation, but I would like to know how Detective Cassidy will figure into it from here."

"He doesn't," Doloviski answered, directing his words to me. "The detective needs to go home and take care of himself. As bad as it is around here right now, the police department won't fall apart if he takes a week or two to recover from his injuries and," he faltered for a moment, "everything else."

He checked his watch yet again. "Now if you'll excuse me, I need to meet someone five minutes ago. I trust you can find a ride back to the police station?"

"Sure," she said for both of us.

"Get some rest, Michael," Doloviski said, patting my shoulder on his way out.

After he had left, my attorney packed up her briefcase. I could tell she was not ready to move on just yet.

"Will you be all right, Michael?"

"Sure, Anna. I mean I will be," I answered, far from convinced of that. "And thanks for sticking around. This has been quite the day."

"Yes, it absolutely was," she responded. "I'll check in on you in a few days, make sure you're doing okay."

My response was interrupted by loud footsteps and excited voices drifting in from the hallway.

"I know, right?" said a man with a high voice. "You'd think the guy would at least say something in, what has it been, almost a week?

Strand said he's been on his knees the entire time, prayin' or some damn thing."

The steps halted just outside the doorway. I didn't want to hear this, but neither Anna nor I could do anything but listen.

"No shit? That's crazy," a lower voice chimed in. "So why's he coming here? Why don't they just keep him locked up?"

"One of the paralegals told me they found some evidence at his place. The dude has some 'splainin' to do."

"Yeah? Well, check it out." The second voice dropped to a conspiratorial whisper. "I hear internal investigations is pushing some conspiracy crap, something about the Surenos."

"What is it with those guys?" said the first voice. "Sounds like bullshit smokescreen to me. All I know is Orlando's in some deep shit."

I had known what they were talking about. Yet when I heard Nate's name tossed out in such an offhanded, vile tone, the words were like rocks hitting me in the face. A brown hand patted mine. I looked down in surprise at my own clenched fists. Anna's expression mirrored at least some of my own outrage.

Like my fists, my feet operated on their own. In a single movement, I was up and out the door, making a sharp turn towards the lobby and sprinting down the long, narrow hallway past the two obnoxious young prosecutors. If they hadn't hugged the wall, I would have knocked them into next week.

My amped-up senses allowed me to hear quiet conversations in the adjacent offices, a distant phone ringing, and the *snick-snick* sound of high heels on carpet. My attorney was trying to catch me. I kicked it up a notch, running with reckless abandon and leaving her in a cloud of carpet fiber.

I had no clue where I was running, only that I'd been sitting on my ass for far too long. Somewhere close by was a man who'd just lost his career, his purpose, his freedom and, worst, the woman he loved. This man had saved my life. Twice. And by God, I was going to repay my debt. One way or another.

Hang on, Nate.

CHAPTER 27

Dashing after her client, Anna caught a heel in the rug. It had been a long time since she'd run full out, and she barely caught herself in time to prevent a nasty fall. She recovered quickly and saw Cassidy was well ahead now, running full out for the lobby.

What is that fool doing? she thought. It was rhetorical. While she was considering his career, which was still salvageable, that tormented man was chasing after things he could never catch. She set those thoughts aside for now, gaining speed despite the damn shoes.

Bad day for heels.

The heavy security door that safeguarded the prosecutor's office opened with a savage yank. Anna pirouetted past the receptionist, who merely glanced up from her screen, and then Anna slowed her pace to navigate the lobby's slick marble. Taking two quick, short steps as she turned down the hallway, she headed for the main entrance. There, a row of metal detectors stood sentry before three sets of glass double doors, while a phalanx of security guards stood idle nearby. Their attention was directed outside.

One of the doors burst open, and loud voices spilled inside, echoing off the foyer's marbled walls. A large crowd had gathered in the courtyard just outside the entrance. Several people held large objects in their hands. She recognized one of them as a local television reporter and then identified the boxy objects as video cameras, each with a different news logo. The reporters, two women and a man, wore flashy business attire, their cheeks covered in flesh-colored make-up, their hair stiff with spray. The remainder of the crowd was a gaggle of nondescript individuals with cheaper clothes and scant makeup, many of whom clutched slim recorders similar to Doloviski's. Print journalists.

Anna wasted no more time on them. She turned to survey the smaller group inside and immediately spotted Cassidy. He was on the far side of the foyer leaning against a wall, his arms crossed over his chest. Breathing a sigh of relief, she began walking in his direction when a distracted woman with frizzy hair and thick glasses carrying a bundle of files bumped into her. Anna recognized her as a former law school classmate. The two exchanged a clumsy hug.

"You must be here for the deposition!" the woman said with obvious excitement.

"Which one are you talking about?" Anna answered, trying to keep one eye on her client.

"You haven't heard?" her friend exclaimed as she readjusted the glasses perched atop her thin nose. "They're bringing that Tacoma police lieutenant over from the jail for an interview. You know, the one arrested for killing his wife? You must have read about the case."

"A little bit, yes," Anna said, trying to detach herself.

Her friend pressed on, oblivious. "Well, I think it was supposed to be a secret, but you know how that goes around here," she said, rolling her eyes.

Anna mumbled a few words and broke away. When she approached Cassidy, his attention was focused on a man who had just bypassed the metal detectors.

He was just under average height with the wide shoulders and thick legs of a lineman and dressed in a black suit with the requisite white shirt and bright blue tie. His pink skin was smooth, his salt-and-pepper hair receding. She knew him to be in his early fifties but thought he looked ten years younger. He stopped in front of her and hooked his thumbs into his belt, exposing a gold shield and sidearm.

Strike the pose, asshole, she thought.

Instead of addressing her, Captain Jack Strand reached past and shook Doloviski's hand. The internal investigations captain had silently appeared behind them, a look of concern sharpening the contours of his weary face. Studiously ignoring Cassidy and Best, Strand lowered his head and spoke into Doloviski's ear in hushed tones.

Best gritted her teeth. As a rookie, she had spent a grueling two months on Strand's crew, enduring his aggressive and self-centered tutelage. At the first opportunity, Best had requested a transfer, a move that had earned her Strand's unending enmity. Up until that moment, she had never regretted the decision. But now he was the commander in charge of a high-profile murder investigation, one that most certainly concerned her. She realized that she had begun to form very emotional opinions based on what she'd heard today.

Strand would be savoring every second of the media circus. The thought just pissed her off.

Doloviski spoke quietly with his counterpart. When he nodded in her direction, Strand's bright eyes studied her over the top of horn-rimmed glasses she assumed were nothing more than a prop to make him look less like the jack-booted thug he was.

Forget the asshole and stay on task, she chided herself.

Cassidy shoved off the wall next to her. In a single stride he stood before Strand; the latter continued to ignore him. Anna looked around, thankful no one else seemed interested in them. She had no idea how this would play out.

"Captain Strand, pardon the interruption," Cassidy said in a calmer voice than she would have expected.

Strand tilted his head and studied the detective as if he were a piece of inorganic matter beneath a microscope.

Shit, she thought. *This guy is Cassidy's boss. Correction, his boss's boss's boss.*

But the officious prick was *the* man today. He had direct influence over the direction and outcome of the Barrajas woman's murder. She braced herself for a volcanic response.

"Detective Cassidy," Strand responded, lifting a palm to forestall Doloviski's objection.

In a smooth and surprisingly gracious motion, he reached for Cassidy's hand and shook it. Standing at rigid attention and ignoring the stern look of reproach from Doloviski, the detective locked grips with Strand.

"Look, I understand that the investigation involving Lieutenant Orlando isn't my assignment, and I apologize for my presumption, but, but," Cassidy stammered, "but I believe that if you were to listen to what I have to say, you'd realize that charging him with homicide could be a huge mistake for everyone."

"Detective," Doloviski answered for his colleague in a tight voice. "I've been keeping Captain Strand informed of your statements throughout the day. He knows everything you've told me."

"With all due respect, Captain, I have to say this," Cassidy plunged ahead, still speaking directly to Strand. "Let me make it plain. Your investigation into Desiree Barrajas's death is off track. In the last few months, there's been a war within the Surenos that was intentionally instigated by operatives working for a large drug network. I don't know if it's one of the Mexican cartels or not. But I do know that there are people involved in the violence who could have killed Desiree Barrajas for intensely personal reasons."

He continued, his voice gaining strength. "This is all about the gang war, a war of attrition with the winner gaining exclusive rights to sell meth, cocaine, heroin, whatever they want, out of our back door. They'll do anything to win—instigate murder, infiltrate the police department, execute rivals—"

For a moment, her client looked like he might choke on the words. She put a hand softly on his shoulder. All thought of silencing him was gone. Michael Cassidy was purging himself and, to a lesser extent, punishing himself. Whether right or wrong, she owed him this opportunity. And so she remained silent.

"I'm sorry, I-," Cassidy stumbled on before finding his place again. "I know this sounds like a conspiracy theory, but if you knew everything that's happened, if you knew Nate Orlando, you'd know . . ." He faltered again, and this time he could not go on.

Strand was now glaring at him, his slim patience evaporated. A door opened behind them. The rising level of volume cut off Strand's reply.

Anna spun around. The crowd outside was now densely packed around the entrance. It seemed that whatever everyone had been waiting for was about to arrive.

Doloviski and Strand sensed the change as well, the latter turning back towards Cassidy with the same haughty expression Anna recalled from years past.

"As you can see, Detective, we have things in motion today," Strand said. "I want you to understand something. The decisions that brought us to this point were made with careful consideration of the facts, which may or may not fit in with your so-called theory." He puffed his chest out a bit more. "To suggest we have missed something is insulting. I may pity you, but I will not let you tell me how to do my job." Strand gave him a scathing look. "Now if you'll kindly get the fuck out of my way."

Anna shook with rage. Twenty years fell away, and she was once again a raw recruit in the cliquish realm of police officers. Some had been strong and good, some had been lethargic worker bees, while some, men like Strand, had used the badge as a ticket that gave them exclusive rights to do whatever the fuck they wanted.

The sensation passed. Anna recalled her place and how she fit into this madness. She represented a troubled man, by all accounts a decent cop and human, who, for whatever reason, was in desperate need of her help. But even as Best reached for Cassidy, concerned he might react violently, he shocked her once again by kneeling down and grabbing Strand by the hand.

"Captain, please!" Cassidy pleaded, shouting to be heard over the din outside. "For God's sake, I'm giving you everything I have! I've been in this since the beginning, and I'm telling you that we're being manipulated! We're playing into the hands of criminals! What can you possibly have on Nate to refute that?"

Strand's face flushed. He rudely ripped his hand away. Lowering his head to Cassidy's ear, he spoke in a hiss. "Evidence, Detective. That's what I've got. No righteous indignation. No fucking intuition. No bullshit theories. Evidence in the form of a murder weapon, found in your friend's goddam car!"

Cassidy reeled as if he'd been struck, would have fallen if Anna hadn't caught him by the shoulders. Doloviski appeared at Strand's side, motioning Anna to get Cassidy away from there. He touched Strand's elbow, but the burly man shook him off with a look of wolfish satisfaction.

"A pillow, would you believe it?" he whispered, enunciating each word. "Your big, badass friend smothered his wife with a fucking pillow!"

Strand abruptly stepped back. He rolled his neck muscles, straightened his tie, and gave Cassidy a last wink before turning towards the expectant crowd.

Doloviski did not immediately follow.

He had known about this, Anna realized, and had kept it from Cassidy. She looked down at the slumped detective. *He's finally broken.* "Well played, Chuckie," she said bitterly.

Her old partner, who looked as if he'd aged during the course of the day, only shrugged. He thrust his hands in his pockets, turned, and walked quickly after Strand.

Surprisingly, Cassidy seemed to revive. He stood up abruptly, teetering for a moment. Before she could speak, the noise level in the lobby rose. With a whoosh, all three entry doors behind them opened, and a mass of uniformed officers swept inside.

The small crowd inside parted. With the doors wide open, she heard the reporters' questions all shouted simultaneously. The cacophony echoed off the hard, flat walls as cameras flashed.

Abruptly, the noise diminished. The stillness was so sudden it felt as if they were in the eye of a hurricane. The incoming officers were formed into a wedge as they passed through the main doors and took a circuitous path around the metal detectors. She counted six cops in the lead with three men in civilian clothes tucked in behind. Once past the entry, the six officers flared out, allowing the trailing three to move into the center column. Two of these three wore matching black windbreakers with badges dangling from chains around their necks—plainclothes detectives—and both were at least six feet tall and well over two hundred pounds. Still, they were dwarfed by the man between them.

Anna Best's five-year tenure had primarily been on graveyard shift. She had rarely crossed paths with Nate Orlando, nor had she seen him in the last fifteen years. Her image of the man had been solely based on the impressions she'd picked up during Cassidy's interview. His words had painted the picture of a heroic figure, which she had dismissed most as sentiment.

Now she realized that description might have fallen short.

Nate Orlando stood a full head above the men on either side. He had a deep chest and thickly muscled arms that were clearly defined beneath a tailored purple dress shirt. He wore black slacks and Italian shoes she knew would have cost several hundred dollars. His stride was fluid and agile, the rhythm of a natural athlete, despite the handcuffs he wore in front.

She studied him closer still. Orlando's whole being seemed to radiate a ferocious energy, and she felt as if she were in the presence of a wild animal. His eyes were black coals that stared straight ahead, and she got the sense of a caged animal. She felt the force of his persona. She wondered if the detectives at his side even knew that they had relinquished Orlando several feet of space on either side. It was hardly a standard position, yet she understood that his powerful presence demanded it.

His gaze took in the foyer, absorbed every detail. This was a disgraced man, she decided, but he was far from conquered. It was easy to see why others might follow him, such was the palpable charisma she felt without even hearing his voice.

Follow, yes. But out of respect or fear? That was the question, wasn't it?

As Orlando and his entourage came abreast, she observed more. From up close, she noticed subtle indications of anxiety: a flicker of the eyes, a hint of moisture on the forehead, a nearly imperceptible lip tremble. Perhaps his stoic demeanor was, at least in part, a façade.

Either way, she thought grimly, *there goes a man living his worst nightmare.*

A commotion coming from the staircase behind them caught her attention. Joe Barrajas erupted into the foyer with an entourage of police officers in close pursuit. He stormed past, dressed in wrinkled clothes with disheveled hair and a haggard face. He pulled up sharply mere feet away from her, and she caught a strong whiff of alcohol.

Drunk off his ass, she thought. Under the circumstances, she found it hard to blame the bereaved father. There was no mistaking the menace in Barrajas's dark-brown eyes, which were aimed squarely at Orlando.

"You bastard!" Barrajas yelled as the hands of several cops caught him by the sleeve. He threw them off as he screamed, "You bastard!"

Jack Strand materialized at his side, whispering softly. Barrajas's rage vanished, and he slumped. Strand motioned the officers to lead him out.

Orlando's retinue began to walk past Anna. Although he had surely heard Barrajas's angry words, he registered no reaction. Until his eyes fell on Cassidy, standing mute next to her.

Orlando stopped in mid-stride. His escorts looked from their prisoner to Strand, their boss, who appeared to be losing his cool as his carefully orchestrated perp walk turned into a farce.

The crowd in the background was silent, everyone waiting to see what would happen next.

"Nate." Cassidy's voice was barely audible.

Yet Orlando must have heard it because his head dipped as if it had suddenly become unbearably heavy.

"Michael," Orlando replied finally. "I . . . I need—"

Next to Anna, Cassidy began to sway as if he were caught in a breeze. She grasped his hand and squeezed.

"Bless me, my brother," Orlando finally spoke, his voice a low rumble, "and forgive me."

Anna felt as if she were eavesdropping on an intensely private conversation. Then several cameras flashed at once, and the moment was gone. Orlando rolled his thick shoulders, turned his head, and resumed walking. His surprised escorts hurried to catch up, while reporters thrust microphones at him.

"Why'd you kill her?"

"Are you going to confess?"

"What made you do it?"

The entourage disappeared around the corner as the last of the hurled questions echoed off the marbled wall, unanswered.

The foyer was immediately quiet. Several in the crowd shot inquisitive looks in Cassidy's direction, though none seemed interested enough to pass through the gauntlet of metal detectors to talk to the distraught man with his arm in a sling. The gathering broke apart into smaller groups and headed outside where the department spokesperson was holding court.

Anna Best felt as if she had been holding her breath. She gave Cassidy a reassuring pat on the back. After a moment, he thanked her with a nod.

"You okay?" she asked.

"No. Not really," he answered in a boy's heartbroken voice. He scrubbed the moisture from his face. "I'll be okay. Someday. Not today."

"So, what was that between you two?"

He gave her a smile that stopped halfway up his face. "I never . . . I mean . . . I just don't understand," he stuttered, looking again like a lost boy.

But Anna already knew what he was thinking. All this time Michael Cassidy had been defending his friend against the accusations of murder. Then Strand had dropped his bombshell. Worse, whatever had occurred during the exchange with Orlando seemed to have shaken the detective to the very core of his being. She considered what to do next, only to be startled when Cassidy bolted towards the main entry doors.

She was about to chase after him yet again when he stopped in front of a petite elderly woman. The two embraced fiercely, the woman giving him gentle pats on the back with a papery brown hand.

The woman stepped back. She was dark-skinned with the unlined face common to many of African descent, though Best estimated her to be in her mid-seventies. The woman had high cheekbones, a confident bearing, and eyes that practically radiated intelligence. Her identity was immediately apparent.

Cassidy walked the old lady towards Best, one arm thrown protectively around her narrow shoulders.

"Anna, this is—"

"Ms. Orlando, I assume. I'm sorry. It's just that your son looks so much like you."

"That's all right—Anna, is it?" Rochelle Orlando answered, taking Best's hands. Her skin was soft, her grip surprisingly strong.

"Yes, ma'am," Best answered automatically. "I'm the attorney for the police guild. Michael has told me about you, Ms. Orlando. I'm sorry to meet under such terrible circumstances."

"I'm pleased to meet you too, Anna," the older woman answered warmly, releasing Best's hand. Then her smile collapsed, and she turned to Cassidy with a stricken expression. "My boy, Michael," she choked. "My boy." The words were immediately followed by a silent flood of tears. She did not bother to wipe them away, and soon tears ran in rivulets down her parchment-thin skin. She gripped Cassidy's outstretched hands tightly.

The air around them seemed to compress as Best watched them wrestle with the horrible knowledge. Twice Cassidy opened his mouth to deliver soothing words, but twice the words never came. Instead, Rochelle Orlando was the one to finally dab her eyes with a worn handkerchief and pat his cheek lightly. He dropped his head to her shoulders.

"He's caught in the whirlwind now, my poor boy. Too strong, too stubborn for his own good. Straight as a board and all hard edges, but that's my fault, Lord forgive me. Somehow I knew a day like this might come. I feared it, I prayed against it, but the good Lord has his own plans."

Rochelle Orlando rubbed her hands together and looked at Anna as if she held the answer to a particularly difficult question. "Oh, it just breaks my heart," she said more calmly. She turned to Cassidy, all the strength drained from her proud figure. "I lost him, Michael. My boy is already gone."

Then Anna Best lost her own battle for composure. Her chest heaved, and she covered her face as the tears came. Moments passed until a gentle hand stroked her hair, and with that touch came a soothing warmth that loosened the knot in her throat. The hand lifted away, and Rochelle Orlando smiled at her through her own tears.

Best gave her a rough hug. Over the woman's shoulder, she observed Cassidy. He looked as if he'd just seen a ghost.

"What is it, Michael?" Best said.

"No," Cassidy whispered in a haunted voice. "No!" he repeated, shouting this time.

Security guards turned to stare, but he ignored them and backed away.

"Watch her, Anna," he said in a frantic voice. "Please!"

Before she could respond, he was sprinting back in the direction Orlando had recently taken, his heavy boots taking long strides, his arms pumping smoothly as if he weren't injured. She watched him pass the reception desk and disappear inside the prosecutor's office so quickly that the receptionist never even glanced up.

With a head pounding, Best turned back to the older woman holding out a tissue for her.

She may look like a china doll, Best thought. *But this woman is all pit bull.*

Together, they looked back towards the prosecutor's office.

Rochelle Orlando shook her head. "It's too late, Anna," Rochelle said, her smile so sad that Best's tears threatened to return. "It's already too late."

"I don't understand, Ms. Orlando. Where is Michael going?"

"He's trying to save my son, Anna. But it's too late. He's already lost."

Despite everything Best had heard, somewhere in this grieving mother's clear brown eyes she caught a brief glimpse of an awful truth.

She was just opening her mouth to ask the first of several questions when she was interrupted by a single gunshot.

CHAPTER 28

I sprinted those fifty yards, the length of the courthouse lobby faster than I'd ever run. All the pain and exhaustion was washed away, replaced by a reservoir of energy I'd never known existed. I gave it no consideration because I was busily working through the worst idea that had ever crossed my mind.

I arrived at this point in a roundabout way. Up until ten minutes ago, my faith in Nate's innocence had been unshakeable. Or so I had thought. Not even when Strand had divulged his poisonous little secret could I bring myself to believe that the man I'd known for more than half my life, my best friend, was capable of such an atrocity.

Then I saw Nate, had read something in his eyes, which I hadn't seen in years, if not decades.

Guilt.

Those dark eyes of his had always been my conduit into Nate's thoughts. With the likely exception of Rochelle, I was the only one who could anticipate him. As our friendship solidified, I finally understood what drove him on, what forces propelled him to achieve his goals, no matter the cost. Only later did I realize that this insight also placed me in the role of his backup conscience.

Because Nate had a temper. Yeah, it took a helluva lot to piss him off, but when he blew, it was a lot more than just sound and fury.

Though I had only seen him at full throttle a handful of times, the most recent episode had sent two gang-bangers into the afterlife.

Just now, when Nate stopped in the lobby and said my name, I had read the guilt in his eyes as if it were a large sign. That there could be blood on his hands—my God, Desiree's blood!—had been a shock of seismic proportions.

And if that were true, then nothing in this world made sense.

Then Rochelle—his mom and my surrogate mother, the person I trusted above all others—had flipped my world upside down yet again with a single sentence.

I lost him, Michael.

Where others might have read this as an admission of her son's guilt, I knew my mistake immediately. For the first time, I had misread the tea leaves floating in Nate's eyes. Because of that, I had betrayed the faith of the man who'd been my best friend since we were two awkward teenagers navigating the lonely, fucked-up path to adulthood.

And he had asked *me* for forgiveness.

My boy is already gone.

The words rang in my head as a precursor to the unthinkable.

And so I ran, my fear galvanizing every muscle. I blew past the reception desk again, maneuvering the office hallways on instinct. At the end of one long corridor, my legs finally began to fail. I slowed, my head whipping back and forth in search of any sign of Nate.

I spotted a green sheet of paper taped to a door, the words "Interview In Progress—Do Not Disturb" written in permanent marker. Regardless, I grabbed the doorknob and twisted. Locked. I scanned the hallway, but no one was in sight. I lifted one heavy boot to take down the door when a loud noise erupted from inside.

Even now, I can hear that sharp, quick sound as if it were on a slow replay—stretched over time, it began with a tremor that I first felt when my fingers touched the doorframe, then struck my eardrum like the blow of a hammer and sent a pressure wave of surprise and despair through me. Luminescence danced down the hallways as I gasped for breath, my lungs filled with lead. My knees buckled first, and I sank to the ground. But slowly, slowly.

Time passed. Rude shoving roused me. Several bodies converged. Hands smacked the door, rattled the knob. Shouted commands, the sound of impact, squealing metal and breaking wood.

Then I was alone again.

My head settled. I stood up on wobbly legs. Ignoring the now open doorway, I wandered down the hall to the next office. Its door was also wide open, and I stumbled inside and collapsed in the only chair at a long table. I blinked once. On top of the table was a video camera pointed towards the wall in front of me, which turned out to be a wide window. With an effort of will, I looked through the window into the next room.

I knew what I would see there. My eyes refused to focus, yet I could not look away.

My vision soon cleared. There were several men inside the adjacent room, all of whom I recognized from the major crimes unit. Every one of them was in a state of agitation I'd rarely seen in seasoned cops. Their heads bobbed up and down, their arms pointing, their mouths wide as they spoke with obvious excitement. On the floor between them was yet another man. I recognized him as well. He had been one of the detectives escorting Nate into the building.

He looked as if he'd just woken up from a long nap and automatically reached for his right hip, an instinctive gesture I knew all too well. His hand came back empty, his face confused. The detective craned his head to get a better view of the far side of the room, and his eyes went wide.

Unable to keep my head from swiveling, I turned and looked as well. For a moment, my mind refused to process the image. Then I saw far too much.

A spray of bright blood in the rough shape of an oval ran up the wall, with chunks of flesh and bone spattered inside. Barely visible in the dense red center was a small hole, a deadly exclamation point highlighting a grisly Rorschach drawing.

Beneath it lay the prostrate form of the man who had been my brother for nearly twenty-five years. Nate lay where he had fallen. His legs were drawn up beneath him, his hands together over his chest as if his last thoughts had been a whispered question to the God who'd given him so much, yet taken everything. Inches away from his hand, with a finger encircled by a thick gold wedding band, was the silver pistol he'd undoubtedly taken from the stunned detective.

It was too much suddenly, and I turned away. But an objective voice in my head intruded on my grief.

Notice that victim's head, it whispered. *It is untouched. There is a spot on the shirt where the material is darkest, where the arterial blood spurted and then pooled on the floor. The spatter pattern on the wall behind is consistent with a shot to the chest from the kneeling position. Based on the position of the hole in the wall, the round exited the victim's body with an upwards trajectory.*

A part of me comprehended the mayhem, understood what had happened. The other part, the one tormented by alcohol, enticed by women, driven by wants and needs both subtle and primitive, wanted to jump off a cliff. For a mad second, I thought I could do it, could kill myself if only to convey how much Nate's loss had cost me. Instead, I whispered a prayer—to God or to Nate, I don't know—for the lost spirit slipping out of the broken body on the other side of the window.

I leaned against the window, facing away.

Why? The simple question challenged me, infuriated me. To my shame, I hadn't thought about the fears that might have pushed Nate, both to achieve and to destroy. Had I considered that, the answer would have been obvious—failure. It's just that he had never failed at anything, whether it was school, sports, his career. Nate had committed every ounce of his being to the singular pursuit of perfection. Yet I never considered the darker aspects of this mindset, where the fear of failing might propel someone to consider options others might not. Cruel fucking irony, it had been both the key to Nate's greatest success and to his ultimate destruction.

And Inigo had discovered that key. *Goddam him.*

Now that I saw the costs spelled out for me in Nate's life's blood, my ambitions appeared infinitely shallow by comparison. And yet here I was. Alive.

With a constricted heart, I forced myself to turn around. The gold crucifix was right where I'd guessed, dangling from the chain clutched in my friend's bloody fist. I clutched my own, closed my eyes, and tried to pray. This time I failed. Instead, I traced the ancient sign of the cross—forehead, chest, shoulders—and anointed myself in fresh tears.

Touching the window lightly, I whispered, "Goodbye, Nate."

CHAPTER 29

The landscape was hellish. Hills of pulverized rock and scorched trees, the sky an opaque charcoal save for an angry swirl of red, the ground a vat of boiling mud.

Somehow I knew it was a dream even as I took a hopeless step forward. A tremor shook the ground and then stopped. When it struck again, I heard a faint buzzing as well. I turned back from the blighted view and began a long, ponderous swim back into groggy consciousness.

The buzzing turned out to be my cell phone. The vibrating ceased as I put my fingers on it. I cracked open an eye. A stinging blue glare forced it shut. When I roused enough to realize it was a computer screen, reality fell into place.

I was at my cubicle in the station. Writing materialized before my crusty eyes. It was a desperate memo I'd attempted last night when events had still been fresh in my mind. It was gibberish.

The station was empty, quiet. I rolled my head and flexed, groaning from all the accumulated aches and pains of the past week. A blanket slid to the ground. Someone must have draped it over my shoulders as I slept. I grasped the blanket as if it were a lifeline, choking up over the uncommon kindness.

The horror of the previous day remained at the forefront of my thoughts, like a vulture waiting for an injured animal to die. The memories had invaded my dreams, though at least my subconscious was trying to process some of this crazy shit. With that slightly coherently thought, I considered what had happened over the last few hours.

After leaving the observation room, I'd nearly collided with Captain Strand. That ass had been the last person I wanted to see, but as much as I wanted to pound his square jaw into mush, I couldn't summon the anger. His normally ruddy cheeks were pale, his eyes wide and lifeless, his mouth slack. He looked as if he'd had a stroke. If anything, he looked more torn up than I was.

Strand gripped my forearm as he passed. He said something, but I was too distracted to hear, much less give a shit. I stumbled past, wandering the hallways looking for an exit. Despite the many times I'd been in the prosecutor's office, I was unable to find my way out. Guilt was taking huge, voracious bites out of my mind while a mad voice in my head was screaming, *Your fault! This is your fault!* It was hard to disagree.

A young patrol officer tapped me on the shoulder. I saw myself through his eyes, dazed and talking to myself, stupid with grief. I was undoubtedly in shock. He led me to an empty office and found a comfortable chair. I tried to relax and think, but I was more than a little delirious. I imagined that all the terrible events were just symptoms of a virus, a sickness that had somehow infected my friends. I had survived, at least for the moment. That knowledge gave me no peace.

But the virus did have a name.

Rafael Inigo.

Some indeterminate time later, one of the major crimes detectives found me there, in a dark room quietly perusing even darker thoughts. He was a pleasant enough guy in normal circumstances, but in my state of mind, he was just one more bit actor in a tragic farce.

"Just need to ask a couple of questions, Michael. That all right? You understand how it is."

"Sure," I replied, laughing. Even I noted the trace of hysteria in my voice. I decided I didn't give a shit.

He chose to ignore my reaction. "Did you witness the alleged suicide?"

"No," I answered.

"How long had you known the deceased?"

"Nate?" I asked, confused for a moment. "Oh, since high school."

"Did you enter the crime scene?"

"No."

"You were seen running there just before the shooting—did you know what was about to happen?"

"I guessed."

"Guessed?" he asked, incredulous.

"Yeah," I said, reliving the moment. Eventually I heard his next question.

"I said you guessed what had happened, based on what?"

And how much of myself was locked up in that question? In the span of minutes, my faith in Nate's innocence had come full circle. He had taken no part in Desiree's murder, had killed himself rather than accept life on terms dictated by anyone other than himself, of that I had no doubt. But there had been a moment, however brief, when I had let my faith slip away like grains of sand.

None of that mattered, at least a not to the detective sitting across from me waiting for an answer. *Fuck it*, I decided.

"Just a guess," I repeated.

It had continued from there. When the detective finally stood up, patted me on the back, and walked out, I just sat there. Then I felt the touch of warm fingers on the back of my neck.

And Echie was there.

In her anguish, she was more beautiful than ever. I reached up and wiped at the tears magnifying her eyes. A black sling that looked all too familiar supported her injured wrist. I gently pulled her in towards me. She buried her face in my chest and sobbed.

We walked out of the office, and I turned numbly away from the sight of the yellow crime-scene tape. I was half-afraid I'd get sucked in the doorway, so I hugged Echie tighter.

A clicking sound caught my attention. It had come from the room next door, the one with the window that had showed me the unspeakable results of Nate's decision. The door was ajar. Unable to help myself, I peeked inside. Behind me, Echie squeezed my elbow, wondering what the hell I thought I was doing. It was a fair question.

Jack Strand was seated at the small table with a laptop open. A wire connected it to a video camera mounted on the wall. He clicked the mouse again as I silently stepped in and peered over his shoulder. Echie's grip on my elbow tightened. But as Nate materialized on the screen, I couldn't have moved even if I'd wanted to.

Nate squished himself into a small chair and rubbed his wrists. Across the table, the soon-to-be unconscious detective was folding a set of handcuffs.

A tug on my elbow made me turn. Echie raised a brow and shook her head. But when she saw the expression on my face, she relented. I turned back to watch my friend die.

"I'm sorry if the cuffs were too tight, Lieutenant."

"It's all right, Stan."

"First order of business. The Miranda warnings, which I read on the way over, still apply. Do you understand these rights, which I have explained to you?"

"I do."

"And knowing these rights, do you wish to waive them and answer questions at this time."

"I do."

"Well then, sir, it is my painful duty to bring up the matter of your wife's death."

"Desiree."

"I'm sorry, sir?"

"My wife's name was Desiree, Detective. Desiree Barrajas. You knew her by that name as well."

"Yes, sir. Well, as you know we have some questions for you regarding her—"

"Let's cut right to it, shall we?"

Nate pulled his chair in close to the table and clasped his hands. The detective, a veteran of the game, waited patiently.

"Yes, silence is the correct response, Detective. When an interviewee starts talking, just let him run his mouth."

Nate was still as a statue, but his eyes shone with fervor.

"I want you to understand exactly what it is I've lost. Before I came to know Desiree, my wife, I never really understood the vast realm contained in one simple word. Love. I caught glimpses, certainly. Love of *family, friends, my church, my God. I also saw it through the lens of literature, music, poetry. But at a distance, if you see what I mean. That was how I wanted it because my goals were inconsistent with something so all-consuming. Then I fell, truly fell, in love with Desiree, and all those books, poems, and songs suddenly made sense.*

The detective's slight smile caused Nate to give him a nod.

"If you've been lucky enough to know that, then you don't need further explanation. If you haven't, I won't diminish it with metaphors. I will only say that it poured out of me until I would have believed I was empty, and yet I had never felt so full. It was chaotic. It was exhilarating. And I embraced it.

Nate cocked his head to the side. *"I've lived a purposeful life. I had to fight to be my own man, not somebody else's version of me. The only tools, the only weapons I had, were faith in myself and in my God. But these carried me through because I never lost sight of my goal. Never."*

Nate looked at the camera, which he knew was there, of course. It felt as if he were staring at me through a lens of time. He continued, *"But then I allowed another voice to sway me. It was clever, cunning. It knew my strengths as well as my vulnerabilities. It bent my love for those closest to me, corrupting that which I hold most dear with whispers. For the first time in my life, I considered the word 'disgrace.' I came to the brink of hate, I'll admit that. But I paused. Why? All I can say was that grace saved me, made me understand the truth. Michael and Desiree had never, could never betray me.*

Those words struck my core. Guilt rose up like bile in my throat.

"I believed again that anything was possible, that even if my path had changed, what I held in my heart could only make me stronger. In my arrogance, I believed I could still shape my own portion of the world, could remake it the way I had always known I could. But as the saying goes," Nate said with a grin that held no warmth, *"'Man plans, God laughs.'"*

"This may not be welcome news to you, Detective," Nate continued, *"but I did not kill my wife. Nor can I help you piece together that puzzle because the penance for my lost faith is that I will have vengeance."* His voice lowered. *"I was too late to save her. And now it's too late to save myself."*

Nate's right arm shot forward. The bony heel of his hand struck the detective's chin squarely, and the man immediately slumped in his chair. Nate leaped forward, surprising me again with his speed, and lunged for the detective's belt. With a savage jerk, he yanked out the detective's pistol.

He stood up to his full height and examined the firearm as if he were testing it at the shooting range. Satisfied, he stepped across the room and wedged his chair beneath the door handle. After checking the detective's pulse, Nate returned to his place at the table and dropped to his knees. His whispered "Bless me Father, for I have sinned" was followed by loud shouts and pounding outside the door. Nate ignored it, looking directly at the camera with a serene expression.

"Michael. Take care of my mother."

The words roared in my head. My hands trembled as I reached out, willing Nate not to do this. Blows hammered the door as he placed the end of the barrel over his heart and, with his eyes raised to the ceiling, to God, he pulled the trigger. The sharp crack was followed by a spray of blood on the wall behind him.

Nate bent forward and then slowly crumpled to the floor.

Echie caught me as I, too, collapsed. In a daze, my eyes drifted to the wall clock. The second hand continued to move. *Tick, tick, tick.* Somehow that offended me, as if my grief were so massive that even time should pause. Then Echie, solid and real beside me, squeezed my hand, and the sensation ceased.

She helped me stand up straight and then motioned down the hallway. Strand still hadn't noticed our presence, so we slipped out without a word and were outside a minute later. The last rays of the sun were touching the building tops, and in my grief, I imagined the golden glow was Nate's departing spirit.

Echie and I drove Rochelle home, and I tried to comfort her. She had always been strong, stronger than I had ever been, so we mostly sat there, content to be close. When she'd finally gone to bed, I convinced Echie to drop me back at the police station. To her credit, she recognized that the demons driving me—guilt, rage, grief—required exorcising. Based on the garbled shit on the computer screen, dreaming had been more productive.

It was time to put matters in perspective. Yes, I'd failed a man I'd loved like a brother. Was I angry with him for taking his own life? I was. But I had long ago realized that Nate wasn't malleable like most of us. When he had traveled out to the rigid edges of his character, it had all snapped beneath the weight.

So I forgave him. Sending out a silent prayer, I asked God to forgive him as well.

Since I could not forgive myself, I decided to put my guilt into that same box already stacked deep with the rest of my unresolved issues. Sooner or later, I would need to deal with it, with all of them, but not today.

I stood up and stretched. The knife-edge pain in my arm had settled into a dull ache. My phone buzzed again, and I realized I'd forgotten to check it. When I saw the number, I ground my teeth in fury.

I hit play and listened to Inigo's message.

"Hey, Miguel. Long time no see. You probably think you've figured everything out, but you'd be wrong. For now, I think I'll spare you the details. The reason I called is, well, I got a problem. Yo se, I know, helping me out is the last thing on your to-do list, but just listen up for a minute."

There was yelling in the background that was quickly muffled by a hand over the receiver.

"Sorry, don't want you to figure out where I'm at. Not yet, anyway. Look, I've got a lotta shit to answer for, but I can't do that if I'm dead, now can I? Mira, the dudes looking for me are what you might call badasses, you know? Sure you do.

"I don't trust anyone at the station, especially those putas at internal. But you, you want to know what happened to your people, right? I need you to be the good guy one more time, mijo."

There was a pause. Inigo's breath hissed into my ear.

"I'll call you again in an hour. Be in your car and find a good parking spot on the East Side. I'll give you a location, and you come get me then, all right? No patrol, no SWAT, just you, Miguel."

The message ended. I replayed it several times, digesting the information hungrily. My hatred was bittersweet. Of course, this was just another one of Rafael's slick games. The clever little fucker had proven he could play the game much better than I could, which meant I would need to cover every corner. Quickly.

There were few options. A SWAT deployment was about as unobtrusive as a nuclear bomb. Inigo's extensive network of confidantes meant I couldn't trust informants, and I had no way of knowing how many other detectives had been swayed by his charismatic bullshit. Inigo knew us, knew what we looked like, knew our methods. Since the last thing I wanted was to send him further underground—if he disappeared I would always wonder if he was drinking Tequila on a Mexican beach or laid out in a shallow grave—I needed someone I could trust to help me.

Someone with skin in the game.

I dialed a number from memory.

"The fuck you want."

"I need your help, Joe."

On the other end, Joe Barrajas laughed mirthlessly. "Why? You wanna tell me some more of your fucking conspiracy theories? Maybe goddam space aliens murdered my daughter, eh?"

Barrajas' voice had a hint of crazy. I ignored it, let him vent. Fortunately, it was short-lived.

"What do you want?" Barrajas asked again, this time in a subdued voice.

"Inigo just called me."

"I don't give a fuck about him anymore. If your friend, that jumped-up asshole everyone worshipped like he was Jesus Christ hadn't come along, my daughter would still be alive!" His voice took on a dangerous note. "I would kill that son of a bitch with my bare hands if he were alive, the dirty coward." His voice lapsed back to a monotone. "So, I ask you a final time, Cassidy—what the fuck do you want?"

"I want you to help me find him, Joe," I said.

This was met with silence. I pressed on.

"Look, you know how much I cared about Desiree. I could spend hours trying to convince you that Nate didn't kill her, but I won't. Instead, I'm offering you a chance to help catch the man who spread all those lies about your daughter, who pushed Nate's buttons, who manipulated everything for his own agenda. You told me Inigo wasn't my friend, do you remember? Are you saying that he's your friend now? Or do you want to be a part of this?"

This time I waited through the silence.

"Tell me," Barrajas finally grunted.

For the next several minutes, I relayed Inigo's message. Then I added a few details he hadn't known about. "He wants to give himself up, Joe. Says he wants me to wait somewhere on the East Side. He'll call in an hour with his location."

Barrajas was silent.

"Look, he's not gonna show if we call this in," I continued. "The chief will want SWAT to handle the arrest."

"Garcia!" Barrajas said with vehemence. "I begged him not to trust Orlando, but he brushed me off. I don't give a good goddam what that asshole wants."

I ignored the outburst. "There's no way Inigo is going to wait around while we set something up. I'm guessing he just wants to avoid taking a perp stroll for the media. He'll want the back door entry at the jail, a hand-picked attorney, and bail. VIP treatment. To get all that he needs us on a short leash."

"Yeah, all right," Barrajas answered. "So, we're gonna keep this just between you and me, right?"

"You, me, and Inigo. Yeah."

"You trust him?" Barrajas asked after a moment.

"Why the hell do you think I called you?"

Cold laughter. "You're learning, Cassidy. Too bad it's too damn late."

"That's not an answer."

"The man has nothing to lose. He'll try to play you again." Barrajas said.

"I know that."

"So, you have a plan to find him?"

"I do," I answered, though I was far from confident.

There was silence for several seconds. "Pick me up in twenty minutes," Barrajas commanded.

The line went dead.

There had been so much to tell, I'd forgotten all about Inigo giving me Desiree's scarf. That was—*Hold up*, I thought. That evening when Inigo had suddenly showed up at the courthouse, when Nate's SUV had inexplicably sat in the parking lot . . . I considered the implications for less than a second.

Fuck!

Somehow Inigo gotten hold of Desiree's scarf and then given it to me as a gift for Echie. Nate must have spotted it at my desk that same night, which would explain his uncharacteristic animosity. He also must have overheard my conversation with Inigo in the parking lot the next day. I had to give credit to Inigo—he was a clever piece of shit. He had played us. Nate's last words floated through my head, reminding me that Inigo hadn't managed to poison our friendship after all.

I didn't spend two seconds wondering how or why Rafael sold us all out. There was and is an unspoken bond between cops, a deep sense of trust, which includes people we may not know or even like, that allows us to stick our necks out day after day. Apparently, he never bought into it, but at this point, I didn't know or care what reason Inigo had for all the destruction he'd caused. All I knew was that he had pushed Nate into the corner, and now my friend was gone. For a moment, I imagined Inigo's face in my gunsights, those cunning eyes raised in sudden panic as I pull the trigger. And I understood in that brief second how a man could coldly take a life.

Does that make me like him? Or is corruption measured on a sliding scale? *Fuck it,* I thought again. *Enjoy your thirty pieces of silver, Rafael. I'm coming for you.*

CHAPTER 30

Rafael Inigo set his cell phone down and leaned back on the ratty couch. One way or another, the phone call to Cassidy had been a game-changer. Not that it mattered. Neither of his current options, prison or death, was all that appealing.

He had never been one to sit idle while others determined his fate. As always, he was playing the cards he'd been dealt. If there was a wild card, he'd find it.

At least he hoped so.

He chuckled and stroked the bushy hairs sprouting on his chin. He hadn't bothered to shave since, *What's the legal term? Abscond? Quite the fucking way to describe running for my life.*

Inigo scanned his current refuge. The crappy little one-bedroom had peeling paint, curtains made from blankets, a couch that looked as if it had been dragged through a cesspool, and carpet with just enough shag to hide the lice, fleas, and bedbugs, which had been feasting on his wanted hide for days. It was better than the street, though not by much.

"*Mierda!*" he hissed to the vermin sharing his living space.

Inigo had put all his savvy, ambition, and drive on the line, had risked everything. If everything had gone as planned, it would have been worth every second he'd spent polishing the boots for a long line of assholes, from the sociopathic gang leader who'd recruited him into the Surenos to the stupid, cocky brigade commander he'd chauffeured around Iraq to Orlando, the officious prick whose rotting corpse would be feeding rodents soon enough.

And yet here he was.

Inigo wasn't unfamiliar with this kind of life, however. He'd joined a gang early on, lured by *la vida loca*, the crazy life, but found it wanting—too much pointless shooting for too little profit. The military had been no better. He had been assigned to a rigid asshole of a colonel, tasked with driving him from one bullshit meeting to another. His entire tour in Iraq, throughout most of Desert Storm, had been extremely dull with one exception. Drunk and high, he'd crashed his commander's Humvee into an abandoned Iraqi tank and then stumbled back to camp with the improbable story of an attack by Iraqi soldiers. Nobody believed him, but in the chaotic days following the invasion, there had been a rash of screwups by overzealous soldiers, and public affairs officers handled this sort of mess frequently. Instead of discipline, he'd received a purple heart and an honorable discharge.

Returning home, the former soldier had fallen into his old habits. That included the Surenos. Like many of the neighborhood kids, El Moto, or Juanito Rodriguez as he was known then, had been intrigued by Inigo's exaggerated accounts of the war. Soon the boy was part of Inigo's set, the East Side Posse. By the time the gang became known as the East Side Criminales, little Juanito was a respected enforcer and had earned the nickname of the Machine.

Yet again, the gang life lost its appeal, and Inigo drifted. Too restless for most jobs, he began attending classes at the community college. On a whim, he took a criminal justice class and was surprised to discover that despite—or perhaps because of—his history, he had an aptitude for it. Inigo had the sudden inspiration to try his hand at police work. It was the opposite of the track he'd been on, but he reasoned, it offered its version of the ultimate prize for an East Side kid with ambition.

Power.

Thanks to his embellished war record, Inigo was able to downplay his criminal record and earn a spot at the police academy. Several months later, he graduated at the bottom of his class and hit the street. He quickly became enamored with his new authority, especially when the worst of the gang-bangers—whose dead eyes had always made him nervous as a young banger—were forced to offer him a grudging respect.

From his vantage as a detective, Inigo became intimately familiar with a wide array of criminals. He learned that most of them, especially the drug dealers and gangster OGs, viewed Seattle to the north as inhospitable for the drug trade. Inigo understood. The larger city was rife with federal agencies and large drug task forces, while Tacoma, Seattle's ugly stepchild to the south, was largely off the federal radar. What surprised Inigo, however, was that Tacoma actually had much to offer criminal enterprises—a deep seaport, an international airport minutes away, and an interstate freeway bisecting the city. As he saw it, the City of Destiny was a logical place for a narcotics hub. And so Inigo had waited for the drug overlords to come to him.

When one of the main drug distributors finally made contact, his only shock had been the identity of the messenger.

It was his childhood friend, Juan "El Moto" Rodriguez.

Inigo had lost track of Rodriguez in the last few years, knew only that Rodriguez had been doing time in a federal lockup for gun trafficking. What he didn't know was that little Juanito had used that time to earn a spot within La Eme, the infamous prison gang. Inigo had been quietly impressed.

Rodriguez had kept tabs on his former mentor, knew of his aspirations, and was actually in Tacoma at the behest of La Eme's shot callers in California. So the two began an ongoing conversation about the drug trade and Tacoma's potential. Rodriguez's report was well received. The two got to work.

They singled out their own former set, the East Side Criminales, as their street representatives. If his former gang were to move, sell, and distribute large quantities of meth, heroin, and cocaine, Inigo knew they would need a clear field. Thus, their first order of business had been to reignite a gang war.

It had been simple.

With rumors and innuendo filtering onto the streets, courtesy of Inigo's long list of informants, gang members had taken the bait. Sureno sets began criss-crossing the city, tagging rival neighborhoods until the inevitable bullets began to spray throughout the East Side.

The police department had been just as predictable. Inigo put forth no effort to secure his position in the reformed gang unit and quickly used his role as the intel officer to bring in Rodriguez's associate, Luiz Gutierrez, as an informant.

El Feo had been a disappointment, a clumsy, brutal man, incapable of any amount of tact. On their last operation, Gutierrez had contacted the wrong dealer and nearly been shot down in the street. Those had been dangerous, wanted men who would have killed Cassidy if Orlando hadn't put them down.

The mistake had triggered Inigo's first anxious moment. The situation had gotten complicated enough, but the two trigger-happy dealers could have ruined everything. Orlando had done him a favor; if only they could've shot straight and taken Cassidy out. That would have solved most of his problems.

Despite the setbacks, his East Side Criminales had stood on the sidelines while their rivals decimated each other, with the help of the gang unit. That done, City Hall's attention had drifted to other matters. His and Rodriguez's efforts were recognized at a hastily set-up meeting on the tarmac of a nearby airport. They had made a brief report to the Gulfstream jet's single passenger while the engines continued to spin. That glimpse of the wealth and power behind the scenes had both excited and terrified him. While he could certainly imagine that level of success and more, his instincts told him that they were now dealing with an entirely new player.

The man in the plane, dressed in casual clothes worth more than Inigo's most expensive suit, was most definitely not part of the Mexican Mafia. If Inigo was any kind of judge, the man was from a cartel.

Yet the recent collapse of Inigo's plans made it all moot. Did it really matter whether the contractor who dispatched him was hired by La Eme or some cartel? *Fuck no.* He was under no pretense about his current situation. Cop or not, he knew what to expect after such a spectacular failure.

Inigo could admit now, at least to himself, that he'd gotten way too cocky. He had been unable to resist the vendettas that had been gnawing away at him—his hatred for Orlando, who represented every motherfucking *jefe* who'd ever told *him* what to do, and that *puta*

Cassidy, who thought he was better than Inigo. Despite the risk, Inigo had quietly inserted his agenda into their carefully laid plans.

But he hadn't been the only one to screw up. It had taken over a month of whispering in just the right ears to bring ESC's biggest rivals together in the biggest shooting match the city had seen in years. Three dead shot callers in one night! It had effectively removed two sets from the playing field, but "El Feo" Gutierrez had fucked it up. He'd shot that OG, Escalante, from the gas station, creating an angle that would immediately push the investigation in another direction. If Inigo had not stepped in, risking exposure, and scooped up Gutierrez's spent rounds, Cassidy would certainly have found them. Worse, Gutierrez had left his fingerprints on the metallic window frame. Even Inigo couldn't get away with destroying evidence, so he'd refiled them and hoped for the best.

El Feo's next screwup had been Oso Negro's "suicide." Instead of just getting the job done, he'd actually partied with the guy. Drunk, high or both, Gutierrez had blown the shot and split the gang-banger's face. Fortunately, Cassidy had been all too willing to close that one out. Inigo'd thought the time to settle the score with Orlando and Cassidy had finally come.

Inigo had noticed Desiree's effect on his boss, how Orlando's attitude changed the moment that *leva* with the gorgeous tits walked into a room. And she'd shot him down as if he was a *puta*, so fuck her as well. Since he'd sniffed out Orlando's weakness, Inigo'd take care of them both. Cassidy, the *pendejo* who'd stolen his promotion, would also play a part. Inigo despised the pathetic alcoholic, a so-called supervisor who had no *cajones* and had to rely on friends like Orlando to help him get ahead. Inigo had scratched and clawed his way up, never taking any help from anyone. Not that anyone had offered.

He'd started with Cassidy. Betting on his pathetic need to fit in, Inigo lured him to the Spar using Echie as unwitting bait. He set the hook with a well-timed drink it would have been difficult for Cassidy to turn down, and Inigo had judged his target correctly. Cassidy had downed his glass without hesitation, but he'd surprised everyone by standing up to Montgomery. But even that hilarious fight hadn't been the best part. That had been the ass chewing Cassidy had endured while Inigo eavesdropped.

That scripted scene brought a sly smile to Inigo's face. His teeth gleamed briefly in the scant light.

After ruining Cassidy so easily, Inigo had turned his attention back to Orlando. That had been far more difficult, and he'd walked a fine line for days. He needed to snare the pussy-whipped lieutenant, convince him that his beautiful new bride was a cheap *leva* who left his bed to suck Cassidy's Irish dick and get him amped enough to do something about it. Little by little, Inigo watched the cracks in Orlando's armor appear. The man just had too much faith in others, too much pride in himself. Those faults were all the leverage Inigo needed.

Still, he'd kept a close watch on his real plans. In a routine check, he'd been shocked to discover that Gutierrez's fingerprints had not only been found but had been processed. Since the case was closed, the results were just waiting for the right person to stumble across. He'd quickly erased everything from the database but not before seeing Desiree's name in the signature block. With no recourse, he'd snuck into the crime scene office and spent a fruitless hour scouring her cluttered desk for the originals.

But the trip had an upside. Her scarf had been hanging on a chair, and he had snagged it out of pure spite. Later, he had the idea to use it to drive a wedge between Cassidy and Orlando. That ploy had succeeded beyond expectations. Seeing his wife's scarf on Cassidy's chair had finally brought Orlando under Inigo's control. The man's anger had been explosive. Quickly following up, Inigo had put Orlando within earshot of Cassidy at the courthouse and steered the conversation, further convincing him of Cassidy's treachery. In the end, Orlando had actually believed that his best friend was sleeping with his wife.

But Inigo had been forced to admit he had underestimated Cassidy's resolve. Despite his humiliating suspension, Cassidy had returned to duty. A man with any pride would have ridden off into the sunset, but the *puta* didn't know when to quit. Not only that, but Cassidy had waded into the territorial waters of major crimes by discussing Inigo's case with the gang prosecutor. That, more than anything, had enraged Inigo. And scared him as well.

Without bothering to check with Rodriguez, Inigo had ordered "El Feo" Gutierrez to take Cassidy out. And the dumb shit had gotten arrested for drunk driving on the day of the hit.

Are you fucking kidding me?

Worse, El Feo had called Inigo's personal phone from the jail. Inigo had anxiously contacted Rodriguez, hoping to salvage the situation. El Moto had taken the news calmly and then personally bailed out Gutierrez. Showing weakness in front of his partner would, Inigo knew, cost him at some point.

But El Feo had failed him again. For the last time.

Dios mio! Inigo fumed. *Fuck!*

Recalling the moment he'd shot and killed Gutierrez calmed him. It had been easy, gratifying even. If only he'd had ten more seconds, he would've put a bullet in the gringo's face as well. But he'd barely made it away before the situation devolved.

His last meeting with Rodriguez had been mere minutes after the shooting. They met at El Moto's favorite strip club outside the city, one of the few places where no one knew Inigo. He'd downed a couple of shots of tequila to calm his nerves, knowing there would soon be hell to pay when Rodriguez learned everything. Whether it was the liquor or his nerves, Inigo suddenly found himself telling his partner about Gutierrez's fingerprints. Rodriguez's thick brows narrowed, and his dark eyes locked on him. Inigo realized his mistake too late, and rather than have his partner leap to conclusions, he blurted the rest. That included Desiree's role in the completed fingerprint analysis. He hoped he'd convinced Rodriguez that the matter was resolved, that El Moto was a stone-cold killer incapable of anything but a savage response. The last thing Inigo wanted was a bloodbath in town, not after all their work to calm things down the last few weeks.

His only leverage was information. Inigo knew that Rodriguez had been after Joe Barrajas's daughter since high school. How, he'd wondered, could he play this to his advantage?

El Moto had been silent, his yellow teeth flashing in a predatory grin. Then he abruptly cut short Inigo's drunken scheming with a dark imperative. "Leave the *leva* to me."

A day later, Desiree Barrajas was dead.

The first twinge of panic rolled through Inigo's stomach.

He had wondered only a moment if Rodriguez would have murdered a police employee and risked the wrath of the entire criminal justice system. But, answering his own question, he knew there was nothing left of little Juanito in the man who had become El Moto.

Given the nature of the murder, Inigo knew instinctively that Rodriguez would be caught. Once arrested, their bond of brotherhood would last about the length of time it took for El Moto to strike a deal. He would tell them everything they wanted to know. Inigo didn't blame him for that—he would have done the same. But when Rodriguez started talking, the *policia* would be looking for him.

Unbelievably, the evening news on the night of the murder had brought a lucky break. First local, then national news stations began broadcasting the news of Orlando's arrest. Inigo had dropped a quick phone call to a detective in homicide, one whose career would be finished if Inigo happened to mention to a fellow cop that his partner was screwing his wife. That's when he learned the details of Desiree's murder, which led him to his last risky move. That same night he'd made a silent entry into Orlando's downtown condo, slipping under the crime scene tape and past a slumbering patrol officer. Beneath glaring halogen lights, he'd surveyed the bedroom for a scant second before grabbing one of the pillows on the bed. He'd stuffed it into his backpack and left without being noticed. From there he'd gone to the police impound lot and pulled out a large set of keys—copies to virtually every car in the police fleet, every door at every precinct, evidence room, and two safe houses—and used one to open Orlando's SUV. He stuffed the pillow under the driver's seat and quickly returned to his apartment.

Yes, he'd managed to point the cops away from Rodriguez and, by virtue of that, from himself. But in the quiet of this little hovel, Inigo quickly realized the extent of his failure. Eventually, the police would wonder where he was, why he was hiding. If nothing else, Hagstrom could charge him for obstruction in the triple homicide. While that possibility alone didn't concern him, once the local street gangs heard about it, there would be hell to pay. Nobody worked with the cops, so the East Side Criminales would be targeted by every set, every banger in the area. They would simply cease to exist. La Eme would lose its lock on the turf. Without his cop job, Inigo would become a liability.

Thus, in the eyes of La Eme, he was already a dead man.

Inigo looked around and sniffed. The apartment still carried the scent from years of burnt meals, unwashed people, and animal *mierda*. Somehow, thoughts of his death at the hands of an anonymous hit man was less repellent than that of being found dead in this shithole. That was no way for a man like him to go out.

Which meant it was time to do what he did best. Roll the dice.

That was why he'd called Cassidy. The cop responsible for his current situation might well be his best bargaining chip. Inigo's last, his only, hope of escaping the noose tightening around his neck lay in the wealth of resources available to La Eme, or better yet the unnamed cartel with untold cash flow. If he were able to spin events well enough, he might be able to pile the blame on Rodriguez. It had been El Moto's idea to bring Gutierrez into the plan in the first place, hadn't it? Gutierrez's constant failures had ruined a year's worth of planning. Didn't Rodriguez share that responsibility?

That is what he hoped to be able to tell his invisible patrons. Better that he himself be the one to bring them the news of Rodriguez's fuckups. *Aun mejor, I'll bring them Cassidy's fucking head on a platter. It could save my life*, he thought, nearly convincing himself. Besides, why eliminate a resource like himself, one with decades of knowledge and a horde of informants? Inigo could still help La Eme set up shop—maybe not here but somewhere else, hell, the fucking moon as far as he was concerned. All he wanted was a chance to live and maybe a little piece of the profit.

They won't throw me to the dogs, no. I'll find a hole in their organization and jump in. I'll survive, just like always.

A floorboard creaked. The sound did not repeat. Inigo turned in a slow circle, trying to locate the source in the dark. He tiptoed to the bedroom and peered through a tear in the blanket covering the window to the parking lot and alley a story below.

It was quiet, empty.

He checked the lock on the window. It was secure, but the wooden rod was on the sill. He had no idea if it had been moved, so he propped it back up and returned to the living room.

Still unsure, he stared down at his phone.

Could someone know I'm here? Who? How?

He hadn't given Cassidy his location. That phone call was still several minutes away, and there was no other means of finding him. Or was there? The realization hit him, and he almost cursed aloud.

It was the phone. *A fucking pen trap.*

Instead of using technology to pinpoint locations through cell towers, Inigo preferred his own, less legitimate, methods for finding people and things. Thus, he had to think hard about the process involved. First, he recalled Cassidy would need to type up a search warrant affidavit. Next, he'd track down a prosecutor for approval, followed by a judge. The submittal would take a while, and even then, it would need to be faxed to the phone company. Still more time would be required to trace the phone through the web of cell towers until its unique signature was located.

That would take hours, he decided. He had given Cassidy less than an hour and only an approximate geographic area. There was no way the little shit could have found him already.

But why leave it to chance?

Inigo reached down and turned off his phone, tucking it between the filthy cushions on the couch. It was time to go. A prickle at the back of his neck stopped him abruptly, his right hand frozen on the doorknob. Slowly, he drew his hand back. His fingers touched his holstered gun.

He was too late.

A brutal blow struck him in the groin, lifting him off his feet. Shards of pain ripped through his testicles. Immobilized and in agony, Inigo collapsed on the stained carpet, hands cupping his genitals. Beads of sweat drenched his face.

Juan Rodriguez surveyed the room. He frowned at the meager furnishings, the dirt-encrusted walls, and the reek of decay and then studied his old friend and mentor with open contempt. "Things've changed, mijo. My brothers ain't happy wit' you. No, no." With his eyes still locked on Inigo, Rodriguez walked in a slow circle, his black clothing and balaclava giving an impression of a crow waiting impatiently for its dinner to hurry up and die.

"I came back to this town to take what was mine! I'm La Eme now, you know. That means *I* bring the drugs, *I* take the money, *I* own the bitches. It's a simple thing, right? But you got plans, and like some fuckin' *estupido* I listen. You wanna fuck wit' people when all you need to do is cap that big black motherfucker, *ese*. Why I let you fool wit' him? Thass my bad, *ese*. I own that one."

Rodriguez shook his head as if he were actually sorry, but his eyes were hard as nails. "You got it all figured out, huh? Well, then how'd they get Feo's prints? *Mira*, you makin' lotsa trouble."

The steps quickened. The circle tightened.

"But I stay wit' you," Rodriguez spat, "even when my people say you sellin' out, that you gonna run you' mouth. I say, 'Naw, naw, this mi hombre!' Stick my neck out fo' you, fool. Even when you come cryin' on the phone. Shoulda heard yo'self, mijo, cryin' like a fuckin' *leva!*"

Inigo heard the footsteps stop next to his head. The pain in his groin was slowly diffusing. He cracked an eyelid. A clear, brilliant white filled his vision. He blinked, and a single white tennis shoe materialized inches in front of his face. Royal blue laces crisscrossed the shoe's tongue, sprouting from the top in a fountain-shaped knot. He focused on the familiar Sureno color, until the foot moved abruptly. He flinched, but instead of kicking him, Rodriguez resumed circling.

"You used Feo for a hit wit'out askin' me. And what happens? What happens?" An icy fury crept into Rodriguez's tone. "You fuckin' kill him. And the *policia*? *Está muerte*? Shit no, he's not dead. Yeah, now *I'm* wonderin' whose side you on, hombre."

The steps passed his head again. Inigo had never seen Rodriguez so agitated. "And I gotta *track you down!* Think that was hard? *Es mi varrio!* Think you can hide from me? Homeys be jumpin' up to snitch you out. Cuz that's what you are, right hombre? A fucking snitch."

All Inigo could manage was a violent shake of his head. After several deep breaths, he felt his strength slowly return. Inigo was no coward. He knew his chances of leaving this room were slim. He would need all his cunning, all his liar's art. He kept his eyes shut, feigning more pain than he felt, waiting for an opportunity.

Rodriguez continued, "I climbed down off the roof and through that window a couple hours ago. Time was you woulda sniffed me out. You gettin' old, mijo. Old and soft." The steps slowed. "Don't know why I didn't come at you then. Guess I wanted to see what you were all about. Heard that phone call you made to the *policia*."

Inigo heard the rage in his former partner's voice. Unable to contain it, a sliver of fear raced through him.

"Yeah, you a snitch, Rafael."

Inigo shook his head savagely. He sucked air in noiselessly between his teeth. His head cleared, and his focus returned, magnified. He heard the snick of Rodriguez' shoes scuffing the sour-smelling carpet, saw a shaft of light through the window, smelled the pungent, sweaty fear leaking off his skin. Time was running short.

As if to accentuate the point, Rodriguez grasped his elbows, roughly hauling Inigo off the floor and shoving him onto the couch. The movement set off a new wave of pain, and he doubled over, squealing in agony. Sweat fell in streams down his forehead, into his eyes. He wiped his sticky face with a sleeve.

A single, metal eye stared at him.

He blinked, and the eye became the barrel of a gun.

Rodriguez hunched over him. He wore blue latex gloves, which held a large revolver steady. He cocked his head and frowned, as if Inigo were a disappointing child.

"You probably been working on a plan to get outta this, am I right? *Mira*, you always got a plan. Got one now?"

An index finger brushed lightly against the trigger, stopped. Inigo watched, mesmerized. The entire sum of his remaining moments were now contained in the millimeters it would take for the trigger pull. He psyched himself up, willing away the pain.

"Too bad, Rafael. You taught me some shit over the years, am I right? Some of it was pure bullshit, yeah. But some of it was good. Like this."

The gun suddenly spun around. Helpless to do anything but watch, Inigo followed the barrel as it swiveled beneath his chin.

Inigo lifted his eyes to his killer, his mind racing at light speed for a word, an action, anything that could save him. But Rodriguez read his mind, his own expression studying his former mentor as if he were already dead.

"No more fuckups, Rafael."

There was a flash of light, a loud bang, and then . . . nothing.

CHAPTER 31

After talking to Joe, I picked up the phone again. Despite the hour, I had a feeling my buddy would be awake. I wrestled my demons during the day. His worked the night shift.

The phone rang twice before a far too awake voice answered. "Hello, Michael. What has you up this late?"

It was good to hear a friendly voice, and at this juncture, Matt Hagstrom's was the one I most wanted to hear. He was already up to speed, so I told him about Inigo's message. I didn't need to emphasize that this was just between the three of us.

"What do you need from me?" he asked.

"Simple. I need the world's fastest pen trap."

Matt started right away on the affidavit, running through the usual questions about my experience, probable cause, warrant parameters, and so on.

"Were you sitting there with a blank affidavit waiting for my call?" I asked, only half-kidding.

He grunted. "Give me a few minutes to wake up the judge," Hagstrom added, "I know just whom to call."

He hung up before I had a chance to thank him.

The drive to the Barrajas home was short. For years Joe, his wife, and daughter had lived in a small but immaculate North End Tudor on the bluff above Commencement Bay, not far from my place.

Though he lived alone now, from the street it looked anything but the home of a grouchy bachelor. The lawn was manicured, the roses flush and trimmed, the front door freshly painted beneath an ivy trellis. It was tranquil and pleasant and totally at odds with the son-of-a-bitch police lieutenant I knew.

"'Bout fucking time," my former boss said, stepping outside and closing the door.

Probably has a landscaper.

Joe Barrajas had aged over the last few days. As the clouds scudded away from the waxing moon, sharp new creases sprouted along his forehead and framed his sunken eyes. A lingering scowl rested on deep hinges of skin. He brushed past me on the way to my truck, shoulders hunched against the chill night air.

Little more was said during the drive. It wasn't until we crossed Yakima Avenue, the unofficial boundary between the city's South End and East Side, that he finally spoke.

"Where?"

"Pac Ave and Fifty-Sixth," I responded.

I had selected the intersection not just for its proximate distance to most East Side spots, but because the choice held a measure of karma. It was where Nate and I had sat in his van while Inigo and his homicidal informant orchestrated their farce. Nate had saved my life that night. Now it seemed as if it had happened to someone else a long time ago.

Barrajas took the news in silence.

My phone buzzed. "Detective Cassidy."

It was the judge Hagstrom had roused. That had been extremely quick work, though now that he was on the phone, the judge droned on for several minutes. Barrajas decided to ignore me, so I swore the oath while I drove on through the darkness.

"New world record," I said after hanging up.

"Yeah? For what?"

"We've got a warrant for a pen trap."

"I'll get you a fucking medal. Can we go get this motherfucker now?"

"Almost," I said, dialing another number.

A security official at the cell company answered, and I told the guy what I needed. Coordinates arrived via text a couple of minutes later, taking us out to a run-down neighborhood on the East Side I knew all too well. Starting at the edge of the grid, we drove in a rough circle. Not a soul was out, and I was beginning to wonder if this was a wild goose chase when another text arrived from the wireless company. The search area had shrunk.

This was more like it. I studied the two-block parameters, did a rough translation to determine the exact streets, and only then did I realize where Inigo might be.

Correction, had to be.

Barrajas just sat there, waiting for me. I put my truck in gear.

Minutes later, we arrived at a dimly lit intersection. On the opposite corner stood a shabby, nondescript apartment building with a rickety wooden fence sagging outwards as if it were under pressure. The gang tagging covering every spare inch was barely visible; the sign above the courtyard entrance, all too visible.

Villa Fortuna.

Déjà fucking-vu.

Images of a bloody corpse beneath a blanket, a sawed-off shotgun, and a mangled face ran through my head. I sat there unable to move, a deer in headlights, frozen by a surge of guilt. The gangster's supposed suicide had presented a real opportunity to uncover Inigo's involvement in whatever the fuck this was. There was, unfortunately, no denying where the buck stopped. With me. I alone had had the information and the authority to press ahead with that investigation. Could I have proven that Oso's suicide was in fact a murder?

I didn't know, never would know. I simply hadn't tried. What other events could have been prevented if I'd simply followed through? I shoved that malignant thought to the back of my brain. There would be plenty of time for a breakdown later. Maybe.

Barrajas seemed a bit shaken by the location as well. He opened his door and got out, gesturing towards the east. As he headed out, I forced myself out of my truck and trudged off in the opposite direction.

I think both of us knew where the search would end.

Ten minutes later, I had walked every sidewalk, alley, and street within two blocks of the Villa Fortuna. I checked my phone to see if Inigo had called again. Nothing.

As I'd expected, the circle took me back to Villa Fortuna. That night now seemed more vivid than the present—strobe lights flashing off wet pavement, police and fire radios squawking and squelching, the smell of animal feces wafting out from the courtyard. The past was so strangely present it felt as if I could walk there, could undo it all. Had it really been less than two months since I had stood in this same spot, a rookie patrol sergeant desperately trying to prove myself?

It felt like a lifetime.

Crack!

My gun materialized in my hand as I ran in a crouch back to my truck. The gunshot had seemed to come from everywhere. Instinctively, I put my engine block between me and that apartment building.

Footsteps pounded behind me. I spun as Joe Barrajas scrambled in next to me, gun at low ready. He shot me a quizzical look. I shrugged and pointed towards the building. Together, we peeked over the hood.

Inigo is in there. I knew this with a certainty that would have seemed surreal a short time ago. One way or another, our little melodrama would end tonight.

I promise you that, Nate, Des.

Lights flicked on in a few apartment windows. If anyone called 911—never a given in this neighborhood—I didn't want to be the first target, so I yanked out my badge and let it dangle from the chain. Joe did likewise.

All we could do now was wait. Running out into the open seemed like a really bad idea.

"Villa Fortuna." Barrajas hissed. "Feels like we've been going in a fucking circle."

Amen. The first siren began climbing McKinley Hill when I caught movement on the second floor. A silhouette glided along the walkway towards the stairs. The stairs were dark as well, but the size and speed suggested a man.

The sirens were less than a mile away, too far. With my heart pounding, Barrajas and I leaped up together and sprinted side by side through the entryway. At the bottom of the stairs, the ambient light showed me a thickset figure with a hood over his head.

I shouted, "Police, don't—"

"Shut up and run, Cassidy," he panted, starting to fall behind.

The man moved with an easy grace, jumping a short fence and racing along a narrow path behind the building. With gun out and pointed down, I hopped the fence a few seconds later and ran across rutted ground littered with sharp stones and trash.

With less than fifty feet to the end of the building and a hundred more to the street, the hooded man reached the sidewalk and turned right. The first large drops of rain struck the ground as I pounded after him.

At the sidewalk, I turned. He was only thirty feet away.

Unfortunately, he was already hopping into a black El Camino with curls of smoke floating out the exhaust. I caught the briefest glimpse of his profile. Before I could touch the car, gravel churned, and the car leaped forward as if it were spring-loaded. In a handful of seconds, it crested the hill and disappeared from view.

Oh no," I whispered, distraught. "Oh no, no, no."

Barrajas hauled up next to me a moment later, sucking in breaths through clenched teeth.

I holstered my gun and turned to him. "Joe?"

No answer.

"That wasn't him."

Barrajas's head snapped up.

"I saw his face when he opened his car door. Just for a second. It wasn't Inigo."

"So who the fuck was it?" he wheezed.

"The guy from La Eme."

"Rodriguez?" he asked, hatred descending over his features.

I nodded and then turned and hurried back towards the courtyard. The cops would be here soon. Things could get tricky.

"Where you going?" he asked.

"Don't you want to know who he was shooting at?"

Joe didn't respond, but I heard him panting behind me as we retraced our path.

Kapalu was one of the first cops on the scene. He'd been given sergeant's stripes temporarily since we were short on staffing, and he got a handle on the situation pretty quickly. If he was surprised to see us, he didn't show it.

With Barrajas stamping his feet impatiently behind me, Kapalu briefed the dozen or so uniforms that had turned up. The rain began to fall in earnest.

Half the cops were sent after Rodriguez, while the remainder formed up in a line—a stick as the SWAT guys called it—with Joe and me bringing up the rear. We hustled up the steps to the door Rodriguez had exited. When everyone was set up, Kapalu braced himself against the railing and unleashed a heavy boot against the doorknob. The stick followed him inside, fanning out. Shouts of "police" laced with the occasional excited obscenity echoed loudly in the small area.

Without our Kevlar vests, Joe and I had been instructed to wait outside. It didn't take long. When the "all clear" was announced, the lights came on. Barrajas and I stepped inside.

Everyone's attention was directed to the couch. It was facing away from us, so I saw Barrajas's expression before I saw the object of his disgust. I moved around the couch with apprehension boiling out of my skin, passing a familiar cowboy boot and catching the unmistakable coppery scent of blood.

Rafael's body was splayed out on the carpet. His arms were wide, his feet tucked beneath his legs. Without his animated smile, that larger-than-life energy, he looked so much smaller. He still had that hawk nose of his, still intact despite a gunshot wound that had gouged a crater out of the top of his head.

Professional curiosity overcame the swirling emotions. I stooped down to get a better look, saw the entry wound below and behind Inigo's chin. A clean shot this time; it was a small, dark hole just above the Adam's apple still oozing thick arterial blood. The rest was less pretty. The pressure of the blast had caused his head to swell. Blood and other fluids poured out of his ears, nose, mouth. One dark-brown eye partially protruded from the socket while the other stared up at the ceiling and beyond.

Nope. Wrong direction, Rafael.

"What?" Barrajas asked, turning to me with a hint of crazy in his eyes.

I must have said it out loud. "Nothing."

The building, the layout of the apartment, the headshot. It was all too familiar, too surreal. Another staged suicide, and this one might actually have worked. Except that we'd seen Rodriguez run, and, this was my firm opinion, Inigo wasn't the type to kill himself. Most narcissists aren't. No, I knew the revolver resting lightly in Inigo's cold fingers was just another lie, an ironic prop.

"What the fuck?" Barrajas cursed next to me.

I followed his gaze up. A pinkish grey goo clung to the popcorn ceiling.

I laughed without humor. "Yeah, sure," I said. "What the fuck."

✳ ✳ ✳

An hour later, the clouds opened up. A sheet of cold droplets so big they bounced fed into a muddy rivulet that meandered along the gutter and out to the pitted asphalt that passed for a street in this part of town.

The caffeine had long since left my system, my energy reserves were tapped out, and my head and heart were empty. For the first time since I'd walked out of the interview, there was no lead to follow up, no imminent threat, no . . . purpose for me.

The image of Inigo's bloated face was fixed in my head. His remaining eye was wide and glassy, as if he were surprised at the moment of his death. Maybe he finally caught a glimpse of the true power underpinning the world. Who knows.

I forced him from my thoughts, replacing that grotesque image with something much, much better—Nate and Desiree at their wedding, touching hands, the joy on their faces larger than life. But guilt stuck a rough hand into my chest and squeezed. The outline of the Villa Fortuna blurred with rain and tears, and my vision became a kaleidoscope of blue and red flashing lights. I blinked and it vanished.

Back in the present, cops and firefighters slogged back and forth, their heads lowered before the pounding rain. A man wearing a translucent white hazmat suit, the words "MEDICAL EXAMINER" on the back, pushed a gurney out to the street. A familiar paramedic trailed him. Stan, whom I'd last seen at this same cursed building, looked worn out.

"You look rode hard and put away wet," he said with a trace of a smile.

"Ain't done yet, Stan. Whaddaya know?"

"Same shit, different day," he said, waving as he reached his rig. It took off immediately, siren blipping and strobes flashing on the way to another call.

I was suddenly overcome by the need for it all to be over. If that meant that every piece of Inigo's fucked-up mess would be somebody else's problem, so be it. Nothing I could do would bring my friends back.

There, in the rain, I clasped my hands and said a prayer for Desiree. For Nate. For me.

For strength.

Because there was one matter still unresolved. By now I believed Rodriguez, not Inigo, had killed Desiree. If there was even the slightest possibility, then I needed to find this El Moto, this fucking Machine.

I asked myself if I was up to the task. Nate would have known what to do, would have already been well on his way. Yet from where I stood, the path forward was as murky as the water sluicing through my shoes.

A patrol officer materialized in front of me, his young face expressing concern. Then I understood how I must have looked to him. I shook my soggy head, shoved my hands in my waterlogged pockets, and headed towards my truck.

I was fishing for my keys when I sensed someone behind me. "Hey, Joe." I turned.

Barrajas appraised me, his eyes narrowed to slits. "You with me?" he asked quietly.

"With you?" I asked. We both knew what he was asking, but I wanted him to say it.

Barrajas was silent.

"Jesus," I said, nodding. "This is never going to end."

"Oh, it will," Barrajas answered. "One way or another, it will."

CHAPTER 32

A STREET IN SAN FRANCISCO
AUGUST 11
0530 HOURS

If anyone had bothered to look, the man who stepped out of a by-the-hour hotel in Chinatown and glanced warily up and down the street would have seemed out of place. Despite the Giants cap scrunched over my sunburnt nose and bulky grey jacket zipped up against the chill, I was still half a head taller than the crowd of Asian men and women streaming past me in the fog. It was apparently too early for tourists but not too early for the locals.

I pointed myself roughly towards downtown and started up one of San Francisco's famously steep streets. The route took me along a stretch of urban peaks and valleys amid exotic smells and storefronts emblazoned with Chinese characters. Gradually, these were replaced with American-style businesses that preceded more than one ultra-luxury hotel, posh apartment buildings, and a truly impressive cathedral. At Powell Street, the neighborhood changed yet again, giving way to tenements interspersed with the odd tourist shop. The abrupt change and variety were disconcerting.

The homeless were everywhere, and I held my breath against the odor of human excrement. A glassy-eyed man of indeterminate age was stretched out on the sidewalk, asleep on a bed of filthy blankets. In the alley nearby were more figures, all of them sprawled across a tarp with several sketchy-looking mattresses. One of them stared back. He was a gaunt-eyed white kid, lips peeled back from a mouth filled with ruined teeth, bug-eyes that gave him a perpetually shocked expression.

Several blocks ahead was my destination. Minutes later, I stood on a corner looking up at an orange-brick hotel. It looked tired and decrepit, despite the jaunty vertical sign identifying it as the Tenderloin Paradiso. *Sure*, I thought, looking up and down the street. *Why not?*

I stepped over a man sleeping in a suspicious puddle and pushed open the front door. The interior was just as I would have guessed— classic Old-World gone to crap. An elderly man snoozed behind a laminate desk, reading glasses dangling from an ear. I snuck past him to the stairs and ascended to the first floor. The air was heavy and moist, pungent with rotten food, incense, and the acrid smell of crack cocaine.

A light shone to my left. On a door the word "Toilet" was scrawled on a piece of masking tape. I pushed it open slowly, careful to keep it from creaking. The smell inside there made me gasp.

"'Bout time," a voice said.

Joe Barrajas stepped out of the shadows. Despite the stench, he didn't seem put out. His eyes practically glistened, and he stood tall and straight with a loose energy to his movements.

"What can I say? The streets are steep," I said, holding my nose. "What's the status?"

"Top floor, room 12. The whore left right after I called you."

I nodded. "Got what you need?"

"Yeah," Barrajas grunted. "Let's go."

We took the last two flights of stairs in silence. Barrajas stuck his head out for a quick peek of the hallway and then shrugged off his small backpack. I took off my coat and removed my backpack from beneath it. We dressed without a word in dark blue hazmat suits, putting everything else back in the bags. Then Joe pulled out two well-used revolvers.

He handed one to me.

"You ready for this?" he asked.

"Let's just get it done," I said brusquely.

A faint smile creased his lips. He gave me a single pat on the shoulder and stepped briskly into the hallway. I fell in behind. Barrajas moved swiftly to the last door and put a gloved hand on the knob. He shook his head. Locked. Reaching into his backpack again, he took out several small metal tools and started working on the lock. I counted off the seconds as I scanned the hallway until the tumbler gave way with a faint click.

I patted him once on the shoulder. Joe twisted the doorknob, and we rushed inside. I shut the door gently behind us and relocked it.

The room we found ourselves in was small, a ten-by-ten square with walls covered in tobacco grease. The only furniture was a square plastic table shoved into a corner, a single chair, and a nightstand beneath the room's only window. There was no bathroom, hence the communal one down the hallway. In the center of the room was a sheetless twin bed with a single frayed yellow blanket.

On it slept Juan "El Moto" Rodriguez.

It had taken us a long time to track him down. Now that we had, all I could do was stare.

Rodriguez lay on his back wearing green boxers and snoring so loudly we needn't have worried about noise. On the nightstand next to him sat an empty forty-ounce bottle of malt liquor and a glass crack pipe.

"Drunk *and* high," Barrajas said with a self-satisfied grin.

He lifted his gun and pointed it at Rodriguez's head. I moved to the far side of the bed, a set of plastic flex cuffs in hand. Barrajas gave me a thumbs up, and I set my gun on the ground behind me.

I leaped up and then dropped all my weight on Rodriguez. My knees landed on his gut, sending a whoosh of air out his mouth. I gathered up his flailing arms and wrapped the flex cuffs roughly around both wrists. Then I spun around and zip-tied his ankles together as well. When I was certain of my work, I stood up and backed away.

El Moto came fully awake very quickly. He popped up into a sitting position, still sucking in air. Yeah, he was a wreck. Despite looking like a piece of aged fruit, those crust-encased, bloodshot eyes still exuded enough malice to make me thankful the guy was tied up.

"What the fuck is this!" Rodriguez roared, spittle flying.

Barrajas abruptly shoved a wadded sock into Rodriguez's open mouth. He choked on it for a bit, but we waited patiently. When his breathing returned to normal, he put his tied feet on the floor and sat on the edge of the bed.

Joe went down on a knee in front of him, smiling. He was enjoying himself way too much, I thought. I'd been worried about this, had mentioned it more than once. We had a plan, and we had to stick to it.

"Joe?"

He nodded once for my benefit. "Hey, *puta*," Barrajas growled at Rodriguez. "Remember me?"

Rodriguez was eerily still, studying Barrajas as if the situation were reversed. His eyes flitted back and forth between us, missing nothing. He had a calculating expression that made me glad that he was tied up.

"Want that sock out of your mouth?" Barrajas asked, unperturbed. "You utter one loud fucking word, and I shove it all the way down your throat. *Comprende*?"

Rodriguez didn't respond. His gaze met mine, and I suppressed a shudder.

"Are. We. Clear?" Barrajas hissed.

Rodriguez gave a barely perceptible nod.

Joe slid the sock out of his mouth and took a quick step back. I couldn't blame him.

"You're dead, both of you. You gotta know that," Rodriguez said in a voice so bereft of emotion that even Barrajas winced.

"That's what pisses me off about fuckers like you," Barrajas answered, his fists clenching and unclenching. "You assume everyone's gonna shit their drawers when you walk in the room. You're not the only one who knows people." He set the revolver on the nightstand next to the bed, adding, "They were lined up to snitch you—"

Rodriguez's tied hands darted out and grabbed the gun. Barrajas took a step back, shocked. The gangster awkwardly pointed it back and forth between Joe and me. He noted my gun on the ground, and his face contorted strangely. Later, I considered that maybe this was the way a fucked-up sociopath smiled. Then Rodriguez was all business again, and he pointed the gun directly at Joe. "Stupid fucker," was all Rodriguez said. Then he pulled the trigger.

There was a muffled sound. A puff of smoke rolled out of the barrel. Without hesitation, Rodriguez swiveled the gun in my direction. He only hesitated when, anticipating an expression of terror, I just laughed. Next to me, Joe Barrajas stood up straight, uninjured, and moved slowly towards the bed.

"Get the fuck back!" Rodriguez snarled. His eyes gave him away, though. He knew something was up. He pulled the trigger again, but a muffled click was his only reward. I snatched the gun out of his hands while he sat there, confused. I emptied the single blank round out of the cylinder with gloved hands then shook out a handful of live rounds from a pocket. These went back into the revolver one at a time.

"What the fuck was that all about?" Rodriguez said, leaning back on the bed. Give the fucker credit—he could put his game face back on quick enough.

"The point of that was simple," I said. "First, your prints are on the gun."

Barrajas grabbed Rodriguez roughly by the hair and slammed the sock back into his mouth before he could protest. He added, "Second, you've got gunpowder residue on your hands."

Barrajas held out one gloved hand and took the revolver from me, examining the rounds before swiveling the cylinder shut. *Click.*

The sound electrified Rodriguez. Despite being tied up by both hands and feet, he somehow rocked his body forward and shot up from the bed like a coiled snake, hands outstretched for Joe's neck. It happened much quicker than I would have imagined.

But his eyes had given him away. I launched a split second before him, dropping my shoulder and zeroing in on the man we'd hunted for too long. Every ounce of rage and pent-up grief transformed into fluid motion, and in that instant, I saw again the gun barrel and felt myself flying backwards, not forwards. Then that sensation was gone, and my shoulder drove into Rodriguez's side with a crunching sound.

Bones broke, not mine. A wave of relief and horror washed over me.

Recovering, I stood over Rodriguez. Beads of sweat formed on his brow. His eyes were scrunched tight. The blow had flung the sock out of his mouth, but he uttered no sound.

Barrajas knelt down next to him. He held out the revolver, let Rodriguez inspect it.

"You don't have the balls," Rodriguez' grunted, eyes mere slits.

"And if I don't?" Barrajas responded.

"Take me back to Tacoma. I don't give a fuck. You ain't got nothin' on me. I got alibis, resources, money, attorneys. My people will fuckin' devour you, hombre."

"You think La Eme can help you, huh?" Barrajas asked.

"Yeah." Rodriguez opened his eyes. He spoke through grunts of pain, but his voice held all of his former menace. "Oh yeah, they'll help. And when I walk, man, we gonna eat you fuckers alive and spit out the bones."

Barrajas looked up at me. His "I told you so" look was unmistakable.

I knew it might come to this. Oh yes, I hadn't deluded myself. Rodriguez and Inigo had created nothing but carnage. They were responsible for the deaths of a score of gang-bangers, all of them young Hispanic men whose opportunity to alter their courses over a longer life would never be realized. The two had terrorized my town and welcomed in a horde of savage criminals who could and would have done worse.

They had also destroyed the lives of my two closest friends. If I thought Rodriguez might confess to killing Desiree, I would have asked. That would have been wasted breath.

Barrajas watched me process this. The effort left me numb.

We had rehearsed every step of this. Instead of responding, I reverted to training and handed Joe a face shield from my backpack. I donned one as well. The clear plastic fogged up as I tugged it over my mouth. It was strange to see Rodriguez on the ground now, as if I were watching him on a television with lousy reception.

Joe's eyes were glowing with energy. His body seemed to vibrate as he donned the shield.

Rodriguez watched us, more curious than afraid.

Barrajas turned his attention back to Rodriguez. He studied him as if he were about to perform surgery. The revolver spun in his hand until the trigger pivoted away. That got Rodriguez's attention. He began to thrash, squealing against the pain it must have caused his broken ribs. I dropped my knees onto his legs, pinning him to the ground. The revolver's sights touched Rodriguez' throat, and the muzzle tucked up beneath his chin.

"Bet this all looks familiar, eh?" Barrajas said in a dusky voice. He cocked his head to the side. "*Salude al diablo.*"

"No!" Rodriguez screamed. "No, Jura! Don't."

The gun barked loudly.

The top of Rodriguez's head exploded upwards in a cloud of smoke, blood, and flesh.

Seconds passed. Joe just stood there, fixated, his face shield splattered with gore.

My ears rang. I released my grip on Rodriguez's lifeless body, letting it slump over. Blood bubbled out of his open mouth. The ragged opening in his skull pooled with blood and pink brain tissue, leaking onto the floor slowly.

I reeled backwards, wanting to throw up. But not because of the fucked-up mess of Rodriguez's mortal remains. No, my guts were churning and churning in tempo with my tortured thoughts. Rodriguez had called Joe by a name I'd thought belonged to a dead man.

"Cassidy!"

I heard the voice as if I were coming out of a dream. Hands shook me once, twice. The spots that had begun to dot my vision faded.

"Yeah," I answered.

A blurred face appeared in front of me. Joe studied me from behind the fogged-up plastic face shield. I couldn't summon words. He turned, leaned over, and gently placed the smoking revolver into Rodriguez's palm. I barely heard the snip-snip of the zip ties being cut. My gorge rose, but I forced it back down.

When things go to shit, revert to training. Joe tossed me a towel, and I wiped my feet without thought. The masks, gloves, and suits got stuffed into the duffel bag. Still dazed, I watched him scan the room for any evidence of our presence. Neither of us looked back as we quietly slipped out the door and walked quickly down the hall to the fire escape. Barrajas had already disabled it, and so we descended to the alley in silence, barely attracting the attention of a flock of pigeons. Every step was slow, unhurried. Each beat of my heart echoed in my head. I was unable to process any part of what I'd just done. Or seen. Or heard.

A block away from the building, we turned the corner and faced each other. Neither of us spoke. Barrajas's face had lost its energy.

He looked, if anything, like a tired old man. He smoothed his gelled black hair back into place but could not hide the shaking. Thick brows hooded his eyes, hiding his thoughts from me. But I knew he was appraising me. Seeing what I would do. Maybe that's what he'd been wondering all this time.

What would Cassidy do?

I handed the duffel bag to him, and he accepted it with a nod. We took off in separate directions.

I didn't look back.

I moved forward, unsure now where to go. During the past week, we had put this operation together, including our exit plan. We had each made our own separate and circuitous route to the Bay Area after tracking Rodriguez here. We had spent hours poring over the building schematics, considered all the potential risks, hashed out the endless scenarios that could play out. It had gone exactly as planned.

Except for one detail. *Jura.*

I looked ahead at the now-crowded streets, wanting nothing more than to put distance between myself and the Tenderloin Paradiso. I walked. Time passed.

My wayward feet eventually took me across Market Street. The scent of spiced meat and the swift and luscious cadence of Spanish music drew me forward. A row of storefronts, each sign written in Spanish, stretched out for blocks ahead. I paused, savoring the warmth of a stray sunbeam.

A block later, a small church materialized on my right. It looked as if it were centuries old, its exterior, smooth, white plaster below an adobe roof, an aged steeple perched above and topped by a wooden cross. The ancient doors stood open, inviting me inside. Without conscious thought, I found myself climbing the clay-colored steps.

My fingers grazed the marble cistern inside the vestibule, and I crossed myself with holy water. The ritual reminded me of Sunday mass back home, Nate standing next to me reciting the liturgy along with the priest.

A ball of grief expanded in my throat. I swallowed it and stepped into the church's cool, damp interior. The pews were old, wooden, and worn. The twelve Stations of the Cross were the only source of exterior light, each one a stained-glass window that created a pleasant mixture of colors inside the dark church. Ahead, the altar was a swirl of saints, frescoes, and statues all paying homage to the crucified Christ, life-size and golden in the gleam of a thousand candles.

The air smelled of worship.

In another time, such a beautiful old church would have felt comfortable, like a worn but favorite pair of shoes. Now the candles were accusatory eyes, the angels a mocking jury. I could not lift my head up to the cross.

I heard a creak. Two doors were to my left, one with a red light above it. This one opened, and an elderly Mexican woman stepped out, hobbled to the front pew. She knelt down and bowed her head. Behind her, the red light above the door became green. The light tugged at me. Before I knew it, I was opening the door, which was remarkably heavy, and entering. My knees dropped to the cracked leather of the confessional. I buried my face in my hands.

A small panel slid open inches away. A voice spoke. "*Buenas dias, mi hijo.*" The priest's voice was deep, his silhouette thick and substantial behind the mesh filter.

I was unable to speak.

The priest was silent, patient. A minute passed.

Then I found my voice. "Bless me, Father, for I have sinned."

Epilogue

Town of Gig Harbor
August 13
0730 Hours

On a bluff above a small fishing village across the narrows, I stared east. Just below the jagged ridges of the Cascade Mountains, the green promontory of Point Defiance on Tacoma's northwestern tip was limned by the arrival of the summer sun atop the trees. *Home.* It tasted of salt air, carried along a light breeze, and looked as if it had been scrubbed clean.

A diesel motor from a fishing boat anchored within the heart-shaped harbor roared to life. A dog barked, the sound echoing until it was joined by others. A few early risers walked the shoreline promenade, their voices drifting up.

I turned from the view to the single-story home behind me. Warm and inviting, smoke wafted from its chimney to mingle with the scent of fresh-cut grass. Blinking against the brilliant pinks and peaches of the rising sun reflecting off the bay window, I put a boot on the bumper of my truck and considered my next move.

Despite the soothing vibes surrounding me, I was in a very dark place. Not to be melodramatic, but everything I'd experienced, every action I'd taken over the last few days had left a stain on my soul. My head was saturated with thoughts I couldn't share. As much as I wanted to be here, as much as I wanted to walk through the door and unburden myself of this shit, I couldn't do it. Let's face it; there was some precedence for bad things happening to people I cared about

So my next move was what, then? Run away? Where? And do what? Stupid idea, since I would only be relocating my baggage.

I had unloaded all of it onto the priest in that humble missionary church in San Francisco. If he had told me to turn myself in, I would have done it. Hell, I would have willingly leaped off the highest spires of the Golden Gate to get his absolution.

But enough melodramatic bullshit.

Despite confessing to such a heinous crime, not to mention mortal sin, the soft-spoken priest seemed unfazed. He'd probably heard the same or worse. Either way, he had a response cued up, "Vengeance is mine, sayeth the Lord." It was a classic line and full of power.

The penance was less destructive than my plans had been. My confessor told me to go home and set things right, an enigmatic response in my opinion. How does one go about "setting things right" when the wrongs include murder? But when I asked for clarification—did he want me to raise the dead?—he merely added, "And say ten Our Fathers."

Nothing like the old Catholic traditions.

So I'd stumbled out of the church still in a mild state of shock. A large wad of cash got me a cab ride well north of the city, where I used the last of my money for a train ticket to Tacoma. The train chugged towards home with my mind on spin-cycle. I don't know how many times I relived the sights and sounds of those few minutes in the rancid hotel room where Joe Barrajas and I murdered Juan "El Moto" Rodriguez.

But that was not the worst of it. What sent goosebumps up my arms and a wave of nausea through my empty stomach was infinitely more subtle. It was the slight quiver of Barrajas's lips, the guilty look in his eyes when Rodriguez addressed him as "Jura."

Was I surprised? Massive understatement. Until that moment, I had been working under the premise that "Jura" was Inigo's nickname. So, yeah, I was surprised. In the last few days of wandering, I'd worked through an even worse, unspeakable line of thought. What if Inigo hadn't murdered Desiree? What if Rodriguez hadn't been the killer either?

What if Joe Barrajas had murdered his own daughter?

Both Inigo and Rodriguez had motive: Desiree had processed the fingerprints that would have implicated El Feo in the big gang shooting. Inigo and Rodriguez would have fallen like dominoes after that evidence was made public. But what convinced me of their relative innocence, however, was the pen trap we had used to locate Inigo and, later on, Rodriguez. Neither phone had been anywhere near Desiree and Nate's place on the night she'd been murdered.

But I had since learned that Joe's phone told a different story. He'd been there.

Then I'd recalled Joe's behavior the night he appeared in my hospital room. He had been manic, distracted one minute and hyper-focused the next. If the timing were considered, he would have just come from—

Enough. I couldn't go there now.

The rest had been assumptions. Joe and Rodriguez could have started corresponding any time after the latter first reappeared in town. It was likely that they knew each other because Rodriguez and Desiree had been classmates in high school. Did he seek out the daughter this time or the father? Would the old cop be willing to help an old friend? I didn't know the answer to that, but I believed the two men had found plenty of common ground this time around.

My guess was that Joe saw an opportunity to stir up a little trouble, enough to create an opportunity for him to outshine Nate. If the gangs started shooting and Joe were the one to make it stop, it would be a fantastic coup. He would be a shoe-in for the chief's position when Garcia pulled the plug and retired. Instead, Nate had been offered the choice position, commander of the gang unit. In this light, Joe's behavior after that announcement, his rage, was easily understandable.

But Joe Barrajas had clearly never trusted Rafael Inigo. By dropping little innuendos against him, Joe meant to rid himself and the department of Inigo at some point along the way. The reason for that, at least, was obvious. Joe had gotten involved with Inigo's people, and Inigo was never one to keep a secret. Not if he could profit by telling someone.

Still, I could have—should have!—known what was happening. So many opportunities presented themselves, and I'd blithely ignored each and every one. The role of the unwitting fool, the *chota*, had been mine. That was simply one more bitter truth in this tragically fucked-up mess.

I don't belong here.

The words in my head propelled me into motion, and I hopped back into my truck. Ignoring the view, I shoved the key in the ignition.

Then a silky finger touched my forearm.

That simple physical contact had a profound effect. A depth of understanding and concern was transmitted to me in an instant, in a manner as intimate as sex. An unseen weight on my chest seemed to shift, and I inhaled as if just emerging from deep water.

The hand lifted as Echie opened the truck door. I collapsed into her, my lungs emptying with a wracking sob. She held me up, fingers caressing my neck, and I cried until I ran out of tears. I held her as tightly as I dared, unwilling to sully the moment with words.

Nothing would be the same.

True, I admitted. But it was also true that nothing was preordained. This much I knew—my life was my own. Maybe there was a way to do my penance, to quiet the guilt that had ravaged my heart and soul since the very moment we'd taken Rodriguez' life. As I held Echie's smooth hand, it actually seemed possible.

When we eventually stepped back from each other, I had the strangely pleasant sensation she was reading my thoughts. She leaned forward and kissed me, first my forehead, then my eyes, and finally my mouth, her lips lightly brushing against mine. Then she led me to the open front door of her small house where a host of pleasant smells enveloped me. A shaved head lifted off the couch. Ernesto gave me a blurry nod.

Hand in hand, we crossed the threshold as a fishing boat sounded its horn on the way out of the harbor.

Acknowledgments

The author would like to thank his law enforcement brethren whose expertise, camaraderie, and courageous efforts inspired this story. A huge thank-you goes as well to Patrick O'Callahan, editor and mentor, for the helping hand; to editor emeritus the late Hillel Black, for his tutelage; and to the family members who helped proof the crumpled manuscript of a cop and would-be novelist. The author would further like to apologize to his wife and sons for any and all bad moods they endured while he struggled to finish this book. Thanks for your patience. Love you all.